BLACK WILL SHOOT

a novel

JESSE WASHINGTON

SISE

SIMON SPOTLIGHT ENTERTAINMENT
New York London Toronto Sydney

This book is a work of fiction. Any references to historical events, real people, or real locales are used fictitiously. Other names, characters, places, and incidents are the product of the author's imagination, and any resemblance to actual events or locales or persons, living or dead, is entirely coincidental.

SSE

SIMON SPOTLIGHT ENTERTAINMENT
An imprint of Simon & Schuster
1230 Avenue of the Americas, New York, New York 10020
Copyright © 2008 by Jesse Washington
SIMON SPOTLIGHT ENTERTAINMENT and related logo are trademarks of Simon & Schuster, Inc.
Designed by Gabe Levine
Manufactured in the United States of America
First Edition 10 9 8 7 6 5 4 3 2 1
Library of Congress Cataloging-in-Publication Data
Washington, Jesse John, 1969-
Black will shoot : a novel / by Jesse Washington.—1st ed.
p. cm.
ISBN-13: 978-1-4169-3879-8
ISBN-10: 1-4169-3879-6
1. African Americans—Fiction. 2. Hip-hop—Fiction. 3. African
American musicians—Fiction. 4. Music trade—Fiction. 5. Street
life—Fiction. 6. Drug abuse—Fiction. I. Title.
PS3623.A8675B57 2007
813'.6—dc22
2007024993

"We, verily, have made music as a ladder for your souls, a means whereby they may be lifted up unto the realm on high; make it not, therefore, as wings to self and passion." —Bahá'u'lláh

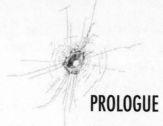

PROLOGUE

I awakened in a tiny room—four paces square, low ceiling, concrete walls and floor. The buzz in my eardrum told me it was busted. Usually I heard so much in silence.

"Wake up," rasped my brother, Dontay, slumped against the far wall. "We in the basement. They taped us up, but I got loose and untied you. Them cats ain't too smart."

"Smart?" My voice hammered the inside of my skull. The pain made me feel alive. "They was smart enough to get us."

"They ain't get *us*. They got *you*," Dontay spat.

"Nigga, they came to kill *you*!"

I lurched to my feet and staggered toward Dontay with violence in my heart. I don't know what I would have done if I hadn't seen his leg stuck out at an odd angle. There was a hole in the inner thigh of his jeans, surrounded by a huge, wet stain.

"It's still bleeding," Dontay said. "It won't take long."

"Won't take long for what?" I said, unthinking.

Dontay said nothing.

How many times had I contemplated Dontay's miserable death, hoped for it, even? Now I was about to be free of his curse at last. Only I had never put myself in the picture.

I took my bandanna and tried to tie it over the bullet hole. Dontay just lay there humming that tune under his breath. *Who's that knocking at my God's door; it's a face I seen before. . . .*

As I worked on him, I felt something inside my Jordans, rubbing my left foot. I reached inside the sneaker and withdrew my mini digital recorder. They must have missed it.

I'm not proud of what I did then. Of all my shameful acts that summer, hiding that recorder behind my brother's back was the worst. But pride and anger lead to regret. Now, as I play back Dontay's words, I can tell he wouldn't have cared anyway. On some level, he knew I had no choice but to finally hear him out.

"Dontay."

His eyelids were half-closed, lips like chalk. I shook his skinny shoulder with one hand and slipped the recorder up against the wall with the other.

"Dontay. This could be the last time we ever speak. So I got to ask . . . would you do anything different?"

"I shoulda made you listen to me from the jump—that's what I woulda done different. You heard me? You got that short-nigga attitude, always been hardheaded."

"And you always been a crackhead," I responded.

He laughed bitterly. "And there you go talkin' greasy. I can't even feel that no more. I'm too tired to hurt. It's time to think about the next life. And you need to think about what's left of yours. 'Cause there ain't but one street nigga in this family—"

"And that's me," I mouthed along with Dontay's stock speech. I tuned out and let the tape roll. If I had learned any lesson from the countless hours wasted on Tay's tales over the years, it was that you can't rush him. He'll say what he has to say in his own way.

I tried to remember how they jacked us. Did I open the door, or did they smash through? I see my hand on the knob and then boots raining down on my face. I flinch and the blow lands near my temple instead of crushing my nose. A man stands over me, gun in hand, braids dripping down his head, red eyes peering from above the black bandanna covering the rest of his face. The sticky, sick sound of duct tape unrolling.

The shame hurt more than my head. Ya blind, baby, blind to the facts. Crack logic. Everything I despised in my big brother manifested itself in me. Next thing you know I'd claim Jesus had returned to walk the earth. Sure enough, Dontay started on that religion.

" . . . I ain't scared of death, yo. The Blessed Beauty has a special place for me in the Abha Kingdom. Everybody will be there. My man Large is waiting for me right now. He understands what happened—with me, with him, with all of us. You wanna know what's happening with black people? Just listen to our music. . . ."

The sins of the father are visited upon the son—that's what Mom always said. I wish I did have a father to blame. But all I ever had was Dontay.

CHAPTER 1

You could say I had a pretty good life heading into that summer, but I always felt something was missing. I just never knew exactly what until Taylor Whittingham called me about writing for *Fever* magazine.

I tried on three different outfits the morning of my interview. Riding up the elevator, I was pleased with my reflection in the shiny, steel doors: gray suit and royal blue dress shirt, open collar. But as I squeezed into the *Fever* waiting area with a dozen other people seeking access to the "shrine of hip-hop," my feet felt like flashing police lights. No one else wore wingtips. They wore boots or sneakers, or square-toed loafers for the lawyers. I knew they were lawyers because I overheard them talking about suing some guy named Hassan over an unpaid invoice.

Only one person was standing, chocolate colored and gap toothed, talking into an outdated celly headset like something from the Burger King drive-through.

"Reddy is wit it, I'm telling you. He's down." Gap Teeth dropped the superstar's name as if it would get him into the *Fever* faster than the rest of us. "Reddy did dat? . . . You on fire right now, son. . . . 'Cause he got that swagger, kna'm sayin'? . . . Aiight, I'ma see you at Mamadeaux—"

The door opened and we all looked up expectantly.

"Where Marq Wise at?" Taylor's secretary asked, cracking

her gum. I didn't need my watch to know I'd been waiting half an hour.

I'd expected the *Fever* offices to look like a music video, but it was more as though my old college dorm hall had been dropped into Manhattan. Mustard yellow industrial-grade carpet, low ceiling that looked as if it had been pierced with a thousand pencils. A row of offices along the far wall blocked the only available natural light. Two dozen cubicles with head-high partitions were arranged in the center around a wide circular staircase. Scotch-taped to the outside of a tall file cabinet was a big picture of Whitney Houston and Bobby Brown with an *X* drawn over Bobby's face. The faint smell of cigarette smoke hung in the air, making me think of Dontay.

Briana was a stunner—dark skinned; short, natural haircut; lot of lip gloss. She took baby steps through the office, as if her green-on-gray Nikes hurt her feet. I followed her down the center stairs and she deposited me onto a sofa next to a light green door. "Can I git you something? Some water?" she asked, her last word sounding like "wuadah," standing sort of close.

"No thanks, I'm fine."

She gave me an interesting smile, returned to her tiny desk, and called someone on her cell. Briana was hot but I didn't sweat her. My girl, Holliday, left no room for improvement. We had been living together six months, and I still had to pinch myself when I woke up next to her. But still, I felt better about my shoes.

About ten minutes later Taylor Whittingham opened his door. He was a full head taller than me, razor thin, with a pretty dark brown face and long eyelashes. Every centimeter of his faintly metallic suit was tailored to his angular frame. He looked much younger than his thirty-nine years.

I was confident that I knew everything Taylor was about to ask me. I'm a reporter. I get information; that's what I do. We exchanged the secret handshake—one of our fraternity brothers had recommended me for the job—and then Taylor sat down and pulled out my résumé.

"So what are you listening to these days?"

That was exactly what they said he'd ask. I pretended to think about it.

"I'm feeling guys like T.I., DipSet, UGK, Game," I said, trying to hit all the geographic regions. "Stuff like that, you know what I'm saying?"

That last phrase felt awkward, even though I had practiced it. Journalistically I was overqualified for this job—I'd been working at *Newsweek* since college, even had a cover story to my credit. Now all I had to do was prove I belonged.

My feet felt hot.

"Who do you think is the best ever?" Taylor asked, raising eyebrows so perfect they looked airbrushed.

"I have to say Rakim. He created the cool, conversational rhyme flow." I had read that somewhere a few years back. I had read everything when it came to rap. "Before Rakim, MCs were all yelling. So he's the best ever, even though his album didn't work out with Dr. Dre."

I had practiced calling Dre "Driz-zay," but changed my mind at the last minute.

"What about Don Imus and his nappy-headed hoes. Do you think it's fair to criticize hip-hop for that?"

"Hell no! First of all, the ghetto took insults like 'nappy' and 'nigger' and turned them into a point of pride. We have the right to use that language to describe the reality of our community. Don Imus doesn't. Second of all, there are plenty of positive aspects of hip-hop. The mainstream media is just focusing on the negative like they always do."

"But even Nas is saying hip-hop is dead."

"Nas is the greatest MC of all time, but he got that one wrong. There's a lot of good music being made. Rap still means something important. Like Ludacris says, 'Hip-hop ain't dead, it lives in the South.'"

Taylor shook his curly head and smiled. "I agree with everything you said except one thing. You forgot about Large."

"Large?"

"Large. *He's* the greatest MC of all time. I met L at the *Fever* first-anniversary party, like a year before his first album was out. He was just the fat, ugly guy hanging around with Reddy, rapping about black power and crooked cops. His first single was making noise, but nobody really knew him yet—that incredible personality was still under wraps. Based on his looks, nobody would have thought that he would be a star, let alone become an actor, let *alone* win the Oscar. And Reddy, he was just a loudmouth kid who couldn't even dress yet, driving a Volkswagen Cabriolet. These dudes were so new, they were opening for Patra. L is getting ready to go onstage, and he needed somebody to introduce him. He was first to perform. The music came on to 'Think Twice,' and you could feel the crowd come alive. I had never experienced anything like that before. I just happened to be on the side of the stage, holding the microphone, and when the music came on, I decided on the spur of the moment to go out there and introduce Large. He came out and dropped it, and the crowd went bananas. His energy was unbelievable, like he was transformed from a misfit into a prophet. It felt like he was speaking directly to me, personally, and everybody in the spot felt the same way. And I kind of stayed onstage. I was like his hype man! I was backing him up, like, *Smart missile to ya crew, now the beef's cooked through.* . . . And Large was just killing it. The energy was off the meter. It was a wrap, right there. I knew at that moment he'd be a huge star. That's why I say that Large, rest in peace, was the greatest MC of all time."

I didn't say anything. It was one of my best tricks.

"You got plans for tonight?" Taylor asked.

CHAPTER 2

The sun never shone on that last room you got me, the one in Bed Stuy. I mean literally.

I had only one window down there, so lookin out, my chin is at street level. And the street ain't but so wide, the buildings is yay tall, so e'y day the sun only hit St. James Place for about two hours. But even then the angle was wrong, so no sun rays could penetrate my basement. You know that feeling you get chillin in your crib, relaxed, just in your creative zone, you know, and a beam of sunlight drop down and you see specks of dust dancing in the air?

I bet you do, Marq. But I never had that feeling. Not since Large was here.

I met Large one night walking through the hood. This was way before he was famous, before Reddy messed e'ything up. L and his crew was posted up on the stoop

smoking blunts and drinking Private Stock. Large was
wearing a leather backpack and a lumberjack-plaid hat.
When I walked past, something told me to look him in the
eye. Dude had magnetism. That moment changed my life.
Strangers never speak in Noo Yawk, kna'm sayin? You say
your name to someone on the street don't know you, they
either gonna bounce or come out with the burner. But
something in L's eyes made me tell him my name.

He asked me, "What's your hustle?"

I told him I make beats. And he busted a freestyle
right there, on the spot, straight a cappella. He was like:

Tall nigga, name of Dontay
I rap tight like turbans in Bombay
Best restaurants, the best entrées
Blow like volcanoes in the land of Pompeii . . .

Now you gotta remember, I done rocked wit the
best. When I was like twelve, thirteen years old? I
was sneakin out to watch Cold Crush Brothers in
the park. I used to trek all the way up to Vyse
Avenue in the Bronx to buy tapes from this Spanish
kid, back in 1980 before rap was on the radio. I
was scared getting off the train way up there. Them
Bronx gangs would rock your knot. But I needed that
hip-hop. I seen all the great ones live and in the
studio. Grandmaster Caz, KRS, Rakim. These dudes
is MCs, man, Masters of Ceremonies. A rapper is
someone who wraps gifts. I seen KRS take out Melle
Mel in a battle. I seen Supernatural versus Craig G.

I been at Harlem World, the Rooftop, Disco Fever, Latin Quarter. And I got mad tapes, thanks to that Walkman you gave me back then with the microphone in it. My collection should be in a museum. That's real talk. When hip-hop is all up in the Smithsonian in a few years, people gonna be buying my collection for millions. Don't forget I got all my radio tapes too. Mr. Magic, Red Alert, Chuck Chillout, Teddy Ted and Special K, Marley Marl, Pete Rock's Future Flavors, Stretch and Bobbito. That's the real, not that Massive 99 bullshit you be listening to. Mad niggas been tryna buy my tapes but them joints is priceless.

What I'm saying is, I can recognize talent. And I ain't never heard nobody nice as Large. So when I first heard duke do his thing like that, right off the bat? I knew it was destiny. I got my equipment, and we went down in L's basement and recorded The Joint that night. The song was so hot, it seemed like the next day everybody knew my name. Back then I thought I was set for life. And it never woulda came to all this if Large ain't got kilt.

Now all I got left is The Joint.

Most of the time that's good enough. It's like the drums chip away my pain. The melody reminds me of the man I really am. L's voice come in strong and heavy. Tall nigga, name of Dontay . . . That beat I made is so simple. Just bass, rim shot, snare, high hat, and a simple loop, chopped twice. Eight bars. It came to me one night on the D train, riding back to Brooklyn over the Manhattan Bridge. I was alone in the empty last car. The Wall Street skyline looked like it was shooting rockets of *stone and light into the sky, like city fingers reaching for the stars. It's my masterpiece. And now it's going to help me reclaim my rightful place in hip-hop.*

CHAPTER 3

Taylor's platinum Range Rover floated down Broadway like a magic carpet. It was a warm night, early summer, so the streets were thick with bodies. Holliday's little Audi TT was fly, the perfect size for the two of us, and we turned heads in it, especially with the top down. But this was a much different experience. Riding high above the river of pedestrians, I felt like royalty carried on a litter. As we crossed Houston Street, I watched the walkers through the tinted glass. They stared at our vehicle, seeing only their own reflections. Did they wonder who was inside this magnificent ride? I almost couldn't believe it was me.

Taylor pressed a button on his wireless headset to answer his phone. I took the opportunity to pull out my Sidekick and text Holliday.

    WE'RE GOING TO PAYDAY LIKE I THOUGHT.
    MEET ME THERE IN A HALF HOUR.

Holliday had a BlackBerry. She called my Sidekick a "ghetto laptop." Holliday was like that when it came to rap—she said it degraded women and brought out the worst in the black community. She stuck to R&B and lite jazz instead.

Taylor pulled up in front of Payday, a hot spot they were

always talking about on Massive 99. Directly across the narrow street was a large, boxy truck, like a UPS vehicle but painted flat black. On the side were two slitted windows, like on an armored car, which made the truck resemble a scowling face. I recognized it from Slow Creep's music videos. They were one of my favorite groups, ever since I read an article in the *Source* about them years ago. Slow Creep consisted of two Brooklyn MCs, Trophy and Bizack, about my age. They met one night on the basketball court at Tillary Park in Brooklyn, where I played all the time. Their bond was cemented when, trying to scrape up enough money to record a demo, they stuck up a bread truck on Myrtle Avenue and decided to keep the vehicle. That was the very same truck, legend had it, that was parked outside Payday.

Taylor tossed his keys to the valet and knifed through the throng. "Catch the *Fever!*" he said to the bouncer while extending his business card. People were getting patted down but Taylor and I walked through untouched. I followed in his wake as he strode inside like LeBron James walking onto the basketball court.

Payday was half restaurant, half bar, and fully packed. The new T.I. record was blasting loud enough to make conversation difficult. The long, curved bar was shoulder to shoulder with folks wearing everything from suits to white T-shirts to miniskirts. I found myself looking at all the diamonds. Up close, the rocks were spectacular.

As we made our way to a rear table, Taylor greeted at least ten people. He introduced me to each one, the blur of names lingering in the air like incense. *Bam Tammy Chris Mongo Platt Shaka Dee Ferguson Boo* . . . They all greeted Taylor like old friends. Taylor kissed the ladies' cheeks and gave fellas "pounds," grasping their hands and then wrapping his free arm around their backs. Holliday called that move the "hug-shake."

I wished she were with me. I felt uncomfortable, out of my element. We rarely went to clubs. Movies, restaurants, museums, and the gym were more our speed.

Someone pointed admiringly at Taylor's watch. Several supplicants who were beneath introduction whipped out their Sidekicks and pushed them toward Taylor, trying unsuccessfully to get his number. The only people in the whole place I recognized were the rapper D. Rex, standing over in one corner, and Trophy and Bizack, holding court at a big table surrounded by waiters.

Taylor stopped by the table and briefly introduced me to Trophy and Bizack, which gave me a charge. I had all their albums. They gave Taylor pounds without rising from their seats and threw me a glance. They were both extremely light skinned, with identical close haircuts faded bald on the sides. Bizack had a round baby face and a thin line of barbered hair tracing his jawline. Trophy was lean, with wispy brown facial hair on a narrow Doberman face made sharper by his trademark scowl. A few seconds later, Taylor plowed straight through the crowd over to D. Rex.

"What's good, baby?" Taylor said, giving D. Rex a pound. "That new single is banging."

D. Rex grinned and nodded. I wasn't a huge fan—he had too many love raps and used his South Carolina drawl as much for singing as rapping. He was walnut colored, about my height, much shorter than he looked on TV. He wore loose jeans, a tight wifebeater, a belt with a large oval buckle, and a white do-rag over tight cornrows. His muscular arms were around two beauties, both much taller than him.

"Thanks, playboy," D. Rex said. "I just try ta do me, kna'm sayin'?"

"I'm looking forward to you performing at the Fever Fest this year. Felix said you're confirmed."

D. Rex's smile faded.

"I ain't fuckin' with Felix like that right now. That's real talk."

"Word? He's still managing you, though, right?"

"Felix Billings can kiss my black ass," D. Rex spat.

"No problem," Taylor said. "I hope you can get busy at the Fest again. Yo, say hi to my man Marq. He's gonna be my newest star writer."

D. Rex ignored me. Taylor gave him another pound and we moved on.

"Who is Felix Billings?" I asked Taylor.

"He manages a lot of artists, has his own record label," Taylor said. "A very powerful guy." He was interrupted by a dude wearing a headband around his tattooed neck and three terry cloth wristbands. As they spoke, I unclicked my Sidekick from my belt and messaged Holliday again.

WHERE ARE YOU?

Finally we reached a table. "I'm not going to beat around the bush," Taylor said after we ordered twenty-seven-dollar coconut-shrimp appetizers. "You're just what we need at the magazine right now. Ever since I started the *Fever* almost twenty years ago at Howard University, ever since we ushered in this new era of black culture, I had this vision of how to set the whole world on fire with passion and knowledge and entertainment. Hip-hop is poised to make that next step right now, where our visions of wealth become reality. We can expand the parameters of our magazine, the hip-hop community, our very culture, to include the Halle Berrys, the Denzels, the Shaqs. We are a broad people with diverse interests. You're the type of journalist who understands that it's imperative to transcend the boundaries of our culture and simultaneously deliver a black voice. . . ."

Behind Taylor I saw a giant cross pendant, studded with at least a hundred diamonds, swinging from a long platinum bejeweled chain. I accidentally locked eyes with the owner. He pulled back his teeth in a feral grimace, startling me with a mouth full of diamond-studded platinum teeth.

". . . and we do speak to our people, perhaps a little more effectively than *Newsweek*."

The expression on Taylor's smooth brown face told me it was my turn to talk.

"*Newsweek* has a circulation of two point three million, though."

Taylor shifted forward in his seat. "*Fever*'s readership is on par with that. But the power of our readers is magnified beyond their numbers. We are the very beating heart of American culture. We are hip-hop. We are magnified by our drive, our creativity, our purpose. This is what I see in you, Marq. At the *Fever* you have the opportunity to penetrate to the heart of our culture. You can make a difference for the people who need it most. I've been trying to do certain types of stories for years, groundbreaking investigative pieces, but the editorial personnel hasn't been up to par. Now you and I have a chance to do some award-winning work."

"*Fever's* circulation is eight hundred fifty thousand," I said.

Taylor's expression told me I had the advantage. "Yes, but an average of seven people reads each—"

"And you missed that number five times last year," I interrupted. "That Big Brawls cover, the pink one, with his wife and kids? That was the killer."

I told myself to breathe normally. I was pushing the negotiation, although I would have taken the job for subway fare and a pound from Slow Creep. I was tired of working at *Newsweek,* tired of being around all those stuffy people, tired of writing dumbed-down 650-word articles on hip-hop, the sound track to my life.

"But that's all beside the point," I said. "If you're offering me a job, which it sounds like you are, this is the point where you make me a salary offer."

Taylor's features shifted into a smile. "Well, our budget for the year is already allocated, but I've managed to free up some money to get you on the team."

I was making eighty-five thousand dollars at *Newsweek,* having recently been promoted from reporter/researcher to full-fledged writer.

"I was thinking eighty . . ." Taylor said. I didn't blink.

"Maybe ninety . . ."

"That's not any better than my current situation," I said. My heart was pounding in my ears.

"Okay, I can do one hundred thousand. Final offer."

"Plus a ten thousand signing bonus, plus a year-end bonus if you meet the benchmarks in my employment contract."

"Contract?" Taylor briefly flashed dismay, then gave a broad smile. "No problem. Welcome to the fam."

Champagne came. We clinked glasses and Taylor drained his. I took a healthy swallow—my first taste of Cristal. It felt light and expensive on my tongue, a long way from my usual Heineken.

A hand fell onto my shoulder. Holliday slid into the seat beside me, directly across from Taylor, and rested her briefcase on the table.

I loved to watch guys react when they first saw Holliday. Taylor's eyes darted from her to me, back to her, then struggled not to drop to the open buttons of her white silk blouse. She was wearing a dark navy pantsuit that clung to her athletic shape and brought out the glow in her cinnamon skin. She took off her glasses, rested them atop her shoulder-length brown hair, and punched me hard in the shoulder.

"Marquis! You didn't tell him I was coming, did you?"

"Marquis?" Taylor said, regaining his composure and raising his perfect eyebrows at me.

Holliday always called people by their given name. I went by Mark as a kid, then brought back the *q* when I got my first byline at my college paper. I wanted people to remember my name.

"Taylor, I'd like you to meet my attorney, Holliday Watkins." I placed my hand on top of hers on the clean white tablecloth.

Taylor looked at our hands. "Isn't that a conflict of interest?" he asked Holliday.

"Absolutely," she said with a straight face. "I thought that would be appropriate for a music-industry transaction."

Taylor looked down at her briefcase. It was by Jack Georges, shiny brown leather, wide and square at the bottom. It cost me $550 on her twenty-sixth birthday. "Would I be wrong to guess that your contract is in there, Marq?"

I grinned and poured Holliday a drink. We all clinked glasses. Taylor made small talk with Holliday until she slipped her glasses back on and started explaining the deal points in my contract. I was calculating the amount of my new monthly paycheck, minus my rent and Dontay's allowance, when I heard the sound of glass smashing at the bar.

The hubbub of conversation died down for just an instant, leaving only Mary J. Blige's soulful wail pouring through the sound system. Then there was an explosion of noise—chairs scraping, feet scuffling, shouts and yells and screams. A knot of men formed at the bar, the outer ring tugging and pushing futilely against the center. Someone leaped on top of the knot, a green bottle held high, and swung the bottle down with another smash. The crowd surged toward the exits. Taylor was standing up, craning his neck. I jumped on top of my chair so I could see over the fleeing crowd. The bouncers reached the knot, plunged in, and broke it apart. At the center was Trophy, a river of red cascading down his head, gripping a knife. A burly guy was holding his hand to a red stain on the stomach area of his white T-shirt, shouting at Trophy as he was dragged off by two bouncers.

"You through, son. You through!" the stabbed man shouted. "You better get your paper up 'cause it's war, son. If y'all set foot at the Baller, y'all *dead*!"

Bizack appeared from nowhere and landed a huge punch on the stabbed man's jaw. Another bouncer dragged Bizack away, kicking and cussing. The stabbed man was hustled out a side door.

Holliday pulled me down from the chair. I started to run with the herd toward the front exit, but she yanked me hard toward the kitchen.

"Taylor, this way," I said as Holliday dragged me away, her briefcase in her other hand. Taylor followed us through the kitchen to a back door.

We emerged into an alley next to a fragrant, overflowing Dumpster. I was full of adrenaline and Holliday was breathing hard. She glared at me through her glasses, which were slightly askew on her face.

"That was really, really ghetto," she said, looking as though she had a bad taste in her mouth.

Taylor ignored her and broke into a smile. "Welcome to the game, Marq," he said. "I think we just found your first assignment. What's the deal with Slow Creep?"

CHAPTER 4

Holliday didn't say a word as she sped us through Manhattan. After the Range Rover, sitting in the tiny Audi felt as though my butt were scraping the ground. Holliday accelerated down Broadway past a Denali pumping Biggie, and the music pulled me back into Brooklyn.

It was two days ago. I was driving Holliday's car home from a basketball game, top down, on one of those cool June afternoons when the impossibly blue sky makes the gray concrete ditch of Fulton Street seem almost cheerful. I was stopped at the corner of St. James and heard Biggie's *where Brooklyn at, where Brooklyn at* emanating from a record store. And as I rolled past the store, I heard the unmistakable sound of Dontay's cough, a deep, wet grating that seemed to recycle cupfuls of phlegm.

He was standing in front of a cloudy bodega window stacked with detergent and potato chips. Haircut six weeks old, dark skin sweaty, arguing with a skinny dude wearing a head-band that squeezed the middle of his peanut-shaped dome. Dontay's lanky frame didn't have an ounce of extra meat, and I could see his tensed-up arm muscles in the sleeveless tee I'd bought him a few weeks back. Peanut Head dug into a pocket and flung something into Dontay's palm.

Damn. My brother was still smoking that crack.

I wanted to punch him in his face. I doubted myself and thought of a dozen other small objects that could have just passed into my brother's hand. Then the doubts vanished beneath a ten-year mountain of circumstantial evidence, only to creep up again as soon as the anger receded. It was so much simpler just to stay mad.

Holliday's voice chased away the memory. We were barrel-ing up the Brooklyn Bridge, warm evening air whispering in my ears.

"Didn't I tell you this *Fever* thing was a bad idea?" she said.

A statement disguised as a question was a bad sign—she was entering lawyer mode. Holliday was a steel-trap corporate attorney, although emotionally she was tissue paper. Our first date was a year ago after being set up by mutual friends. At din-ner that night she told me her father was in prison for killing her mother when she was in high school, and that she wasn't going to talk about them again. She never did. But I could see the damage in her long silences, abrupt mood swings, and grim determination to assemble a tranquil and thoroughly average life.

"Wouldn't the smart move be to stay at *Newsweek*, where your future is secure, instead of jumping into a volatile situation where you have no experience?" Holliday generally hid her vulnerabilities behind the blunt force of her logic.

"What do you mean, no experience?" We were descending the other side of the bridge, Brooklyn spread out before us in a squat, twinkling panorama.

"With these rap guys. That was crazy in there tonight! Weren't you scared?"

Actually, I had felt the same kind of tense, invigorating excitement as when my editor chose me for a one-month stint in Iraq. I turned down the volume on Holliday's John Legend CD.

"We talked all this over before, baby. This is the right move for me."

"That was before people started getting stabbed." She calmly swerved the little car from the left lane into a sharp right turn on Tillary. Holliday's only real vice was her love of fast cars. And she drove them as if they were dent proof.

We found a parking spot up the block from our Brooklyn Heights apartment. Holliday walked ahead of me up to the third floor, hung her purse on the HOME SWEET HOME rack behind the door, and went straight into the bedroom to change.

I shrugged out of my suit jacket and retreated into my office, the smaller of our two bedrooms. After fifteen quick pull-ups on the bar at the top of the doorway, I pulled out Slow Creep's *Killer Theater* CD from the shelf and sat down at my wooden desk. My Mac laptop blinked to life, and I checked allhiphop.com for anything on Slow Creep. Bingo.

Slow Creep Beefing with Label, Bidding War on Tap
By Scrap Thompson
06/03/2007 10:30 a.m.

Drama is brewing between Slow Creep and their longtime label, Pump Records, with the duo claiming free-agent status. MCs Trophy and Bizack are reportedly unhappy with the promotion of their latest CD, Fire in the Hole, *which has sold only 175,000 copies in four months on shelves.*

Since hitting the scene seven years ago with the classic album Killer Theater, *the Creep have sold a combined 13 million units on the Pump label. But sales have been sliding amid the industry downturn, and* Fire in the Hole *bricked despite high-profile guest appearances by the likes of Ghostface Killah, Lil Scrappy, and 50 Cent. When Pump Records offered less than half their usual advance for their next record, the Creep balked.*

"We ain't gonna starve just because the label is out of touch with the streets," Bizack told allhiphop.com. "We got an overseas tour this summer. After that we gonna take our new material to the How To Be A Baller convention and see who gives us the best offer."

Sean "Diddy" Combs, Jay-Z, Tommy Daminion, Ludacris, Meyer Mahl, and Dr. Dre have all expressed interest in signing the critically acclaimed act to their respective labels. But Pump Records president Stan Ross said the group is under contract for two more albums.

*"*Fire in the Hole *actually sold well in this new industry climate," Ross said. "We moved a few hundred thousand ringtones and plenty of cell-phone wallpaper. But*

everyone has to realize that downloading has changed our business forever. Pump Records is the leader in using new technology to connect fans to their favorite artists."

Daminion, reached by phone, hinted that the contract might not hold. "All I'm saying is me and Stan go way back," he said. "And when I want to sign someone, I usually find a way to get it done."

I peeked over my shoulder down the hall into the living room. Holliday was on the couch reading *O*, the Oprah magazine. I could tell she needed more time, so I changed into workout gear, grabbed my basketball, and slipped out the front door.

It was a five-minute dribble to the park. I'm only five foot eight, but I can play. Once I hit the empty asphalt, my body automatically began the routine: Dribble the length of the court and back five times. Sink twenty-five midrange jump shots. Now twenty-five lefty layups, twenty-five righty, twenty-five three-pointers. Last comes twenty-five free throws, the motions unconscious, leaving my mind free to ponder and plan as I stand at the line: Bounce, bounce, bounce. Breathe, bend, flick, swish. Make the last five in a row or keep shooting. Dribble back home. I could write a whole story in my head over the course of one workout. By the time I showered and fell onto the couch next to Holliday, I was ready.

She was watching the news, wearing a T-shirt and a pair of my sweatpants. Her hair was pinned on top of her head. She held the remote in her left hand and a pen in her right, poised over a legal folder open beside her on the couch.

"So it looks like Slow Creep is going to sign with someone at the How To Be A Baller convention," I said to break the ice.

She visibly tensed, then started twirling the pen between her fingers.

"There are some bad people behind the Baller," she said, eyes still on the TV screen.

"How can you be sure? You don't pay any attention to hip-hop."

"Daddy's friends used to talk about the Baller."

I was stunned. She had never even spoken his name. I waited eagerly to see what else she would say.

"Daddy was a drug dealer. Not a corner type of guy, but a big-time wholesaler on Long Island where we lived. He was a powerful man. People were scared of him. And at the end of every summer, he would head to Miami with all his cronies for the Baller convention."

I moved closer to Holliday and rubbed the back of her neck as I tried to process this revelation. Whenever I pried about her past, she would slip into a depression that lasted for days. "Things have changed," I said. "The Baller is mainstream now, corporate. Besides, I can handle the *Fever*. I've handled worse at *Newsweek*."

Holliday leaned into my backrub and kept her eyes on the TV.

"What is it with you and hip-hop all of a sudden?" she asked, twirling her pen. "Can't you just listen to the radio like everyone else?"

Rap is something you do. Hip-hop is something you live.

That was from KRS-One. Rap quotes were always jumping into my head. I had learned to trust them.

"I want to be a great writer," I said. "To do that, you have to write what you love."

There was silence while she watched the end of her show.

Holliday clicked off the TV and pulled me on top of her. "Then what are you going to write about me?" she said, her embrace signaling surrender. I don't know if I was more excited by the promise of her body or the *Fever*.

CHAPTER 5

Heads swiveled in unison when I spoke Tommy Daminion's name in my first *Fever* staff meeting. I'd been working there three days.

"Are you serious?" Rosa asked. "How is *he* a story?"

Rosa De Leon was editor in chief, a brassy six-foot-three Dominican with heavy makeup and perfume that filled the room. She'd barely said hello to me before now. I'd done my research, so I knew she and Taylor were enemies. In the twenty years since founding the *Fever*, Taylor had changed editors like cuff links. Then he sold his magazine to the Versatize corporation six months ago for sixty million, staying on as CEO. Rosa was the number-two editor of another Versatize magazine, and the corporate bosses put her in charge of the *Fever*—over Taylor's objections.

Taylor had wanted Willie Stripp as editor. Stripp sat glowering in a corner, chair tilted back against the wall, with black smoker's lips and stone-serious features carved into a dark face. I'd been reading his column for years. The rest of the editorial staff lounged around the scuffed conference-room table. They were young, multicultural, attractive, and casually but carefully dressed. The cast included several sets of dreadlocks, on both men and women; a white version of 50 Cent down to the muscles and tattoos; a young male Hispanic contingent wearing extra-large, flat-brimmed baseball caps; and Rosa's deputy, a tall light-skinned brother with a crooked hairline in the front.

None of them had gone out of their way to say hi to me. I felt alone, out of place. Just getting inside wasn't enough—I needed to earn some respect.

"My story is about Tommy Daminion, the guy who started the How To Be A Baller music convention," I declared. "He's about to sign Slow Creep."

My first day on the job I had called Pump Records. The publicist said Trophy and Bizack were out of the country. I asked to speak to Stan Ross. She took a message and I never heard back. After that I called all the people the allhiphop.com article said were trying to sign Slow Creep. None of the publicists got back to me—but I couldn't find any number or company for one person: Tommy Daminion.

The name sounded like an alias. I called one of my frat brothers who was an NYPD detective. He didn't want to tell me anything, since he could lose his job over leaking info. "All I need is a real name," I insisted. He came back with Thomas Clark. I plugged that into Lexis and some online criminal databases. They revealed that Clark/Daminion had spent five years in prison on a second-degree murder conviction, then was hit with a federal narcotics distribution charge about a year after he got out. Facing a life sentence, he went on the run and evaded authorities for six years. While on the lam he started the Baller convention and released three hit albums under his Daminion Entertainment label. He was finally captured a year ago and was now jailed downtown, awaiting sentencing.

"But what does he have new?" Rosa demanded, removing a chunk of pineapple from a heaping fruit plate with long, light pink fingernails. "He got any music coming out?"

"*He's* not even out. Of jail, that is," I said. "But he's still gonna sign Slow Creep at the Baller." That last part was an exaggeration, but I had to sell this story.

"They're signed to Stan Ross at Pump Records," Rosa said. "How can Daminion sign them?" She leaned back and lifted her feet onto the table. They were shod in giant pink and gray Nikes. I saw a few people exchange glances.

"Because Daminion has Mrs. Ross locked up in his basement," someone said. The room busted out laughing and conversation bubbled to life.

"Yo, you remember that time at the Baller with Dark?"

"You wasn't even there, son."

"But remember what they said? Dark was producing a session with like twenty dudes in the room. Daminion came in and told everybody to turn around and face the wall, then pistol-whipped Dark half to death for selling a piece of his production money to another manager."

"What you mean, sold his production money?"

"You know how these broke producers do. Take fifty, sixty grand up front in exchange for a percentage of whatever they make. And the whole time Daminion is smashing Dark in the face, he's saying, 'My contracts don't end. Ever.'"

I had assembled a thick manila folder documenting Daminion's legal history. But none of my facts carried the weight of that one story.

"Maybe we could write about how Daminion got Large shot up," someone said.

A tremor cascaded down my spine. This was something new. I fell in love with Large's music back when my brother produced a record for him, before L was famous. The song even got a little write-up in the *Fever* way back then. After that I bought every record, single, and mixtape Large put out. What really grabbed me was the way he condemned drugs and drug dealing. I was just starting to confront Dontay's addiction at the time, and Large made me feel as though someone sympathized with my situation. My first *Newsweek* byline came when Large survived five bullets in a robbery attempt outside Junior's restaurant in Brooklyn. And my first cover story was after Large was killed at the premiere of the *Dark Alliance* movie.

I thought I knew everything there was to know about Large. But I had never heard Tommy Daminion's name mentioned in connection with him before.

"Daminion ain't shoot Large. That's just Internet rumors."

"Daminion was the one who invited Large to Junior's. Maybe Daminion got tired of Large talking about how hustlers be killing the ghetto. It was a setup. How else would the shooter know he was at Junior's?"

"Nigga, he's Large! The biggest celebrity in Brooklyn! A thousand cats coulda saw him go in there and just waited for him to come out."

"All I know is the streets don't lie," murmured the white 50 Cent.

That's when Willie Stripp leaned forward in his chair, the front legs hitting the floor with a bang.

"Whatchu know about the *streets*? Ain't you from Connecticut?" Stripp said.

White 50 turned red. "Fairfield is right next to Bridge-port—"

"And Rosa," Stripp interrupted, turning toward the head of the table, "why don't you stop frontin' on the Daminion story in the first place? You just scared to keep it real."

Rosa's mascaraed eyes narrowed. "I'm *never* scared to keep it real," she said. "But only when it's in the best interests of our readers."

Stripp turned toward me with a scowl. The whites of his eyes were yellow. "I been telling these fools we need to do a story called 'There's One on Every Payroll.' All these labels got gangsters for hire. Mafia, gang members, felons, whatever. It's like nuclear weapons. You don't wanna use 'em. But you gotta have 'em."

Rosa popped open a can of Sprite. "Look, this ain't *Don Diva* magazine," she said, slurping. "Don't get it twisted."

"But we can freak it like they can't, though!" Stripp was so excited, he rose from his seat. "They say hip-hop journalism is dead—I'll show y'all some *journalism*. Y'all talking 'bout a hip-hop history issue. Yeah, give Kool Herc 'n' Bambaataa n'em they props. But you got to give props to the game. This rap game was made by hustlas. But y'all don't know. Can anybody here name the first rap record?"

"'Rapper's Delight,' son."

"Wrong, *son*. That was the second one, on Sugarhill Records, which was distributed by Morris Levy, who was an associate of the Gigante Mafia family, the crazy bathrobe Chin and his priest brother. Levy was one of the all-time biggest crooks of the record biz—he snatched publishing like they snatched chains back in the day. And he had the Birdland club too—took it from a guy with debts to the Gigantes. But Levy did the second record. The first rap record was put out by Garry Ross, who's connected to dozens of mobsters across the country. Garry's dad, Steven, was a major mob figure, a top guy.

"And," Stripp said, pausing to remove a cigar from the breast pocket of his navy blazer, "Garry's son, Stan Ross, owns Pump Records."

There was silence.

"What the *fuck* are you talking about," Rosa said.

The room broke up laughing. Stripp's face could have cut glass. He laced Rosa with a glare and stalked out.

"This has been another public-service announcement from Willie Stripp," Rosa said, imitating Stripp's gravelly voice. "In our next installment, we will analyze DNA recovered from the knife Young Buck used in the Vibe Awards stabbing."

The laughter was uproarious, and Rosa basked in it.

"Marq, about that Daminion article," she said when the noise died down. "Unless you get an interview, you can forget about it."

CHAPTER 6

I saw you that day on Fulton Street, driving your girl's car. You think I was buyin crack, dontcha? I wasn't buyin nothin. Peanut owed ME money. You always on me about this crack. But you know what's worse than crack, Marq? Cigarettes.

The juicer is gonna get rid of all that. The Newports, the drugs, the whole nine. I don't need to smoke crack—it's just a symptom of all the terrible things that's been done to me. And with Dr. Walker's juice I can beat it. Dr. Walker is a genius. Fresh carrot juice has sodium, potassium, calcium, magnesium, iron, phosphorous, and sulfur, plus silicon and chlorine. But for it to work right, you gotta have the right machine. Dr. Walker's juicer costs two grand, but it extracts thirty times the nutrients than the cheap juicer you bought me.

After I saw you that day, I went out to buy some carrots, took myself a long walk because I hate being in that room. When I finally get back to the block, there's a crowd of fiends on Boo's stoop, two buildings down from me. He hit a number for a few grand and wanna party hard. It used to just be Stanley the mailman up in there, getting high around Boo's rickety green kitchen table. Stanley spend more time in Boo's crib than on his route. I knew all them cats from the block. Now Boo's spot is swarming with crackheads. Me, I'd never set foot in that place. That's what makes me different.

I'm trying to figure out how to get home safe when I see Gutter's Suburban parked across the street from my building. Behind it was a dusty black Hummer, the old kind that was real wide and rugged. Gutter ran things around my block. Coke, herron, weed, pills. All the little corner-hustling niggas bowed down to him. And he owned my building, bought it after somebody defaulted on the mortgage. He had a stash spot in the back. You know that room on the other end of the hall from mine, the one with the metal door? It went down into a deeper basement where Gutter did his dirt.

Gutter's sittin in the truck and I go over to say what up. I used to keep an eye on things for him around the way—that's why he ain't stress if my rent was late. When I get close to the car, I hear he's playin Tupac's "Hit 'Em Up," that song where he came at Biggie over the "Don't Look Any Further" beat.

I can't stand Pac—his rhymes was nursery school. But I love that beat, love how the bass waterfalls at the end of them eight bars. I used to vibe off that track with Large. He always said he'd make a song to it. It was gonna be about how niggas don't look any further than today; we always actin in the short term. This was before Large got signed, before he changed. He was a real peaceful dude then. Reddy is the one who told him to play that drug dealer movie role, and Reddy is the one got him kilt. Large ain't never bust no guns; he never sold no crack; he was smarter than that. He was a beautiful dude.

One day I looped up the "Don't Look Any Further" beat for one whole side of a sixty-minute cassette. I brought it over by Fulton, on the corner by the liquor store. Large n'em was out front. They had an old Volvo parked at the curb; Nice & Smooth was on the stereo. I just walked up, reached in the driver's side window, and popped my tape in. This kid got heated but L was like, "Nah, chill, I know my

man Tay got sump'n I can rock to." The beat came
on and Large put his head down and listened. He
was looking hard at the pavement, you know? Someone
passed him a long, droopy blunt rolled in one of them
frontal leafs. I remember L exhaled a big cloud of
gray smoke. The air was all still and moist, and the
cloud hovered around his head. He took a swig from
a bottle of Hawaiian Punch, looking like some kinda
greasy dragon. He had on one of them brown Karl
Kani sweatshirts with the metal plate on the front.
And then Large freestyled for the whole tape, kid.
Nonstop.

The nigga rapped for thirty minutes straight. He
was flawless. Nothing fazed son, not the people coming in and out of the liquor store, not the jakes rolling past. Everything he saw he incorporated into his
rhyme, and he ain't stumble once. Nothing could stop
the flow. Niggas gathered round—other dudes is
wantin to rhyme but they scared to take the plunge.
L saw one dude bite his tongue and was like:

I see you quiet in the corner, don't hold the Dutch
Speak now nigga or forever hold these nuts . . .

There was no space in that cipher for anybody
but Large. When the tape finally ran out all of a sudden, he kept going, like:

Tape stops with a pop like a kernel
The beat might end but my rhyme is eternal.

The whole corner went crazy off that line, niggas jumping up and down, yellin, smashing bottles, spilling into the street. Cars couldn't get by. The nigga L stopped traffic! It was a classic moment, pure and free, no videos, no fame. No damn Reddy Rock Records. I just lay back in the cut, leaning against the window of the liquor store. I caught L's eye and we shared the moment. We ain't have to even speak. Our vibe was that tight. Then L went back to just standing there on the corner, lazy and content like he just ate a whole box of Kennedy Fried Chicken.

The point is, here's Gutter in Brooklyn, which is like the Jerusalem of hip-hop, and he's playin Tupac! Brooklyn's biggest enemy! Gutter shoulda known better. It's a matter of respect.

So I'm heated when I walk up to duke's ride. Gutter slid down the window. I see he got on a red Yankee cap, so I know he's got on some red sneakers. That's how Gutter did. Every day of the summer, he wore a white T and a brand-new pair of sneaks that matched a brand-new hat. He never wore the same pair of kicks twice. That was the uniform every single day of the summer: white T, new kicks, new hat. In the winter, though, he went all out. Furs, gators, yellow leather suits, the whole nine.

I see a dude I don't know in Gutter's passenger seat. There was growls coming from the back of his truck, so I know Gutter got his dogs with him. He had two big-ass black rottweilers. I don't know if they had names or not, cause Gutter always called them the Bitches. Their cage was bolted into the floor of the back of the truck where the third row of seats should be.

Gutter and the other dude get out the truck. Gutter say dude's name is Julien. Julien got a real squeaky, raspy voice, like Puffy the first time he rapped on Supa Cat's "Dolly My Baby" remix. He got his hat pulled low on his forehead, and he's wearin the biggest watch I ever seen in my life. Gutter brought a lot of hustlers around, but this cat took the cake.

Gutter opened up the back of his truck and I could almost taste that pissy dog smell. We was about four houses down from Boo's spot. Them fiends was all over the place, running back and forth to the bodega, arguing and fighting and e'ything. Just disgusting. Gutter leashed his dogs and they sat down right next to him, real well trained. Then he start askin me about Boo, why the block was so crazy, sayin I should say something to him about it. I was like, "Nigga, I don't work for you." Then Gutter gets real disrespectful, talking bout late rent, woop woop woop. We get into it and he's like, "Don't fuck with me or I might have to let the Bitches get at you." Right when he said that, he unsnapped the leash and said sump'n to them dogs.

Man, them two rotts started running at them fiends so fast, I heard their dog nails scratching the pavement. Stanley saw the dogs first. He jumped off the steps and jetted toward Fulton. But he was the only one who ran. Everyone else scrambled up the front steps. They was scrabbling and scratching at each other like a sack fulla cats. This one tall crackhead manage to climb up on top of the front door; she was squattin on that little overhang. I'll never forget that—she had her skinny arms spread out for balance, lookin like some kind of addicted bat.

The dogs run right past the stoop and chase Stanley, and before dude run ten steps, he fall flat on his face. Usually Stanley change out his uniform right after work, but tonight he still got on the mailman shorts, them snug blue joints. In about two seconds they was ripped clean off. In another two seconds Stanley's tight white draws is bright red. He's screamin and thrashin around. I was standing there in shock until I heard something strange and realized Gutter and Julien was laughing. Julien had this real crazy laugh that sounded all sandpapery, like sump'n from a cartoon.

I run over to Stanley and his thighs look like hamburger. One dog had her mouth clamped around his elbow and was dragging him back toward Gutter. The other dog was just barking its head off. I heard Stanley moaning, "Lawd, please, make it quick. Please, Lawd." I picked up a rock and beat at the dog on Stanley, but she kept dragging. I was looking for something bigger when both dogs all of a sudden turnt tail and ran back to the truck. They jumped up in their cage and Gutter slammed the car door shut. All the fiends was just standing around, straight petrified. I mean literally they was too scared to move.

*Gutter started the car and slid down his window.
He said, "I'ma be in the basement on Thursday. Tell
Boo to calm this spot down, or he'll be next."*

CHAPTER 7

A week after the staff meeting, my story was stuck. Tommy
Daminion was locked up downtown and his lawyer wasn't
returning my calls. Taylor was out of town. None of the publicists were calling me back. The few times I spotted Rosa in her
office, she was on the phone and waved me away.

I felt even more alone than at *Newsweek*, where my col-
leagues, almost all white, seemed willing to accept an educated
black man. There were two types working at the *Fever*: thugs
and thug-nots. The thug-nots included all races and were intelligent and well spoken, even with their slang and faux-ghetto
accents. They were cordial to me without being friendly and
gave me the briefest possible responses to any small talk I initiated. They seemed to spend most of their time in their cubicles
or offices hunched over their new Sidekick 3s. I had a two-year-
old model, which felt like a brick on my hip. When Briana
brought me a new one, courtesy of Taylor, I didn't put it down
for an hour.

The thugs were all black and seemed as if they'd come to
the office directly from street-corner shifts selling crack. They
congregated in a lounge area on the lower floor near Taylor's
office, engaging in loud PlayStation battles and talking on a
single phone plugged into the wall next to a battered brown
couch. I couldn't come up with a pretext to talk to them. When

our paths did cross, they never even said hello, just gave a stone-faced up-nod if eye contact was unavoidable. Those hard stares told me that even though I had a college degree, earned a six-figure paycheck, and could bench-press 250 pounds, they were more powerful, more paid, more potent than me. And in the fleeting seconds when we actually looked at one another, we all knew I wanted what they had.

When the thugs weren't in their lounge, they were coming and going through a door leading to the fire escape, which was the designated weed-smoking area. Everyone called it Knots Landing, or just Knots for short. That was the only place where the thugs and thug-nots mixed. Finally, out of desperation, I went out there late one afternoon. Two thugs and the crooked-hairline managing editor were passing around a blunt and dissecting a basketball game they had played against Reddy Rock Records. Apparently Reddy had shown up at halftime with the streetball star Main Event, who proceeded to take over the game. There was some heated debate over whether Crooked Hairline had gotten dunked on. I'd smoked weed only a few times in college and generally avoided it, but when the blunt came around, I was grateful to be included. After a few minutes it kicked in. Every sound and movement became swollen with flavor and meaning, without that unbalanced alcohol feeling. Next thing I knew, all four of us were floating up to a club called Kaya.

"Step out your kicks," the bouncer said. He peered inside each of my Stan Smith adidas and felt up my legs to the very edge of my crotch.

"Open your mouth," he demanded. "Lift up your tongue."

Lift up my tongue? What was he looking for? Then his meaty paw squished into my back and shoved me into Kaya.

I went to the bathroom to make sure my outfit looked right—orange patterned Marc Ecko shirt, new Rocawear jeans. I bought a Heineken at the bar and played with my Sidekick for a few minutes. Walked around the half-empty club a few times. Then I was out of things to do, so I just stood at the bar and let the sounds flow through me like hot coffee on a cold day.

If I had to choose between sight and hearing, there's no question I'd go blind. My earliest memories were sounds— Mom's soft hymns, Dontay's beats, rain on the window, coins passing from hand to hand. I befriended those random noises when I was little. They were often my only company.

Kaya was shaped like a large rectangle with a dance floor sunk in the middle like a broad, yawning pit. The sound system was scaffolded to the ceiling. A balcony jutted out like the upper deck of a stadium. Beneath the overhang were bars and long, low couches. The music was rattling around the space, so I could still hear the conversations.

Polow did the beat . . . in the building! . . . Fresh Beat sounds classic, dun. . . . Nah, not the kid . . . Pharrell was there. . . . Them niggas was scrubs, girl. We left them at Howard Johnson's . . . Hot like the real fever . . . Shawty trill fa sho . . . Diddy n'em . . . Budget was only fo' hunnet. . . . Mark Pitts . . . YO, NIGGA, WHAT THE FUCK YOU LOOKIN' AT?

A stocky dude was scowling at me. The white towel draped over his head framed heavy eyebrows, a lead pipe of a nose, and black jaw stubble. He wore a blue T-shirt with SPANK ME in big white letters on the front.

He took a step closer and expanded his barrel chest. "I said, what the fuck you lookin' at?"

My heart banged in my chest. I contemplated defending myself with the Heineken bottle in my hand, then decided I would flee if the situation deteriorated any further.

The stubbly scowl relaxed into a smile.

It was Chunk.

Relieved, I grabbed my childhood friend into a hug, then got embarrassed and released him. He laughed and pulled me back in, then took a step back to look at me.

"Damn, you swole!" Chunk said, looking at my chest. "You look good, son! But what the fuck you doing here?"

As a boy I saw Chunk every Sunday and Wednesday at church. We used to write Christian raps together. My mom was deep into Jesus, to the point where she nixed any activities unrelated to school or the Bible. My restrictions got even worse after Mom found weed in Dontay's closet and kicked him out. Dontay was eighteen; I was twelve. So when Chunk stopped going to church and started selling crack, I was doubly afraid to be in the same room as him. But our shared love for hip-hop kept us together. We'd meet on the Fulton Street Mall in downtown Brooklyn and spend hours perusing the record stores. My favorite rappers were Wu-Tang and Nas; his were Tupac and Large. When I went to Rutgers, I would tell Mom that I was taking the train back to school, then have Chunk pick me up in one of the cars in his ever-changing fleet of vehicles. We spent long hours listening to Funkmaster Flex on the radio, reading the *Fever*, going to Rutgers parties, and debating whether Jay-Z, Biggie, Tupac, or Nas was the greatest MC of all time.

Then, my sophomore year, Chunk got arrested by an undercover DEA agent at a bus stop in Toledo, Ohio. He was carrying five kilos of cocaine.

Prison created a vast gulf between us. Our places in the world had changed—I was now free from Mom, and Chunk was trapped. I sent letters and mixtapes, but when Chunk got out five years later, everything felt different. He even listened to rappers I thought were wack, like Master P and DMX. He came by my apartment once or twice, and then we stopped calling.

My Sidekick vibrated. I eagerly whipped it out, but the caller ID showed Dontay's number. I let it go to voice mail.

"Uh-oh, this nigga got hisself a Sidekick!" Chunk said. He detached his own Sidekick from his belt and we exchanged contact information. The DJ slid into the Mobb Deep song with the "She Blinded Me With Science" sample. Chunk laughed and bopped his cinderblock of a head. He still had that mischievous smile and a habit of glancing sideways, which made him look like a little kid thinking about grabbing candy off the table.

The club was filling up now, the low couches full of couples, people guarding their places at the bars. Four paces from the couches, a railing encircled the first tier of the dance floor. Those who didn't have a place on a couch or at a bar were pushed in never-ending circles around the dance floor, which had layers deeper and deeper, like an upside-down wedding cake. The innermost pit was the fullest, a tangle of wriggling bodies melted together in pairs.

The funk-filled air had me in a full sweat. Chunk removed the towel from his head to mop sweat off his face, revealing long, straight cornrows that fell back over his bulldog neck. I was one of the few men without headgear of some kind—do-rag, hoodie, T-shirt, stocking, too-large flat-brimmed baseball cap, or some combination thereof. The women had their bodies packaged like steaks in the supermarket. It really did look like a music video, only the girls weren't all gorgeous.

"I can't believe I'm looking at you, son," Chunk said. "But for real though, what you doing here? This the last place I'da expected to run over you."

I smiled as I remembered Chunk's habit of mangling everyday expressions. Despite his bad English, Chunk was fiercely intelligent and a good guy at heart. The reason he fell into dealing drugs was his father, a sociopathic hustler who reappeared in Chunk's life when he was thirteen. We used to argue about who was worse off—him with a twisted pops or me with none at all.

I knew my father's name was J.D., but that was about it. All Mom would say about him was that he was going straight to hell. I remembered seeing him only one time, when I was very young. It was late and Dontay was out in the street someplace; he was six years older than me and just starting to run wild. I heard a knock and peeked out the bedroom door. The man walked in, hugged my mom, and lay his coat and hat down onto the couch. There was a long blue feather stuck into the band of the hat. They went into Mom's room for a long time. I got tired and returned to my bed. When I woke up, it was morning. My heart leaped and I rushed out of my room, but my father was gone. After that I tried to convince myself that you can't miss what you never had.

"I just started a new job at the *Fever*," I said.

"Get outta here! So we in the same game now."

"What game is that?" I asked, eyeing Chunk's long chain, diamond cross, and heavy wristwatch.

"The rap game, nigga! Check it—I'm Young Spank's manager now."

I was shocked. Young Spank was the newest platinum artist on Fresh Beat Records, the greatest rap label of all time. His Dirty South anthem "Spank Me" had started the biggest dance craze since Soulja Boy's "Crank Dat" dance. And Chunk was his *manager*?

He motioned to the bartender, who poured three skimpy shots of Hennessy in front of us. The third glass was taken by a tall dude with sleepy, green eyes and an overbite, who'd been standing next to Chunk.

"This my homie Wop," Chunk said as we grabbed the drinks. Chunk whipped out a fat knot of bills and extracted two twenties. He saw me looking at the money, grinned proudly, and nodded his head.

"That's right, ya boy gettin' that gwop." He held up his glass. "Love is love."

The brown liquor disappeared down his gullet. The DJ blended into T.I.'s "Why You Wanna."

Wop disappeared into the crowd and returned a few minutes later with two girls wearing leggings and tube tops. Chunk waved the bartender over and ordered a bottle of Dom Pérignon. He peeled off five hundreds from his knot of bills and tossed the money onto the bar.

"It's nine," the bartender said.

Chunk flinched, peeled off another four. We all clinked glasses.

"Spank Me" came on. The two girls started doing the dance, throwing their butts back and forth and singing along: *Spank . . . Spank Spank . . .*"

Wop gestured at one of the tube-top girls, who was stumbling drunk. "You see them lips, son?" Wop said to Chunk. "She remind me of that bitch sucked my dick in the bafroom at the Tunnel that night."

"She had some crazy lips," Chunk agreed.

Wop tugged on his crotch. "Watermelon through a straw."

My head was starting to float from the alcohol. "So how'd you become Young Spank's manager?" I asked Chunk.

"I was in the fed with this nigga who's down with Tommy Daminion from way back. Me and P did some things together, and he put me in the mix with Daminion Entertainment."

The music faded and the dark room instantly righted itself. *Bingo.*

"I found Spank at the Baller two years ago," Chunk continued. "I brought him to Daminion and we signed Spank to a production deal."

Wop grabbed one of the tube tops by the elbow: "Ay, ho, c'mere." He pulled her close and said something into her ear, one hand on her curve of a hip. She shook him off and kept dancing.

"Daminion Entertainment?" I said. "I thought Spank was on Fresh Beat?"

"Yeah, but he's signed through us."

"What do you mean, through us?"

"Fresh Beat pays us, and we pay Young Spank. Now we platinum, son. So welcome to my world."

Chunk rubbed his hands together, then gestured grandly into the dimness.

"Check it," I said casually. "I'm doing a story on the Baller and I've been trying to interview Daminion. Can you get me in with him?"

"No problem, my nigga." Chunk laughed and draped a heavy arm around my neck. "Marq is in the building! I always knew you was gangsta."

CHAPTER 8

Is there any remover of difficulties save God. . . ?

There ain't none, you can bet on that. Especially for me. I never had nobody in my corner my whole life. Especially Moms. I know you always take her side, but you just gonna have to listen if you wanna hear my story. There's a lot you don't know. See, before Moms got saved, she was a drinker, a cusser, and a fighter. She kept two things on her night-stand—a bottle of Jack Daniel's and a pistol. She was so bad, me and you was about to get took by the state. After them social workers almost put us in foster care, though, Moms grabbed on to religion as a last resort, and she grabbed on tight. She stopped sinnin but her personality ain't change. She put away the Jack, but the pistol stayed. And she turned all that self-righteous anger on me. That's why I left.

So whenever I got into trouble, I had to say the prayer: Is there any remover of difficulties save God! That's what I was saying after them dogs went wild on the block. But I still ended up outside of Oldie's spot.

It ain't like I stop what I'm doing and say, "Lemme go smoke some crack." It just creeps up on you from nowhere. And when you're in the situation I was in, with no friends, nobody at all got your back, it creeps up with a quickness. So I have no idea how I got there. I mean, I know I walked there, but it's like I'm floating, and all the while I know I'm going to smoke crack, even though I don't want to, and I can't believe that I'm actually going where I'm going, because I'd rather die than go there. But here I am.

I went down to the bottom door of the brownstone and knocked. Oldie opened it and I followed him down the hall and into the kitchen. A few pots was cooking on the dirty stove. Oprah was on a tiny TV on the counter, next to a sink that stayed full of dirty dishes. Nicky and two youngsters I ain't know was sitting at a metal foldout table counting out a package. Nicky was watching the rocks, her big forehead all sweaty. It was always hot as hell in Oldie's spot.

Oldie was about sixty but looked eighty, with real bad teeth and eyes that bulged out like a frog. Back in the day he held down the dope flow in all of Bed Stuy. Now he stayed in his house and let the clientele keep him high. People kept Oldie high because he always had good dope and he could provide any kind of sex you wanted.

Nicky looked up from the metal table with her pretty green eyes. I tried not to look at her. I had some history with her, but so did a lotta cats. She was a sheisty one. Nicky might as well have been Oldie's daughter. After her moms OD'd, Oldie took her in and been looking out for her forever. She was stone-cold gorgeous—the finest crack smoker you ever seen.

I asked Oldie if he heard what happened to Stanley. He said yeah, but he ain't have no sympathy. He was like, "Stanley's a mailman. The mailman should know how to deal with a damn dog." Oldie knew all about Gutter, but I asked if he knew this guy Julien that Gutter had with him, the stocky nigga. He told me Julien's from Flatbush, got in the game by hanging around Tommy Daminion and the rest of them crazy Untouchables gangsters. He said Julien's a stickup kid—sell a few keys when he can get his hands on it, but really he wanna rob you for what you got. That was the first time I heard Daminion's name. Oldie said Daminion had Brooklyn sewed up before the feds got on him. He said after Nicky Barnes got knocked, things was up for grabs in the city, Colombians and Dominicans fighting, and then this Harlem nigga named Danny Hobbs started moving a lot of Colombian weight through Daminion, Alpo, AZ, all them cats.

Nicky came over and told me the young boys wanted to buy some beats from me, but I ain't pay her no mind. These kids don't know what hip-hop is. I gave Nicky a hundred dollars and she went out the back door on the other end of the kitchen. Oldie went to the stove to scramble some eggs. The two kids pocketed they stash and turned to look at me. Punks. Street-level scramblers. Prolly not from around here if they was willing to pay Oldie's commission. Cause Oldie made it known that he wasn't no real wholesaler, so he was gonna take a nice chunk off your package.

One of the boys looked at me and said, "We got niggas in the studio right now need tracks to spit on. Home girl said you nice. So who you done beats for?"

I told him, "I don't waste my music on broke niggas wit no skills. A G might buy you a few bars—come back after the first of the month when you got enough for the hook."

The kid was trying real hard to grow a mustache. He pulled a knot of cash out his pocket and was like, "Aiight, you got a track record; I can pay for that. So who you done beats for?"

I said, "Does the name William James Christopher mean anything to you?"

Dude ain't even know who I was talking about, but his friend said, "You ain't did no beats for Large. Reddy did all them tracks, him and the Beat Squad. And you ain't no Beat Squad. Smoke Squad, maybe."

I was ready to smash dude until I noticed Oldie wasn't scrambling his eggs no more. He kept an Uzi in the drawer next to the silverware. So I just stepped to home boy and told him that me and Large was making classics back when Reddy was hoppin turnstiles. Ignorant bastard ain't even know I saved his life right there. He put away his cash and left with his friend.

"When it comes to money, you the stupidest motherfucker I ever seen," Oldie said to me. That got me hot. I was about to bark on dude but the thought of the Uzi calmed me down.

"Making music ain't like sellin drugs," I told him. "I can't do it with just anybody. I don't even know why you bother with cats like that."

Oldie was like, "This why, nigger." Funny how old-timers pronounce that word. And he tossed a baggie with two big rocks onto the table.

I knew I was in trouble then. Is there any remover of difficulties save God! I pulled out my phone and tried to call you, but I got a message about needing to make a payment. I tried calling you on Oldie's phone but you ain't pick up. So I had no choice but to get high. And it was your fault. See, you think I'm nothing. But all these gangsters you wanna run with? I deal with them e'y day. And they all show me respect. Even a killer like Julien.

CHAPTER 9

Holliday was working late, so she stopped by Kaya to pick me up.

"Are you drunk?" she said as I fell into the Audi.

"No, I'm working. Guess who I saw in there? You remember Chunk? And he's gonna hook me up with Tommy Daminion."

Holliday gave me a disapproving glance and gunned the engine. We flew down Broadway and across the Brooklyn Bridge, Corinne Bailey Rae cooing to us from the CD player. Leaning back in my seat with the warm wind rushing past, eyes half-closed, my girl by my side, I felt as though I owned the city.

Holliday pierced my contented cocoon. "I hope all this drinking isn't going to be a regular thing," she said. "It's gonna hurt your workouts."

We exercised four or five times a week together, either at home with our treadmill and weights or at the YMCA, where I played basketball and she did kickboxing.

"No, I just needed to get some leads for my story," I said. "It's not a big deal."

As usual, Holliday cut over from the left lane to make the right turn off the bridge onto Tillary. The car she cut off drove up next to us at the light. It was a BMW convertible with a young brother in a suit behind the wheel.

"So not only do you look like Halle Berry," he said before screeching off, "you wanna drive like the bitch too."

Holliday found a parking spot. As we approached our building, I heard that wet cough. My heart sank.

Dontay was on the stoop, the hood of his velour sweatshirt pulled over his head. It was one of those muggy, still nights when the humidity seems magnified by the concrete. I had bought the sweatshirt for him last winter. It was matted with dirt that absorbed the blue-tinged street light.

"'Sup, bro," Dontay said, then turned toward Holliday. "Hey, lady. You aiight? Sue anybody lately?"

"Not lately." She smiled. Holliday knew all about Dontay's

problems. I knew he made her skin crawl, but she still treated him with respect, and I loved her for that.

We all stood there awkwardly.

"Your landlord tried to run me off the stoop, but when I explained I was your brother, he left me alone. I asked him about vacancies."

"I'm going to head on upstairs," Holliday said. "Dontay, it was nice to see you." She used her key on the front door and closed it behind her. My brother and I stood on the stoop.

"You should call before you come over," I said.

"You should answer your phone. Plus, my cell is off."

"Off? I just put the money into your account."

Dontay ignored that fact. "I tried to contact you everywhere. And *Newsweek* said you didn't work there anymore. What happened, you lose your job?"

"No, I just started a new job at the *Fever.*"

Dontay gave me a startled look, creases digging into his dark forehead. He was still a handsome dude, tall and graceful, although the scraggly beard he had tonight made him look shifty. Then Dontay started to rap, dark eyes glittering beneath the shadow of his hoodie.

Back in the day we slept on them floors
Now it's world tours, stepping out Benz doors
Way back I never thought I'd blow
Now I stack dough, hundred Gs per show
Put in so much work the street owe me dues
Flow cold like sleet so it froze these dudes . . .

I waited for the lyrics to stop rolling off his tongue. My brother was always quoting Large. He had an incredible memory for lyrics, although when it came to things that happened in real life, he could twist things so crazily. But he never forgot a syllable of Large's catalogue. And he was still trying to live off that one song he produced for Large back in the day.

> Real ain't really what you seem to be
> I make it real by the force of personality

Dontay looked at me as if he had just proved something. "You know where that last line's from?"

"Of course. The *Dark Alliance* sound track."

My brother cocked his head to the side. "What you think L's movie said about dope dealers?"

Dark Alliance was based on Gary Webb's book claiming that the CIA allowed tons of coke into the country so the proceeds could benefit groups fighting Communism in Central America. Thousands of kilos ended up in the hands of Freeway Ricky Ross, the LA dealer credited with starting the crack epidemic in the early eighties. In the movie, Large played Freeway Rick, trapped between his Central American suppliers and the CIA.

"Large hated drug dealers, and he portrayed Rick as the essence of evil," I said. "It was true genius the way he portrayed this archetypal drug dealer—it was like the highest form of satire."

Dontay's jaw twitched. "Then why all the dope dealers love that movie?" I started to answer but he cut me off. "How come Large won an Oscar for glorifying the dude who brought crack to America? I'll tell you why. Because once Large got signed to a record deal, he turned into somebody else. All the leeches changed him. E'ything that made him special got lost, and he turned into just another ho getting pimped by Hollywood—"

"Okay, okay," I said, cutting off the familiar speech. Dontay couldn't deal with the fact that Large got famous but he didn't. "So why are you here?"

"I have to leave that apartment. Things are dangerous for me there. If I didn't have so much respect on the block, I'd be dead now. I told you it wasn't a good place for me at the beginning. Plus, I need someplace where I can do my work, so I can get back on my feet. . . ."

I tuned him out, but even watching Dontay's lips move was excruciating. I ached to confront him about that day I saw him on the corner with the crack, but that would just prolong the encounter. Besides, I didn't need confirmation. I knew.

For the past two years, I'd been putting $900 in Dontay's account on the first of each month—$500 for rent, $75 for electric, $250 for food, and $75 for the cell phone. And he still came up short every month, asking me for money, not paying his bills. At first I would give it to him sometimes, until I got tired of getting played for a sucker. But he never stopped asking. Ever.

The cough. Dontay wasn't talking anymore.

"So what da deal?" Dontay asked, his face screwed into an angry frown.

"What's the deal with what?"

"You got some vittles up there or what?" Dontay took two strides up the steps toward the door to my building.

"Oh . . . my fridge is empty, man. Here." I pulled out my

wallet and angled my body so Dontay couldn't see inside. All I had were twenty-dollar bills. I gave one to Dontay without looking at him. As soon as the bill was out of my hand, I felt worse than before.

I always held on to the hope that Dontay would change. That was the only way I could stay with him. He had the talent. All he had to do was be in the right place at the right time to sell a few beats . . . but I still knew Dontay was going to get high. Tonight.

"Thanks, bruh."

I hated it when Dontay thanked me.

"I gotta leave that apartment," he repeated. "Bad things are happening there."

"Like what?" Now I was angry. No matter what place I got him to live in, he always said he needed to move.

"You couldn't even imagine. But I need to get out from under all this stress."

"What you need to do is stop smoking crack," I blurted. The words felt cathartic coming out of my mouth. "You're always trying to move. But no matter where you go, there you are."

Dontay glared at me and shook his head. "What I do to deserve this kind of abuse?"

"How are simple facts abuse?" I felt myself losing control and almost enjoyed it. "Why anytime I speak my mind you call it abuse?"

"See, you're acting crazy. I would never say anything like that to you. I could ruin your whole life with just a few words."

"If you have something to say, just say it. Your threats mean nothing, just like everything else you say." I could swear we had exchanged these exact words a thousand times. The urge to do something, anything, was overwhelming. I kicked an empty soda can, sending a tinny staccato rattling up the quiet block.

Dontay just stood there. I turned around and pulled out my keys.

"Yo, Marq."

"Yeah."

"Marq!"

I looked back over my shoulder. Dontay's glare was stony.

"Be careful with these rap niggas, ya heard me? You ain't built for that hustle. If you took the time to learn about your father, you'd understand why. *I'm* the only street nigga in this family."

"Yeah, whatever." I double-locked the door behind me and went upstairs.

Holliday had already taken her shower and was in bed with her glasses on, reading some legal papers. When I came out of the shower, the light was out and she was asleep, or at least acting like it.

I stood in the dark, looking at her shape in the bed. Her rejection was more than I could stand. I walked into the living room, standing helplessly, then throwing furious punches into the air. The liquor sloshed inside me and I felt wobbly. I dropped to the floor and started banging out push-ups.

One through fifty: *Dontay is the worst. Dontay is the worst.*

Fifty through eighty: *Where is my father?*

The burn flooded my brain, and I collapsed on the wooden floor before I could reach one hundred.

CHAPTER 10

Big stories made me feel as if rubber bands were squeezing my lungs. It wasn't a nervous sensation, because I knew I was prepared. More like anticipation mixed with exhilaration. As I slid into the metal chair across the table from Tommy Daminion, I dealt with the tension by envisioning a *Fever* cover story with my byline.

I had done prison interviews before, but only with low-level guys who wore defeat like a dirty coat. Not Daminion. His narrow face was ageless and serene. He was a few inches taller than me, with fuzzy, intricate braids clinging to his scalp. A faded scar ran down the side of his cheek, with another peeking from beneath the rolled-up sleeve of his khaki jumpsuit. The marks had been almost completely absorbed by his dark brown skin. He didn't seem dangerous or frightening. Despite the stone and metal surrounding us, he seemed in control.

Looking at Daminion, I wondered if I could survive in this place. Just how different could we be?

"A Salaam Alaikum, my brother." Daminion shook my hand, the regular way. We were in the main visiting room, alone at the corner of a long metal table. My heart pounded as I pulled out a yellow legal pad. The guards had refused to let me bring my little recorder inside.

A faint smile traced his thin lips. "A lot of people have been after me to do interviews," he began. "One reason I denied all the requests is that I've been in continuous turmoil with my legal situation. Now all that is about to be over. Once I get this last case out of the way, my battle with the government will be finished." He waved a hand in the air as if fanning away smoke.

I stayed silent and felt my interview face slide into place— open, receptive, eyebrows slightly raised.

"I know some people in the industry perceive me as dark, but they confuse darkness with staying in the shadows. So I want to be clear about one thing."

Daminion's index finger poked out at me.

"I feel like I can talk to you because Chunk put in a good word. But I ain't doing this interview to come out looking worse than when I started. Y'unnerstand, man?"

The word "man" was grunted out like "menh," the accent pure Noo Yawk. I automatically nodded my head with a sincere expression and said, "Of course."

"Good. So you wanna know about me and Slow Creep."

I waited.

"It's like this. I been a consultant for Stan and Pump Records for a long time and helped him out of a lotta jams. Matter of fact, I'm still getting paid a hundred and fifty thousand dollars a year from Pump, even in here. You can check my W-2s. So we have a relationship. At the same time, if the Creep don't wanna be on the label, Stan's gonna have to let 'em off. Unhappy artists don't make money for nobody. And right now it looks like they really don't wanna be on the label. Plus, Stan got a lot of problems right now. He got dudes beefing with him, Sony's ready to pull the plug on his whole operation. By the time the Baller rolls around, I should be out of here, and then we'll see what happens. Plus, I started the Baller, menh. It's my joint. So I'ma have the home-court advantage."

"How exactly did you start it?"

Daminion leaned back in his chair, laced his fingers across his chest, and looked up at the ceiling.

"Back in the day my cousin was a DJ. He got hooked up with this theater across the river in Jersey. They needed someone to finance it, so I stepped in. I needed a place to invest in with money from some of my other ventures."

Other ventures. Selling cocaine.

"Financing the theater brought me into the fold of hiring acts and trying to make money off parties and shows. I met a lot of managers and a lot of artists. But the money wasn't too good, even though I was primarily interested in it at that point for the laundry facilities, kna'm sayin'? It didn't take long to figure out that I wanted to be the one taking the money instead of paying it. That's when we started How To Be A Baller."

"Who's 'we'?"

"Me, my man Black out of LA, and a guy named Danny Hobbs, who's locked up now and never getting out."

"Locked up for what?"

Daminion's eyes dropped from the ceiling and made contact with mine. His expression indicated he was merely tolerating my questions.

"Hobbs was a real cocaine cowboy. He also was into music—he discovered D. Rex."

My brain flashed to the club scene with D. Rex and those two chicks draped over him.

"Hobbs was like, We got plenty of money, we gonna buy our way into the music industry. We gonna fly all these players down here and disguise it as a birthday party for Ricky Sixx from MTV. We chartered a plane and brought down like sixty people. We had MTV, BET, the *Source*, *Billboard* magazine, all the rappers, Teddy Riley, Aaron Hall, Shakim from Flavor Unit, all the Def Jam acts. We put up all the major players at the dopest hotel in Coconut Grove, all suites and penthouses. We had limos for everyone, catered meals—it was fly."

Daminion's eyes wandered dreamily for a moment before regaining their sharpness. "We had a bash Friday night on Fifth Street and did it again Saturday night. For Sunday brunch everyone went to Hobbs's crib. He had two tennis courts, a pool. He had a Porsche, a Benz, the 850 and 740 Beemers, and a Ferrari"—his fingers counted the cars, pinky first—"parked in the driveway. He even had off-duty police directing traffic to his house. There was a redneck cop standing right at the front door, in uniform, eatin' fried chicken. Niggas' jaws just dropped, menh. It was lavish."

I smiled into my pad as I scribbled as fast as I could. Lots of articles had been written about the Baller, but they always referred to the organizers as "a music management and production company." Now it could be told: The Baller was started by drug dealers.

"How much was the tab?"

"Maybe two hundred thousand. Hobbs spent the most money, since he was really benefiting. I dropped like fitty thousand. What that weekend did was introduce me to all the major players. Now I was on a first-name basis with them. The next year, 1995, we did it again and it was even bigger. Cats paid their own way. A few hustlers were there. We didn't spend as much, maybe a hundred thousand, and it was bigger than the last one. Word spread through the industry. That was the year I really came into the game. When you call Russell Simmons and say, 'Hey, I got you a suite at the Delano,' he looks at a nigga different."

Daminion paused and looked me in the eye, making sure I heard him clearly.

"Reddy was there, Puffy, Russell, Andre Harrell, J. J. Jones, Meyer Mahl, Tracy Waples, all the A&Rs. We bought out all the clubs and sold different nights to the labels so they could showcase their acts. They were all vying to get the best nights, the best slots. They wanted to knock the other labels out of certain positions. I would hook them up depending on who was who. It was crazy, bigger than anything done before." He shook his head as if still amazed, then cleared his throat.

"That's when I met Large, at the Baller that year."

All right. Here we go.

Before that first *Fever* staff meeting, my years of reporting on Large had made his history seem so clear: Large was wounded outside Junior's by robbers who took all his jewelry. Then he was killed eighteen months later exiting the premiere of *Dark Alliance*, by Central American drug cartels that were embarrassed by the movie's exposé of their operations. No arrests were ever made.

But after the meeting, when I Googled the word "Large" with "Tommy Daminion," blogs popped up claiming that Daminion had invited Large to Junior's in order to have him shot. And they said some guy named Julien did the shooting.

I took a breath and delivered a carefully calculated question: "So why did you shoot Large that night at Junior's?"

Daminion laughed. That was a surprise. I had no reason

to believe my statement was true; I just wanted to knock him off balance.

"How could I shoot L if I was inside the restaurant when he got shot? Ask anybody who was there. I was inside. Large caught them slugs on the corner of Flatbush and DeKalb."

"So you had him shot, then."

"Why would I do that? I invited dude there to talk about bankrolling his next film. He was the hottest nigga in the game, about to cop an Oscar. I'm financing a surefire hit movie and I'ma shoot duke *before* the cameras roll?" Daminion looked at me, eyebrows raised. One hand lightly strummed the table with long fingernails. "I'm on the run from the feds and I'ma shoot this cat on the busiest corner in Brooklyn? I'm a lotta things, but I ain't stupid."

His logic made a lot of sense. "So who shot him, then?"

Daminion looked away. "Large got himself mixed up in some shit that was too deep for him to handle."

He obviously knew more than he was saying. He probably didn't want to say it outright.

"So it was this guy Julien," I said.

Daminion's fingers stopped strumming the table. "Like I said, I wasn't there. But Julien did have reason to be mad at L."

"Why?"

Daminion re-established eye contact. "A week before the shooting, Large was talking about Julien in the paper. There was a picture of Julien in there with L saying how Julien is a lowlife, woop woop woop. I get a call from Julien like, 'You see what this nigga said in the paper?' Right there I knew L had problems."

"How did Large and Julien even know each other?"

"It's like this," Daminion said, exhaling hard. "I knew Large from the Baller. He knew me as a nigga with a whole lot of money who kept a gun with him at all times. One time we run into each other and he's getting ready to make *Dark Alliance*. He says he's playing a drug dealer in the movie and wants to hang out with some niggas doing some things so he can get an image for this part."

My mind reeled. In the worldwide acclaim that followed the controversial movie and Large's Oscar, no one had ever written that Large spent time with actual criminals to prepare.

I looked at Daminion and realized that the scar on his face was exactly the same as the one Large had in *Dark Alliance*. For a second, it felt as if I had fallen into my own movie.

"Now me, I'm not a flamboyant dude," Daminion continued. "I got the Rolex, yeah, and I like a nice car. But I ain't dripping in diamonds. I like to stay in the background. Some people would think Julien is the epitome of a gangster. To me, he's a clown. But to someone who's not in the game, they think that's what a gangster is supposed to look like. He had the BMW 850, the Rolex busting out all over with diamonds, the chain encrusted with diamonds, and all that. This is when rappers were still wearing gold. So I introduced Large to Julien and it was love at first sight.

"The three of us start hanging out. One time we're riding through Queens in Julien's 850. We're at a light in Jamaica and DTs roll up. I'm wanted by the feds. I ask if everyone's clean and Large is like, 'Nah, I ain't clean.' Luckily the police didn't pull us over. We got away from there and I told Julien to stop the car. Me and L got out and I screamed on dude: 'The fuck are you carrying for? Don't be holding no guns around us. I'm facing *life* for what I'm running from. This ain't no movie. You need to relax 'cause this ain't that typa party.'"

Daminion's voice rose in anger, and then he caught himself.

"I think L felt disrespected," he said, calming down. "It was like I wasn't a real G to Large. He looked at Julien as the gangster, but he didn't know that Julien is like my son. So I started to show Large things, probably showed him a little too much. Guns, a million in cash, kilos. I took him around a lot of Jamaican dudes, Brownsville niggas, introduced him to major well-known hustlers from Brooklyn. In the back of my mind, my intention was to manage L."

"Manage him?" I asked. "But Large was the antigangster! All due respect, but how could he be running around with y'all after building his career calling drug dealers the cancers of the black community?"

Daminion's face darkened, and for the first time I felt a flash of fear.

"Large was a fake-ass hypocrite," he spat, face crunched into a fierce frown. "Worse than that, he was a coward. How you gonna run with Gs just to do some movie, then vanish after it's done? You can't turn back that clock, menh. You build a whole image as this smart, righteous dude, then all of a sudden you rolling through Brooklyn packin' gats but you don't want nobody to know? That's like the master runnin' up in the slave house, then denying all the yellow babies is his."

My mind felt like an old computer trying to run a brand-new program. Large was really living the gangster life? It all came down to how much I trusted Daminion's story. When we caught each other's eyes, he knew I was hooked. At that moment, he seized total control of our conversation.

"So Large does *Dark Alliance* and all of a sudden he's the black Al Pacino," Daminion said, settling back into his chair. "His head blows up and he wants to direct his next movie. To Hollywood he's still a nigga, though. So where does he turn for money?"

Daminion chuckled. "They always come back to us for that. We're like the venture capitalists of the hood. One minute they call us scum, the next they got they hands out. Anyway, I line up J. J. Jones as my movie partner and invite L over to Junior's to close the deal. The spot was filled that night; all of Brooklyn was in there. We talk and then L leaves with his boys. Next thing I know, there's sirens and lights all over the place. I see duke on the ground and I call Julien and tell him, 'Are you outta your mind? Shooting this nigga at my meeting?'"

I was scribbling so furiously, my writing hand was starting to burn. I flexed my fingers and thought fast.

"How can I get ahold of Julien? I'd like to talk to him about this."

Daminion's eyes went cold.

"I'ont really know. Dude is one of the suspects in me being here right now."

"Julien? Why would he do that? I thought he was like your son?"

There was a pause. He looked at me, measuring me with his eyes. When he spoke, his voice was icy calm.

"I fronted him one time to rob some Colombians. It was forty-eight thousand. That's Julien's thing—he sets up drug deals and then robs the niggas who show up. Everybody in the game got they specialty. And I gotta admit when it comes to that, Julien's a brave muhfucka. But this time he comes back and tells me he gave the money to some Spanish dude in a car who drove off without leading them to the dope. I was like, 'You took a loss. I want my money.' I had him on my 'To Kill' list, but he's worth more to me alive than dead. I waited three months for my money. What part of the game is that? Finally he calls me and says this dude in Queens has three, um, *things* he wanted to get rid of—each one was twenty grand, sixty for everything. So I go see the dude and I tell him, 'Julien owes me forty-eight thousand, so just transfer that.' I paid him twelve grand, told him Julien would come through with the other forty-eight, and bounced."

Daminion smiled treacherously.

"Julien called me and said it was fucked up what I did to him. Right after that, the police was on me. They went to my landlord and asked to put a camera in the hallway. Somebody gave them my beeper and cell numbers and they tracked me to Miami. I was down there with my boo, Sugar, you know, from the group Sugar 'n' Spice. I used to be with her."

I remembered that group. Which one was Sugar? All I saw in my mind was an asymmetrical haircut and a big butt encased in spandex.

"I left her in the hotel, paid for two nights, and went to LA for the Soul Train Awards. After I left, she said room service came in while she was gone but she didn't order nothing. Four days later I was arrested in LA. They had my alias and everything."

I was writing furiously when I heard someone clear his throat behind me. A young, muscular dude whispered something in Daminion's ear, then left.

"My brother, I'm sorry, but my son and my wife just got here," Daminion said, rubbing a hand over his face. "We're gonna have to continue this conversation at a later date."

My mind raced for one last question. "So . . . the Baller is legendary now. Do you feel like you're missing the boat, locked up in here?"

Daminion winced. "That's why this sentencing is gonna be so crucial. Fifteen years, menh . . ." He stared into space for a few seconds. "I'd be fifty when I get out. A lot of my peers, guys who came into the game the same time as me, right now they're presidents of record labels, major figgas in the industry. These guys came in as managers, just like me. I got a lot of catching up to do. If I can get out by the end of the summer, in time for this year's Baller, that would go a long way toward putting me back where I belong."

A knee-high boy burst into the room and leaped into Daminion's arms, followed by a young, attractive woman wearing an expression that said she'd rather be somewhere else.

I stood up. "How can I get ahold of some of the other guys from the Baller?"

"Hobbs is doing life with no parole," Daminion said, cradling his boy. "Black, he's chilling out in LA. Go talk to Chunk. He can get you in touch with Black."

CHAPTER 11

I was sitting on my stoop with a glass of juice when Gutter and one of his boys showed up. Julien was with them, carrying a gym bag. The dope had to be in there.

The block was quiet. After Stanley came home from the hospital with his face lookin like shredded wheat, the fiends was smoke in the wind.

Gutter came through the gate into the little concrete yard next to the steps. He pulled out a big ring of keys and went to open the basement door. Gutter's lieutenant and Julien were standing behind him next to some garbage cans, waiting for Gutter to find the right key. He was fumbling through the ring looking for the right one. It was hot as hell, but Julien was wearing all black velour, real baggy. And dude was staring right at me. I put up with it for a minute before I asked him what he was lookin at.

He pointed to my juice and said, "Look like a pussyclot, bruddah. Yunno?"

I laughed. You know how apple and carrot juice makes that orange-reddish foam stick to the top of the glass? People always bug off how it looks, until they taste the goodness.

I took a minute to check Julien out. His skin

was real black and sweaty, but when I looked close at his face, he had a minefield of little round pimple scars on his forehead. I told him, "Yo, you should try some of this juice—it'll clear your skin right up." He scowled and looked away. I told him that right there in Dr. Walker's book it shows how a mixture of carrot, spinach, and lettuce juices will heal even the worst acne.

I was about to offer him some of what I had in my glass when Gutter finally got the door open, turnt around, and looked at me. "You call my cell if anybody comes to this door."

See, Marq, you have no idea how close you came to getting me kilt.

You had messed up with my cell again and it was cut off. I couldn't tell Gutter my phone was off. And if somebody ran up on him and I didn't call to let him know, I'm good as gone. You think you're my father the way you dole out that measly allowance. If I hadn't got Nicky to turn the phone back on for me, I'da been in real trouble.

When I axed Nicky for the hundred dollars, she scrunched her pretty face into an ugly mask, but I knew she'd come up off the gwop. That's why it was so hard to ask. History hurt. Nicky was a dime piece, even after all this time on the pipe. She used her looks to rip niggas off. She was a master of the okey-doke—loading up a pipe, then taking out the screen when you wasn't looking and loading up another screen like it was the first one. Niggas would spend hundreds of dollars with Nicky and only smoke 25 percent they own dope. She'd smoke for days off them suckas. On the rare occasion when she actually had to give it up for a hit, the girl was so fine, she could squeeze a dick between her hand and thigh and niggas swore it was pussy. They just couldn't believe they crusty asses was that close to such a beautiful woman.

That, and the crack played tricks on the jimmy.

I peeped her game, though. I ain't pull her card until one night she had the nerve to say my whole eight ball was gone. So I told her, "You know what, Nicky, you pretty slick the way you rip all these dudes off." She sat up so quick, the bed squeaked. We was upstairs at Oldie's house. She was like, "What you tryin t'say, Dontay?"

"You know what I'm saying. I know what time it is. I ain't like all these other niggas. If I was a little different, you'd be dead. I like you as a person, whether we gettin high or not. But when I expect certain things and you don't give them to me, I get angry. And at that point, if I was a different kind of person, I could kill you."

She started cryin and apologized and it was all good after that. That was one of a thousand chances I had to hurt people, but I never did. That's what makes me different. And that's why Nicky came up off the cash that day. Now tell me it ain't messed up that I gotta borrow money from a crackhead to turn my phone on when you won't *give me a dime. But that's my life right there.*

Anyway, Gutter went down into the basement. His lieutenant went down next. Julien went last, but before he walked through the door, he stopped and looked at me.

He said, "Carrot, spinach, and lettuce? I might try dat." Then he disappeared into the hallway.

CHAPTER 12

"Uh-huh," Willie Stripp grunted when I knocked on the door to his secluded office in a back corner of the floor. I entered the dark, smoky warren. Stripp was hunched over his computer with his back to the door, *XXL* magazine's Eye Candy site on the screen. Redman's "I'll Be Dat" was thumping from waist-high old-school stereo speakers in the corners of the room. The cover of one speaker was missing, exposing a vibrating woofer covered with graffiti. Stripp clicked off and spun around in his leather swivel chair.

"So I talked to Daminion," I said, moving a stack of newspapers off a stool and sitting down.

Stripp squinted. "And?"

"What can you tell me about Julien?"

Stripp's eyes widened. The whites were brown from smoke. He spun back toward the computer, reached under the desk, and raised the volume on Redman, then swiveled back toward me.

"You know what you doing, son?" he asked, rolling closer. "How you even decide to write about Tommy Daminion in the first place?"

"Taylor gave me a Slow Creep story. Daminion wants to sign them. He said he's been a consultant to Pump Records for years—he's still getting a hundred and fifty thousand dollars per year from them even while he's locked up. He says if Creep wants off that label, Stan will let them off."

Stripp removed a cigar from the breast pocket of his battered blazer and placed it unlit into his mouth. I thought he was massaging the cigar with his teeth until I realized he was talking just loud enough to be heard over Redman's lyrics.

"The fact that Taylor put you on this assignment makes it suspect from the jump. Dude always has an agenda when he asks for a story. But first things first: Why you think Stan Ross pays Daminion? What exactly does 'consultant' mean?"

I didn't say anything. I really didn't know the answer.

"What does Daminion have that Stan needs?" Stripp prodded, then answered his own question. "He has a name, a name that people fear. Stan needs people like Daminion so niggas won't run up in his office, hang him out the window, and shake him until all his publishing falls down onto the sidewalk. Stan had problems with Wu-Tang a while back, and Daminion helped him solve that amicably. But when the problems went away, you think Stan can stop paying Daminion? Your boy from Connecticut got one thing right: Daminion's contracts don't end—ever. So at what point does it turn from consulting into extortion?"

I hadn't thought about that. "If Daminion is so tough, why isn't Julien scared of him? Because Daminion said Julien is the one who shot Large outside Junior's and then told the feds where Daminion was."

The song was ending. Stripp leaned down to adjust the shoelace on his red-on-white Nike Cortez and waited for the next track to start. The Nike stripe matched the red band in his stingy-brim hat.

"No one really knows the deal with them two. Word on the streets is that Julien did get at Large outside Junior's, but it wasn't nothing Large ain't have coming. And the streets don't lie. I only got one more thing to tell you—be careful with Taylor. Now if you'll excuse me, some of us got work to do."

Stripp's warning about Taylor was hard to believe. I had been out a few times with Taylor since starting the job. It seemed as though no club was closed to him, no celebrity VIP lounge off-limits. And his secretary, Briana, kept bringing me a steady flow of perks—the Sidekick, clothes, CDs before they were officially released. So why would Stripp say the Slow Creep story was suspect? Taylor put me on it because of the stabbing that happened right in front of us.

I needed to make sure I wasn't missing anything, so I grabbed my ball and headed to the gym. The high-end Reebok Club—Briana said I could expense it. As I was finishing up my free throws—bounce, bounce, bounce; breathe, bend, flick, swish—something occurred to me.

Slow Creep's label drama must have been brewing before I saw that stabbing. Otherwise there wouldn't have been an article online when I got home that night. So Taylor probably had the assignment in mind for me when he contacted me for the job.

I showered so quickly, I was still sweating afterward. The overcast afternoon sky was a humid bubble over Manhattan as I hurried back to the *Fever*. Taylor wasn't in his office. I found him next door, in an office decorated with Pittsburgh

sports memorabilia and photos of the rapper Leak with various
celebrities. I'd never heard Leak on the radio, but I copped his
albums after he was on the cover of the *Fever*. He had some
nice beats.

Taylor was putting golf balls through a hole cut into an
empty Prada shoe box. He looked up at me and smiled, then
looked back down at the small white ball.

I smiled back. I had the edge because he still thought I was
clueless.

"So how'd it go with Daminion?" Taylor asked.

"Great interview. He talked about starting the Baller, and
it looks like he has a good chance to sign Slow Creep. Now I
need to go to LA and talk to this dude, Black. He's part of the
Baller and should have some good information about what's
gonna go down there."

Taylor's eyes stayed glued to the ball as he made a putt.
"Daminion talk about what happened at Junior's?"

Something told me to play dumb. "What happened at
Junior's?"

"You know, with Large."

"Daminion had something to do with him getting shot? I
thought that was just Internet rumors."

Taylor made another putt. "Ask Black about it. I bet he'll
have something good to say. Back when—"

Rosa burst into the room, wearing painted-on lowrider
jeans and huge neon green and yellow Reeboks. Her pretty
eyebrows were twisted into a scowl.

"You need to talk to your girl Lonnie," she spat at Taylor,
looking past me as though I were another piece of furniture.
"She's trying to front on the cover."

The office was in an uproar trying to finish the new issue. I had heard people talking about the Lonnie McCready photo shoot all week. She was the sexiest R&B singer out.

"What's wrong?"

"It's already been shot. We all agreed ahead of time she'd be naked. Lonnie wants to keep her panties on during the shoot, no problem—we can take them out digitally. But now the photographer won't turn over the prints! She showed them to Lonnie—which I can't fucking believe—and now Lonnie is having second thoughts. We're closing on Friday. I'd like to wring that little bitch's neck."

Rosa looked as if she could do it with one manicured hand.

"Don't worry about it," Taylor said. "Felix Billings is her manager—lemme call him and straighten this out."

"You do that," Rosa said as she stomped out. "Putting her on the cover was your idea in the first place."

The door had barely closed behind Rosa when Leak walked in, the heels of his unlaced Timberlands making a scuffing sound as they dragged along the industrial-grade carpet. Taylor got up, and I was surprised to see Leak take the seat behind the desk. He lifted his brown boots up onto the table, heavy jewelry clanking with every movement.

This is Leak's office?

"You still playing that bitch-ass game," Leak said, nodding at the golf club in Taylor's hand.

Taylor ignored the comment. "Leak, this is Marq, a new dude on the team. Marq, this is my partner, Leak."

Partner? Nobody told me Taylor has a partner.

I got up and gave Leak a pound. He had a strong grip. He

was slender and brown-skinned, with a gleaming bald head and no facial hair on his round face. Two tattoo tears were inked beneath his left eye. As we separated, I got a close look at his diamond-coated medallion, a giant *F* made of three arms, each gripping the next with a bulging fist.

"What that bitch want?" Leak asked Taylor.

"She's just mad 'cause Lonnie ain't give her no pussy at the photo shoot."

Leak and Taylor laughed hard. "She be stressing me, though," Taylor said. "I think we need a jump-off."

Taylor picked up his Sidekick and tapped out a message. A dude walked through the door a minute later, scratching at his high-yellow acned face. He was wearing the exact same Sean John outfit, down to the stain on the sleeve, that I'd seen Taylor in a few days earlier.

Taylor said to him, "Yo, it's time for a jump-off."

Acne Face grinned and grabbed his crotch. "Ah, yeah. You want me to holler at your boy, get them hoes from last time?"

"Indeed. Them bitches was smokin', son!" Taylor and Leak laughed uproariously, slapping hands. I chuckled, at what I didn't know. Acne Face left.

"LA sounds good," Taylor said once he was gone. "Briana will get you the ticket. Now let me straighten out this Lonnie business with Felix." He put the phone to his ear and started to dial.

I went back to my office, turned on some Young Jeezy, and went online to check the weather in LA. So Taylor wanted me to pursue the Daminion angle. I didn't mind playing along. Whatever happened at Junior's was probably connected to Large getting killed in LA. Despite all the by-the-book reporting I had done on Large while at *Newsweek*, it felt as if a different story was calling me from the parallel universe of the streets. And I was powerless to resist.

CHAPTER 13

Julien came out the basement by hisself.

He was carrying the gym bag, had Gutter's keys, and was trying to lock the door behind him, but it wasn't working cause he ain't know you had to lift up the door to get it shut. I offered to help him and he got agitated, told me to keep back. The back of his neck was mad sweaty. He finally got the key to work and turned around, breathing hard.

That's when I stepped to him. I pulled the juice book out my bag and told him, "This dude, Dr. Norman Walker, is a genius. He lived to be a hundred and seventeen years old by drinking only fresh juice. This book will change your life."

That's the same thing I told Moms, but she never believed me. She got mental problems, you know that. The juice woulda cured her, but she didn't want to talk about it, same way she'd never talk to me about my father. She avoided all my questions about Pops, told me to come back when I was older. But I was never old enough. Until one day I exploded and demanded to know where I came from.

That was the first time I ever saw Moms scared.

She sat down at our tiny kitchen table and lit a cigarette. Moms might act like she holier than thou, but I bet she still keeps a pack of Winstons around for emergencies. She was rubbing her thumbs over each other. That thumb shit drove me crazy. She didn't want to look at me, either. You know how she usually demands your attention with that hard glare. But this time she just looked out the window and rubbed her thumbs over each other. Finally she said, "Your father was no good, period. He was a con man, a dope dealer, a gambler, prob'ly even a killer. You want that kind of father? Better to have none."

I didn't dare ask how she could make a baby with someone like that. I thought she mighta shot me. And the whole conversation she ain't look at me, not once. That's when I finally recognized what she's hung on me since the day I was born.

It's shame.

Moms is ashamed of Pops, and she's ashamed of me. Not you, though, Marq. You're different. But you don't wanna hear about that.

The only thing I could remember about Pops was the name J.D. Something inside told me he was still in Brooklyn, and one day I started searching for him. I looked for seven years. I wanted to know what part of me was him. Did he wake up to melodies falling through the air? Why am I even on this planet? If God controls everything, how can he put me into a situation where I'm forced to do the things I did? Is it cause I'm plain bad inside, like Pops?

One day I was in this Crown Heights speak-easy on Park Place. Musta been about '94, cause I had money. The joint was a hangout for the Franklin Avenue Posse. About a dozen of the crew had just rolled in from a boosting expedition, so they was all Poloed down. Somebody'd even stole a mannequin—not that hard when you flood a store fifty deep, snatch armfuls off the racks, and then scatter like roaches. The mannequin was posted by the door of the bar, sporting a bright yellow Polo cap turned to the side. I was parlayin with this kid about some tracks when the bartender caught my eye and said, "That's J.D. right there."

He was sitting in one of the two booths, his back to the bar. I slid in across from him. My father has a smooth, dark face, just like mine, only puffy around the eyes and mouth. Pencil mustache, long fingernails. His maroon suit matched his wide-brimmed hat and his cuff links matched his gold chain. He wore a medallion with some saint on it.

I had so much planned for this moment, but I just sat down and said, "You're my father."

J.D. looked up from his drink with a squint and said, "Who yo momma?"

"Althea Wise."

He winced and downed his drink. "Where she at now?" he asked. I told him Brooklyn Heights.

We looked at each other. He pulled out a Kool. I broke out a Newport and we smoked in silence. Then he said, "You might as well take my phone number."

And that's how I got my father back.

I hope you hear what I'm saying when I tell you we looked at each other. You remember that prayer about the remover of difficulties? That's from the Báb. That means "the Gate"—he was like John the Baptist who opened the door for Jesus. After the Báb came Bahá'u'lláh—that's pronounced Ba-hah-OO-lah. He's the founder of the Bahá'í Faith. That's my religion. And Bahá'í's have a saying that "the eyes are the window to the soul."

So when I looked into my father's eyes, I knew who he was. And I knew I shoulda been with him my whole life. That woulda solved a lot of the problems I have now. But Moms kept him from me. All the bad things she said about him, they all went out the window when I looked into my father's eyes. Because the eyes are the window to the soul.

Ever since that day I been able to see inside of people when I look in they eyes. And when Julien came up from the basement and looked at me, I got a bad feeling. There was something behind his eyes I had seen before in the most dangerous people.

My hand was still stuck out with the book in it. Julien snatched it from me and opened the gate. He said, "Okay, bruddah, I'ma read this book. Gutter said for you to wait here until he come up. Don't move."

CHAPTER 14

Black was very black.

We were in the parking lot of a high school in Simi Valley, California. A group of men stood about, blunt smoke and stories in the air. Black was in the driver's seat of his Mercedes S500, door open, one leg on the ground, rummaging through his glove compartment.

He looked to be in his midthirties, with close-cropped hair and a barbered mustache. The June sun raised a sweat that ArmorAlled his skin so it matched the tires of his car. A baggy blue adidas sweat suit almost hid his potbelly, and he wore white-on-white shell-toes, silvery sunglasses, and a floppy white bucket hat.

I had chosen to wear a forest green track suit, carefully avoiding anything blue or red. Still, I was kind of nervous. According to Chunk, Black was a member of the Rolling 60s Crips, one of the most notorious sets in LA. What if a Blood rolled up and tried to shoot him? When I had told Holliday about the purpose of my LA trip, she had gotten up from the couch, gone into the bedroom, and stayed there for half an hour.

The parking-lot crowd disappeared along with the weed, and I finally had Black to myself. He locked up his ride and we started walking toward the stadium.

"So tell me about this article, cuz," he said, lobbing the

words to me in his Cali twang. "Whatchu need to know from me?" The cheeks on his round face bunched up when he smiled.

"I'm writing a history of the Baller. How 'bout we start by telling me how you got into the music business."

I had a pen and fat pocket-size notebook in my hands. My tiny digital recorder was tucked into a pocket, turned off. It didn't seem smart to use it right now.

"My cousin was DJ Cheetah," Black said, rubbing the back of his neck. "Cheetah was in Uncle Jam's Army, the biggest black party promoters of all time in LA. They gave dances at the Sports Arena, the Forum, places like that. There'd be ten thousand people in there, just dancing to a DJ, no performers or nothing. Cheetah started out carrying crates for the DJs in the Army like Alladin, Battlecat, DJ Pooh, Egyptian Lover. Cheetah would do errands, pick people up coming in from out of town. I would roll with him, hop in the van, just do whatever. About this time I was also gettin' into the streets. My crew was called the Tiny Locos—we was young teenagers. This was like '82, '83."

"How old were you when you were initiated into your gang?"

Black cocked his head to look at me as we entered the gate to the stadium. "Initiated? That's something from the movies, dude. That's for outsiders. Initiation is when you play football in the street with your cousins and they all 60s. Initiation is when it go down and you right there. Initiation is when the poh-leece"—it rhymed with "snow fleece"—"put you on the wall with everyone else and write 'Rolling 60s Crips' in they book next to yo' name. Ain't no initiation. I was born into it."

"So what happened with Cheetah?"

"He went to a DJ contest in New York. It was the New Music Seminar, CMJ, sump'n like that. He ain't win, but he hooked up with J. J. Jones, and he became Big Brawls's DJ."

I remembered Cheetah now. The legendary Big Brawls had recorded ten albums for Fresh Beat Records.

"Now Cheetah's in New York all the time, in the studio with Brawls, out on tour, the whole thing," Black said. "I would be around him. I had my own money, so I'd travel with him, party, get at bitches. I'd fly to the different places, maybe ride the tour bus for a lil' bit. I saw that I had more paper than Brawls. That was the first time I noticed all these rap niggas wanna be like us hustlers. They change their names and personalities like we do. Hustlers, they go and do something, they'll change their name to throw the poh-leece off the track. That's us. I would get a gold chain, Brawls n'em would want to mimic it. I knew how to spend paper, to enjoy paper. They wanted my jewelry, I didn't want theirs. They wanted to come to my hood, I didn't want to go to theirs. Me and my home boys was like, We can do this music thang. We don't even need these busters, these cornballs. Let's get our money together, make us our own Big Brawls."

Black fell silent. We were inside the stadium now, near the front of the packed bleachers. All of a sudden Black ran to the railing encircling the track, paunch jiggling.

"Run, Kyree, run!" he shouted. "Dig dig dig dig dig! Ruuuuuunnnnnn!"

A swarm of knobby young knees churned by. Black stood on his tiptoes, hands on the rail, until his son passed the baton to a teammate. I walked up and stood beside him.

Black waited for the race to end on the far side of the track. His son's team did not win. A rueful smile spread over his face as he rubbed the back of his neck and continued talking.

"So I started knowing all the music dudes from being on tour with Fresh Beat. I already knew all the LA niggas. I grew up with Dr. Dre in church—his grandmom was our Sunday-school teacher. I still got the Bible she gave me. So I started comanaging Cheetah and some other groups I picked up here and there. I got a little deal for like forty thousand from bitch-ass Stan Ross at Pump Records to develop this group I had."

We walked over to a crowded refreshment stand and took our places at the back of the line.

"But he expected me to do a whole album for forty Gs. We did a few songs; he wouldn't put them out, and he wouldn't give up any more money to make no more music. Plus Stan don't like black people. You can quote me on that." An edge started to creep into Black's voice. "Stan only respects two things: money and fear. So he lies to everyone, and then he surrounds himself with bodyguards. And it ain't no excuse that he's white. You don't see a white dude like Meyer Mahl walking around with bodyguards. Meyer may have got his nose broke a few times, but he's man enough to face that chance. Meyer don't care who gets paper, as long as he gets his. Stan wants to pick and choose who gets paper. Stan didn't earn his paper—he got it from his daddy—so he don't respect it. I had my own money when I met Stan, so he was scared of me. He tried to pay me peanuts, so I had to do what I had to do. You can't tie me to no office. I would disappear for six months and still be getting checks from Stan. I brought all kinds of groups in there. I brought Eminem to his office; he said no. I sat him down with the Neptunes—no. In three years he never let me sign one group, and I'm supposed to be West Coast director of A&R for Pump Records. How can I go in there and kiss his ass and then go home and tell my sons to be a man? I got a little heated with him. I guess he got scared, and he was like, 'Do you know who my daddy is?' Like I'm supposed to be scared of the Mafia. I told him, Fuck yo' daddy, nigga—I'm from 60s! I don't give a fuck about no Mafia. I'm Six-Oh Crip. And Black will shoot, nigga. I *will* shoot. You can ask anybody. That nigga Black will shoot."

He was speaking with a laugh in the back of his throat as if it was incredulous that anyone would challenge him on this fact. I looked around to see if anyone had overheard us. We had moved up to the middle of the refreshment line. For the first time, I noticed that the crowd of several thousand parents and children was almost entirely white.

"That's about when I met Hobbs at a concert in Miami," Black continued. "He said he was looking for some partners for the Baller and he needed about sixty thousand dollars. I was wit it. Now the music niggas had to come to us. They were our guests. That really put me in the music game in a big way. After that I could go to people and make deals, because it was like, How can you deny me when you was my guest?"

Black paid for six hot dogs, two sodas, and four bottles of water. He handed me a dog and a Coke, then balanced the box in one hand and stuffed half a hot dog into his mouth with the other. We climbed the tall bleachers and sat down beneath a banner reading VALLEY ROADRUNNERS amid a dozen black men and women, casually dressed but wearing watches and jewelry that betrayed expensive tastes. Several of the men had prison physiques and blue clothing. The whole group seemed oblivious to the all-white surroundings.

"So why do you think Slow Creep wants to leave Stan?" I asked once we were seated.

"He prob'ly cheating them out their money."

"You think Daminion will be able to sign them?"

Black chewed on a hot dog and spoke without taking his eyes off the track. "Could be. I got half a mind to go start my own label."

"You mean bump heads with Daminion?"

"Ay, Tommy is like my brother—I love that dude. Whenever he come to LA, I got whatever he need waiting for him—guns, money, whatever. Matter of fact, he's locked up now for a gun I gave him, and I put up the bail money that he skipped out on. Ain't no problem, though. I would do anything for that man. So we'll see how things work out with his legal situation and take it from there."

I hesitated, then sprung the question I had been waiting to ask all morning.

"What about Julien? You cool with him, too?"

"Course I am. Dude called me the other day."

"Word? You could hook us up?"

Black pulled out his phone and hit a few buttons. He had a wireless headset stuck to his ear. "Whatup, nigga, it's Black. . . . Don't get mad at me—I'ont know why he did that. . . . Naw, that ain't work out. . . . So I got this writer here from the *Fever* magazine—he doing a story on me and he wanna holler atcha. . . . Uh-huh . . . Aiight, I'll see you there."

Black clicked off. "Julien said he don't do interviews."

I decided against asking for Julien's number. "So what's up with Julien and Daminion? They having problems now?"

"Them dudes always beefing, like schoolgirls or sump'n. One minute they best friends, the next they wanna kill each other."

I lowered my voice so no one could hear my next question. "Were they friends the night Large caught it at Junior's?"

Black shot me a quick glance out of the corner of his eye, then returned his gaze to the track. "I'ont know nothing about that. But Tommy was braggin' about having that movie meeting with Large. He even called me up about that."

"So he could have called Julien, too, and tipped him off."

"Not on some 'come get this dude' shit. Julien musta made his own move on that."

So it's true. Julien shot Large in Brooklyn.

Now I needed to figure out who really killed Large in LA. As I scribbled in my notebook, two young boys materialized and jumped onto Black's back.

"Daddy, you got sodas?" the older one said, reaching into Black's gym bag. The boy pulled out a water bottle and made a face.

"Soda'll tire you out," Black said. "Drink water and you'll win your next race. You know I don't tolerate no losers around me. Kyree, Kijana, say hello to Marq. He's writing a story about me and the rap industry."

Kyree, the older boy, had fuzzy cornrows and hazel eyes. "I already won twice today, Daddy," he said. Kijana was trying to climb on top of Black's head.

"That's why you my favorite son, Kyree," Black said, shrugging Kijana into his lap and tickling him. "Now drink that water like I told you." The brothers each grabbed a bottle and skittered down the steps.

My Sidekick vibrated. It was a message from Chunk.

YO, WHAT DA DEAL? WE JUST LANDED AT LAX.
IT'S GONNA BE CRUNK TONITE AT SCRUPLEX

"Yo," I said to Black. "What da deal with Scruplex?"

CHAPTER 15

"Daddy, turn this up."

We were in Black's Benz, rolling down the 101 freeway, listening to a New York mixtape with an old Ghostface song on it. Three small brown heads in the backseat bobbed to the music. The twinkly beat sounded rich and full through the speakers.

I live it out. . . . Special Delivery . . .

"I spit it out." The whole family rapped together.

Special Delivery . . .

"My crib now is aiight—it's in the Valley, got it for like seven hundred and fifty thousand," Black was saying. "I'm about to sell it and move to this other house. I should make like three hundred off it. The new house is like a million something. I own about ten million in properties. That's the best investment there is. Your house is like your bank account. You put money into it every month. It ain't like that money is gone—you just saving it for later, and you get back more than you put in. I mean, it's a sure shot! 'Scuse me."

Black pressed the button on his wireless cell-phone headset, spoke to his wife for a few minutes, and then clicked off.

"Kijana, you put on that lotion?" Black barked.

The smallest boy looked pained.

"You know he didn't," said one of the older brothers, the one with a lopsided Afro that showed evidence of a recent unbraiding.

"Lotion is poison," Kijana said solemnly.

"Go in the bag and put on some of that lotion or I'ma pop you when we get out this car," Black commanded. There was movement in the backseat and the littlest boy reluctantly rubbed his elbows.

"Daddy," he said when the song was over, "yesterday, when you were talking to that man on the phone about money, if we were using the curse jar, you woulda owed us five dollars and fifty cents."

"That's why I told you I'm not doing the curse jar." Black was trying not to smile. "That's for y'all kids."

"Curse jar?" I asked.

"Every time they curse, they gotta put fitty cents in the jar. 'Scuse me." Black pressed his headset button.

"Hello? . . . Nah, dude, that's impossible. . . . There's no way that could happen. That's why I said you were under. . . . You do that math, then. . . . Twenty-eight times four . . . That's almost two—am I right or wrong? Am I right or wrong?" The Benz was in the fast lane.

"Okay, okay, it's all my fault. You just keep everything," Black said. He yanked the headset out of his ear and picked up the cell phone. "That's my kids' spending money—you can just keep that, take that from out my kids' mouth, then."

Without moving my head, I glanced at the speedometer. Seventy-five.

Black listened for a long time.

"You got a real problem with raising your voice at me," he finally said. "You got a real problem with that, dude. I get real offended by that. I don't never raise my voice at niggas, 'cause I don't like it when they do it to me."

The Benz was riding the bumper of a Toyota 4Runner. We were so close, I could see the Toyota driver's eyes in his rearview mirror. I peeked at the speedometer, but the needle was so far to the right it was beyond my view.

"Don't tell me that, dude. That's impossible. I stayed in the house doing *just that*. That's why I was late. I was doing *exactly that*." Black was holding the phone directly in front of his mouth like a microphone. "I never had this type of problem with any of my transactions. I don't make mistakes. . . . Three and a hee-zalf over . . . I'm telling you, dude, *I don't make mistakes*."

Black's tone was sandpaper on plastic. He was driving with his knees, large white teeth flashing against his ebony skin.

"I'm guaranteed, dude. Ask anybody about me. Ask ten niggas in ten different cities. *I don't make mistakes!* . . . I'm not finna argue over this with you. It ain't worth it. For a thousand bucks? I give that to my kids every month, every two months. So they'll be a little short for the month. . . . Look, dude, I told you about raising your voice like that."

I tried to think of something Black could be talking about besides drugs.

"Yunno, I'd rather you just keep it and we can keep being friends. Our lives depend on this, dude. Our lives! *Especially yours!*"

Black hung up and tossed the phone into a space beneath the stereo. He looked in the rearview mirror.

"Lemme see them elbows, Kijana. They best not be ashy."

We dropped the boys off at Black's house in the Valley, showered, and changed. Black's attractive wife said a quick hello. Then Black and I jetted into LA.

I asked Black a series of questions about his history, trying to lead up to what I really wanted to know: Did Central American coke dealers really kill Large outside his LA movie premiere? As obviously connected as he was, Black had to know something. I finally saw an opening when he mentioned that he had helped finance the *Dark Alliance* movie.

"So you were at the premiere?"

"Course I was. It was the flyest shit ever."

"Until Large got shot, though, right? That must have been crazy."

"Crazy ain't the word."

"So was it really those foreign cats who did it?"

"That's what the papers said."

"The papers also said Large got shot in Brooklyn after a stickup, but it was really Julien behind that. So I'm assuming there was something else going on in LA."

Black was silent as he exited the metal river of freeway traffic and piloted the Benz onto a city street. "I'ont know nothing about that. I was inside when it happened."

"It just doesn't make sense now that I think about it. Large wasn't a drug dealer; he didn't know any Central Americans. Why would they be mad at him?"

Black silently steered the car. I waited him out.

"You know, all the dirt I done did, I never snitched on nobody and nobody ever snitched on me. And I ain't see what happened that night, because I was inside." He reached over and turned up the music. It was Nas, the *Stillmatic* album.

That's how we pledge allegiance to the alliance
Of underworld killers and thugs, though the science
Of a nigga's still yet to be found
So light up some green and pass it around . . .

Once we hit South-Central, Black pointed out a dizzying list of gang-related landmarks, boundaries, and historical sites until we pulled up in front of one of those little single-family houses, the kind that Cuba Gooding Jr. had in *Boyz n the Hood*.

"My homie Big Emp gon' ride with us. He just came home and he need to get at summa these hoes."

"Home from where?"

"Lompoc, nigga, fifteen years for armed robbery. And I'ma tell you"—Black fixed me with a red-eyed stare, the result of the blunt that he'd sparked as soon as his sons were out the car—"this nigga is the devil. Even in the Rolling 60s, he was considered crazy. And mind you, that was before he went in. He my big homie, like forty-two years old. This nigga ran Lompoc. All them Mafia niggas in there all had to bow down. You can ax anybody. My nigga Big Emp is in-sayne. He used to catch niggas in bed and beat them with hammers, and *they was from our own neighborhood*. He did that to 60s! That's why they used to call me Lil' Emp."

"You used hammers on niggas?" The last word, which I

rarely used, felt natural coming out my mouth. I had taken two hits from the blunt.

"Nah, but the first time I ever shot someone, when I was thirteen, he was from 60s. That's why they say you can't trust nobody from 60s."

Black abruptly jumped out of the car and embraced a short, square man with arms so muscular, they poked out from his sides. It was dark, but he wore narrow gangbanger shades, jeans, and an old Eddie George Tennessee Titans jersey. Where the back of his shaved brown head met his neck were three large, meaty wrinkles.

Emp got into the backseat. I turned around and gave him an awkward pound. I felt a brief flash of wonder at shaking the hand of a killer. Then I remembered Black was probably just as lethal. Somehow Black seemed more benign than Emp, who appeared to be straight out of gangbanger central casting.

Black turned up the stereo and we rode in silence.

Pardon I got a question of life now
Look at the nigga next to you right now
Is he real, fake, or scared?
Do it like this nigga's right hand in the air
I shall stay real stay true stay holding figgas
Never put a bitch over my niggas
I shall never
Cooperate with the law
Never snake me I'll always hold you down in war
If they take one of mine I'll take one of theirs
I'll never break the oath to the death I swear

I swear, that's how we pledge allegiance to the alliance
Of underworld killers and thugs, though the science
Of a nigga's still yet to be found
So light up some green and pass it around . . .

"That's some of the realest shit Nas ever wrote," Black said. "'I shall never cooperate with the law'—that shit is real right there. I got respect for Nas, that song says it all."

I knew the song. I knew the whole album, line for line. Before, it was a story, a movie. Now it felt real. I was always left out as a kid. Mom had me on the Jesus train and hip-hop was the forbidden fruit.

Look at the nigga next to you right now

The Benz felt like sitting on a couch made of speakers. We passed another blunt around. I heard every tiny piece of the music, individually, the notes separating and then blending back together in a vivid symphony. Leaned back in plush leather, barreling eighty miles per hour into the most exciting story I'd ever touched, I finally felt as though I belonged.

"Let's stop fo' some grub," Emp said from the backseat. His voice was surprisingly high-pitched. "Whassup wit Roscoe's?"

Black turned a corner and turned up the music. It took about ten minutes to get to the restaurant. About two dozen black people were out front, including a huge man wearing a rusty maroon sweat suit.

"See that big nigga right there?" Black turned to me. "That's Big Sam. You got to meet this dude. He the nigga brought me on tour where I met Tommy n'em." Black pulled out his cell and hit one button. I looked in the side-view mirror and saw the big man put a phone to his ear.

"Whassup, you chicken-eatin' muthafucka," Black cackled as he wheeled his Benz around a corner. "I thought they banned you from Roscoe's for eatin' all they food. . . . Who else was there? . . . So they was heated? . . . Fuck 'em, then. . . . Yeah, I got them tracks. . . . Aiight, I'ma see you in a minute." Black slipped the Benz into a space in front of a residential home and clicked off the ignition.

"I'ont know why you fuck with that slob-ass nigga," Big Emp said from the backseat.

Black popped the trunk as we exited the car. "It ain't like when you went away, Emp," he said, rummaging through the trunk. "It ain't war on the streets no more. This nigga, Big Sam, done plugged me into a lotta paper, even though he is a Blood. Like right now, I'm finna get these CDs out the trunk 'cause he wanna buy some tracks off me for this group he got."

"Sam got groups?" Emp grunted. I was surprised to see that I was taller than Emp. But he was definitely bigger, by a lot. I needed to find a gym out here and get my workout on.

"Sam is like the O.G. of the whole music game on the West Coast. In the 1970s after he came out the pen, Sam used to work for Glen Spivey at Sunburst Records. There used to be a gang of Bloods up at Sunburst. Sam would drive Spivey around, bodyguard and stuff. Eventually he became Spivey's right-hand man. When I was getting in the game, I was managing a group that was cool with Sam and we got tight. Sam took me on tour with Bobby Brown, with D. Rex—a whole bunch of tours. That's how I met Danny Hobbs, at a D. Rex show in Miami. That's when I got down with the Baller."

Black was leaned way into his trunk, digging through a gym bag. I heard something clatter to the ground by Black's foot.

"Fuck!" Black clutched the waistband of his sweats and shook his leg.

I saw two things: a small silver pistol on the ground, and a police cruiser up the block, headed in our direction.

"You tryna get me violated already," Emp muttered.

I stooped down as if I was tying my sneaker, picked up the gun, and slid it into the front pocket of my hoodie. I didn't think about it at the time. It just felt right.

Rap is something you do. Hip-hop is something you live.

Black kept rummaging through the trunk. I stood there with my mouth dry as sand and all the blood in my body rushing to my head.

The two black cops rolled by slowly and looked at us, hard. Emp stood there, swollen arms held out from his body, grilling the police back.

The cops didn't stop. As the cruiser turned the corner, my body tingled with adrenaline.

Black said to me, "You ain't as square as you look, huh?"

I reached into my jacket pocket and felt the gun's cold steel. It was the first gun I'd ever touched. I was surprised by how small it felt in my hand.

Big Sam was a tall Buddha of a man, with gray creeping into his goatee and low Afro. He was sitting on a bench outside the front door of Roscoe's, tree-trunk legs spread, massive belly hanging low. He wore a faded black sweatshirt with the sleeves cut off at the shoulders, exposing arms as big around as my thighs. He was surrounded by a clutch of younger men who were talking to each other but clearly hoping that Sam was listening.

Black and Sam went right past the pound and straight to the hug. Black introduced us, said I was writing a story for the *Fever*. Sam's wary eyes flicked over me.

"So how long you been workin' with Black?" I asked Sam.

"Sheeit, a long time, long time. I got to give these younger dudes a chance to get into the industry like I did. That's why I work with people like Black and Tommy Daminion and Julien. We can get into this game and do our own thing without worrying about what the white man thinks."

He turned his attention to Black. "So you got them tracks?" Black slid him the CDs.

"Whassup with that concert tomorrow night?" Black said. "You know Nas my nigga. And wifey wanna see Mary J. Blige."

"I ain't got no tickets on me, but be outside before the show start and just call me. I'll send somebody out for you."

Black had a CD in one hand and was rummaging in his duffel bag with the other. "I thought I had these other beats for you, but they must still be in the car. I'ma run back and get 'em."

Black peeled himself away from the crowd. I followed. Emp saw us leaving and hustled to catch up, rooster-walking on his short legs.

Sam's voice boomed out over the hubbub. "Ay! Don't be runnin' up on my nigga like that!"

Emp whirled, wide nostrils flaring. "Fuck you said, slob?" he snarled.

"I said, watch out who you rollin' up on like that."

Black tried to intervene. "Sam, this my big homie. It's—"

It was too late. As swollen as Emp already was, he seemed to expand like one of those spiky fish.

"The fuck you say, *fat boy*?" Emp emphasized the insulting phrases by wagging his sweaty, bald head side to side. "Huh, *fat boy*? Who you t'say I cain't *walk* with a nigga?" He moved forward, jeans sagging on his short legs, and came within arm's reach of Sam. "You know who you fuckin' wit, mutha*fucka*?"

Emp was so short, he would have had to hop to punch Sam in the face. Sam stood with his arms crossed in front of him. He outweighed Emp by at least one hundred pounds.

"Get the fuck out my face," Sam said, just loud enough for everyone to hear.

Black slid between them. "Aiight, aiight, this all a misunderstanding. Relax, my niggas. Ain't no problems."

Emp turned his glare onto Black. "'Sup, lil' homie? You ridin' wit this slob over me?"

"Naw, Emp, it ain't like that. But Sam cool, though. He ain't know you was my big homie. He was just—"

Emp was suddenly standing in front of me.

"Gimme dat gun," he demanded.

My heart felt as if it had turned to concrete.

"Gimme dat!" Emp started grabbing the sides of my sweatpants, trying to feel out the piece. The harsh smell of his sweat stung my nostrils. Over Emp's shoulder I saw Black, eyes wide, frantically shaking his head.

Emp had huge hands. One was clamped onto my shoulder and the other roughly searched the front of my pants, grazing my nuts. I prayed that he wouldn't look in my jacket. Emp pulled my notebook out of my jeans, looked at it, slammed it to the ground. Behind Emp's back Black was drawing a hand back and forth across his throat and mouthing, *No!*

I wrenched away from Emp. "It's in the ride," I said.

Emp stopped. He turned and looked at the scene for a murderous moment. Two dozen people waited to see what he would do.

Emp roostered off, walking quickly across the street and disappearing around a corner. I tried not to let anyone see how hard I was breathing. Conversation bubbled up and people started leaving. Black turned to face Big Sam.

"That's Big Emp, Sam. He just came home from fifteen at Lompoc. Ask your homies about him." Black lowered his voice. "You gotta get outta here."

Sam snorted with disdain. "That nigga trippin'."

"Please, Sam, I'm beggin' you. Emp is the devil. If he come back, I ain't gonna be able to stop him."

They exchanged looks.

"I *cain't* stop him, know what I'm sayin'?" Black was pleading. "That nigga brought me into this shit. Ain't no telling what he might do. So please, Sam, please, just leave."

Sam didn't budge.

"Please, man, please." Black's voice quavered. "Please just go home. I'm beggin' you, Sam. Please."

Sam took his time, but he did it.

When we got back to the Benz, I took the gun out of my pocket and gave it back to Black. He stashed it in a door compartment. Emp was nowhere to be seen.

Black and I looked at each other. He started laughing and I joined in, relief washing all the tension out of my body. Black lit a blunt, started the car, and pulled away from the curb, shaking his head.

"He really woulda shot him," Black said. "That nigga Emp is the devil."

CHAPTER 16

It felt like hours since Julien left, and I needed some cigarettes.

There was only one way out that basement. Every brownstone on the block was flush up against the next. Each yard was surrounded by three other yards, two on each side and one opposite. So the only way out the basement was through the door I was watching.

I needed some cigarettes. I left a twig leaned against the basement door so I would know if anybody opened it, and I went to the corner store. My friend Mo smiled when I walked in. He took out my Newports, a New York Times and four Dutches and put them on the counter.

We started talking Iraq, as usual. Mo is from Pakistan, with skin darker than mine and a wife and five kids back home that he sends money to every month. Mo always says Bush controls what the newspaper sees, what the TV sees. "Bush uses the Jewish newspaper to do his bidding," he said. I tried to tell him the Times hates Bush. He'd always say, "Yes, but they love Americans, and they love Israel even more, and that means they hate Islam." Muhammad is a good dude, but when it comes to God, he needs to understand that the social laws of Islam were designed for the seventh century. God sent Muhammad to solve the problems of that age. Now the world got new issues, and Bahá'u'lláh is the only answer for those.

Peanut walked into the store, talking all loud on his cell. He asked Mo for some Dutches and a pack of Kaboom, that ginseng sex thing. While Mo was getting it for him, Peanut starts yellin, like, "Hurry up! Fuck you think, I got all day?"

I wanted to punch him in his face. Peanut always treated Muhammad like trash, because on the street Peanut was a nobody.

Mo's head stayed under the counter. Peanut kept cussin him out. Mo got the Dutches out and said, "Five dollars." Peanut yelled, "Five dollars!?! The 'Boom is two bucks and Dutches is a buck each." All the while knowing Dutches been $1.50 since last year. Mo stayed real calm and we all looked at each other. That's when Nut decided to mess with me.

He was like, "What the fuck you lookin at?! Best watch out 'fore that ass get wetted." Then he starts talking in his phone, like, "You got the hammer, son? Cause this nigga Dontay don't think his ass will get shot up." Then he smacked a pile of change on the counter and limped out.

Muhammad counted out the money with one finger, each coin scraping the plastic counter. It was $3.60.

The only thing keeping me from chasing Nut was the thought that whoever was on the other end of his phone really had a gun. Peanut was a bully and a coward. But it was possible his crew did have some heat. I looked at Mo. His dark eyes were on fire. He said, "In Iraq, I would kill him in the name of Allah."

You think I ain't got no reason to hate Peanut. But you don't have no idea what it's like on the streets. I watched Peanut and his crew sell crack to pregnant mothers, rob people, have girls do the worst sex things in exchange for crack. He was the kind of person who victimized the weak and the helpless. And he thought he could do the same thing to me.

I kept one eye out for Peanut as I walked back to the stoop. The twig was still leaned on the basement door, so that meant Gutter hadn't come outside while I was at the store. I needed to calm myself down, so I popped The Joint in my CD player.

Large had been so amped for the session. We had to walk right past Miz Christopher to go down into the basement where we recorded. Large wasn't fat yet, just chunky, but he wore a down bubble goose that made him look huge. His eyes was bloodred from the chronic. Coming down the basement steps, L's coat ripped on a nail and feathers went floating through the air. After the session we bought a fifth and got pissy on the stoop, pumping the new tape in the Ack. Mad heads came through. When L told cats

I did the beat, they started throwing money at me for more work. I had a pocket full of money back then. Brooklyn was full of my beats. All because of The Joint. My Joint.

Borough to borough
Nuts like a squirrel
Fight the power like COINTELPRO heroes
Intellectual
But I'll stab you with a fork
Magnitude greater than all New York . . .

That was the night I realized I was in the presence of greatness. But Large was so humble about it, not like mosta these egomaniacs. It only took him one take to lay down the verse, right off the top of his head. No notebook or nothing.

"What you think, Tay?" he asked me after we listened to the playback. And I knew he meant it, by the way he looked at me. I told him, "It's perfect." A big smile cracked his face. Large never smiled in pictures. But those of us who knew him best saw the child inside. And The Joint is still perfect. It's as good as any record he's made since. Better. More pure, more free. As soon as I get it into the hands of the right people, all my troubles will be over. . . .

My life woulda been so much different if Large was still here. For example, Peanut never woulda tried to kill me that night.

That's right. You ain't believe me when I told you,

and look where we at now. I was sittin there on the steps, waitin for Gutter to come out, when the steps exploded in my face. It was bullets, and they were meant for me.

CHAPTER 17

Darkness dragged a thick cloak of haze over Los Angeles. Black pulled up to the back gate of Scruplex. It was guarded by a large man with a huge woolly beard and an ancient gait.

"Whassup, Sha-Ron," Black said. "This my nigga Marq from the *Fever*. He doin' a story on the club."

Sha-Ron scratched his upside-down Afro of a beard, matted and gray. A long, filthy olive jacket hung from his shoulders, flapping in the gusting wind. He was at least sixty years old, still hard as a safe. His red-rimmed eyes looked like something out of a horror movie.

"Better watch yourself, young fella," he said, cracking the gate.

The parking lot was crammed with shining automobiles, men, and a few strippers wearing tall boots and flimsy cover-ups over panties and bare breasts. Auto sound systems rubbed against the beat pounding from the back door of the club, creating a grating sensation in my ears. The weed in my bloodstream made every sound a falling water balloon, about to burst.

I saw Chunk in the far corner of the parking lot, talking on his cell and leaning against the rear fender of a big-body Lexus with dark tinted windows. He was wearing another SPANK ME shirt. A few other dudes in SPANK ME tees lurked nearby.

Chunk greeted us with pounds and hugs while still talking

on his phone. Black wandered off to talk to some people. Chunk was clutching a manila folder bulging with papers, Post-it notes, CDs, and all kinds of other scraps. I remembered back in the day his room had looked like a bird's nest.

"Stop frontin' or there's gonna be problems. You know Daminion don't play. That's real talk!" Chunk exclaimed into the phone, then clicked it off.

He gave me an exasperated look. "Fresh Beat is trippin' with this money, dude. They actin' like we ain't gonna sell another two million albums."

"I thought Spank's album sold one point two million."

"Whatever is whatever, man. Wanna see something crazy?" Chunk asked me with a sly, sideways grin. He opened the front passenger door of the Lexus and motioned me in.

Settling into the seat, I was enveloped by the overripe smell of sex. I turned and saw Young Spank slouched in the corner behind the driver's seat.

I almost didn't recognize him. Spank always wore shades in his videos, and now I saw why. His eyes had a hollow, hard-drug glaze and were weighed down by enormous dark satchels that puffed out like used tea bags. A sleeping woman lay across the rear seat with her head on his lap. Another was lying across the floor, sleeping, her head resting against the side of Spank's skinny knee.

As my eyes adjusted to the dimness, I realized both women were naked.

"This my man Marq from the *Fever*." Chunk was in the driver's seat. "He gonna put us on the cover." Out of Spank's sight, Chunk made a "play along" gesture.

"'Sup, homie," Spank slurred around his mouthful of

diamond-encrusted teeth. He slowly reached his hand into the space between the rear seat and back windshield, found his sunglasses, and gingerly placed them on his face, then adjusted the giant S medallion on his chest.

I was having a hard time not staring at the girls.

Chunk slid a disc into a slot on the dash. TV screens in the front sun visors and center console flicked on and a woman's moans came to life over the sumptuous sound system.

There was a cornrowed man having sex on the screen, doggy style, his back to the camera. A large tattoo of a roaring dinosaur spread across his sweat-slick shoulder blades. The man turned around, looked at the camera, and smiled.

"Ohhh, shit!" I exclaimed. It was the rapper D. Rex.

"That ain't nothin'," Chunk said. "Watch this right here."

Another man appeared in the frame and approached D. Rex's partner. He lingered near her head for a few moments, then moved toward D. Rex.

Chunk started giggling.

The man rammed himself into D. Rex from behind. D. Rex let out the same war whoop that had won him six Grammys.

I remembered meeting D. Rex at Payday with Taylor and searched my memory for any sign. Not a thing.

"Chunk, this is incredible!" I tried to contain my excitement. "Who knows about this?"

"I got the only copy, son. But everybody 'bout to see it unless D. Rex come up off that gwop."

"Whaddya mean?"

"He's frontin' on the cash."

"What cash?"

Chunk looked sideways at me, shook his head, and laughed.

"Man, that's just how the game go. You either a shark or a
guppy. Kill or be still, muhfucka. D. Rex got to pay or this tape
gon' end his career."

I wasn't sure how this tape fit into my Baller story. Maybe
it would have to be a separate piece.

"Much money D. Rex got, he can buy him a new career,"
Young Spank mumbled from the backseat. My eyes jumped
to the plump mocha buttocks squished against the car's center console, inches from my left hand. Chunk popped out the
DVD and Jodeci came on: "Come and Talk to Me." Behind
the bass I heard the wind blowing outside.

"You ready to get at some more hoes?" Spank said. His lips
were the color of eggplant.

"I was worn ready," Chunk said, twisting another phrase.

Faster than seemed possible, Spank was out the car. The
woman whose head had been in Spank's lap looked around,
confused, brushing long auburn hair out of her face. She lay
her head back down in the space Spank had just vacated. The
woman on the floor bolted upright and looked right at me.

"Aww, hell naw, nigga," she rasped. "Who the fuck is
you?"

Chunk opened my door and punched me in the shoulder.
Someone else slid into the seat as I left the car.

Spank was standing next to the back entrance of the club
doing a jiggly shuffle-hop dance to the frenetic bass line pounding out of the doorway. His SPANK-shirted entourage buzzed
around. They danced, careful not to come too close to one
another. Gave pounds, talked loudly on phones, punched their
Sidekicks, wearing determined looks. Two blunts were circulating. The leader of the pack was wearing braids that slid sideways

down his head. He spoke with his body, elaborate moves accompanying his words. *Yeah, nigga! . . . Let's do this, fool! . . .* One hand clutched a fifth of Hennessy, which he distributed into cups like a mama bird feeding gaping baby beaks. I watched him orchestrate the weed cipher, keeping the blunts passing in the right direction. When one was smoked to a nub, he produced another, fully assembled, from the pocket of his warm-up jacket. The blue flame that leaped from his stainless-steel lighter hardly bent in the whistling wind.

The ringleader approached me, produced an empty cup from deep within his jacket, and said, "Boom."

"Thanks." I was more than ready.

"Boom," the dude said, raising the bottle to chest level and holding it there. I tapped the fist clutching the bottle with my own fist and held out my cup. "'Sup, I'm Marq from the *Fever.*"

The ringleader wore gangbanger sunglasses beneath his fuzzy sideways braids. "No doubt. Boom. Love is love, baby." He glanced into Chunk's cup, slopped a few more ounces in, and moved on with more loud pantomime. *Keep it crunk in this beeyotch!*

Chunk was hollering into his cell. "We at the back—where you at? Spank right here with me. Let's do this. Aiight, I see you." He snapped his phone shut as a bright pink shirt materialized at the entrance. Black was nowhere to be seen. Chunk rubbed his hands together, grabbed Spank by one shoulder, and steered him through the door. The posse collapsed around us and I went with the flow. Two shallow steps deposited us into the club. I couldn't see through the thicket of bodies, but as Spank made his appearance, high-pitched syllables and excited words pelted my eardrums like hail. The music—*to the window, to the wawl*—thudded in my chest. Bodies pressed at the perimeter of the posse, which hardened in response. Spank's thugs transformed into storm troopers as they plowed through the club. I looked over the head of the dude to my left and caught a glimpse of two brown breasts, bouncing languidly. They were attached to a woman on a low stage. She was not paying attention to anything. The DJ zigga-ziggaed into "Spank Me" and the club popped like water in hot grease. The posse flooded into a U-shaped booth. Spank in the middle, Chunk next to him, me next to Chunk. I recognized Wop, in the pink shirt, from that night at Kaya. Two of the biggest dudes stood in front of the table, repelling a steady stream of fans. No one had gotten within six feet of Spank since the parking lot.

It wasn't my first strip club. Some of my frat brothers from college were connoisseurs. Their joints were seedy Jersey dives, though. Not like this. There had to be two hundred people in here, solid black. There were more than a few women in the crowd, and not dykes, either. Best of all, no fat guys with yellow teeth and comb-overs.

The main stage ended directly in front of our table. The performers floated atop a roiling swell of arms, hands, eyes, and mouths. Boom poured another Hennessy, and another. . . . I was drunker than I'd been in a long time. Then I saw the Ass.

It was beyond perfect. Bisected by a bright red thong, it made moves I thought impossible. One cheek bounced. Then the other. One against the other. Both in unison. . . . *Wait till you see my . . .*

". . . Stoute? I'ma holla at dude right now." Chunk was squeezing out of the booth. "Be right back after I handle this bidness." We all got up to let him out. When we sat back down, I ended up next to Wop.

"I know, I know," Wop whispered, breath hot in my ear. "Thas the most incredible ass in the whole spot. Trust me, I know. You wanna get at that?" I didn't say anything, but I kept watching.

The posse erupted. The dancer on the main stage had done something in front of our booth. A shower of bills and shouts of "Make it rain on them hoes!" fluttered through the air. Spank delicately flicked one bill after another off the top of a thick stack of currency. The dancer squatted to collect all the money. A drink spilled and dudes shrank from the wet. It was creeping toward Chunk's big folder. I snatched it up and saw there was a contract on the top.

Agreement made this third day of November, 2006, by and between FRESH BEAT RECORDS, INC., at 215 Lexington Avenue, New York, New York, 10019 ("Fresh Beat") and CHUNKZILLA ENTERTAINMENT, INC., at P.O. Box 4096, Los Angeles, California, 90019 (individually and collectively, "Grantor") . . .

"Marq! Yo, you with this or what, playboy?"

Wop and Chunk were standing in front of the booth with three strippers. One of them had the Ass.

I shoved the contract into my pocket. "Am I, uh, am I with what?"

"VIP, nigga!" Chunk angled his eyes toward a far corner, where a double door was guarded by double bouncers. Wop fidgeted as if he had to piss.

Chunk walked behind the booth and tapped Spank on the shoulder. "We gonna scope out the situation for you, be right back." The rapper sat there behind his shades, jerking his head to the pounding beat.

"This Shortcake," Wop said. She turned and brushed the Ass against me, grabbed two of my fingers, and started walking.

I found myself reclining on a love seat. A tiny sober voice deep inside my head was shouting at me to leave. I had never had a lap dance before, and I was in love with Holliday.

But it was too late. All Shortcake had left was the thong. The Ass melted all over my lap. She turned, straddled, twisted. I heard her breathe. I saw her eyes for the first time, small and buried in blue powder. A single lower tooth, turned forty-five degrees. Beautiful.

CHAPTER 18

After Peanut tried to kill me, first thing I did was get me a gat.

Zee was in his studio. He's a Rasta straight from Jamaica, vegetarian and all that, with a pipeline to some of the purest weed I ever smoked. He got a nice lil' setup over by Putnam. He an aiight engineer—lotta reggae cats done joints in his studio—but his real talent is hooking niggas up with what they need. When I told him I needed a burner, he laughed and shook his fuzzy dreads. When I told him I had money, he got serious. Dude ain't stupid, but he's greedy. He went in the back

room and came out with a small, black automatic
pistol.

I had no idea how to work it. It'd been years since
I held a piece. That last one was a little Saturday-night
special I got after these little punks tried to rob me up
on St. John's. It came with the bullets loaded, and all
I had to do was cock back the hammer with my thumb
and pull the trigger. Zee's gat had a trigger, but after
that I ain't know what to do wit that thing. When I
asked him how much, he looked up at the soundproof
foam on the ceiling and said, "Four hundred."

I tossed the gun back onto the table. Zee flinched
hard to one side and was like, "Relax, bredren! Yuh
nuh toss dis round when it's low-ded! I give-a you
for tree fiftee."

I told him all I needed was some simple old-school
shit. Six shots, six bullets. Zee looked at me, then
went in the back and brought out a silver snub-nose.
I could see the bullets in the cylinder.

"You still got dem records?" Zee asked me. "I
trade you straight up."

I laughed at him. My collection is priceless.
I have the only set of complete Large recordings,
on vinyl, signed by the man himself. You can't put
a price on that. Just for kicks I pointed at his
forty-eight-track recording console and told him
I'd trade my records for the console. He told
me the console cost a quarter mil. I was like,
"Exactly."

So I talked Zee into letting me hold the piece

for nothing. That's the respect I get. Once I was strapped, I took a walk to figure out whether I should go find Peanut or just wait for him to find me. I tried calling you, but you were too busy with your woman and gave me the runaround. I couldn't believe it. Here I am telling you I just got shot at and you're talking bout, "This isn't a good time for me to talk." That hurt me to my heart. And what kind of woman would let her man treat family like that?

I had to hang up before I lost my temper. That's when I realized I was clutching the pistol inside my bag.

Bahá'u'lláh is the only one who kept me from murdering someone that night.

Mosta my life I felt like a despicable person. Corrupt, hopeless, immoral, all that. I couldn't figure out why I was having all these problems. After all I sacrificed for you, how could you leave me to suffer among the lowest of the low?

Then I met Billy Bob. He's an old artist cat who used to hang around the block. He started giving me the Bahá'í books and explaining how God sends tests to people so they can improve themselves and get ready for the Next World. The more tests he sends, the more special you are. Ain't nobody had more problems, more tests, been kicked around more than me.

And guess who did most of the kicking, Marq? That would be you.

CHAPTER 19

To the windoooooow . . . to the wawl . . . till the sweat drip down my bawls . . . till all these females crawl . . .

I awoke in my bed with the music from Scruplex inside my head. Holliday was still asleep. I shook off the noise and tried to erase the specter of the stripper from my brain. It made me cringe. I had never even thought about cheating on Holliday. But there had been no sex in LA, no kiss. It was just a lap dance. Right?

I slid out of bed and got my duffel bag from the living room, where I had dropped it after arriving home late last night. Chunk's contract was on top. Underneath was the Sean John sweat suit I had been wearing at Scruplex. I took it out and saw a stain on the crotch. The garment smelled like smoke and wet grass. I dropped the sweat suit into the kitchen trash, went out the front door of my apartment, and dropped the whole thing down the trash chute. Then I took a hot shower.

When I got out, Holliday was awake and sitting in the breakfast nook with a grapefruit and some cottage cheese, leafing through a furniture catalogue. She had on one of my wife-beaters, no bra, purple panties, and bare feet. Her briefcase was open at her feet.

"You got a case?" I kissed the top of her head, feeling as if the words "strip club" were branded on my forehead.

"Uh-huh. A good one, but it'll be a lot of work. Do you

like this bookcase?" She pointed to a page. "It would be perfect in the hallway."

Holliday was on a constant home-decorating mission. "Looks great," I said, catching sight of Chunk's contract on the edge of the couch. "Hey, can you translate this into English?"

She slipped her glasses down from the top of her head and scanned the thick document, flipping pages every minute or so.

My cell rang with a 718 number. I thought it might be someone for my story calling me back, but it was Dontay. He sounded high and was talking crazy. I tuned him out and watched Holliday reading the contract.

". . . Marq? Marq! Are you listening? I said I need to get out of here!" Dontay said. "I'm not gonna make it if I don't leave. I need to sit down with you and go over this situation."

Same old thing. "Yeah, okay," I said. I wondered if Holliday had heard me take out the garbage. Dontay hung up so I snapped my Sidekick shut as Holliday put down the contract.

"Your friend has a lousy deal. And his artist, Spank"—she screwed up her face when she said the name—"he's got it even worse because he's trapped inside this contract. So how is your story coming?"

"LA was off the chain. This dude Black owns a piece of the Baller and is trying to sign Slow Creep, even though his friend Tommy Daminion is too. Both of them are friends with this guy Julien who shot Large in Brooklyn. And I saw D. Rex on tape getting done by another dude."

"Getting done?" Holliday's eyes went wide.

I told her about the tape and my visit with Black. I left out Big Sam and Big Emp. When I was finished, Holliday just stared at me, twirling a pen through her fingers.

"Why hasn't this story been done before?" she asked, entering lawyer mode.

"Huh?"

"These guys have all been around for years. The Baller has been going strong since I was a teenager. Why is all this opening up now?"

She had a gift for this kind of thinking.

"Because Slow Creep is trying to get out from their contract?"

"But why you, though? No offense, baby, but you're new to this whole scene, and all of a sudden the story just lays itself out for you?" She frowned behind her glasses. "Something's just not right."

I tried to think quickly. "That's because I'm bringing real journalism to the table. None of the people at these magazines approach it like a real reporter." I convinced myself as I spoke. "They're too close to the music industry—they do business with all the people they need to be investigating."

"Okay, I guess so," Holliday said, pulling a thick folder from her briefcase and opening it on the table. "But keep in mind that you work for these same people, too."

Back at the *Fever* office, Taylor couldn't keep the grin off his face when he heard about the D. Rex tape.

"You're doing big things, Marq, real big things. So you got the tape?"

"Nah, my man Chunk has it."

"Chunk?" Taylor frowned. "Who's he?"

"Young Spank's manager."

"Spank is managed by Tommy Daminion."

"Yeah, Chunk is down with that whole crew."

Taylor got a blank look on his face for a few seconds, then smiled. "Okay, let's think about how we can do this. We gotta make Rosa think it's her idea, because anything that comes from me she'll automatically think is wack."

I thought about Holliday's warning. "So you and Rosa got beef, huh? Is that why she won't talk to me?"

"No, no, that has nothing to do with it. Rosa was totally on board with your hiring. Okay, let's do this. Tell Rosa that you found this tape and want to write about it, but don't say that you found it after I sent you to LA. That way she won't think I had anything to do with it."

I needed to think, so I pulled out my Sidekick. People at the *Fever* did that all the time—in the middle of a conversation, they would start thumbing away and expect you to keep talking to them.

I messaged Chunk and tried to decide how to play the Taylor angle. I still didn't know why he wanted me to write about Daminion. Best to let him think he was still leading me along.

"Aiight," I said. "So about my Baller story. What do you think is my next move?"

Taylor smiled. "The Hamptons."

I couldn't help but get a shiver of excitement. I had never been. I was thinking about what to wear when Briana came into Taylor's office with a huge pile of clothes.

"These just came over from Ecko, the new fall line," she said, dumping them onto the couch. I found it impossible not to watch Briana's tight pink skirt as she walked back out the door.

* * * *

Later that day I entered the bathroom and saw a slender dude with his back to the door, his shiny bald head hunched over the tall garbage can between the urinal and the sink. He appeared to be constructing something. Probably a blunt.

Then I recognized Leak. But he wasn't rolling up weed. He was dismantling a gun.

It was a machine pistol, large and clunky, with a long magazine jutting out of the handle and small ventilation holes on the barrel. The entire thing was made of a metal that looked like gold. Leak carefully detached each part and polished it with a small, white cloth, bringing out a dull glow.

I zipped up and went to wash my hands. Leak screwed the barrel back on and finally looked at me. There were four Sidekicks on his belt, three on the left and one on the other side.

"What's your name again?" Leak asked. He was a few inches taller than me, wearing a long French-cuff button-down shirt, untucked over deep navy jeans. Up close he looked much older than on his album covers.

"Marq. What you got there?" I asked. I suddenly felt bold after my trip to LA.

"It's a gun," Leak said.

"Is that gold? I never saw a golden gun before."

Leak's jewelry clanked as he shrugged. "You know how I do."

"Actually I don't."

Leak didn't like that. He shoved the gun into the front of his jeans and covered it with his shirt. "So you work for Taylor, huh?"

"True."

He looked me up and down. "You a pretty nigga. You must catch a lotta hoes."

I didn't say anything. I wasn't sure where this was going.

"So you know if you work for Taylor, you really work for me."

I didn't like that. "Taylor never mentioned you before," I said.

"He didn't, huh?" Leak chuckled to himself. "Let it be known, then. I'm the nigga holding shit down in this muhfucka. That's real talk."

I decided to play along. "So what I gotta do to get a raise around here?"

Leak didn't hesitate. "Loyalty," he said, staring hard. "Those who show loyalty will always be family. Those who don't . . ." He pulled up his shirt to reveal the golden gun. Before I could come up with a reply, Leak walked out.

My Sidekick vibrated. Chunk.

YEAH I GOT THE TAPE. YOU READY TO GET THIS MONEY?

CHAPTER 20

Holliday liked to unwind on Friday nights, so we headed to a party she knew about at a brownstone. Holliday dropped the top on the Audi and Erykah Badu funked it up on the stereo as we zipped up Myrtle Avenue in the sunset's glow. Holliday turned right onto Washington and parked near the corner of Fulton.

There was a big guy standing guard at the front door of the house.

"Security at a house party?" I asked.

"I know, it's terrible," Holliday said. "Roxanne said the last party they threw, the neighborhood thugs just flooded in."

The guy at the door gave me a cursory pat-down and waved Holliday in. The huge, high-ceilinged living room was shoulder to shoulder. The DJ was in a room to the left, spinning from a big wooden desk. Somebody was on the mic.

This is for everybody who's ridin' instead of slidin'. Brooklyn style!

It was a bougie set. Professional, with a few artistes and a sprinkle of pseudo-thugs. Soul II Soul's "However Do You Want Me" thumped in off the a cappella. Holliday was a wonderful dancer, with total command of her body. She moved against me in the living room, and I closed my eyes and let the bass fill me. "Genius of Love" mixed into "Fool's Paradise," the original and then Mary J. Blige with Jay-Z. Two women appeared, Holliday's college friends who had invited her to the party. "It's All About the Benjamins" electro-shocked the dance floor, and I was surprised to see Holliday and her two friends fall into a dance routine. They ran through a catalogue of classic steps—wop, cabbage patch, snake, butterfly, running man, Harlem shake—each showcasing an individual yet synchronized version. A circle of people formed and Holliday shook herself like an untamed animal. Then she laughed and moved back against me, and we took our places in the Soul Train line that allowed everyone his or her moment in the sun.

"I didn't know you knew all those dances," I said, our faces close in the moist room. She smiled shyly, took my hand,

and walked toward the kitchen, which was filled with a dozen people. I found myself a Heineken and got Holliday a white wine.

"You still going to the Hamptons?" she asked.

"Yup. Sure you don't wanna come?"

"No thank you. That's not my scene." She hesitated. "I don't really think it's yours, either."

That stung. "What do you mean?"

Holliday smiled and hugged me around the waist. "C'mon, baby. You're a nice guy. You take care of your family. You like to peruse the *New York Times* on Sunday mornings over bagels and cream cheese. What do you have in common with those people?"

A song snippet flew into my head. "We're all young, gifted, and black."

Holliday snorted. "I'll tell you what. Young, gainfully employed, and good credit sounds better." She gave me a look and then went across the room to speak to her friends.

I thought about it as I watched her make her way through the crowd. So Holliday was worried about me changing. But this change would make me stronger. How could I call myself a real black man if I was cut off from the heart of our culture? And this story was my opportunity. I slugged down my Heineken and looked around the party for leads.

It took only fifteen minutes for me to hear something.

"*What?* That nigga look like an extra from the Land of Oz. I'd like to see *his* law degree."

A woman at least six feet tall and pushing three hundred pounds was talking to two men and a woman about the president of Soulstacks Records.

"Me and Kemmy never slept together. Not that he didn't try. I just wasn't with it. Back then I was a hundred and thirty-eight pounds, honey. Brothers was tryin' to holla. Kemmy came to the Baller when he first started managing Polytonic. Hopped out that stank bus wrinkled as a *muh*fucka."

There was laughter. I eased over and joined in.

"Now he's rolling with bodyguards and limos and whatnot. I just think it's funny."

She had to be forty years old, wearing the biggest Rocawear sweat suit I'd ever seen.

"Which Baller was that?" I asked.

"They all run together after a while," she said, and I moved closer. "All these big shots—back then they were all a bunch of linty *scrubs*." She shook her girth to emphasize the point. "Puffy, he was always jumping into some picture. He stayed very accessible. Big Brawls—when we get to Miami one year, I see him at Macy's trying on *hats*. I screamed on him—I said, I know you ain't standing here trying on hats when I just seen you backstage at the After Midnight in Philly banging that girl against the wall and her back was hitting the light on and off. Now you in here buyin' hats with that big ol' Mr. Potato Head you got. You need a visor, not no *hat*!"

Someone laughed hard enough to spit liquor.

"J. J. Jones was always asking who you were and what you did. That, and bumming cigarettes. He tried to holla. I was one hundred and thirty-eight pounds. I had a shape instead of something you hide under a carpet." She forlornly popped her collar, plucking at the shoulders of her sweat suit with each hand. "And Meyer Mahl, he was just the big bully of rap."

"Bully how?" I asked.

"Back in the day, Kenny Gamble, Sherry Atkins, and them did a so-called Black Music Association event. And they couldn't book Derrick and Farris."

"You mean D3OG?" someone asked. An old-school rap group.

"Yeah, but to me they were my boys Derrick and Farris. So I hook them up with the BMA joint. This was like '87—there's no real money involved. A few hundred dollars. Meyer is their manager. The day of the show comes and Meyer sends his flunky down to Philly to get things ready for the group. A blizzard hits, like a foot. The show's canceled. I'm in New York with D and Farris. They're broke, bitchin' and whinin'; we're parked in a garage in my Datsun B210. I give them money to take the train home to Long Island, buy them some cheesesteaks. I was working at an optical store at the time. The next day the doctor says, 'There's a Meyer on the phone for you.' The doctor liked me—I was a hundred and thiry-eight pounds back then. I pick it up and Meyer's *screaming*, like, YOU BETTER HAVE MY FUCKING HUNDRED DOLLARS! I'M FUCKING MEYER MAHL! DON'T ACT LIKE YOU DON'T KNOW WHO THE FUCK I AM! I SENT MY ROAD MANAGER DOWN THERE AND IT COST ME A HUNDRED DOLLARS! YOU'RE GONNA PAY ME OR I'LL RUIN YOU!"

Silence.

"Did you pay him?" I asked.

"I told him to go fuck himself."

This chick was crazy. Which was good for me and my story. The rest of the group had wandered off, but I was just happy to have her to myself.

"Tell me what the Baller was like back in the day."

"After Daminion went away, it was pure chaos." She
rolled up her sleeve, exposing wide terry-cloth wristbands, and
mopped her soaking forehead. Her face was dotted with large
freckles. "They had it at Disney World one year, like '95 or
'96. Death Row rented an airplane, took over the lobby, set fire
to the hotel. There was sheer fear on the faces of them white
folks. You saw their perception of what black America was.
I saw this woman from Europe literally running for her life,
holding her daughter's hand and dragging their suitcases out
the hotel. I saw niggas grab a girl, tear off her clothes, grab her
pocketbook, and throw her into the pool."

"Are you serious? It was that bad?"

"*What?* They were tossing TVs off the twentieth floor balcony.
People got jacked in front of hundreds of bystanders. Jim Freakly,
you know, the radio promoter? He had a broken arm. He said
some guy came up to him in the hallway, saw his camcorder, and
said, 'Give it to me.' Freakly said, 'Fuck you!' So the guy broke
Freak's arm and took the camcorder. Then Mark Cockburn calls
me from his room whispering for me to come over. I'm thinkin'
I'm gonna get some dick. I get there and Burn is scared to death,
talkin' 'bout 'They killed somebody.' Turns out the guys in the
next room had murdered some dude and used his money to get
to the Baller. They were talkin' loud all through the walls and shit,
like, 'Yo, I don't know who killed him—we all got a shot in.' And
then they beat another dude's ass right there in the room. It was
incredible. I heard the whole thing."

She mopped her forehead again, breathing heavily.

"Were you scared?" I asked.

"*What?* That shit got me hot," she said. "I was a hundred and
thirty-eight pounds. Cockburn made that a night to remember."

* * * *

Someone's jacket got stolen. From the upstairs bedroom.

The DJ made the announcement, half laughing. Holliday and I were wedged on the dance floor, forty-five minutes into an old-school set . . . *Street life, it's the only life I know.* . . . She kissed my ear and whispered that it was getting late.

Outside the cool night air cleared my head. Holliday spotted some friends in the tiny concrete front yard and started tugging me down the steps.

That's when I saw Dontay.

He was standing outside the gate, talking to two dudes wearing bright yellow Busta Rhymes T-shirts. The strap of his shoulder bag pinched the chest of his plain maroon T-shirt, and he had two CDs in one hand.

My first instinct was to avoid him, but there was no way I could get through the gate without him seeing me. So I bit the bullet, grabbed Holliday's hand, and pulled her over there.

He jumped as if I were a ghost. Snow in the winter would shock Dontay.

"Whatchu doing here?" he said, then continued without waiting for my answer. "Listen, these guys are major players with Busta Rhymes. We're gonna put together some tracks for Busta to rock with, and there'll be a fashion line attached to that." Dontay turned his attention to the yellow T-shirt guys. "This my little brother, Marq, from the *Fever*, and his girl, Holliday. She's a lawyer."

"What up, ma," one of the Squad said to Holliday. "Don't I know you from someplace?" His partner was eyeballing the other females in the small concrete yard, which was enclosed by a wrought-iron gate.

"No, you don't," Holliday said. She walked away to speak to her friends.

Dontay coughed into his hand and said, "I need to talk to you." I steered him down the sidewalk, next to a thick tree growing from a square hole in the cement.

"I need something to eat," Dontay said. "I ain't eaten in a while. I can't have serious discussions standing in the street. What you and Holliday about to do?"

He looked tired and dirty. Half of me wanted to run and the other half wanted to help.

"What's so important that you need to talk about?"

"All of my money problems are history."

I waited.

"I can start handling all my own finances now. Soon as I get the money from Busta, the first thing I'ma do is move. There's too much stress on me where I'm at now. I gotta move as soon as possible."

"You're relying on those guys"—I looked at yellow tees, who were arguing with the doorman—"to get you in with Busta?"

"You always so negative. Everything I try to do, you say it ain't gonna work. You say you wanna help me, but you never do what I ax you to do. You don't really want me to succeed!" His eyes shifted up and down the block and he coughed hard, shoulders hunching with the effort.

"I bend over backwards to help you!"

"No you don't. You gotta look at the real. Like with this phone." Dontay pulled his purple Kyocera from his bag. "If you would just take care of this phone, in three months all this garbage would be behind me."

A subway rumbled past beneath the pavement. I was pissed off. I wanted to be home with Holliday, not talking to my begging-ass brother.

"I gave you money for the phone. And how a phone gonna stop you from smoking crack?"

Dontay clenched his jaw and exhaled loudly through his nose. "You better watch yourself, nigga. Be careful. I'll bring the whole thing down all around you. I could destroy you with just a few words."

It was so easy to lose control.

"Fuck your words! All you do is talk, then you don't do shit but blame your problems on someone else. It's a fuckin' cop-out. . . ."

As I cursed my brother, a burning sensation filled my mouth. When I was in the fifth grade, Mom caught me muttering "shit" under my breath while working on some tough math homework. She pried open my jaws and emptied half a bottle of Tabasco inside.

Dontay took a step back and gave me a look of pure hatred. "I will kill you, do you understand! I'll blow your brains out!" His face seemed to pulsate, like something from a horror movie. "You don't talk to me like that! I'll destroy you!"

"You ain't doing *shit*," I said. "You ain't doing a fuckin' thing except wasting your time and my money. You ain't—"

Dontay collapsed into the gutter. He just fell out, right there in front of me.

My heart flooded with hope that this was the end, then guilt. I knelt between two car bumpers next to my brother's head.

Dontay was groggy, trying to struggle to his feet. His limbs flailed weakly in my arms.

"Are you okay? Dontay, say something." I tried to look into his eyes, but he avoided me. "Come on into the party. We'll get you some water. Come on in."

"Nah, man, nah. You don't want me in there. You're ashamed of me. Just leave me here."

I tried to get my arms around him. "Come on with me."

He wouldn't move. I left him sitting on the curb and went to find Holliday. She was laughing with three girlfriends. I pulled her away.

"I gotta take Dontay home."

Her whole body tensed up. "To our house?" she said, looking around for him.

"Nah, nah. I'ma go to his spot."

"What's wrong?"

"He just passed out in the street."

"Oh, Marq, I'm sorry." She grabbed my hand and squeezed it tightly. "Are you okay?"

I'd been taking care of him for so long, this was just another bump in the road. And it would be over soon.

"I'm aiight."

"Do you need me to drive you guys?"

I didn't want Dontay and Holliday in the same car. "Nah, we'll take a cab. Lemme walk you to the car."

My brother was still sitting on the curb, his head between his hands. I deposited Holliday into the Audi and then jogged back over to Dontay.

"Let me take you home," I said.

"I don't have a home," he said, the words sharp and bitter.

"Look, you need to lie down for a while. Lemme take you back to your place, then I'll go get some food for you."

Dontay sat there hunched over for a few more minutes, then struggled to his feet. We walked around the corner and up Fulton Street. Bright storefronts lit up the night—bodega, cleaners, Jamaican takeout, Kennedy Fried Chicken, record store with blaring speakers parked outside.

I'm not a biter I'm a writer for myself and others
I sell you Big's verse I'm only biggin' up my brother
I'm big enough to do it, I'm that thorough . . .

It was the same place I'd seen him buy the crack.

There was a crew of dudes standing outside the record shop. Dontay put his head down and sped up as we walked past. At the corner of St. James we turned left onto his block. I hadn't realized it was so close.

The window in the front door of his building was shattered, tiny glass pieces littering the vestibule. I followed Dontay as he shuffled down the steps into the basement. On the plasterboard wall outside his door hung a framed picture of Large, wearing a black suit and smoking a huge cigar. The cigar smoke spelled out his name in cursive letters. I recognized the picture from an old issue of the *Fever*. Dontay brushed his fingers on the picture as he walked past and inserted his key into the flimsy lock on his door.

The room looked much worse than the last time I'd been there. A stained pillow with no case rested on the low, thin futon. Books and old copies of the *New York Times* were strewn everywhere. His CDs were in three bulging binders. Dontay's SP1200 drum machine and keyboard lay in a jumble of wires under a cinder-block shelf next to the bed. The top shelf was covered by a clean,

black cloth. It held another framed picture of Large. He was hanging out the side of a blue convertible, derby cocked on his head.
The picture was flanked by two candles, uncased CDs and tapes,
an almost-empty fifth of Hennessy, a Garcia-Vega cigar still in the
wrapper, and a single empty crack vial with a blue top.

Dontay struck a match, lit the candles and then a cigarette.
"I haven't been here in three days," he said.

Once this room held the promise of a new beginning, just
like the Lower East Side one-bedroom with garden access, the
loft in Williamsburg, the cottage in Poughkeepsie. . . . "I can
make my music right here," Dontay would say each time. "I
have no excuse now."

I took the one chair. Dontay paced the brown linoleum
floor, seven steps each way. Finally he sat on the edge of the
futon, knees by his shoulders.

"I need something to eat," he said.

I got up and looked in the cube of a fridge. A bag of apples,
a half-dozen oranges, and a five-pound bag of carrots. Dontay
didn't move.

"I've decided that I'm moving to Atlanta. That's what I
been trying to tell you," Dontay said. "I need to get away from
all this stress around here, away from you, away from Moms.
You two have a lot of similarities. Moms never encouraged me
with my art, never said, 'Oh, that sounds nice.' She always
said it was the devil's music and wouldn't allow it in her house.
Always told me to get a job at the supermarket or the post
office or some other menial position. I never had the support I
needed to accomplish *my* goals. Mine, not hers. When—"

"You thought about getting some help?" I interrupted.

He looked at me blankly. "Help?"

"You know, like counseling, rehab."

Dontay scowled. "Have *you* thought about gettin' some help? Because all this comes back to you. If you knew how to act, I wouldn't be in this mess. It's always been like that with you and Moms. . . ."

I tuned out and got up from my chair. It was a nice-size room, really. It was cool in the summer. I heard laughing voices through the wide, flat window tucked into the corner of the wall and ceiling. I wished I could just float out of Dontay's life forever. But that would make him homeless, I was sure of that, and a part of me didn't want that to happen. There was no reason Dontay couldn't make his music right here. I flipped through his CD binder, then saw a stack of Con Edison electric bills and opened one up. It had a past-due balance of $745. The number made my head swim.

"Moms will never understand that Jesus has returned. Marq? Hello? Are you listening?"

"What?"

"I said, Jesus Christ has returned."

I refused to take the bait. The Con Ed bill was on fire in my hand.

"That's him right there." Dontay pointed to a strange inscription on a piece of paper tacked to the wall. It looked like Arabic. "That's the Greatest Name. Bahá'u'lláh."

"Aiight, Dontay, whatever, but what you gonna do? How many years I been paying for your mistakes? When you gonna change this situation?"

"It's you I'm worried about right now," Dontay said. "Running around in the rap game. It's a den of thieves. You don't know how to deal with these typa niggas. Here in my hood

I'm connected at the highest levels. You need me to have your back."

I screwed up my face.

"I know what you're thinking," Dontay said. "But every single person out here, from the lowest to the highest, they all respect me. No one will mess with me. Because they don't know what I might do. They don't know if I'm gonna shoot them or not. The type of guys you're dealing with, you need them to think that if they mess with you, they're gonna get hurt. You have to let them know that."

Black scared of Dontay? Tommy Daminion? Please.

"So when you gonna change your situation?" I said.

"As soon as I move from here and get out from under all this stress. I can get down to Atlanta and do my thing."

"Atlanta? Whatever, man. Where you gonna live until then?"

"I can rent a new apartment, I can stay a bunch of places, aiight? Anyplace but with my own brother."

"Whatever. But from now on I'm gonna send the rent directly to the landlord."

"Say what?"

"I don't know what you doing with the money I'm giving you," I lied, "but you ain't payin' no bills. So just gimme an address and I'll send the rent there myself."

"That's exactly what I'm talking about!" Dontay said triumphantly. "That's the kind of attitude that's holding me back. You won't let me handle my own business."

"Because you can't handle it, that's why."

"So you're saying I'll run out and smoke up the rent money."

"I didn't say that. I don't know what you spend your money

on." I held up the Con Edison stack. "But it damn sure ain't no bills."

I waited him out.

"I think you better leave," Dontay said.

My hand was on the knob when Dontay said, "You ain't leaving me no cash?"

Incredible. "No, I ain't leaving you no cash."

"I'm hungry! That's why I passed out back there, not from no crack!"

"I ain't leaving you no paper right now."

Dontay sprang up from the futon quicker than I expected, fists clenched.

"You ain't just walkin' outta here like that! I'll bust your head wide open! I'll kill you, you heard me? I'll blow your muthafuckin' ass away!"

Over his shoulder the wall of exposed bricks teased me. I could rush Dontay and smash him right into that wall, crack his skull.

I stepped into his face. There was a dull roar in my ears.

"What, you gonna hit me now?" I said, hoping he would. "Go ahead, do something. Do something for a muthafuckin' change."

Dontay flung a jab and backpedaled. His fist tapped me weakly in the nose. I charged forward, batted aside another punch, and grabbed both of Dontay's wrists. They felt snappable, like pretzels. Dontay crumpled to his knees, head in his hands. I let him slip down through my arms, then turned my back and left him in a heap on the floor.

Fuck it. Just fuck it. I'll clean up this mess later.

CHAPTER 21

I shoulda shot your ass that night.

As soon as you left, I got the burner and went over to the window. I watched you walk down the block with my finger on the trigger. After you turned the corner, I sat there for a long time looking at that gun. I wanted to end it. I was just so tired. Tired of taking all the abuse, of being so alone in the world. Tired of nobody having my back. I tried to think of something I had to live for. I ain't scared of death, you know? Large is waiting for me in the Abha Kingdom. But real niggas don't kill theyselves. We just got to play the hand we're dealt.

I put down the gun and got the prayer book Billy Bob gave me. My favorite section is Tests and Difficulties. "Thou wilt never cause tribulations to befall any soul unless Thou desirest to exalt his station in Thy celestial Paradise and to buttress his heart in this earthly life." See, that's how I know I'm special. Who got more trials and tribulations than me?

I see the expression on your face. You laughed at me that night, too, when I told you Jesus Christ has returned. But check this out: I dunno if you still consider yourself a Witness, but I know Moms made sure you learnt the history. So you know the Witnesses came from Charles Taze Russell of Pittsburgh, Pennsylvania, who was a Seventh-Day Adventist. And the Adventists come from a Baptist preacher named Reverend William Miller. Back in the day Miller did a bunch of mathematical calculations to figure out exactly when Jesus would return. The Book of Daniel talks about 2,300 days, but a day is a year in Bible prophecy. So Daniel said The Messiah would come 2,300 years after the decree to rebuild Jerusalem. That decree was made in the year 457 B.C. Subtract 457 from 2,300 and you get 1,843. But Christ was born 456 years after the decree, so subtract 456 from 2,300 and you get 1,844. William Miller said Jesus would return in the year 1844. All of Miller's people got together the night Jesus was supposed to come back, but when nothing happened, they fell out and some of them formed the Adventists, and then Russell formed the Witnesses outta that.

My point is this: The Bahá'í Faith started in 1844. So Jesus really did return then. It's just that nobody noticed it. He came back just as he said he would—like a thief in the night.

After you left, I stayed in that room praying, taking long showers, drinking my juice. You always talking about rehab, but Dr. Walker shows exactly how to detoxicate your body. I drank three glasses of salt water every morning, to draw all the impurities into my intestines. All that dirty fluid comes out your behind. To replace it you drink fresh citrus juice mixed with a lot of water. Then you take a high enema with a thirty-inch tube, but I skipped that part. After three days I was cured.

I went out that morning and saw my homie Mister P getting a cut in the barbershop. When I walked in, I felt the barber's eyes on the back of my neck. The hair was like an inch deep back there. It took P a few seconds to recognize me. You know P—he DJ at a lotta clubs, he got that show on Massive 99. And he helped Large make the demo that got him signed to Reddy's label. He used to play my beats all the time when he did parties. We talked for a little while about how Massive 99 banned my music from the station. Reddy was behind that—he ain't want me to shine because niggas might come across all the hot joints me and Large did back in the day. You know how I get down. Them joints make all Reddy's producers look like straight doo-doo. That's why they froze me out.

P was like, "Yo son, say what you want about Reddy, but he took Large to the top, kna'mean? And L had love for Red—I seen that with my own eyes. Reddy took duke from off this block right here and made him a superstar. Hollywood, Japan, Europe, cars, money, hoes..Who else coulda blew duke up like that? You think L wanted to stay on the block the rest of his life? Yeah, Reddy wanna control things, he wanna put his name on e'ything. But he made Large happy."

I hated Reddy for stealing L from me. For years I agonized over all the strange shit that happened before L got kilt. Why L wouldn't put me on. Why The Joint wasn't on none of L's albums. But what P said felt right, maybe because they confirmed a lotta things about L that I knew was true.

I had The Joint on me, so I played it for P, plus some other beats I had. P liked what he heard, he said he was making a demo to take down to the Baller and I should come through his studio that night. It had been so long since someone believed in me, I almost cried.

When I got to the session that night, the studio had one of them real big mixing boards. You don't need all that equipment to make hot beats, but dudes these days hide a lack of skills behind technology. There was about ten dudes in there scribbling in notebooks, rolling blunts, jerkin around with their pagers and whatever. After a while they put on one of my beats and this kid went into the booth. He was like, "Yo, turn the bass up." The engineer twisted one of his thousand knobs and the bass line just got distorted. I went over and started twistin knobs but the sound just got worse. Dude in the booth was one of these young cats—he was like, "I said turn the fuckin bass up!" I told dude, "Just rap, nigga, I'll handle this." The engineer ain't know what he was doing so it took a minute to get shit straightened out. Dude said his rhyme—it was average. And then I hear this kid laughing at me.

It was a skinny boy wearing one a them white T-shirts down to his knees. I walked over and stood in front of him, like, "You got something you wanna say?" He laughed some more and crossed his arms like I had mine crossed. He was like, "What you think this is, Flashdance?" His friends started to laugh and that souped him up, so he shuffled through some fake b-boy moves. My beat is still playing over the monitors, and the kid starts to freestyle. He was like:

Old school comin' through with the hole in his shoe
Style stuck back in 1988
Not even Crazy Legs can save you from your fate
So go write some graffiti on a subway train
I'll be in the Range gettin lovely brain
Straight insane nigga you got no shame
I rock the white tee plain while you rock ketchup stains
Tight-ass jeans like an old-school rapper
Fuck the old school cause here come the next chapter
Clap ya with the fifth make ya brain matter splatter . . .

Dude had skills, I'll give him that. I done rocked with the best, so I know. All his boys started whylin out, pullin out they guns and yellin, "Buck buck buck buck" and bumpin into one another. It's real stupid the way these youngsters need to get all hyped up just to rhyme. You know how Rakim recorded "Check Out My Melody"? He was sittin on a couch in Marley Marl's apartment.

So now they all in the moment, freestylin, and this other kid steps up and starts rappin, like:

Unh nigga what
Layin in the cut
Niggas get bucked if they fuck wit us
Get ya throat slit when a Young One spit
Rollin in the whip wit the fifth in my grip
Spit three hits while I hit three chicks
Fuck bitches so hard they think I got three dicks
Keep grindin like niggas from the Clipse
Flip three birds so I can get these chips
Push work on my block and you get pistol-whipped
Fuck Kool Herc, I started this rap shit . . .

The rhyme was straight wack to me, but from the way these kids was carryin on, you'da thought they just recorded the greatest song of all time. I was about to put 'em in they place when a voice rang out, like, "Ay yo! Can't y'all see I'm doing an interview here?"

E'ybody got quiet real quick. All eyes jumped to this big, light-skinned cat sitting in a corner of the room, next to a Chinese dude holding a tape recorder. The big one stood up. My beat was still playing in the background. Dude was muscular and real lean—you could see the cuts in his upper body through his shirt. His hair was cut low, almost bald. He scowled around the room and ended up looking right at me. He was like, "You don't remember me, do you?" I had to admit I didn't. He axed me, "This your beat?" I just nodded. Dude walked into the booth, clamped on the headphones, and closed his eyes. When he opened his mouth, his voice was like a cinder block and I instantly remembered his name—Cox. And his rhyme was devastating, like:

I see a million lil' niggas on a million blocks
Bustin a million caps over a million rocks
But if you ax these lil' niggas to invest in stocks
And bonds, they brain locks
What kind of drugs you on?
Why you worship hustle'n like it was the Koran?
If your foundation's weak then you can never be strong
Word bond, my rap sheets up in these streets is long
I put in work with legendary hustlers who long gone
Ripped shows with legendary MCs wit classic songs
And every time the crowd bows down to the real don
Paid my dues in the '80s nigga recognize
This old nigga put new bullets right between yo eyes
So while you crumb-snatchers buyin up chains and whips
I sell one of my three houses for three million chips . . .

I had met Cox more than ten years back, when I was doing some beats for Eric B at his studio in Queens. Late at night, Cox would come alone to the studio and work with the engineer on his own album. Eric had a rough crew, full of Brooklyn killers, Supreme Magnetic, Rap, the original 50 Cent. And they all gave Cox incredible respect. Cox had crazy skills on the mic—illmatic voice, hard-core lyrics, dope delivery. But if his album ever came out, I never heard it. He was a ghost.

Cox ripped off the headphones, came out the

booth, and told the engineer, "Gimme the tape." Then he gave Mister P a pound and walked out without a glance at anyone.

I jetted after him and jumped into his elevator just as the doors were closing. Cox just stared straight ahead. I didn't know what to say. We came out the elevator and onto the street. We was in downtown Manhattan and the sun had just gone down. There was a Lincoln Navigator at the curb, sparkling white, with a beautiful woman in the driver's seat. Cox finally looked at me, and we made small talk for a few minutes about people we used to know in common. He gave me his number. When I axed him if he had a record deal, his face got real hard and his look felt dangerous. He said, "Fuck a record deal. I just do me." Then he got into the car and they drove off into the bright night.

The thought of going back into that studio seemed crazy. So I just walked to the subway and got on the first train I saw.

CHAPTER 22

"I swear to God, Chunk. Sometimes I wish that nigga was dead."

We were back in New York, Chunk's silver Benz CLK320 coupe encased in Times Square traffic. Young Spank was popping his *spank . . . spank spank . . .* on Massive 99. The neon crawling up the steel canyon walls washed out the night sky.

"I just be so frustrated, like it ain't never gonna end. But then I can't let him kill himself either."

"You know that's your fam, though," Chunk said. "Everybody got a fiend in they family. You just got to deal wit it."

"You right, I could never do that. But what's that going for these days? Just curious."

"What's what going for?"

"You know, knockin' somebody off."

I was just curious.

Chunk looked at me sideways. "Depends on a lotta things. Could be as low as three thousand or as much as fifty. But whatever, nigga. You ain't killin' no Dontay. You afraid Jesus'd send you to hell."

He was right. Not that I bought Mom's spiel. But there had to be a God. There just had to.

"So bust it, how much you think I'ma get for this tape?" Chunk said. We were on our way to Massive 99 with the D. Rex DVD. "'Cause a nigga damn sure need it right now. Fresh Beat be trippin', dude. They gettin' real stingy wit the advances. They owe Spank fifty Gs right now. My 20 percent manager's fee comes to ten thousand. I got moves I need to make with that paper—it's already spent, ya heard? They don't want a nigga to have to start running no jooks."

"Jooks?" It rhymed with "books."

"Jack moves. Robberies."

I had known the truth about Chunk since we were kids, but this was the first time he had ever openly acknowledged being a criminal. I had never even seen him mad.

"You ever feel bad for anybody, Chunk?"

"For who?"

"People you rob, or people who buy your drugs."

"I ain't got no love for them cats, 'specially no fiends. I ain't targeting nobody innocent. If they ain't get it from me, they'd just get it from somebody else. Plus, the government could put a stop to all this cocaine traffic if they wanted to. I know you seen the *Dark Alliance* movie, dude. Crack came here 'cause the CIA was letting them Central American niggas bring coke into LA so they could pay for their war against Communists."

One thing about Chunk: If he didn't want to talk about something, he'd find a way around it. "We was talking about how you're going broke and you might have to do these jooks," I said.

Chunk acted nonchalant, like the first time he had showed me a big wad of bills from selling drugs. We had been around the corner from my building. I was supposed to be out buying some milk. "It ain't like I'm snatching pocketbooks from old ladies," he said now. "These niggas got it comin'. I mean, I ain't no professional robber or nothing, although there are niggas who specialize in that."

Chunk's comment nudged something in my brain. Daminion had said that Julien's specialty was robbing drug dealers. I had to get more information for my story.

"So why did Julien shoot Large outside of Junior's? Was Large selling drugs or something?"

Chunk wrinkled his nose as he parked the Benz on a side street in lower Manhattan. "Nah, Large was a buster, not a hustler."

"So why did Julien do it?"

"He felt disrespected by Large. And he ain't actually do it himself. He sent his peoples. But whatever is whatever. So you ready to get this gwop or what?"

We walked into a building and showed ID at the lobby desk. Chunk's said Anthony Turner. Back when we were kids, his ID said Charles Wilson.

"You ready?" I asked as we rode the elevator to the fifteenth floor.

"I was worn ready."

"Don't you mean *born* ready?"

"Whatever, nigga. I'm ready to get this paper, that's what."

We gave our names to the receptionist and sat down in the waiting area, all sleek silver metal and leather. I was hyped. I'd been listening to Massive 99 my whole life, but the place where those magical beats came from might as well have been a castle in the clouds. And now here I was, flying high.

It was at least half an hour before a young intern came out and took us to Gloria Menendez's office. Gloria had been on the radio for years and was one of the best-known personalities in New York. I recognized her from a few rap videos. She greeted Chunk by name and was all smiles when he introduced me. She was bantering with Chunk about mutual friends and current music when the door opened and a middle-aged white guy stuck his head into the office.

"Don't forget the new tagline today, Gloria. From now on it's 'Get online with Massive 99, keeping it real with hip-hop and R&B.'"

"That starts today, the 'get online with Massive 99, keeping it real'?"

"Today. You know we always keep it real," the man said, throwing a proud glance at me and Chunk.

"Okay, I got it." She threw an intro our way: "Chunk,

Marq, this is Josh Green, the station manager." Josh nodded at us and left.

"So you brought the tape, right?" Gloria finally asked. "I'm on the air in a few minutes."

"No doubt," Chunk said. He removed a DVD from its case and popped it into the player. I watched Gloria's face as it was bathed in blue light. At the moment of truth, her expression went utterly blank.

"Oh my God," she said, dropping her face into her hands. "Oh . . . my . . . God. I can't believe he's going out like that. This is unbelievable." She whipped out her Sidekick and started thumbing.

Chunk froze it on the frame where D. Rex's ecstatic face was fully visible. "You better believe it. That nigga D. Rex is a homo. So let's talk bidness."

Gloria looked up. Her face was wet with tears and her eye makeup was running. I wondered if she had been with D. Rex or something.

"Yeah, lemme talk to the station manager and get that together. I gotta start my shift, so holla at me tomorrow and we can get that done. Aiight?" She jumped up from her desk and hurried out, thumbing her Sidekick.

On the way out through the lobby, we passed a tall, heavy-set black man at the security guard's desk. Two women standing next to him were wearing long coats despite the heat.

"I'm here for Josh Green," the man said. He spotted Chunk and shouted him out. Chunk walked over and gave him a pound. One of the women turned around and my pulse quickened.

It was Shortcake. The Ass. Her tiny eyes looked through

me, unrecognizing. Her mouth hung slightly open and I saw her crooked tooth. Despite my embarrassment, I felt myself getting aroused at her memory.

Thankfully Chunk separated himself from the big dude and we walked outside. Chunk was irate as we slipped into his Benz. "Gloria better not be playin' around. I need to get this paper." He turned on Massive 99.

Gloria's theme music was just going off. "This is Gloria Menendez, gettin' online with Massive 99, keeping it real with hip-hop and R&B. I got some real talk tonight. I know all y'all been talking about this D. Rex tape. The streets is burning up over this topic, so you know we here at Massive had to address it. It's been a crazy few days since it all started, and I just want all you listeners to know that Massive is on the case, keeping it real, letting you know what the deally is. Now, if this tape is for real, and if D. Rex really is having sex with a man on there, it could probably be the end of his incredible career. And stakes is high right now with his new album dropping, *Sex for Days*. Matter fact, we got a new joint from that album to play for you a little later. So we just wanna be up front with everything in this piece, ya heard?"

Chunk was grinning.

"Now, I haven't seen the tape, so I can't be the judge of whether it's really him or if it's a fake or what, 'cause I haven't seen it. So until this thing gets sorted out, I just wanna send a big shout to D. Rex and tell him keep ya head up. . . ."

"Fool me once, shame on me," Chunk told me. "Fool me twice, shame on a nuh who try to run game on a nuh!"

He asked Rosa for five thousand dollars just to see the tape.

"Five Gs?" She had on bright pink Pumas the size of small floats in the Puerto Rican Day parade. "Get outta here!"

"Stop playin', ma. You the first magazine I'm coming to. The tabloids will buy this from me in no time phat. If I let you see the tape, you can write, 'We seen the tape and blah blah blah.' At this point, you don't know what to believe. It could be a setup. It could be a fake. Without this tape, you out the game."

"Aiight, send me an invoice."

"You think I'm stupid? It's now or clever."

Rosa picked up the phone and asked to speak to a Samuel Fogel. "I got the tape," she said when he picked up. "It's gonna cost us, though. . . . That sounds about right. . . . He's right here."

Rosa pressed the speakerphone button. The voice was old and nasal.

"This is Fogel. Who am I talking to?"

"The nigga with the tape," Chunk said.

"It's really him? The tape is real?"

"As real as that bunion on Rosa's toe."

The phone laughed. "I would be very disappointed if I came down there and the tape is a fake."

"And I would be disappointed if you came down here with any less than five thousand dollars."

"Okay, sonny. I'm on my way."

Rosa punched the button. "Marq, you seen this tape?"

"No doubt."

"And?"

"It's the real."

Rosa shook her head and laughed. "I don't know how I'm gonna get out of this one."

Rosa turned to her computer and started typing as if we weren't there. Chunk whipped out his Sidekick, so I did the same and sent Holliday a message.

HEY SWEETHEART. WHERE YOU WANNA EAT
TONIGHT?

She hit me back in less than a minute.

WANNA? WHAT HAPPENED TO YOUR GRAMMAR? I
PREFER SEAFOOD.

I typed back "AIIGHT." Just to tease her.

HERE'S SOME SLANG FOR YOU, MARQUIS WISE.
DON'T PLAY YOURSELF.

I was trying to figure out exactly what Holliday meant by that when Fogel walked in. He was at least seventy, with a full head of white hair, gnarled fingers, and wide fleshy lips. He was smiling as he shook hands all around.

"Okay, forget the coming attractions," he said, smirking, settling into Rosa's couch. "Bring on the feature."

"Fa sho," Chunk said, and pressed play. As the man entered the frame, Rosa said, "Uh-oh, it's a wrap."

I looked at Fogel. His big lips were spread in a gleeful smile.

When Rex hollered, he jumped off the couch and grabbed Rosa's arm. "Whoa, Nellie! Woo-hoo! Did you see that? Wow! He just impaled him! Pa-*dow*!"

Rosa shook free. "Get your dirty hands off me, Sam."

"We have to put a screen grab on the cover," he exclaimed. "The one where his face turns around in ecstasy. We'll sell more copies than with Tupac and Biggie combined. What's the title of his album?"

"*Sex for Days*," Chunk said.

"The cover line can be 'Sex for Gays!' Woo-hoo! D. Rex, you're incredible!"

Fogel tossed a stack of bills onto the table, pocketed the DVD, and left. Chunk snatched up the money and started counting it.

"Marq, I need to talk to you for a second," Rosa said.

Chunk walked out, still counting the money.

"So what's up with you and this tape?" Rosa asked. She was leaned back in her leather chair behind her huge glass desk, which was covered with a mess that resembled a trailer park after a hurricane.

"Nothing's up. Chunk is my man since way back. He showed it to me, and I knew right away what a big story it was."

"How much of that five Gs are you getting?"

"None of it. I don't pay sources, and I don't take money from them, either."

Rosa just stared at me, saying nothing. She wasn't bad looking, even though she was a giant. And she had a body, too.

"How did your man get the tape? Who gave it to him?"

Good question, one that I didn't think to ask.

"C'mon, yo. I got to protect my sources. How you gonna ask me that? Matter fact, I got some questions for you, too. Like who the hell is this Sam?"

"Sam's the editorial director."

"You mean to tell me an old white man runs the *Fever*?" I asked, shocked.

"I know how to handle Sam. He ran some very profitable magazines for Versatize back in the day and now they keep him around to look after things. I bet your boy Taylor didn't tell you all that, right? Just like he told you not to tell me that this whole videotape thing was his idea."

Finally we're getting somewhere.

"Like I said, me and Chunk grew up together in Brooklyn. Taylor had nothing to do with me finding that tape. What is it with y'all, anyway? And does this have anything to do with me not getting any assignments? I been here more than a month and haven't written a thing. I've pitched stories to three different editors, but I never hear back from anybody." The pent-up frustration made my voice louder. It felt good and I let it roll. "I mean, what the fuck is going on? I'm better than anybody you got here, so why I'm stuck on the bench?"

A smile crossed Rosa's lips. She leaned forward to tie a pink shoelace, exposing her creamy cleavage.

"I have nothing against you personally, Marq," she said gently. "As a matter of fact, I kind of like you. I know you have skills, and I'd love to see them. But yes, there is a situation with Taylor. Are you saying you don't know anything about it?"

I didn't, so I said nothing. She laughed.

"I'm liking you more and more every minute. So I'ma let you in on a little secret: Taylor is on his way out."

"Out?"

"Out. Ghost. Swayze. Audi 5000. Peace. One."

"Why?"

"Because the *Fever* ain't his personal fucking playground

no more," she barked. "Versatize don't play that shit. This is a Fortune 500 company we're talking about. You think they'll allow some uppity Negro and his gangster pal to run around exchanging ad money for good record reviews, holding editors hostage in their own conference rooms, leasing Bentleys, bouncing payroll checks just to shoot music videos that nobody ever sees? It ain't gonna take Leak long to run through his half of that seventy-five million."

"Leak's half?"

"Half at *least*. Leak's been extorting Taylor since day one. Taylor didn't even wanna sell the magazine, but Leak made him do it because he wanted to buy this crib out next to Russell Simmons and P. Diddy n'em. Leak convinced Taylor that they could sell the *Fever* and then stay on to run the show like always. But Leak didn't realize there's some people you can't intimidate with big guns and a bunch of Pittsburgh thugs."

"All this is very interesting," I said. "But you still haven't explained why I'm getting frozen out."

Rosa hit a button on her remote control and an unfamiliar track came on. The voice sounded like Young Dro, but I didn't recognize the song. Must not have been out yet.

"You know Mini-Mack, right?" she asked.

"Fa sho," I said. "I'm feeling that song where he goes, *'Undersized since the Mack was baptized / Now I'm four foot three with raps that's Shaq's size.'"*

"Yeah, that joint is mad catchy, right? Well, Taylor wanted him for one of his compilation albums. So he went behind my back and got one of my writers to do a story on him. Mack gives us the interview, sits for a photo shoot, the whole nine.

Problem is, he don't want anyone to know he really ain't no midget."

"Mini-Mack ain't a midget?!"

"Hell no. Everybody in the industry knows who he is. Mack's almost your size. What are you, about five seven?"

I winced. "Five nine."

"Yeah, he's just a little shorter than you. Anyway, he tells Taylor not to say nothing because he's about to drop his first album and the midget thing is the whole gimmick. I don't know nothing about this, so when the story comes out, it says dude's normal size, and there was a picture of him standing next to some little kids and he was, like, taller than all of them. Mack goes nuts and it was almost a real problem. He called me up screaming when Fogel was in the office, and Fogel banned Taylor from having anything to do with any of the editorial content of the magazine."

"Fogel can do that?"

Rosa sighed. "Yes, he can. So when you pop up all of a sudden, hired by the infamous Taylor Whittingham, you're immediately suspect."

I thought about the situation. It was clear what I had to do.

"Well, Taylor did hire me," I said. "But it ain't like I got love for dude or nothing."

Rosa smiled.

"This song is tight, right?" she said. "Young Dro is in town; he got a new album dropping. Why don't you knock out a story for me."

CHAPTER 23

The first time we spoke after that fight we had, I was standing in front of the supermarket on the corner of Fulton and St. James. A woman with a shopping cart full of cans was feeding them one by one into a redeeming machine. Just looking at it made my teeth ache.

There was a pay phone there. When's the last time you had to use a pay phone?

I was shocked when you actually picked up. I asked where you were. You said, "Just taking a drive," but I could tell you were lying. I could always tell. I explained how me and Cox was working together now and how all my problems were over. All I needed you to do was turn on the cell phone so I could make these moves and get on my feet. You started getting real agitated. I heard beats in the background and thought about when you was little, when you'd sit for hours listening to me make music. Beautiful hip-hop music.

You thought I was smoking crack. Wrong as usual. I told you I was finished with all that because I had detoxified myself. But you were bugging out. That's when I knew we had to separate for good. I said, "Just turn the phone on and that'll be the last you hear from me." And you hung up in my ear.

Next thing I knew, I was in front of Oldie's house.

I know I said I was done with crack. But it was you that made me go back.

Oldie opened the door with his gap-toothed smile. He ain't even look in my bag this time. The front room was steamy and a tall pot was boiling on the stove. Nicky was wearing a robe, eating greens from a paper plate, and watching home shopping on the tiny TV on the kitchen counter. Billy Bob was on the sofa, wearing shades. It looked like he was asleep.

I sat down at the table and told them how Peanut tried to kill me. Oldie stopped stirring his pot. Nicky passed me a pipe. I usually don't smoke no stems. I might sprinkle a lil something in the blunt, but that's it. Stems is some real crackhead shit. But you just had my insides so torn up, I grabbed that glass tube and took a long pull. It felt like a shotgun blast of ice to the front of my forehead. It was like I was on a jet plane flying through thick clouds and then all of a sudden the sky was completely clear and sunny.

I told them the whole story about what happened with Peanut n'em.

Oldie was like, "Peanut ain't the one tryna kill you. It's Julien you need to worry about."

I didn't believe him.

"How many times Nut say he gonna shoot some-body?" Oldie said. "And how many times he done it?"

I thought about it. Peanut was a punk, indeed.

"Bet you ain't seen Gutter since then, have you."
I hadn't.

"He dead, that's why. And since you the only one seen Julien come out that basement, you next, nigger."

All of a sudden I felt alone, like a bug under a microscope. Oldie was an evil dude—I'd watched him beat a woman half to death with a cast-iron skillet in that same room. But he knew the streets. That's why he'd been doing his thing from that house the past twenty years.

I realized that Nicky was rubbing my shoulder. Soon we were upstairs.

Nicky had a little vanity table in her room overflowing with beauty products. She checked herself in the mirror and started brushing her hair. It was long and bone-straight, shiny-fresh from the shop. The skin on her face was flawless, except for the burn marks on her lips, but she always covered that up with lipstick. She looked at me in her mirror as she brushed. I could smell her sickly sweet scent.

When you smoke crack, a chemical reaction explodes in your brain. You got no control over it. It's the law of nature, just like if you drop something in the air, gravity will bring it down. That chemical reaction makes you smoke more crack. And it makes you need sex, too.

Nicky lay back on the bed and threw open her robe. She was naked underneath. I stood up and started undressing. When I turned around, Nicky's legs were raised like begging hands. Her eyes were rolled back in her head as she took a hit off the pipe. Her vagina was a vertical scream that hit me like a sledgehammer right between the eyes.

My stomach heaved. I jumped back into my pants and jetted out the door so fast, I was on the sidewalk before I realized that I left all my dope in her room.

CHAPTER 24

I was listening to Dontay with one ear and Taylor with the other.

Botha them was full of shit.

"The cleansing takes place through the skin, the kidneys, and the bowels," Dontay was saying. I was sitting in the passenger seat of Taylor's Bentley, speeding through Long Island toward the Hamptons. "The sweat removes toxins that can injure the body. The kidneys get rid of what the liver metabolizes. The bowels eliminate more than used-up food—also dead cells and tissues that are the result of physical and mental activities. . . ."

"Forget about demographics for a minute," Taylor was saying into his phone. "See, the power keepers try to exclude people by breaking down everything by race, by age, by gender. That's an ancient way of thinking that emphasizes differences and divisions instead of cultural forces that bring people together. . . ."

I thought I'd become numb from all the years of Dontay's nonsense. So why was I so tight inside? Maybe because I wanted to let him go. He'd end up homeless for sure. But if I let him destroy himself now, all my pain would be for nothing. Plus, I was the only person on the planet who would help him.

"America is embracing a new culture, baby," Taylor said. "That culture is us. It's time to break free of outdated definitions and categories. It's time to embrace all that is urban. . . ."

"All these ulcers and cancers and diseases don't just come from a deficiency of live atoms," Dontay ranted. "What about jealousy, fear, hate, envy, frustration. But the carrot-juice molecule is analogous to the blood molecule. . . ." There was some crazy grinding noise coming from Dontay's phone, so I clicked off and looked at my new Rolex. Chunk had hooked me up with a discount.

Taylor hit a button on the dash of the Bentley, exhaled loudly, and shook his head. "Sorry I've been on so long. I can't believe I still have to explain to these corporate cats the value of our culture. You'd think they'd recognize by now the power of the hip-hop nation."

I said nothing while I chased Dontay from my thoughts and focused on the task at hand. I had investigated Rosa's claims about Taylor. They were all true.

"You aiight?" Taylor smiled. "What, the Bentley ain't your style? You liked the Range better?"

I waited.

"I know, I know, you're pissed, Rosa's buggin', she won't give you assignments, whatever. Don't worry about that. There's some things going on that you don't know about, and I can't speak on a lot of it right now, but Rosa's not gonna have that job for long."

That's exactly what Rosa said about you.

"So who's gonna be the new editor?" I asked.

He gave me a reassuring smile. "Why do you think I brought you here? But we'll make that call after the new ownership team is in place."

"Who are the new owners?"

"I can't disclose that right now." The Bentley plowed ahead. The front passenger seat felt incredible, plusher than a king's sofa. "The main reason I want to buy it back is because it kills me to see Rosa running it into the ground."

"What, profits are down?" I feigned concern.

"I'm not talking about money. I'm talking about having some values, about not letting white corporate America take over hip-hop and allow all these white rappers to sell all the records so there are no sales left for real niggas who stay true to the culture. When I sold *Fever* to Versatize, they were scared to let a black man run the whole operation. Plain and simple, they were scared. They had never seen a black man who wasn't going to bow and scrape and beg them for a place at the table. So Versatize insisted that they be able to appoint an editor and I would be CEO. Now, what does Versatize know about hip-hop? What can they tell *me* about urban culture? I created this niche. Before *Fever* came along and explained to the advertising community the power of the urban audience, Versatize wouldn't touch anything black with a ten-foot pole. So they put Rosa in charge and they tell me to stay out of her way editorially, but she's fucking up the integrity of the product. And I can't let that happen. So I'm making moves, starting with bringing in a strong black man such as yourself to make sure the flavor stays in the magazine, you know what I'm saying?"

"I heard Versatize wanted to make sure that you and Leak didn't chase out any more editors."

"Excuse me?"

"After the sale, Versatize wanted to make sure you didn't sneak any more stories about Leak into the magazine. The kind of stories that would, say, make your entire editorial staff quit."

"Who's telling you this?" Taylor asked.

"Sources who say that back in 1994 Leak was walking around the office threatening editors with guns, threatening to drag niggas out in body bags if they didn't give his album a good review. They say after they closed an issue and sent it to the printer, you went behind their backs and inserted a story about Leak into the magazine."

Taylor kept his eyes on the road, but his voice was smiling. "Those editors, who I assume are also your sources, they were gonna ruin the magazine. They were writing crazy, unfair, biased stories about people. Meanwhile I'm the one out in the streets who has to ride for what's printed. Do you know how many rappers stepped to me over shit they read in the *Fever*? Do you have any idea what that's like? Do you have any idea what it's like to see copies of the magazine you created burned onstage at a concert? The editors were alienating the industry to the point where we were about to be blacklisted. And when it came to Leak, they had a terrible attitude. Sure, me and Leak go way back. We met at Howard when I started the magazine. But I never was his manager—"

"I never said you were his manager," I interjected, although I had photocopied a page from an early issue of the *Fever* that said just that.

"I never was his manager," Taylor continued as though I hadn't spoken, "and I never gave him special treatment in the magazine. He *deserved* that article. Back in '94 Leak had been putting in work for years, the hard way, the classic way, doing shows in hole-in-the-wall clubs, selling records out the trunk, and he had finally gotten his first record deal. He's from Pittsburgh, which is unique because not a lot of rappers come from there. But the editors had something stuck up their ass about Leak, and they just wouldn't listen to reason. And Leak has done a lot for the magazine. He's been there since the beginning. He's like family, and you don't turn your back on family, no matter what. I believe in loyalty, Marq. Do you?"

I remembered Leak using those same words in the bathroom, with his golden gun. Taylor's spiel was fairly convincing. But I had more questions.

"How badly did you get beat up by Mike Hyatt?" I continued. Hyatt and several other editors had described a fight in front of the old *Fever* offices after Taylor snuck the Leak story into the magazine. They said Hyatt pounded Taylor's head into the pavement like a basketball.

"I didn't get beat up by Mike Hyatt."

"He said so, and so did three other people."

"I'm telling you, it didn't happen."

"You didn't go to the hospital with a concussion?"

"I did not go to the hospital with a concussion." Taylor said it as if he were ordering food at a restaurant. I hadn't expected total denial.

"So what about your next editor?" I demanded. "The one Leak trapped in the conference room with the whole staff? They said Leak cursed them out for like three hours, had his crew holding down the door so they couldn't leave. They finally let them go after your editor in chief broke down in tears."

"Look, Leak can be forceful with his opinions. But no one was in any danger. He just wanted to discuss some legitimate issues he had with the coverage of his third album. It's tough for Leak to get a fair shake because he's Leak, a street nigga, for real for real. In the streets, if you have a problem with somebody, you go handle it. If dude couldn't handle the way Leak brought it to him, then maybe he wasn't qualified to be editor of the magazine."

"If that's the criteria, maybe you're not qualified to be CEO of the magazine."

The silence lasted a full minute. The highway had turned into a dark two-lane road flanked by thick trees.

Taylor sighed loudly. "Marq, I have no idea what you're talking about. These sources of yours, they sound like haters to me. They sound bitter and angry that we're shining without them. They see us in Bentleys and at the Fever Fest and the award shows and wish they were still down."

I counted to ten in my head before speaking.

"Why did Leak have that gun on you?"

"Leak never had a gun on me, Marq. I don't know where you're getting this stuff."

"Someone said that back in the day they walked into your office late one night and Leak was holding a pistol on you and you were crying."

"I can't believe that Elliott Michaels would tell you that."

I hadn't wanted to bring up Elliott's name, because he hadn't spoken to me directly. A former *Fever* writer had told me that Elliott had told *her* that. Elliott had not returned my calls, pages, or e-mails. I searched my vocabulary for the right combination of words.

"Yeah, Elliott said that."

"Nah, I can't believe Elliott told you that. Look, Marq, like I said before, Leak is fam. We've been through so much together, back when we didn't even know if we had enough money to pay the printer to get out the next issue. He's been there since day one, and his vision has been instrumental in making this magazine what it is. That's why when we sold it to Versatize, he got paid just like I got paid, and now it's a dead issue. He's not an owner anymore. He doesn't work for the magazine. Sure, he's affiliated with our record labels and recording studios and the TV show and other entertainment properties, but as far as the magazine goes, that's ancient history."

The Bentley turned onto a long dirt driveway crowded with cars. Flashing white lights were visible farther into what looked like woods. Taylor parked behind a BMW X5 truck with fogged windows.

Taylor stepped out and adjusted the Sidekick and new iPhone clipped to his Gucci belt. His boy with the acne face was standing nearby, next to Taylor's Range Rover. Taylor patted the truck's platinum hood. "The Range ride smooth, don't she?" he said. "You gonna love this whip."

He turned to look at me.

"I know you must feel confused right now, but you have to trust me. I brought you here to do great things for the magazine and for your community. Our mission to educate and uplift has just begun, and we need you to get there. All this stuff you've been hearing—those people are just player haters, baby. Here we are, riding in a quarter-million dollars worth of automobile, about to rub elbows with the most powerful people in the entertainment industry. And there the haters are, stuck somewhere in Brooklyn, digging in their pockets for change to buy some potato chips. So let's forget about the haters, Marq, and go get this money. You feel me?"

I thought about it. The evidence against him was overwhelming. But Taylor was so sure of himself, he just might be right. It wouldn't be smart to cut him off at this point.

Especially when I was about to make my debut in the Hamptons.

CHAPTER 25

Harlem is a different kind of hard. It's a lot more American than Brooklyn. B.K. is full of immigrants just glad to have a job, any job. But Uptown niggas ain't happy to be Uptown. That's why Harlem niggas always look so fly—out of defiance.

So here I am, walking up Frederick Douglass Boulevard toward 155th Street. Every T-shirt is crisp, every hat is cocked at an impossible angle. Grade-school kids is wearing jewelry.

And I'm rocking Billy Bob's old shoes.

I had run into Billy coming outta Oldie's spot. He was out front in his rusty-ass Honda. He was like, "Dontay. Look at your feet." I looked down and realized I'd run out of Nicky's room in my socks.

Billy lived in a studio high-rise apartment up at the Junction, by Nostrand and Flatbush. He pulled a pair of scuffed Reeboks from under his bed and gave them to me. He said his son gave 'em to him. The sneakers fit in fine at the Junction, where most everybody is straight off some Caribbean island. But in Harlem they made me feel like a junkie. I kept my eyes straight ahead and didn't look at nobody. Then I fished through my bag for the Roots CD and turned my headphones all the way up.

Sometimes I wouldn'ta made it if it wasn't for you
Hip-hop, you the love of my life and that's true . . .

I stopped at a hamburger stand and counted my money. The cook slapped a fresh batch of meat on his crusty black metal. I had twenty-four dollars left, in fives and ones. There was a lot of people out, flowing up the ave like a river, heading to Rucker Park to watch a ball game. A water balloon exploded on the ground. Everyone flinched, then looked up. The kids on the rooftop scattered, and that's when I saw Large.

The billboard was three stories high, an ad for Reddy Rock Records. It was their fifteenth anniversary. L's black face was like a dark cloud hovering over Reddy's shoulder. Reddy's chinky eyes were looking through them damn sunglasses. The image gave me the chills, but I couldn't stop staring at Large's face. Fifteen years . . . back then my whole life was ahead of me. I had money. I had Large. And then Reddy stole him from me.

There was this guy from my neighborhood who had a little studio down in Fort Greene, did a little A&R, too. I took The Joint over there and played it for him. Home boy said he already had a Large demo from Mister P, but he played The Joint anyway. That's when Reddy rushed into the room, wearing a Washington Redskins cap with the R on the front. His red Afro stuck out from under his hat like clown hair. I knew who he was—his name was poppin from the parties he was promoting. He told my man, "I wanna hear what new stuff you got. I'm bout to start my own label."

We played The Joint. Reddy gave me a pound and snapped his head to my rhythm. He was like, "That nigga nasty. You got any more of his stuff?" We played Mister P's demo and told him Large was signed to P. I fished one of my beat tapes out of my bag, slipped it to Reddy, and was like, "Yo, I'm a producer, been working with L for a minute. We got a real connection in the studio. If you make some moves with my man, hopefully we can do some more work together."

Reddy gave me a pound and told me, "No doubt, home boy."

That's exactly what he said. I'll always remember that. "No doubt, home boy." And that was the last time we ever spoke.

Close to thirty, most of the niggas she know is dirty
Havin more babies than Lauryn, she started showin early

As of late I realize that this is her fate
Or destiny to bring the best of me it's like God is testing me
In retrospect I see she brought life or death to me . . .

So there I was, standing in front of that bill-board, and the next second I'm at Pops's door. I don't know if I black out or what, but that kind of thing happens to me all the time. I'll be one place, and then all of a sudden I'll be someplace else with-out even thinking about it.

J.D. was standing in his doorway wearing a frayed maroon bathrobe and slippers embroidered with a crest. He said, "Hello, son," then turned and shuffled inside.

I stood in the doorway. This was only the third or fourth time I'd ever seen the man. I finally fol-lowed him inside the tiny living room and sat on the dusty couch. J.D. sat in a cracked vinyl recliner, glass of liquor and an ashtray on a TV tray beside him. Our knees were close enough to touch.

J.D. looked out the open window. We were eleven stories high in the Polo Grounds projects. You could see Rucker Park and hear the announcer on his microphone.

He asked me, "How's your mother?"

I told him I ain't know cause she ain't wanna see me. J.D. grunted and stared out the window.

I had all these thoughts inside me, and none of them made sense. So I decided to just let it all out. I asked him, "How'd you two get together, anyway?

How she meet a guy like you being so religious and all?"

J.D. chuckled and said, "Yo' mama ain't all what she would lead you to believe." He fidgeted around with his cigarettes for a while and then said, "I was on the subway one day, mindin my own business, and she ended up next to me. She was a cute lil' thing. We start talking, and I can tell she likes me. So I invite her to this restaurant I had on the Lower East Side. We went over there and talked damn near all night long. About what we wanted to do with our lives. I had never met anybody who was so straight, you know? She wanted to save up and buy a house and get married. I didn't want none of that. I had things, money, a restaurant, a nice car, two or three girlfriends. But yo' mama just wouldn't let go. We moved in together. She was good for me, tell you the truth. And when she got pregnant, we decided to get married."

See, Moms never told us she got pregnant out of wedlock. But I believed the man, I swear I did. He looked at me hard, eyes all yellow, and said, "Lord knows what kinda lies you been fed. Your mama's fam'ly had it in for me the moment they met me. I loved that woman. But we never had a chance. She prob'ly told you all the bad things I did, and they mostly true. But there's a lot of things she ain't tell you too."

I was scared to ask him what. Now that I think about it, I knew already. Moms ain't tell me a damn thing, ever. Not about me, about being a man, about life, about God. I deserved better than that. I deserved someone who loved me. My father coulda loved me, but she ain't tell me about him, neither. All I ever had to go on was memories of a damn hat.

It was wide brimmed, light brown with a big blue feather. I couldn't take my eyes off the feather. I only saw the hat twice, sitting on top of a man's leather jacket on the couch. I wanted to touch it, but I was scared to leave my room. You weren't born yet. I was supposed to be asleep, and Moms would beat my ass if she found me creeping around the house. So I just looked at the feather through a crack in my door, imagining what it would feel like in my fingers.

After a while J.D. flicked his butt out the window and said, "So what's this problem you got? Must be some street shit, cause I cain't think of any other reason you'd call me."

I told him the whole Julien story.

"What you want me to do?" he said when I was done. "I'ont know this Julien cat."

I told him I just needed some cash to get down to Atlanta. He was like, "Sound like this Julien cat'll find you in Atlanta easy as he'll find you here. Runnin ain't gon solve a thing."

We looked at each other like strangers.

J.D. got up, went down the narrow hallway, and opened one of the two doors. I wanted to leave, but I didn't. When J.D. came back, he was dressed in an olive suit, black hat—no feather, though—and shiny black gators.

There was money in his hand.
"Forget about Atlanta," he said. "We gon squash this right here in Noo Yawk."

CHAPTER 26

The RZA beat throbbed in the salty, humid air as Taylor and I walked around the side of the enormous house. The hum of many voices danced atop the bass line. We came around the corner onto a wide stone patio overlooking a huge backyard filled with several hundred people. They were standing in clusters that divided and regrouped like cells under a microscope. I recognized many industry people and at least a dozen rappers. Thonged girls lolled around the pool. A parked helicopter squatted in the distance. Taylor stepped off the patio and waded into the crowd. The throng washed over us, a deluge of names and pounds. *Shante Boots Matt Das Life Def Marvet Jef Daddy Rich Britto Man Child Ike Sunz Jef Jam Burroughs Carlito Jimmy Wright Wong Thorough Power Suave Raynard Upski . . .* Everyone first made small talk with Taylor, and then one of two things would happen—the person would ask Taylor for help in some deal or project, many revolving around the Baller; or, less frequently, Taylor would propose something of his own. No matter what, each exchange ended in assurances of "Let's make it happen."

I felt like one of the accessories clipped to Taylor's belt. I didn't come all the way out to the Hamptons to be nobody's sidekick. So I started listening for an opening.

I found it in a sharp, odd accent slicing through the background noise like a new razor through flesh. I turned to see an older white man with a full head of too-dark black hair. He wore a crisp white Polo shirt, pressed jeans, and gray New Balance sneakers. His arm was around Young Spank. Chunk was nowhere to be seen.

"He's been riding on your back awl this time. He's dependent on you for his livelihood, not the other way around." The accent was strange, almost foreign. "Don't get it twisted, my friend. You're a smaht guy—this is no shockah. They are eating off you. They are thirsty, and you have the water. You are the artist. He should be building you as a brand. Is that thorough? Is that . . ."

Taylor was in between convos. He produced a long cigar and lit it with a tiny blowtorch. "Who's that?" I asked, gesturing toward Spank's companion.

"Him? That's Meyer Mahl."

The memory of Meyer's unreturned phone calls, back when I first started at the *Fever,* settled in my chest like phlegm.

"What's up with dude?" I asked.

Taylor blew smoke. "Meyer's the most ruthless executive in the game. He's got all the top artists, and he refuses to accept anything less than total domination. Not that he's gangster—Meyer is strictly legal. And he refuses to be defeated—ever."

"For example?"

Taylor puffed contemplatively for a few seconds. "Back in the day before his name rang bells, when he was just another manager trying to make sure his artists got paid, Meyer is on tour at some little club in the middle of nowhere. After the show the club owner tries to say he doesn't have the rest of Brawls's performance fee. They're arguing about the gate count and the guy keeps saying he doesn't have the money, he'll send it to Meyer later. Meyer's not having it and he won't leave the club.

Things start getting heated and the club owner starts making threats. He's telling Meyer to leave but dude just stays right in his face. Finally the club owner calls security, Meyer says something he shouldn't have, and security punches Meyer dead in the face. Meyer's lying there on the ground, knocked out."

Taylor paused, working the moment. The sound system pumped out Big Pun's *I'm Not a Player*.

"Brawls's people all run up and it's about to jump off. But Meyer regains his senses, dusts himself off, goes straight to the security guard—and shakes his hand. Meyer tells the dude, 'You are doing a *great* job.' And when he got back to New York, he sued the club and got triple what he was owed. C'mon, let's go holler at him."

When we finally pushed our way over to Meyer, Spank was gone. Meyer was sitting on a lounge chair next to the pool with an unlit cigar in his hand. An obese man draped in an enormous diamond necklace was reclined on the seat next to him, encircled by a half-dozen hangers-on, all of them huddled over a portable DVD player.

"I'm telling you, that ain't him!" the big man said, pointing at the screen with a pinky bearing a diamond ring the size of a small lemon. "They tryna set dude up, man, cain't you see that?"

"But that's D. Rex's face, pimp! And that's his tattoo!"

"They got computers can put anybody's face anywhere," Big Man said, eyes glued to the screen. "They can put—oooh, that's nasty! Man, turn that off!"

Taylor flicked his blowtorch and Meyer puffed his fat stogie to life.

"Tay-lor Whit-ting-ham," Meyer said, pausing a millisecond between each syllable of the name. "Catch the *Fever*.

I never told you what a great marketing slogan that is. How the hell are you, Taylor?"

His enunciation was so crisp, I could taste each *t*. But there was something odd, almost retarded, in his halting delivery.

"Can't complain. Meyer, say hello to my newest star writer, Marq Wise."

I was starting to hate that introduction. Meyer extended a hand and we shook the traditional way. There were small wrinkles at the corners of his frowning mouth and utterly sober eyes.

"Marq Wise? You sound like you could be one of the tribe."

Taylor laughed. "Meyer thinks everyone's a hidden Hebrew."

"If I were a member of the tribe," I said, my heartbeat quickening, "maybe you would have returned my calls."

Meyer's head jerked back. "Calls? My secretary didn't mention any calls. Taylor, be sure to give Marq my direct number next time. So, Marq Wise, tell me: How did you end up at the illustrious *Fever* magazine?"

"I came from *Newsweek*."

"So you must have skills."

Somehow it didn't sound like a compliment.

"Mad skills," Taylor said. "He's doing a story about the Baller and Slow Creep."

I silently reached a hand into the pocket of my new Evisu jeans and hit the button on my mini digital recorder. The microphone was at the end of a wire dangling inconspicuously out of my pocket.

"Ah, yes," Meyer said. "Very, very interesting story."

"You're trying to sign them," I said.

For the first time, Meyer paused. More people had gathered

around, and Big Man was no longer talking on his phone. Meyer mashed out his cigar so hard that it bent.

"Let me tell you something. If I want to sign Slow Creep, I will, and there's not a fucking thing these assholes can do to stop me. This is Fresh Beat Records, motherfucker. We have more than one hundred platinum and gold albums. I know because I hung them up myself. We are the world's leading lifestyle and music com-pany. If I sign Slow Creep, we'll sell a billion albums. Everyone knows this."

I said nothing.

"Don't fucking look at me like I don't speak the truth. Ask your boss here."

Taylor shrugged. "He's got a point."

"All these would-be moguls make me laugh. They give their artists a twenty-thousand-dollar advance, a car, and a house, and never pay them another dime. Fucking drug deal-ers buying their way into the music industry." He looked at Taylor, who shrugged again. "These guys are crooks! Felons! They shaht Large, for Christ's sake! The guy runs the biggest music con-ven-tion in the industry and he's sitting in prison right now! About to get locked up for twenty-five years!"

"Fifteen," I said.

Meyer looked shocked that I had interrupted his tirade. I heard a subtle intake of breath from the bystanders. It gave me chills—of pleasure, not fear.

Two girls spilling out of their bikinis came over and started dancing in front of Big Man's chair. We were no longer the show. Meyer waited until no one was listening, then reached out and poked me in the shoulder.

"Let me ask you something," he said quietly. "How can

Tommy Daminion be in prison and still be on the payroll of several major record companies?"

My radar started tingling. "Which ones?"

"Off the record? Look at Soulstacks, look at Pump Records. What services could he possibly be performing in prison that would be of use to a record company? What do you think the corporations who own those record companies would think of their money being spent that way? What do you think the *shareholders* of those companies would think? When J. J. Jones and I sold Fresh Beat to Versatize, I understood that I was now a Versatize employee, bound to make the best decisions possible for the people who own that company, for the mothers and grandmothers and pension funds who own that stahck."

A huge guffaw erupted from beside us. Big Man was laughing so hard he toppled off his chair. One of the bikini girls had been straddling a lounge chair and popping her body to the music. A guy had tried to slide underneath her from behind, and his white linen pants had split from his belt buckle to his behind, exposing dangling parts that indicated he was underwear-free.

"Look how he split hisself!" Big Man spluttered. "He split his whole shit in half!"

Big Man's crew followed his lead, hooting and staggering about as the splitter scurried off into the crowd, his shirt tugged as far down as possible. Meyer's body shifted in his chair in a way that indicated he was done talking. He pulled another cigar from a leather case and Taylor's lighter instantly flamed on.

"So when are you heading back to the city?" Taylor asked Meyer. "Traffic's gonna be a bitch."

Meyer stared at Taylor as Big Man dragged himself back onto his chair. The girls resumed their dance.

"Don't patronize me, motherfucker," Meyer said, beckoning toward the helipad. "I'm on the cop-tah."

CHAPTER 27

Pops drove a ten-year-old Cadillac, clean enough to eat off the floor. Once we hit the Harlem River Drive, he told me, "Buy yourself some clothes. You look terrible. That's one thing Harlem niggas unnerstand. If you ain't dressed right, you carry no weight."

We got on the Cross Bronx and then the Deegan. I didn't ask where we was going. I was still trying to wrap my mind around the five thousand dollars in my pocket.

To this day I'm not sure if what I was feeling was love. But the closest I ever came was that moment when Pops put that stack of bills in my hand.

We got off the highway and parked in back of a large restaurant. I followed J.D. to a table in the back. There was a thick brown-skinned dude at a table, with grayish hair braided straight back. He had tiny little scars all up his arms, like old scratches, and a "Southside" tattoo on the back of one hand. I recognized him immediately. Back in the day when Reddy first got with Large, Reddy used to come through the block all the time, and for a while this dude was always with him. Sometimes there would be Crips with him, straight LA, Converse-wearing, gangbanger types.

Pops introduced dude as Pez. Pez stood up and told me to have a seat. Him and Pops walked over to an area near the restrooms and talked there for about five minutes. Then they came back to the table and sat down.

Pez asked me, "All this happened in Gutter's building?"

I said yeah.

He said in a real low voice, "You seen Julien shoot at you?"

I didn't really know. That made him mad. He said, "Did you see the man shoot at you or not?"

I said I didn't see anyone shoot at me—I was sitting there on my stoop mindin my own biz when the bullets started flyin.

"So it coulda been anybody you had beef wit."

"I don't have those kind of beefs. I'm an artist. I make music. Does the name William Christopher mean anything to you?"

Pez pulled out his phone and hit a few buttons and was like, "Ay yo, Reddy. It's me. I got this kid here say he did music wit Large. . . . Name's Dontay—he J.D.'s boy. . . . J.D., who used to run wit yo' daddy, nigga. . . . Aiight, yo. . . . Peace."

Pez hung up his phone and told me, "Reddy ain't never heard of you."

I pulled The Joint out of my bag, slapped it on the table like the last domino.

"I made this here classic with Large when Reddy was still fetching coffees and washing cars. Reddy stole Large from me, so fuck what that nigga say."

Pez looked at me for a long time before he said,

"So you sure ain't nobody but Julien out there tryna smoke you?"

Pops jumped in and said, "It cain't be no coincidence. This one cat just happens to vanish in his own basement, this other dude come out with the bags, and then my boy get shot at? That ain't no accident."

Pez stared into space for a while and rubbed the gray stubble on his chin. Then he told me, "Aiight, check it out. I'ma holler at dude and see whassup. Meantime, pack up yo' shit and leave that spot. Consider yourself evicted."

I was like, "Bet." All the while holding the knot of bills in my pocket.

Pez turned to J.D. and said, "Now lemme buy you a drink, old man, and we can talk about all them bitches you used to have."

"Used to?" J.D. said. Them two gangsters laughed hard together while I sat there planning my new life.

CHAPTER 28

The Range Rover pulled up in front of my building as garbage trucks chewed through the early morning quiet. I had ridden back from the Hamptons with Acne Face after Taylor disappeared about midnight with the party in full swing. Upstairs Holliday was in the shower. Sleep came before I hit the bed. The apartment was empty when I awoke, sweating from the noon sun streaming through the window, Raekwon lyrics—*Let's connect, politic, ditto*—skittering through my head.

I rode the subway to the *Fever*. The humid New York funk made my body feel heavy and lethargic. I needed to get to the gym—it had been four days since my last workout. Inside my office, I took out my mini recorder and checked the sound quality from my conversation with Meyer Mahl. It was good enough.

My Sidekick buzzed with a phone call. The caller ID was blank but I picked up anyway.

"Hello, Marquis," a man said. "We want to talk to you."

"Who is 'we'?"

"Your long-lost uncle."

"Uncle who?"

"Uncle Sam."

When I finally realized it was the FBI, my first thought was that this would be great for my story.

"What you wanna talk to me for?"

"I'm parked in a gray Impala on the corner of thirtieth and Lex. Come on over."

Worry crept into my head as I walked through the crowded streets. *You come from the era when snitching is the shit. . . .* I had seen plenty of STOP SNITCHING shirts in my short time at the *Fever*. I tried to comfort myself with the fact that I didn't know anything incriminating. Yet.

The agent was a block-shaped brother with a Sidney Poitier low-fro. I slid into the front passenger seat and he said simply, "I'm Wilkins."

"So what's this all about?"

"How does the song go? Money, power, and respect?" Wilkins said with no trace of humor. He looked about forty years old. His skin was dark and shiny with sweat. The windows were down but the car still reeked of cigarettes.

"What you need in life," I said, finishing the chorus. That cut made me a Jadakiss fan.

"I'll cut to the chase. You're a smart kid, so I know you want to help us. We have evidence that Steven Richards, aka Leak, who is the head of a large interstate criminal organization in his hometown of Pittsburgh, is using *Fever* magazine to launder proceeds from the sale of drugs, guns, prostitutes, counterfeit merchandise, and unlicensed medicinal products."

"Uh, unlicensed medicinal products?" I said, stalling.

"Sexual stimulants. Specifically, Kaboom."

"Kaboom, guess who stepped in the room?"

"What?" Wilkins looked annoyed.

"You know, the commercial with the Method Man song?" Wilkins just looked at me, so I nervously continued, "Kaboom, guess who stepped in the room?"

Wilkins scribbled on a small pad. "So tell me about Taylor," he said.

"Taylor? He's involved?"

"Of course he is. Him and Leak are best friends, business partners . . . or are they?"

I pretended that my Sidekick had vibrated. "Just a second," I said, and sent Holliday a message:

I'M BEING INTERVIEWED BY THE FBI!

"Listen, man," I said as I hit the send button. "I only started here a month ago. I don't know anything about what you're talking about."

Wilkins said nothing for a long while as a stream of pedestrians flowed down the sidewalk outside my window. Finally he reached into the breast pocket of his shirt and placed a business card onto my lap.

"If you're smart, you'll give me a call," he said. "You don't want me to have to find you."

My Sidekick buzzed for real this time. Taylor.

I NEED YOU IN LEAK'S OFFICE.

I trudged through the heat back to the office. The steel elevator doors closed to reveal freshly scratched graffiti: ABANDON ALL HOPE, YE WHO ENTER HERE.

Upstairs I could see Leak was sitting on his couch, blunt in hand. Taylor was in a metal chair to the side of the wide coffee table. I paused in the doorway and watched. The speakerphone was on.

"Freddie is on it, duke. They workin' out all the clearances. Meyer signed off on it and the check is being cut. Leak gets one track each edition—"

"I need three tracks, plus approval of whoever else gets to rock," Leak interrupted from the couch. "Plus executive-producer points."

"Damn," the voice on the other end said. "I'll talk to duke about it. You want solo joints, collabos, what? That makes a difference, kna'mean?"

"Fuck that. This is a layup. You know how many units they sold of that wack 'Now That's What I Call Music'? We gon' clean up with the *Fever Hits* joint. What kind of promotions budget they talkin' 'bout?"

"We need to put Flex's street team on this project," Taylor said.

Leak scowled at Taylor. "Fuck you just said?"

"We need a street team on this one."

Leak jerked to his feet, jewelry clanking, and started pacing. "You need to shut the fuck up!" he half shouted at Taylor. "You always coming in talking some dumb shit. Fuckin' Flex street team. This is my shit! The only thing you need to be thinking 'bout is how the magazine can support this record! That's it!"

Taylor sat emotionless in his chair, staring at the phone. I almost felt sorry for him. I waited for Taylor to say something, maybe laugh it off. But as he sat there mute, I rapidly understood that all the stories about Leak intimidating Taylor and holding guns on him were true. Taylor's denials during our Hamptons trip were lies.

My sympathy evaporated, and I knew that Taylor was absolutely not to be trusted.

I was trying to figure out how to use this new knowledge when Leak stopped talking and noticed me in the doorway.

"What about snipes?" the speakerphone said.

"Yo, I'ma hit you back," Leak said. He punched a button and nodded his head toward the couch. I sat down.

"So what the feds talkin' 'bout?" he asked. "That money launderin' bullshit?"

I tried to hide my surprise that he knew about the meeting. Someone must have followed me. But as the FBI man's card burned hot in my pocket, I felt as though I finally had some leverage in this situation.

"True," I said.

Leak looked straight at me. "What else?"

"Nuttin' else."

Leak sat down next to me on the couch, inhaled a huge lungful off the blunt, and dropped it into the ashtray. His fingernails were cut long and perfectly manicured.

"You ain't tell them shit 'cause you ain't know shit, right?" he said without exhaling, his voice choked.

"Right."

He blew a cloud of smoke. "Aiight, den. You better keep it that way—that's real talk." He gave me a long glare, then got up and headed out the door, unlaced boots dragging. Taylor took a quick pull of the still-smoking blunt, stubbed it out, and put the ashtray into Leak's desk drawer.

"So where are you with your story?" Taylor asked from behind the desk.

I tried to keep the pity off my face and formulate an answer. Before I could say anything, Briana stuck her head in the door and cracked her gum.

"Ay yo, Marq. Your brother is out front."

"The Jerusalem artichoke makes excellent juice; it's got mad potassium. The name might throw you off, but it's from the sunflower family and grown in Italy, where it's known as the *Carciofo*, or the *Archicioffo-Girasole*, because *Girasole* is Italian for 'sunflower'. . . ."

Dontay was leaning against the receptionist's desk as he spoke to her. His gear was a travesty—tight Levi's, Spalding sneakers, and a plain blue T-shirt, with a ratty black nylon bag slung across his chest. I hated the way he showed up places he didn't belong. I had known it was only a matter of time before he figured out my address here. But still.

The receptionist's name was Asia. She had her neck pulled

back and her eyebrows raised as if she smelled something rotten.

"Let's go outside," I interrupted. Asia looked relieved.

"Here," Dontay said, pushing a scrap of paper toward Asia. "Write your information down and I'll send you Dr. Walker's book."

"You can send it to me right here," Asia said. She was used to getting hit on by every dude who came through the door.

"Aiight, my brother will bring the book for you," Dontay told her as we waited for the elevator. As the scratched doors slid closed, he stuck his head out and yelled, "It'll change your life!"

Hot air fell onto my shoulders as we stepped out of the lobby onto the sidewalk. Dontay coughed and cracked open a fresh pack of Kools. I thought he smoked Newports.

"All my problems are over," he said.

I waited.

"I'm about to move to Atlanta and start over. I'm paying off all my debts, and then I have a few loose ends to tie up before I can get on with my life."

"I can't pay for you to move to Atlanta."

"See, there you go again being all negative. I ain't ask you for a thing. I got my own money. I'll never take a penny from you again."

"Where'd you get the money?"

"Pops hooked me up."

It had been years since Dontay had surprised me.

"That's right," he said smugly when I didn't respond. "Pops hooked me up."

"You know where he's at?"

"Course I know."

"You said you didn't know."

"I never said that. Stop frontin', son. This thing between us is over."

We stood there staring at each other like boxers before the bell. He had to be lying. Our father had never done a damn thing for us. He must have gotten the money some other way and was ashamed to tell me. I needed to know how much he had so I could be ready for the fallout when he smoked it up.

Dontay pulled on his cigarette and looked up and down the block. "'Bout time you started listening to me. Soon as we can get my stuff out that rat hole you call my crib, I'm gone. . . ."

And that was the moment I gave up.

Why then? It was an argument just like any other. I'd spent tens of thousands of dollars the past five years, sacrificed countless hours to his intrusions and fruitless missions and broken promises. Wasn't that a small price to pay for my manhood? For hip-hop? I owed him that much, right?

But standing there inhaling baked oxygen rising from the gum-pocked street, the traffic a slipstream of metal noise, I surrendered. I lay down before the disappointment and hate and disgust and let it wash the pain away.

"Aiight," I said. The urge to run was overwhelming. "But once you move out that spot, you're on your own. I ain't doing this no more. That's real talk."

Dontay started speaking. I let the cacophony of the city drown out his voice and watched his face bones move underneath his skin. God, I missed my brother. Not this corpse standing here. My brother, the man. I tried to conjure up some of those moments when I had loved him. But every second just reminded me of what was gone.

Dontay's mouth stopped moving. His face registered an instant of shock before squinting up the street with a familiar anger. I followed his gaze and saw a black fire hydrant of a man wearing a loose, billowing silk shirt, bright green and open to the waist, with matching green gators. He had a cocky walk and a straw stingy-brim hat riding low on his forehead. He strolled past us and had his hand on the door of my building's lobby when Dontay's voice made him stop short.

"Did the juice help your face?" Dontay called out.

I could tell he was trying to be calm, but his tone held a tremor of violence.

The dude cocked his head and looked at us for a long moment before he walked over. "Wh'appen?" he said in a squeak-rasp of a voice.

"I bet you didn't even try it," Dontay accused.

I watched recognition spread across dude's face like water through a paper towel. He pushed his hat up on his head and scratched his forehead. "Oh, wh'appnin', bruddah? Nah, I ain't tried the juice. How your boy doing, what's his name? You seen him lately?"

"Nah, we don't hang out like that." Dontay had one hand shoved into his bag, his stringy arm muscles standing out in sculpted relief. "Have *you* seen him?"

I started to get the familiar sensation that Dontay was about to embarrass us.

"Nah, bruddah, I ain't seen him," the dude said in his

cartoon voice, staring at Dontay with a strange expression. "He ain't come up that day? You ain't stay and wait for him?"

I could tell where this was going. As soon as Dontay opened his mouth to reply, I stuck out my hand and introduced myself. "You heading up to the *Fever*?" I asked. "That's where I work. The name's Marq."

The hand clenching mine was soft and sweaty. "Wh'appnin', bruddah. Julien."

Bingo.

"Say word? I been looking for you, man."

That was the wrong thing for me to say. I could feel Julien and Dontay tense up at the same time. I wanted to yank Dontay's hand out of his stupid bag.

"I'm doing a story on Tommy Daminion—we spoke about you the other day—"

"Listen, little brother," Dontay interrupted. "Can't you see I have business with home boy?"

"Y'all bruddahs?" Julien frowned, eyes moving back and forth between us.

I ignored both questions. "I was with Black when he called you the other day."

That got his attention. He studied me with onyx eyes and was about to say something when Dontay moved in between us.

"You stay away from my brother, ya heard?" Dontay growled, a caricature of a threat. "He don't have nothing to do with me. If I see you around him, I'm gonna make you wish you never knew either of us. You hear what I'm saying?"

As I stepped in front of Dontay, I was surprised to hear Julien laughing, a grating screech.

"You a funny dude, bruddah. What you got to be mad about? It's a beautiful day, everybody breathin'. Let's keep it that way. I'ma see you real soon." He walked into the lobby, leaving the scent of cologne behind.

I looked up and Dontay was gone.

CHAPTER 29

When I saw you and Julien, it all became clear to me. Like all of a sudden I was a thousand feet high and could see all of New York spread out beneath me, with all y'all running around like rats in a maze. I worked my whole life to keep you away from everything Julien represents, and now here you are with the dude trying to kill me. Put yourself in my position, you feel me? So I knew I had to take care of Julien myself, step to him and explain you had nothing to do with all this. I ain't have nothing to do with it, either, but it was too late for all that. I just couldn't let anything happen to you.

I figured Mamadeaux was the kind of restaurant Julien would be at. Plus, I finally had some money and it had been so long since I bought myself a nice meal. They made me wait ninety minutes to get in, and that was just for space at the bar, no table. It was packed to the walls with cats trying to be Big Willie. Just the sight of them niggas got me hot. I saw a lot of people I knew. Dudes I used to produce

with, dudes from the block. Niggas was in the back
sniffing coke. Your friend Chunk was there, the one
who used to sell that lousy weed. He was flashing
his money around, said he was managing some guy
named Young Spike. He asked if I was still producing. I said yeah. He told me he produced two songs
on Spike's album, whoever that is. I brought up
Julien's name and Chunk was like, "Everybody gon' be
at the Baller." That's when I decided to go.

People started looking toward the door and then
Reddy came in. I saw his little light-skinned moon
face peeping out from between bouncers and friends
and chicks and diamonds. I hadn't seen him since
that day all those years ago he lied to me about
hooking me up to do some tracks for Large's
album. For some reason I didn't hate him. I was
sure that if he heard my sound, I could take my
place in the history of Large and his music. My
talent would be recognized and all my problems
would be over. But when I reached into my bag for
The Joint, I found cold steel instead. That pistol
pulled my life into the present. I laid back and
didn't approach him. People started yelling, "Reddy
bought the bar!" Grabbing two and three drinks at
a time—you know how thirsty niggas do. I start
kicking it with some dudes from around the way.
This one cat Boom had some rhymes and wanted to
buy beats from me, pay me to produce his demo.
See, I had money in my pocket, so I could get into
an environment where I could make more money. I

been tryna explain that to you for years.

Me and Boom go outside to his car to spark an
L and listen to The Joint. My music blew him away.
I remember he had this stainless-steel lighter, and
as soon as Boom lit the blunt, I immediately noticed
that he had rolled a wooler. You know, there was
crack in the weed.

I know you think I'm an addict, but you're
wrong. I had that five grand in my pocket for like
three or four days and ain't smoke nary bit of
crack. That's not something a crackhead can do.

Boom needs to go get some money so we can get
this project started, so we head over to some guy's
house out in East New York. Boom asked him for the
money he owed him. Dude said he ain't have it but
that he could get some cash from another guy. So
all three of us roll all the way back to Manhattan,
the Upper West Side, to this nice building. They get
buzzed in while I wait in the car. When they came
back out about fifteen minutes later, Boom is highly
upset with his home boy, who's actin real funny
style, like all nervous. We stop at an ATM, and him
and Boom hop out and get some money.

So me and Boom, we got real high. He spent all his
money. But I never let him know that I was sittin
on five Gs. See, that's not something a crackhead
can do.

Then I made a real big mistake—I lost my bag.

We dropped the other nigga off and then hit a
bodega for some Dutches. Boom was in the car outside.

When I come back out the store, I see four or five police cars surrounding Boom's ride. They got him in cuffs and traffic's blocked on both sides of Washington Avenue. I watched for a few minutes, careful so they couldn't see me, then found the closest subway and took it. But I had left my bag in the car. I had my money in my pocket, but my phone and The Joint was in there.

I always was careful to keep more than one copy of The Joint. One copy is yours and one is hidden at Moms's house. She don't know it's there. I tried calling you three or four times, but I couldn't get through. And if I lose The Joint, I lose everything. So I had to go see Moms. I ain't have no choice.

CHAPTER 30

The D. Rex tape was playing on the big flat screen when I walked into the *Fever* staff meeting. Someone was rewinding over and over the part where he lets out the war whoop.

"We should loop that up—it could be the hook to a hit song," a voice said. Everyone laughed except for one dreadlocked sister.

"That ain't him," she said, arms crossed over her chest.

"Is you crazy? You using your eyeballs or something else?"

"D. Rex is not gay."

"Nah, he ain't gay. He just likes it up the—"

"Shut up! Just think for a second. A lot of haters out there who would do something like this. They could have spiked his drink or got a look-alike or something. Because I'm telling you, D. Rex is *not gay*."

"Why it always got to be 'haters.' Anytime somebody got legitimate criticism, the guilty parties always blame it on haters. That's what's wrong with hip-hop. It's like a drug addict not wanting to admit they have a problem."

"I heard that," I said.

"But people do be jealous of success."

"If you always stuntin', talkin' 'bout 'I'm richer than you, my rims bigger than yours, my diamonds, my hoes, my whips,' of *course* people gonna be jealous."

"D. Rex do like to stunt."

"What I wanna know is how his manager and his record label could let this happen. Ain't he on Fresh Beat? They supposed to squash that! That tape is supposed to go into the vault with all the Michael Jackson evidence. Who's dude's manager?"

"Felix Billings used to be," Rosa said as she entered the room. "They had some sort of beef and split up recently. But all that's beside the point. What we have here is evidence of the Sasquatch of hip-hop—the mythical gay rapper. The question is, do we put D. Rex on the cover or not?"

Everyone started talking at once until a flat accent sliced through the noise.

"Excuse me. Excuse me! I thought this was where they kept all the smaht peo-ple."

Meyer Mahl strode in front of the TV screen and calmly surveyed our stunned faces.

"Who the fuck let you in here?" Rosa demanded.

"I did," Leak said from the back of the room.

Rosa whirled around in her chair and glared at Leak. "You know you're not allowed in these meetings."

"Ain't no rule about Meyer, though."

"And now that I'm here," Meyer said, "may I have the floor for just a few moments, Madam Editor?"

"Just say your piece and get out."

"Why, thank you. Are you wondering why I am here? Perhaps to make a case for the heterosexuality of our friend D. Rex? No, I am here to talk about integrity and relationships and how we can preserve all of the above for everyone involved. I have in my pocket a statement from D. Rex denying that the man on the tape is him. So it would be irresponsible of you to claim otherwise, both legally and journalistically. Not to mention that I would never allow another of my dozen platinum artists to ever appear in your fucking magazine again. Given these statements of fact, I think we can all agree that putting D. Rex on the cover would be a grave error for all involved. Madam Editor, thank you for your time."

"You're fucking welcome," Rosa snapped. "But don't think you can run up in my meeting without answering some questions. Starting with, if it's not D. Rex on the tape, who is it?"

"How should I know?"

"It looks just like him. You think we're stupid?"

Meyer smiled. "I do not know who is on that tape. I was not there when it was made. D. Rex says it is not him."

"Why would somebody fake a tape of D. Rex having sex with another dude?"

Meyer leaned forward and put both hands on the edge of

the conference-room table. His gray Polo shirt exposed hairy forearms.

"There are a lot of haters—"

"See what I'm sayin'?" someone yelled.

"—who have it in for D. Rex. There is a lot of turmoil in his camp these days. His management situation is unsettled."

"What happened to Felix?" Rosa asked.

"I have no idea. Fresh Beat is handling his management now."

I remembered Meyer with his arm around Spank in the Hamptons.

"How can you be his manager and his record company?" I asked. "Isn't the manager supposed to negotiate the best deal with the record company?"

Meyer stood up and his eyes narrowed in recognition. Then Leak's voice barked from the back of the room.

"Look, bottom line—it ain't good business to put dude on the cover. It ain't fair and it ain't right. Even homos got the right to be proven innocent before presumed guilty."

"Don't you mean presumed innocent?" Rosa said, smirking.

"You know what the fuck I mean!" Leak stalked to the middle of the long table, platinum FEVER pendant swinging from his long diamond-studded chain. "Y'all always tryna stir something up, and that's bad for business. Remember that all y'all eatin' off this magazine."

I wondered if it was obvious to everyone else that Leak had some sort of business deal going with Meyer. I looked around the room. Everyone had downcast eyes except for Rosa, whose red-painted lips were compressed into a thin, angry line.

"This meeting is over," she snapped. "Meyer, Leak, why don't you step into my office."

Holliday was running hard on the treadmill when I came home. I changed clothes, warmed up, and began to struggle through a workout. After Holliday finished and went into the bathroom to shower, I gave up and sat down at the computer.

My story was half-done. It started in the lockup where I talked to Daminion, then segued into his past, the rise of the Baller, his relationship with Black, and the competition for Slow Creep. It was some of the best work I'd ever done, but it needed more reporting. I needed to verify if Tommy Daminion really was on the Soulstacks and Pump Records payrolls. I needed to speak to Stan Ross. And I needed to find Slow Creep.

I showered and went into the bedroom. Holliday was lying back on the tightly made sheets, twilight burnishing her naked cinnamon body. We were deep inside each other when my Sidekick went off with the "Spank Me" ringtone. I looked at it with one eye—a 718 number—and let it go to voice mail. Two minutes later it spank-spanked again, this time with a text message from Taylor.

READY FOR THE GAME TONIGHT? YOU'RE STARTING.

Holliday shoved my pager off the nightstand and rolled on top of me. I closed my eyes and imagined that we were married.

Later our bodies were resting against each other on the bed, me flipping channels on the TV, when my Sidekick spank-spanked again. The caller ID showed it was the publicist for Young Dro. I clicked on and made arrangements to meet up. We kept flipping channels until I saw Large's wide, dark face on HBO. It was the movie *Dark Alliance*, the scene where Large, playing Freeway Ricky Ross, faces off with the Nicaraguan cocaine connection.

I elbowed Holliday and said, "Here comes the look."

It was the defining moment of the movie, the image captured on a million T-shirts being worn around the world to this day. Large glanced sideways at his adversary, eyes slitted, long prosthetic scar carved in bold relief against his onyx cheek. He knew everything—that the CIA was behind the Nicaraguan rebels, that crack was the apocalypse, that he was powerless to resist the mountains of cash born from this deadly poison. But he was still going to play his hand until the bitter end—and enjoy it.

"Life is a hustle," Large said. "I'm just livin'—"

The screen went black. Holliday flung down the remote.

"Yo, this is the best part!"

"That's a terrible movie," Holliday said in a low voice, scooting to the other side of the bed.

"Why you say that?"

"He made the drug dealer into the hero. Freeway Ricky Ross introduced crack to America, and he's the hero."

"See, you have to know Large's music to understand the nuances of this movie. Large hated drug dealers, and he showed Rick as the essence of evil. It was actually genius the way he portrayed this archetypal drug dealer—it was like the highest form of satire."

"Satire?" Holliday sucked her teeth contemptuously. "You

think the audience even understands what that word means? All they see is a guy getting rich turning black people into crack fiends."

"But it was the CIA who was really responsible. They watched the Nicaraguans bring in the coke, and they didn't care because it was only affecting the ghetto."

Holliday was lying on her back, staring up at the ceiling, a beam from the streetlight falling over her body. "I would expect you to have a different opinion of drug dealers given your brother's situation."

Contempt flooded through me. "Dontay has no excuse. There's no reason for him to smoke crack except that he can't deal with the choices he's made in life and the reality of his existence. I'm not gonna blame no dealers for his weakness."

Holliday looked over my shoulder out the window. I waited for her to compose her thoughts. Maybe now she would tell me more about her parents.

"Remember my friend Tammy who came out to dinner with us last year, the teacher?" I nodded. "She grew up down the block from me. Tammy's mom had a good job at the phone company, but then she got hooked on that crack. Tammy started coming to my house all the time, every day after school, like she lived with us. I thought it was because we had nice things, but then Momma told me that I wasn't allowed at Tammy's house no more because her mom was on drugs. Tammy's heat would be off in the middle of the winter; fiends would be coming through at all hours. Daddy was hustlin', but it wasn't obvious to everybody, at least not that I knew. We had nice clothes and toys, you know, but we didn't have no Benzes or stuff like that. That wasn't Daddy's style. Anyway, one day Tammy got sent home from school early with a cold, and she walked into our house and saw Daddy putting some bricks into a suitcase."

"Bricks?" I asked. The slightest bit of street had crept into Holliday's voice. It gave me a strange thrill.

"Kilos of cocaine. Tammy went crazy, gave Daddy a big scratch across his face. He had to slap her down. She thought my dad was selling drugs to her mom. Daddy didn't do retail, but Tammy couldn't understand that. And in a way, neither could I."

"But you and Tammy stayed friends."

"Tammy ran away that same night. She had a terrible life after that. We got back together years later."

I tried to imagine what Dontay was doing at that moment, but it was impossible.

Holliday sat up on the edge of the bed and started to get dressed. She spoke with her back to me. "Daddy used to talk about a dude named Tommy Deuce from Brooklyn who changed his name to Tommy Daminion when he got into the music business."

"Your dad did business with Daminion?"

"I guess so. I know they bought a lot of product from Brooklyn cats. But Daminion was different because he had a hit record at the same time. You remember "Who Me" by Funk Equation? Daddy said Tommy created a new identity for himself that got the government off him."

Holliday walked around the bed and stood over me, silhouetted against the window. Her voice came from an unseen place.

"I never said nothing because I just wished this Daminion

thing would go away. I don't even like to think about those days. The things my family was involved in, nobody should have to live through that."

"Do you think Daminion had something to do with . . . with what happened?"

Her voice went flinty. "Nah," was all she said.

I felt a rush of love for this strong yet vulnerable woman. I took her hand and she sat down beside me.

"You were right about Taylor, by the way," I said, and told her about the FBI investigation.

"You need an exit strategy."

"This story is my exit strategy! All this stuff with Taylor and Leak only makes it better. No one has ever written about how the rap industry has been so influenced by real gangsters. I mean, these guys have killed people, and they do business every day like normal folks. Plus, I can figure out what really happened to Large. Once I get this story nailed down, I can take it anywhere."

A car drove by, low bass rattling, Large's voice riding on top:

Life is a hustle, I'm just livin' it out
I'm 'bout to call the wolves bust the prisoners out
My team deliver weight like a paper route
Triple beam exact, so there ain't no doubt . . .

Holliday saw me listening and gave a mirthless laugh. "I see where your head is at, Marquis Wise. Have you really thought about what you're doing, about these people you're dealing with? Don't front. Do you really want to be like them?"

"I don't want to be like them. I just want to tell their stories."

"Stop frontin'! You're not like these people, Marquis. That's why I fell in love with you."

I didn't want to be that guy anymore. He was soft, a sucker. But I couldn't tell Holliday that. Once she understood the new me, she would love him even more.

CHAPTER 31

Moms opened the door, gave me one of those hard looks, and said, "You got some nerve coming to my house."

I knew she would let me in, though. We sat down at the kitchen table. "So you back on the street again, huh," she said. She crossed her legs under her nightgown and rubbed her thumbs over each other. I can see how you fell for Holliday. Most men always go for women who resemble they mamas. Both of them ladies keep you in deep check, and you like it that way. Not me.

Growing up I was like a piece of furniture, a doorknob or something. Nobody paid me no mind whatsoever. Moms was wild in the streets. Men coming in the house all day and night. Most nights one of her sisters would watch me, and they was only a few years older than me. Foster kids all over the place. A lot of bad things happened then. And through it all I was like an afterthought. As long as I was alive, they thought everything was fine. But I had no idea about anything. I had to find out everything for myself.

There was this one foster girl, I can't remember her name. Kids ran through our house like roaches. Sometimes they stayed a week, sometimes a year. This girl always had her hair braided up tight, and she smelled like singed hair from the hot comb. She was the first person I remember paying me any attention. She would cut her eyes at me and then leave the room. One day I followed her. I went upstairs and she was in one of the kids' rooms with the door open a little bit. I stood outside until she opened the door a little bit wider and said, "Come in here." I did what she said because that was what I was used to doing. Plus she was older than me, a lot older. I was maybe nine or ten. I sat down on the bed and she pulled me on top of her and started kissing me. Her tongue scared me. After a while she pulled me into the closet and took our pants off. I had no idea what was happening.

This particular girl stayed with us for a while. One of the other kids must have said something to Moms, because one time she snuck up on us in the basement. We was butt nekkid on a blanket on that dirty floor. Moms appeared out of nowhere like a ghost. She let out a yell and whapped me with the cord from an iron, with the plug end. I guess she knew what she was gonna find, cause she came down with the cord in her hand. I jumped up and was crying and trying to get away from her, running in circles with my dick poking out. The girl disappeared in a flash. Moms had me blocked in because the door was behind her. She beat me until my legs was bloody, then stuffed me into my clothes and marched me to the police station. She turned me over to the cops, and they put me in a room by myself for what seemed like days. I was asleep on the floor when they came and took me to a van and took me up to the juvenile jail. And of all the low-down places I ever been in my life, Spofford's the one spot I would never wish on nobody. Not even you.

The first thing I did when I sat down at Moms's table that night was to give her some money. I put three hundred dollars on the table and explained to her that I was heading to Miami for the Baller Convention because I had to help you out of a situation. I wasn't even done talking when she said no. Just like that. She turned me down without even listening to what I was gonna ask for.

I asked her why, and she said that as long as I was a sinner, I wasn't welcome in her house. I told her that it wasn't her place to judge me, especially after all she'd done to me. I told her Jesus said let he who is without sin cast the first stone, you know? She didn't like that at all. She starts quoting scriptures fast and furious, and it's like the more she says, the more she's convincing herself. That's when I had to come with the real.

I told her all these years y'all Witnesses been

waiting for the return of Jehovah amid fire and brimstone and hell on earth and all that. But when the Messiah came, you wasn't listening, just like the Jews overlooked Jesus Christ. See, the word "Christ" is a title, the Greek translation of the Jewish word "Messiah," which means "anointed one." Jesus was anointed with the spirit of God. They used to call him Jesus the Christ, but then Peter and Paul shortened it to Jesus Christ. See, Christ is not any one person. Christ is a spirit, part of God's essence, and that essence comes to earth at different points of history in the form of God's Manifestations—like Bahá'u'lláh Him Who Shall Be Made Manifest. The man foretold by Jesus, Muhammad, all of God's messengers all the way back to Abraham.

Of course, Moms comes back at me with John 14:6 "No man cometh unto the Father but by me." So I tried to tell her that I do believe in Jesus, because Christ and Bahá'u'lláh are one. If you're so desperate for Christ to return, don't you at least owe it to yourself to see if what I'm saying is the truth? That's when she went crazy and started screaming at me, calling me the Antichrist and all that. And then she ran into the other room and came out with my CD case.

I had hidden it way at the top of her pantry—I thought she couldn't find it there. She flung open the window and was about to throw my stuff out, screaming and cursing at me. And when I saw my life's work in her hand, I panicked. I grabbed her by her wrists and shook her, trying to get her to come to her senses. She screamed, "Get out! Get out! If you ever come back to this house again, I'll have you locked up for the rest of your life!" And she threw The Joint out the window into the street.

She might as well have thrown me out the window too. Because without The Joint, I'm nothing.

CHAPTER 32

Stan Ross was not at the basketball game against Pump Records. I started at point. Taylor started too, his slight gut exposed by the mesh tank-top Chelsea Piers jersey. I soon realized that my opponent was too slow to guard me. I got into the lane on the first few possessions and fed my teammates for easy buckets. My opponent started backing up, so I dropped a few threes on him. On one fast break, I sensed the defender leaning the wrong way, changed directions, and made him stumble. His own teammates oohed at that one. Layup and one—I'm on the free-throw line: bounce, bounce, bounce. Breathe, bend, flick, swish. The only good player on the other team was a high-jumping six-foot-six cat with a handle, but he had nobody to run with him. I finished with twenty-three points in an easy win.

Afterward a few Pump cats complimented me on my game. I asked what was popping that night. They said they'd be at a spot called the A.C., "and Stan's gonna be in the house, so you know the jump-off's gonna be crazy!"

Turned out the A.C. was a strip club. Sitting at a table with Taylor and his entourage, I tried not to look at the G-stringed women. I still felt guilty about Shortcake. Holliday was superior to her in every way except sheer ass size, yet the stripper with the crooked tooth continued to stain my thoughts.

I struck up a conversation with someone from the basketball game to focus on my mission of gathering leads about Pump Records. Drinks were drank. Fire touched blunts. In less than half an hour, I had found the right person.

"That was back when I used to work at the *Fever*," said a dude named Emmitt with a dark face splotched with patches of light skin around the eyes and mouth.

"Word? Doing what?" I asked.

"I was an editor or whatever, and I did the About to Blow column. That's how I discovered Slow Creep."

"You discovered Slow Creep?"

"Believe that. We used to get a hundred demos a month, and I would listen to them all.

"I'd love to talk to the Creep for this story I'm doing for the *Fever*."

"Word? Them's my peoples—I'll see what I can do."

We were standing at the bar, drinking Hennessys. Emmitt had a pocketful of slender, immaculately rolled joints. A horse-faced dancer came over and whispered something into Emmitt's ear. "I'ma check you later, ma," he told her. "Come holla after Stan gets here."

"That chick's mug could break glass, but check this out," Emmitt said to me as she turned away and walked over to another customer. Her body had the impossible shape of a cartoon.

"Damn."

"I know. When Stan gets here, it's gonna be a problem."

"So you were at the *Fever* back in the day. Musta been a lot different back then," I prodded.

"True indeed. I've known Taylor Whittingham since he was twelve years old. He's really a shy guy, especially around females. But he grew into the business role, kind of grew up with the magazine. Back then it was so new—a rap magazine had never been done before. We were writing about people we had looked up to our whole lives, and most of the time these artists were being critiqued for the first time in their careers. No one wrote about rap back in the late eighties. All of a sudden we were wielding power over our idols. So we had beef on the regular. Dudes tried to roll up into the office all the time, but Leak stopped that pretty quick."

"So you were there when Taylor snuck that article into the magazine about Leak without the editors knowing?" I asked.

"Listen, I was the biggest 'Leak is wack' person in the office, but I never said he shouldn't get an article. Every editor had groups they showed favoritism to. Leak and Taylor really are friends. And Leak may not be the most artistic MC, but he puts his music out every year. He's like a graf artist—he's in your face wherever you go. That's the definition of real hip-hop."

Based on what I'd heard about Leak holding the gun on Taylor, I found it hard to believe they were friends. "You mean Leak isn't extorting him?" I asked.

"If Leak wasn't around, someone like Suge Knight woulda steamrolled the *Fever* a long time ago. I believe that Taylor chose this relationship because long range he saw it as mutually beneficial."

I looked over at Taylor. He was ensconced at a table, talking to an older man in a suit, surrounded by his employees, bottles of champagne, and a half-dozen strippers. The music was pounding—*Never spend dirty money on a dirty dame.* . . . Taylor looked up and caught my eye. He smiled and picked up his Sidekick.

MAKE SURE YOU ASK EMMITT HOW HE PUT LARGE ON.

"So I hear you put Large on," I said.

"Well, I helped. I knew L from Mister P, who gave me his demo for the About to Blow column."

For some reason Dontay popped into my head. "You heard that song The Joint?" I asked, instantly regretting it.

Emmitt thought for a minute. "Yeah, I remember L on that song. It was hot. I did a write-up on it in the *Fever*."

"My brother produced that track."

"Say word! Your brother is Dontay? I used to see him on the block with L all the time. Whatever happened to him?"

Emmitt was an A&R; his job was to buy music for his artists.

I took a swallow of my drink.

"Tay's still around the way. So how'd you end up working at Pump?"

"I wanted to get into producer publishing. I knew Stan from the industry—he had just started his label. This was back in '94. He hollered at me, said he wanted to sign Slow Creep, he wanted to make me the A&R, woop woop woop."

There was a flurry of activity as an entourage made its

way from the front door to a private room at the back. The
group was escorted by at least a half-dozen large, white security
guards.

"Stan's here," Emmitt said.

My Sidekick went off. Chunk.

WHATS CRACKULATIN? BLACK JUST GOT IN
TOWN. WE LOOKING FOR THE JUMP-OFF

I hit him back.

COME THRU THE A.C. THERE'S NUFF HOES UP
IN THIS PIECE.

Emmitt slipped off his stool and headed to the private
room. I knocked back the last of my Hennessy and followed.
We started to walk through the doorway when one of the security guards put a rough hand on Emmitt's shoulder.

He knocked the hand away. "What the fuck, yo. You new
or something? I'm Stan's partner. Chill the fuck out."

The man's beefy face reddened. He had a crew cut and an
NYPD tattoo on his thick forearm. One of the other guards
said, "Let 'em through."

The VIP room had long leather couches up against three
walls. Dozens of bottles filled low movable tables. I scanned
faces through the dim light. About two dozen men were
playing with their mobile devices, talking on phones, rolling blunts, and pouring drinks. Emmitt slid onto a seat next
to a small, white man and introduced him to me. It was
Stan.

He was dressed in Pumas, carefully distressed jeans, and an untucked pale yellow button-down shirt. His longish blond hair was carefully jelled into a spiky style that was too young for his rough, squinty face.

Emmitt poured three shots from a frosty bottle of Grey Goose vodka and slid one each in front of me and Stan. We were about to drink when Taylor entered. He pulled up a chair and Em poured him a shot. We all drank.

Stan spoke while looking out into the room. "How's your lady, Taylor? She close that Benz account yet?"

"Indeed. Thanks for putting in a good word. How's Teddy's soccer camp going?"

"He loves it. His tan is wicked. All the kids think he's black now," Stan said proudly.

Mobb Deep's "Quiet Storm" throbbed over the sound system, Lil' Kim's vocals stabbing the air. A half-dozen strippers came through the door. The men raised bottles into the air and cheered.

"I see you've met my newest star writer, Marq Wise," Taylor said. I suppressed a shudder. "He's doing a story about the Baller."

I couldn't figure out what angle Taylor was trying to play. Normally I would have primed Stan with a few flattering questions, but tonight I decided to be aggressive.

"So what's up with Slow Creep?" I asked.

A stripper was straddling the face of a man clenching a twenty-dollar bill between his teeth. "Whaddya mean what's up with them," Stan said.

"People say they're leaving your label."

"People who?"

Another stripper was on her back with her legs spread. She puffed on a cigarette, inserted the filter end into her vagina, and then expelled a cloud of smoke. The men roared.

I half wanted to run over for a better look. Instead I looked over at Stan, who was wearing a thin smile. He leaned back to pull a thick stack of cash out of one pocket just in time to hand it to a man who walked up.

"Who says Slow Creep is leaving my label?" Stan repeated.

"Look, I don't like to spread people's names around, kna'm sayin'?" I replied. "I ain't gonna leave here and run over to the next dude and say, 'Hey, Stan said woop woop woop.' But dudes is talking about signing Slow Creep, and there must be a reason for that. I'd rather hear the truth from you than have to find out from somebody else. But I will find out. That's real talk."

A busboy cleared an armload of empty bottles. Stan ran a hand through his tousled hair. He looked as though he hadn't slept in weeks.

"I brought Slow Creep into my company before they were old enough to drive," he said finally, gazing at the revelry. "Trophy and Bizack are like family to me. And like any family, sometimes you have disagreements. People get mad, they make up. Slow Creep is not going anywhere. They are under contract to Pump Records. We treat them very well, as we should, because they helped us become a hundred-million-dollar company. Their last album went platinum, the first million-seller of their career."

I needed to shake him up. "So why are they so unhappy with you?"

"Artists are always unhappy with the label," he said calmly. "I spent two million dollars on their last album. They recorded more than forty songs."

"So they haven't got any royalties yet?"

"They got a very nice advance. When Trophy's mom broke her hip and had no insurance, we picked up that bill. We invested very heavily in Slow Creep, we're very happy with the songs they've recorded for their next album, and we anticipate everything moving forward with their next album according to our contract."

I applied a little more pressure. "Given that they weren't satisfied with your promotion of the last record, what are you going to do differently this time to push their music?"

"It's not about music anymore, it's about lifestyle. We sell the lifestyle. There's no difference between Allen Iverson and Puffy. The same kid buying the Puffy record is buying the Iverson sneaker is buying the Slow Creep record. I know how to reach those kids."

Time to flip it. "Tell me about your relationship with Tommy Daminion."

Stan frowned, still looking out into the room. "With who?"

"Tommy Daminion."

He looked at Taylor, who raised his perfect eyebrows and gave a half shrug.

"I have a great deal of respect for Tommy as a music executive, and I've been able to work with him on a few projects."

"So he's on retainer?"

"Retainer?"

"Do you pay him a salary?"

Stan suddenly grabbed my arm and leaned in close. "What kind of games do you think you're playing?" he hissed, not taking his eyes off the room. "Who the fuck do you think you are, asking me these questions?" He flung my arm away and leaned back silently in his seat, gazing at the strippers as if nothing had happened.

I looked over at Taylor, who shrugged again. I had to figure out his angle, quickly. I was about to get up when "Spank Me" electrified the room.

Spank . . . spank spank . . . The strippers jerked and popped, the men grabbed and slapped. A face was buried in a crotch. Champagne splashed through the air. Stan sat back and calmly surveyed the scene. My Sidekick buzzed. Chunk.

YOU IN VIP? COME TELL THIS CRACKER PIG
TO STOP TRIPPIN.

I elbowed my way to the door and found Black nose to nose with two security guards. Chunk was behind him, cell phone pressed to his ear with one hand and Sidekick in the other.

"Y'all muhfuckas the second string and don't even realize it," Black was saying, his head wagging. "Y'all's a contingency plan. Only reason y'all beeyotches is here is 'cause real niggas like me don't have Stan's back no more. Y'all the poh-lice, right? Shouldn't y'all be out robbin' some dope dealers or something? I know that pay better than Stan's cheap ass."

"Look, I don't know you," a security man said.

"You don't wanna know me, nigga. I'm a Six-Oh Crip. And Black will shoot, beeyotch—you can ask anybody. If I wanted to cap Stan, I'da did it when he was paying me to sit in the office next to his. I'm the one who kept Suge Knight from turning Stan into his food."

Black saw me. "What up, my nigga," he said, drawing me into a pound.

Chunk snapped his phone shut and gave me a pound. Someone inside the room came through the door, tapped the guard on the shoulder, and pointed to Chunk and Black.

"Pig," Black spat as he walked past.

All the strippers were now completely naked. Chunk grabbed a bottle of Cristal and took a swig. Black was greeted like a relative by a half-dozen people. We slowly made our way back over to Stan and sat down.

"My man Black," Stan said. "Good to see you. How's your wife?"

Emmitt passed Black a joint and he took a long pull.

"Julien said to tell you that you owe him eighty thousand dollars," Black said.

For the first time, Stan's face darkened. He ran a hand through his hair. "That fuckin' guy," he said. "I told him I'm not signing his group. I don't care what Relativity owed them. I didn't buy those debts. I just bought the catalogue and the groups that are actually worth something. Julien needs to take that up with them."

"Yeah, but you know Julien. He a persistent muhfucka."

"Whatever. So what's up with you these days?"

Black's cheeks bunched up into a smile. "Oh, I'ont know. I was thinking of starting my own label and signing Slow Creep."

I stifled a laugh, which didn't escape Stan. "Very funny. You two know each other?"

"Hell yeah, we know each other. Game recognize game, nigga." Black clinked my glass of Goose with his bottle. "He writing the history of the Baller. Speaking of which, I got you down for a Friday night showcase and two tables at the Willie Awards, aiight?"

"Who else is on the bill Friday?"

"Dr. Dre want a spot—he breaking some new artists this fall."

"I need the last hour. I don't want Dre's guys before mine."

"Dre already put up fifty Gs, though."

"I got you, don't worry."

"'I got you?' Fuck that s'posed to mean?"

"I said I got you. You know I'm good."

"Yeah, you good for seventy-five, muhfucka," Black said, sinking back into the couch and taking a long pull from his joint. "Now shut up so I can get at some of these hoes."

CHAPTER 33

"What happened to all your records?" I asked Dontay. We were in his apartment, packing the meager trappings of his life into boxes, stirring up dust that danced in the sun rays piercing the musky basement air.

Back when I was little, Dontay's large, square LPs stayed hidden from Mom between Dontay's box spring and mattress. We had no record player in our house. Late at night, when Mom would hold window vigils waiting for Dontay to come home, I would take out the LPs and gaze at the young black men on the covers, their bold faces inviting me into Dontay's unknown world.

Dontay was rummaging through a crate filled with a jumble of wires. "Somebody cheated me out of them," he said, his back turned to me. "But I'ma have the last laugh on that one. Besides, I got them all right here." He pointed to a stack of three bulging CD binders.

I flipped through the top binder. The titles were scribbled in Magic Marker on the naked plastic discs: A Tribe Called Quest, Public Enemy, Mantronix, Big Daddy Kane—all old school. I dumped the binders into a box and opened the closet door. Two pairs of decrepit jeans hung from sagging wire hangers. On a shelf were a few yellowed tighty-whiteys and rumpled T-shirts. I started folding them and putting them into a box.

"You can leave all those clothes here. I'm finally going to buy myself a wardrobe. All these years I been forced to wear whatever you wanted to buy me. That's over now."

Something stirred beneath the thick layer of weed and Heineken suffocating my emotions. I had bought Dontay a lot of nice stuff. But I wasn't going to fight with him today, and that meant letting his delusions run free.

"I get a lot of unreleased music at the *Fever*. I'll burn some copies for you."

Dontay snorted, shook a Newport out of a crumpled pack, and fired it up. "You getting me music? I ain't interested in what the *Fever* calls hip-hop. Ain't no soul in that. Niggas just be in it for the money. Cam'ron, Jadakiss, Ludacris, alla them. Them cats ain't got no real skills."

"No skills? You heard what 'Kiss is spittin'? *Prob'ly think I won't murder you the way I smile, but I'ma take a lotta shots A-I style.* . . . Duke is nice. He's like the new Rakim," I argued.

Dontay put down his cigarette on an overturned lid from a jelly jar and removed a CD from one of his binders. His Walkman was plugged into a Radio Shack amplifier that was connected to black speakers, each half the size of a shoe box. Dontay hit a button and the tiny system sputtered to life.

> Sometimes I'm like a white man: Don't trust me
> Sometimes I'm like a black man thinking like a white man:
> All you niggas disgust me . . .

"Who this?"

"Cox," Dontay said, lighting another Newport. "Jadakiss talking 'bout murdering dudes, but Cox mean what he say. Listen to this." Dontay turned it up, the tiny woofers crackling under the crunching beat.

> I'm like Rakim with muscles, no jokin'
> If niggas try to disrespect my melody
> I'm gunnin' for the felony
> There's a lot of questions that really need answers
> Like who the fuck told you that your rhyme style was hot
> You know how Large died, who bust that shot?
> Why is Sammy the Bull still living
> And where the fuck is Pac?

"That's what I'm talkin' 'bout," Dontay said, almost to himself. "Niggas know what happened to L. Y'all need to stop lying."

"So what did happen?" I said, glad not to be arguing.

"It was all Reddy's fault."

"C'mon, bruh. You just mad 'cause Reddy signed L and didn't holler at you."

Dontay was standing in front of the framed Large picture on his shelftop shrine. He spoke bitterly, fingers flitting over his mementos until they came to rest on the single blue-topped crack vial.

"That don't change what happened. You think I'm nobody, that I'm just some crackhead runnin' the streets gettin' high. But I'm connected to the top levels of the game. There's some life and death drama going down right now. I been tryna tell you, but you too busy playing rap writer, messin' with cats like Julien. Dudes like him's the reason hip-hop is so wack right now. And I can tell by the way you dealt with dude that you have no idea what time it is. No idea whatso*ever*."

I pictured myself smacking Dontay in the face. Just smacking him and then standing there, to prove how weak he was.

The room was bare now except for the shrine. Large's onyx face peered into the distance from beneath his slanted derby. The picture, the mementos . . . it was absurd. Hero worship. Dontay might as well be killing chickens down here and dancing over their blood.

"I know a lot more about Large than you think."

Dontay coughed. "That's funny. How could you possibly tell me anything about Large that I don't know? I know L better than he knew himself."

"Word? Then who kilt him?"

"I told you. Reddy did it."

"He pulled the trigger?"

"Might as well have. Reddy got so many people hatin' him, he needed security when he went to the West Coast. So he got with some Crips, but then he ain't wanna pay them niggas. So they got L."

That sounded crazy to me. If Reddy needed security, he could afford professionals.

"I bet you didn't know Julien's people were the ones who got Large outside of Junior's, though."

Dontay jerked his head away from the shrine to look at me with crazed eyes. "Don't play games with me, boy!"

"Uh-huh. I thought you knew so damn much. I only been in the game a minute and done figured that out."

"Who told you that?" Dontay demanded, taking a step toward me.

I felt a twinge of regret. Maybe this was too much information for Tay.

"The streets don't lie," I said.

"What you know about *streets*?"

"I know Julien makes a living robbing drug dealers, and I know him and Large was kicking it before Large made *Dark Alliance*."

Dontay sat down heavily on the edge of his low futon, knees poking up near his shoulders. He held his head in his hands for a few long moments, then abruptly pulled out a giant wad of bills and began counting, moving his lips as he went along.

"*Pops* gave you that money?" I asked.

"Word—five Gs. I been tryna tell you all these years he's a good dude. Moms, her whole family, they poisoned us against him."

"Why he ain't come see us then?"

"Because Moms said she'd kill him if he came back."

When I was younger, I'd often think about the man who had come to visit Mom that night, wearing the hat with the feather. I wondered why God would take my father away from me. Now I pondered why Dontay would be the one to find him.

"Where'd you meet him? What'd y'all do together?"

"I went to his crib at the Polo Grounds projects, and then we went to a restaurant up in the Bronx. He introduced me to this cat Pez, and once I told Pez about me and Large, Pez got Reddy on the phone for me. The door is open now for The Joint to take its rightful place in L's pantheon, so e'ybody will understand—"

"Who was this Pez dude?"

"Some gangster Pops knew from back in the day. Reddy used to bring him around the block. He's probably the one who plugged Reddy in with the Crips out in LA. . . ."

This was good information. I filed it away for future reference.

"Pez said all I had to do was leave this room. And now here we are."

Dontay licked his thumb and started counting the money again. It made me nervous. "So where you gonna go?" I asked, knowing that Tay's existence had long ago ground itself down into moment to moment.

"Don't worry about it. I got plenty of places to stay."

"Like where?"

"I said don't worry about it, aiight? This right here"—he waved a fistful of bills—"means the end to all my troubles. You ain't gonna have to pay for me no more. My whole life is about to change, starting right now."

A familiar tightness crept into my chest. There was no way to avoid what was coming. I walked over to the shrine and started to toss the items into a crate.

"You sure you don't want me to hold on to some of that cash for you, until you get situated?"

Dontay sprang across the room and grabbed my arm.

"Watch out with my stuff!" he rasped. "Nothing else in this room means a thing besides what's on this shelf. Matter fact, I don't even want the rest of that stuff. Throw it all out. All I need you to hold for me are my CDs, my equipment, and Large's things."

"Oh, so you want *me* to hold this stuff for you."

Dontay glared. "I can't walk around New York with all my possessions on my back."

"So you really don't have any place to stay."

"You listen to me! This got nothing to do with you no more. Without you holding me back, I'll finally be able to get back on my feet. Just take these couple crates and I'll pick them up in a week. Then we can be done with each other for good."

I never hated Dontay more than at that moment—for wasting his life, for disappointing me, for shitting on everything I had ever done for him. Tears of frustration stung my eyes and I searched for a way to inject my pain into Dontay's heart. But he was oblivious, carefully emptying the crate of Large's mementos and rearranging them in a careful circle on the floor.

I willed myself to be calm and lugged the boxes outside to the rental car. Sparking a blunt on the front stoop and waiting for Dontay to finish, I mentally visited the entire dingy procession of hopeless spaces I had moved Dontay in and out of all these years. At least this would be the last one.

Dontay came out with one more box. I handed him what was left of the blunt and asked where he wanted to get dropped off.

"Why don't I crash with you just for tonight."

I didn't even bother to reply. After a while Dontay understood my silence. He stood up and shouldered his duffel bag.

Before he disappeared into Brooklyn, he said to me, "What
did I ever do to you that you'd leave me out here to die?"

CHAPTER 34

"I hate that bitch," Chunk muttered.

The prosecutor's slate-heavy voice thudded through the
courtroom, emotionless and menacing. From where Chunk
and I were sitting, right behind Tommy Daminion's defense
table, I could see the back of her calves, fish-belly white beneath
her gray skirt.

"A high-end sentence is absolutely warranted due to the
defendant's severely underrepresented criminal history. The
defendant was charged in a 1991–1992 crack cocaine distribution conspiracy that also involved several attempted murders
in Virginia. Before we could arrest him in that case, he fled
to New York, where he was arrested with a gun. He bought
his way out of Rikers Island and went on the run from federal
authorities once again. And finally, more than five years later,
he's caught with a different gun, in this case a stolen Amadeo
Rossi .38 caliber revolver. . . ."

That was the gun Black gave Daminion. I waited a suitable
interval, then looked toward the back of the courtroom to see
if Black was there yet. He was in the last row, dark face looking
sweaty and uncomfortable. He up-nodded at me and mopped
his forehead with a blue bandanna.

A half-dozen rappers were in the courtroom, a few R&B

singers, and a slew of industry cats. The only dudes I didn't recognize were three older black men sitting toward the back, wearing stylish hats and expensive suits.

"So he was a fugitive and a felon already when he became a fugitive in possession of a gun and a felon in possession of a gun in this case," the prosecutor said in her hard voice. Chunk sucked his teeth and snorted. His beefy shoulders twitched.

I stopped taking notes and rubbed my eyes with two fingers. It had been two a.m. when I dropped Dontay's stuff in my apartment last night. Holliday was asleep and I was too wound up to join her. I considered hitting the park for a basketball workout, then texted Chunk and met him and Wop at a strip club. We had some Hennesseys and some lap dances, and then I woke up on my couch three hours later to the smoky stink of Dontay's belongings and the sound of the front door closing behind Holliday.

A hint of emotion was creeping into the prosecutor's voice. "How can two incidents five years apart, with different guns in different places, be one continuing course of conduct? Where the defendant's asking for a departure—"

"Let's not talk about departures," the judge interjected. He had thick black-rimmed glasses that matched his dyed black hair. "Let's just talk about whether or not the Court computes the criminal history correctly."

I elbowed Chunk and raised my eyebrows. "The sentence depends on a point system," he whispered. I could still smell the liquor on his breath. "The more shit you done did, the more points you get. The more points, the more years. Tommy's lawyer's sayin' the old case is the same as this one, so them points don't count."

"The guidelines don't specifically have an example of a case like this where you actually have someone who's escaped in the middle of all these proceedings," the prosecutor said.

Feet shuffled in the back of the room and everyone turned around. A tall, light-skinned man was making his way to a seat. He wore a black suit, tailored to the exact contours of his well-muscled physique. Everyone he passed reached out to shake his hand, which had an enormous diamond on the pinky.

I elbowed Chunk.

"Cox," he whispered.

I couldn't figure out why Cox was getting sweated so much. He hadn't been on the radio in years.

The judge peered through his glasses, then decided not to say anything as Cox took his seat and the hubbub subsided. The judge cleared his throat and the prosecutor continued.

"The bottom line, Your Honor, is this: The government should seek justice where justice has not been done in the past. This defendant is the definition of a recidivist, a dangerous individual, a violent felon. And by some amazing amount of skill he has managed to spend very little time incarcerated. I mean, this guy has skated in every jurisdiction he's been in."

I looked at Daminion's back, visualizing his calm face from our interview. Was it the face of a killer? I couldn't remember.

"So your argument," the judge said, "is that his two previous cases didn't turn out how you wanted, and you want to make up for that now."

"There's nothing wrong with that, Your Honor."

"Well," the judge said, looking at some papers on his desk, "I happen to agree with the government in this case. I think they're two separate crimes and it's not relevant conduct."

"Fuck!" Chunk muttered. Daminion shifted in his seat, the first time I'd seen him move during the proceedings.

"Now, the defendant's other argument is that a departure is warranted based on delay in prosecution. After his release from federal imprisonment the defendant was convicted in New York of bail jumping and sentenced to eighteen to thirty-six months. Two days before his state sentence was completed, you brought the defendant to this court. The defendant is arguing that this delay precluded him from serving concurrent sentences. . . ."

A soft hand fell onto my shoulder and Holliday slid onto the bench next to me. She kissed me on the cheek, smelling like citrus.

"I was in the neighborhood," she whispered, looking hard into my eyes. She was dressed for work, in a tan pantsuit and peach blouse.

I tried my best to hold her gaze. Was it possible the shower didn't erase the stripper smell? I wished I had joined her in bed last night, but my body was on a different clock than hers now. I tried to remember the last time we had worked out together.

"How'd it go with Dontay?" Holliday whispered.

It was easy to let those troubles rise up and hide the guilt. Holliday saw my emotions bubbling up, gripped my hand, and whispered into my ear: "You can't save your brother. He has to save himself." She turned her attention to the proceedings and I realized that my secret would hold.

The judge and the prosecutor were tossing numbers back and forth. It took me a minute to figure out they were discussing

months, not years. I stopped taking notes—Holliday could translate for me later.

"All right, let me hear from defense counsel," the judge
finally said.

"Your Honor," Daminion's lawyer said, running a hand over
his dark, slicked-back hair, "the sentence that the court decides
upon is really independent of whether my client is a bad person.
It's a question of how much time the government took away from
him by delaying this prosecution. We also submit that it would
be proper to find a downward departure based on Mr. Clark's
conduct and his new sense of purpose in life. He's got a three-
year-old son who's in court right now. His wife is here today.
And he's got an employer here today, Felix Billings, who owns
a music-industry company called Deep Entertainment, and he's
been in business for decades. Mr. Billings is on the boards of
several major civil-rights organizations, and he is married to the
actress Brenda Long, who's here in court with us today—"

"Wow, we have Wanda in the courtroom. Please don't
throw me out the window!" the judge said, speaking of Long's
most famous movie role.

The courtroom chuckled as people craned their necks to
catch a glimpse of Long. Chunk laughed, a bit too loudly, the
sound bouncing through the room like a thrown pebble.

Daminion turned his head and shot Chunk a glare. It was
the only time that day I saw his eyes. For a moment I saw,
shockingly, the slightest trace of fear. It was quickly buried in a
look of pure menace. I actually felt a chill run down my spine.
Chunk ducked his head and looked away.

"No defenestration today," the lawyer said, buttoning
his expensive suit jacket. "But what's relevant here is that the

government filed a pleading with the court listing what they said
was a criminal history of Felix Billings. But this was a rap sheet
for another Felix Billings. This is an outrageous transgression,
Your Honor. It would be libelous if the government didn't have
absolute immunity. They claim Felix Billings has eleven criminal convictions. This man here in court today has no criminal
record whatsoever. I ask that Mr. Billings be allowed to address
the court about the changes he has witnessed in Mr. Clark."

"May I just address one accusation that was made, Your
Honor?" the prosecutor said shrilly. "Defense counsel gave me
no additional information when I talked to him more than two
months ago about running this criminal history."

"But you're supposed to be thorough when you check
these things out. You have the entire United States government
behind you."

"Okay, we've got the entire government, but they have
Wanda on their side."

"Now, that's uncalled for," the judge said. "Mr. Billings,
please address the court."

A short, wide man rose from his seat in the back of the
courtroom, next to the other two men with hats. His skin was
so light, he would have looked white if it weren't for his thick
lips and wide nose. He was dressed like a banker except for the
black fedora in his hand. He walked to a lectern at the side of
the defense table and cleared his throat.

"Ever since my education at Howard University and at the
University of Illinois," he began, "I've tried to help rehabilitate
our young brothers. I've built one of the most prolific organizations in the world at helping young people restore their
lives—it's been operating for more than thirty years now. And

when I became a Muslim, I got even more involved in helping as many young people as I could. That's how I heard about this kid coming out of jail. He was a Muslim, and whether people like it or not, the Muslim faith is good with helping young men succeed using a strong God concept where you have to pray several times a day and touch your forehead to the ground and submit to God. That was the basis of the discussion when I met this young man, and I saw a spark in him. He wanted to live right. He had no father in his life. Where that guidance was supposed to come from, there was a void. . . ."

I tried to conjure up an image of my father. All I could remember was Mom's closed bedroom door, his coat on the couch, and the hat with the big feather in the band.

I grabbed Holliday's hand and squeezed. She smiled at me, my sadness melted away, and I tuned back in. Billings had a deep, majestic voice, like a preacher's, and he spoke slowly enough to enunciate every syllable.

"If these young brothers have no support base, then they don't have a chance in life. So I decided to give this young man a job. I talked to Tommy about Allah, and I knew that he was a believer. I'm planning to give him a job so he will be next to me every day. I'll sit him right next to my other two sons, who run my company with me. Every day I'll see Tommy and know where he is and who he's with and what he's thinking about. I'm not going to worry about his past. I'll worry about his present, because I'm not going to tolerate any nonsense from the kids born to me or from the artists on my label and I'm not going to tolerate it from him. I'll step to any one of these young brothers myself before I let that happen."

It felt as though Billings were talking directly to me. For a moment I wished that it were me instead of Daminion under his wing.

"Give him to me, Judge. He needs a daddy in his life. Give him to me and you won't ever see him in front of you again. I'm asking this not for him, but for all the people around us that need to see some success. There's a lot of thuggery in the black community and in the music business. I knew what it took to duck crime, but this kid needs a chance to do the same thing. And if you cage someone up like an animal, they will continue to be an animal. Tommy needs love now. He needs support. Whatever he did, he did. Whatever we think he did, he did. Just like you were wrong about who I was, you could be wrong about him. We think, hey, here's Felix Billings—he's in the record industry, so he must be a crook. But not only am I not a crook, I love black people. I love white people. We need to come together and destroy some of these problems. There's a lot of young people who need our help.

"I wouldn't stand here in front of you and risk my good name unless I knew that this young man would do right. I beseech you to please give him a chance to fulfill his promise. Give him to me, and if he breaks the law, I'll bring him right back to you. God took the lowest and raised it to the highest. This kid believes in God. I will be there next to him saying, *Did you pray today?* We've got brothers in this room who have been praying hard all the time we've been sitting here. Let that reach your heart. Please let it reach your heart. Your Honor, please let it reach your heart."

Billings walked back to his seat. The courtroom was silent. I tried to remember the last time I had been to church. I heard a noise and saw Chunk wiping his eyes.

"Mr. Clark," the judge said, "would you like to address the court?"

As Daminion stood, the entire courtroom seemed to lean forward in its seat. Daminion's braids were gone, replaced by a low, clean cut. The stiff white collar of his shirt shone between his dark suit and darker skin. He clasped his hands in front of him, then put them at his sides and began to speak.

"First I'd like to apologize to the court and to my family. Your Honor, I would very much like to be there for my son and my wife, and to pursue the things that I love to do. I have found my purpose in life now, Your Honor. Before, I had no objective. I had no plan. I'm thankful that Felix Billings is giving me a chance to redefine my life and my goals. I have a purpose now, Your Honor. Let today be a crystal ball into the future of my life. This is my future, Judge. You have seen my future right there. Thank you."

The prosecutor was rising before the judge called her name.

"I've prosecuted a lot of narcotics cases, Your Honor, and seen many defendants make the same argument, but without such eloquent supporters to back them up. And I've seen these same defendants back in court again."

She sat down. The judge shuffled papers on his desk for what seemed like five minutes.

"All right," he said. "I'm going to depart based on pre-indictment delay, which deprived the defendant the opportunity to serve concurrent sentences. . . ."

Chunk squeezed my arm so hard it hurt. I shook him off and nudged Holliday. She shushed me.

"The defendant, Thomas Clark, is hereby committed on counts one and two of the first superseding indictment to the custody of the bureau of prisons to be imprisoned for a term of nineteen months. Due to time served, he shall be . . . released immediately."

The courtroom bubbled over with noise. The judge peered over his glasses and waited for it to subside.

"You've got a lot of friends out there," he said to Daminion. "I gave you a big break because the government waited so long to charge you with this crime. You have a chance to taste the good life. There's no reason for you to go back to the bad."

"Aiight!" Chunk said. "Time to get paid!"

The hallway was like happy hour. Pounds, smiles, proclamations. Everybody knew everybody. It was an exclusive club, being friends with Tommy Daminion, and today was the best day to be a member.

I spotted Julien by the doorway, talking to the rapper Ton-Ton. "What's he doing here?" I asked Chunk.

"Who, Ton-Ton? Him and Tommy are peoples."

"Not him. Julien. I thought . . ." I didn't want to say anything volatile in front of Holliday, who was holding my hand and staring wide-eyed at the crowd.

"You thought what? That they wasn't boys? That's just how these niggas get down. Some days they best friends, some days they wanna kill each other."

I shot Chunk a scowl at the murder reference and glanced at Holliday. No way she could have missed that. But she was looking into the crowd. I followed her gaze and saw the large, light-skinned man surrounded by a knot of people. Cox. And he was looking right at Holliday.

She had a confused frown on her face. "Whassup?" I asked

her, but she didn't respond. I tugged her arm. "Why you staring at dude?"

Holliday snapped out of it, and her normal expression
returned to her face. "Staring at who? I was just thinking, baby,
that's all."

"Thinking about what?"

She paused, long enough for me to notice that Cox was
walking in our direction.

Men tried to hit on Holliday every single day, even when
she was obviously with me. But I had never seen her respond,
even slightly.

Up close Cox was even more impossible. He had taken off
his jacket, revealing a silky T-shirt that failed to contain biceps
the size of cantaloupes. The skin on his head and face was clean
shaven, the color of a manila folder, and looked soft to the
touch. He was pretty as hell.

"Is that really you?" Cox asked.

"Yes, it's me," Holliday said.

"How are you? *What* are you?"

"I'm great. I'm a lawyer now."

Cox nodded approvingly and smiled with everything but
his light gray eyes, which stayed strangely distant, as if he was
watching someone else at the same time. Then his gaze shifted
to me. I stared up at him and said nothing.

"This is my boyfriend, Marquis," Holliday said. "He's the
reason I'm here today. He writes for the *Fever*."

Cox extended his hand. Unlike the rest of his perfect skin,
the knuckles were blackened and scarred. We shook, no pound.
I squeezed as hard as I could. His fist was stone.

He turned back to Holliday. "I'm 'bout to be out. I hate

courtrooms. I'm glad we ran into each other. Now I know everything turned out aiight."

He stood there and looked at Holliday. I couldn't decipher the look in her eyes. Cox turned and walked down the hall, past the elevator, and through a door leading to the stairwell. He was alone.

CHAPTER 35

Holliday screeched the Audi out of the garage and barreled through Chinatown, scattering pedestrians like pigeons.

We hadn't said a word since leaving the courthouse. The car stereo was off. I tried to wrap my mind around the concept of Holliday with another man.

Holliday hated hip-hop. That didn't mean she couldn't have dated Cox, but it didn't make sense. Cox was a hardcore hip-hopper. If his records were to be believed, he was a violent dude—everything Holliday hated.

I grabbed on to the armrest as Holliday careened past City Hall and on to the Brooklyn Bridge. She drove *this* fast only when she was highly upset.

My Sidekick buzzed. Phone call from Taylor.

"What a story!" he exclaimed. "I know you were in court today, right?"

"Does Al Sharpton go to the beauty shop? Course I was there."

Taylor laughed. "We gotta crash your story into the next issue. It needs to come out before the Baller. Might even be the cover. How soon can you get it done?"

My heart raced at the thought of a cover story, making me

forget that Taylor was supposed to be banned from the editorial side. "I'll knock it out next week," I said

"My man. Aiight, I'll see you at the victory party tonight. It's at Sting. You're coming, right? We got some suites for the jump-off afterward."

"I'm all over it, yo."

"Cool. One."

"One."

As I clicked off, Holliday made a disapproving noise.

I hardly ever challenged her, because she was always right. But now I felt something unfamiliar: jealousy.

"How you gonna be mad at me when some secret boyfriend just popped up outta nowhere?" I said.

"Cox was never my boyfriend."

"Sure seemed like he was special."

She let out a long sigh, downshifted, then swerved into the left lane to pass a yellow cab. We were at the top of the bridge, Brooklyn spread out before us, late-afternoon sun glinting off the East River.

"Daddy introduced me to Cox."

"Yeah, he looks like a drug dealer."

Holliday shot me a disgusted expression that I had never seen before. "Cox never touches drugs." She chuckled mirthlessly. "He's a problem solver."

"What kind of problems does he solve?"

"The ones no one else can. But whatever, I don't even want to talk about it." She gripped the wheel with both hands and stared straight ahead.

It was time for this sensitive act to stop.

"You know what, that's a cop-out," I said. "Yeah, you had it bad back then. But so did a lot of other people. Hiding things just makes it worse."

Just like that, I walked right into her trap.

"So you want to talk about hiding things?" she said in her lawyer voice.

I said nothing.

"I asked you a question."

"A rhetorical one, yeah."

"Let me rephrase, then. Marquis, why are you hiding things from me?"

"I ain't hidin' nuttin'."

"'I ain't hidin' nuttin','" she mimicked, scrunching up her face. "Have you looked at yourself lately? It would be comical if you weren't so serious. So there's nothing you want to tell me?"

What could she suspect? The hoes? The weed and liquor? No way could I admit anything. I might lose her.

"I have no idea what you're talking about," I said, looking directly at her. Our eyes met briefly before she looked back at the road. The light at Tillary was turning yellow. She took the corner without slowing down, the little Audi's tires holding the pavement in a death grip. I had to grab the armrest again to keep from sliding into her lap.

"You're a lousy liar, Marquis. I never realized that until recently, because you never lied to me until all this *Fever* bullshit happened. So I'll ask you one more time: Do you have anything you want to tell me?"

It had to be a trick. We were sitting at a light a half-dozen blocks from our house. *Please don't let me lose this woman.*

"Just tell me what you're talking about," I said.

It was as if I had prodded a wounded beast. Holliday

mashed the gas, popped the clutch, and let the tires scream before peeling up the block. As we raced through the narrow streets, my mind skittered over our year together, grasping at the memories. We pulled up in front of our building and Holliday finally released the steering wheel. When she looked at me, her face was wet.

"This is my fault," she began. "I knew all this was a bad idea."

"All this what?"

"All this hip-hop nonsense. I never should have let you convince me to go for it. You had no way of knowing. But I never thought it would happen so quickly."

"What would happen?"

"The man I love is kind, sweet, and honest. And he never, ever has sex with prostitutes."

"I never slept with any prostitutes!" I yelped. "I never—"

"Think for a minute before you go any further," she interrupted, her voice quavering. "Do you really want to go down that road? Do you want to talk about the details?"

There was a waterfall where my stomach used to be.

"I chose you, Marquis. You have to realize that. I chose you for all the things that you weren't. I needed something different in my life, something nice and safe and normal. I still need that. Because I am not going back to . . . to . . ."

Her voice broke into pieces and her head fell into her hands. Maybe I still had a chance.

"I never slept with another woman, I swear. I wouldn't—"

She grabbed my forearm, so tightly it hurt. "Can you walk away?"

I didn't understand.

"Just leave. Forget about this job and go back to the way we were."

I stared through the windshield, wondering how it had gotten this far. I couldn't imagine what it would be like *not* to know what I knew. Sitting on this story would be as impossible as swallowing my own tongue.

I was trying to figure out something to say when I realized that Holliday was saying my name.

"It's over, baby."

"But I didn't—"

"It doesn't matter. I know you can't let this thing go. Even if you did, you'd just be doing it because of me, not because it's what you really thought was right. And you'd hate me for taking it away from you. If not now, then you'd hate me later."

I don't remember what we said next. I only remember seeing Holliday's car fleeing up the block, the brake lights flashing good-bye.

CHAPTER 36

The week after Holliday left was a blur. Each afternoon I joined the crew on Knots Landing, and from there we hit the clubs. Each night I came home intoxicated, sat down at my computer, turned on my music, and worked on my story. Then I ran into Black at Kaya. We started talking about Daminion, and I mentioned he might be a cover story. Black got an interesting look on his face. The next day we were on a plane to Houston.

As we exited the airport's sliding-glass doors, the velvety night fell over us like a hot, wet coat. At the car-rental office

Black loud-talked his way into a free Lincoln Navigator upgrade. We rolled down the ten-lane freeway that was flanked by a series of strip malls until the downtown skyline poked its head above the flat, expansive landscape. Black produced a blunt he had snuck onto the plane and slid in Slow Creep's new mixtape, *South Coast Creep.*

> Bizack, back to creep up on ya
> Gattin cats Cacalack to California
> I warned ya
> Not to play with these Gs
> Keys move overseas while we breathe trees
> Importation my expectation
> Explanation for the next vacation
> You went down south stopped at the border
> We Gulfstream through and place the order
> Break bread with dons, gonna rub you out
> Fly back get paid then flood the drought . . .

We finally arrived at a plush Hilton tucked into a deluxe shopping mall, showered, changed, and climbed back into the truck. The valet had the AC on full blast. Black tipped him a hundred dollars from the mishmash wad of bills stuffed into his wrinkled black linen shorts.

In ten minutes we were cruising through a dilapidated neighborhood of used-car lots and residential houses with big, scraggly yards. Black turned onto a side street, pulled in front of a large warehouse with three loading docks built for 18-wheelers, and cut the engine.

"Aiight, when we go in there just lay back and chill," Black said, eyes on the rearview mirror. "I been doing business with dude a long time, so no matter what it seems like, you got nothing to worry about. And this is just between us—you can leave it out of the article and all that. I just wanna show you how 60s get down."

We walked through a curtain of clear plastic strips that hung from the top of the loading doors. Inside the cavernous warehouse were more CDs than I had ever seen in my life—spilling out of barrels taller than me, stacked up on long tables, lying loose in piles like spare change. Hulking machinery lay silent in the dim light. A few Mexicans absently swept the floor. I followed Black down a corridor of sky-high stacked cardboard boxes and into a brightly lit office. A dog smell drew my eyes to a large, furry mutt asleep in the corner.

The man behind the battered metal desk looked up. He had crow's-feet at the corners of his blue eyes and three ropes of hair combed across his gleaming pink scalp. He was eating mashed potatoes and a thick piece of steak from a paper plate. He wiped his mouth, hefted himself to his feet, and stuck out his hand with a smile.

"Black! It's about time," he drawled. "How yew been, old devil?"

"I'm good, I'm good. This my man Marq from the *Fever* magazine, he's doing a story about me. Marq, say hi to Dunlap."

The man frowned. His skin was very pink. There were stains on the front of the pale yellow golf shirt that stretched like a sausage skin over his girth.

"Dunlap?" he said. "Yew know that ain't mah name."

"Sho it is," Black said. "'Cause yo' belly done lapped over yo' belt."

The man regarded Black for a long second before he started laughing through his nose without opening his mouth. "Dammit, Black, ya never stop, dewya? Grab a seat."

Black plopped into a dusty swivel chair. I eased over to a cracked leather couch. The walls of the small room were lined with tall file cabinets. There were no windows, only the door we had come through and one behind the man's desk. Fluorescent lights hummed faintly.

The man opened a desk drawer, removed a plain white envelope, and slid it across to Black. Black ripped it open, tossed the envelope onto the floor, and removed a check for $113,000.

"That's it?" Black said, throwing it back onto the desk, almost onto the steak.

"What yew mean, 'that's it'?" the man said nonchalantly. He picked up a gleaming silver fork and a huge serrated steak knife, nudged the check back toward Black with the tip of the knife, then began sawing at the red piece of meat.

"C'mon, Jack. I know we sold more than twenty-six thousand copies!" Black yelped.

"Mmm hmm," Jack mumbled with his mouth full. "It was 26,588. At $4.25 a record that comes to $112,999. So yew owe me a buck."

"How you expect me to believe that when we just got done with that other deal," Black said, shrugging.

"Ah got the paperwork," Jack said. He rolled his chair over to one of the file cabinets and started to slide it open.

"Man, ain't nobody believe them papers you got in there," Black said, anger lacing his voice. "You really must think I'm stupid now. I'm starting to get offended by how stupid you think I am. You don't think I know the game just as good as you?"

Black leaned over the desk and with a quick swipe knocked the paper plate full of food to the floor.

I had forgotten about the dog. It sprang to life and gobbled down the steak in less time than it took to tie my shoes. It ignored the mashed potatoes, went back to its corner, and lay there looking at us, almost curiously, with its big brown head on its paws.

Jack's face and scalp turned from pink to crimson. His knuckles were white around the steak knife. My nerves twanged with tension as I tried to keep one eye on Jack and the other on the dog.

"That was fucked up, Black," he said slowly, as if trying to figure out how to respond. "That was a nice piece of meat right there." He rolled back over to his table and put his silverware in a drawer. "Look, things ain't sellin' like it used to. Kids are burnin' instead of buyin'. They're bootleggin' the bootleggers. Can you believe that?" He laughed through his nose. "Maybe I can make it up on the next one. So what yew got fer me?"

Black picked up the check from the table, stuffed it into his pocket, then pulled a CD out of his pocket and tossed it onto the table with a clatter. It was *South Coast Creep*.

"I manage them now," Black said, sitting back down. "We got all of Houston, Louisiana, and Mississippi on this joint. Paul Wall, Slim Thug, Mike Jones, Lil' Flip, David Banner, UGK, XYZ—all them niggas. I think DJ Screw came up out the grave and got on the turntables. This a bestseller and you know it. George muthafuckin' Bush gonna be bumpin' this here out at the ranch, you feel me?"

"Hey, don't be talking 'bout my president, awright?" Jack removed the paper artwork from the jewel case, turned on a desk lamp, and scrutinized it front and back under the light.

He put it back down onto the metal table and fixed his clear blue eyes on Black.

"One hundred," Jack said.

"Man, *fuck* you," Black said. He stood up and snatched back the CD. "C'mon, let's be out," he said to me.

"One fifty," Jack said before I could stand up. "Plus eight bucks per CD after that."

"Fuck after anything. This a sure shot. I'm gettin' everything up front. Do you understand I just put two million dollars on this raggedy desk? Do you hear what I'm saying to you?" Black stood there, glaring, arms spread wide.

The dog started to whine.

"What about Tommy?" Jack said. "Don't he got a piece of them, too? I ain't fixin' to get hit up twice on this one."

"Is Tommy standing here in front of you with two million dollars? That nigga just got out of jail—he tryna get some pussy right now. He ain't involved in this right here. He gonna handle the official label deal. This here's just the mixtape. Lissen, I'm at the usual spot until tomorrow. Send your boy over with two-fifty. You can thank me later."

Black headed toward the door, the CD in his hand. He stopped to pet the dog's head on the way out and finally cracked a big smile.

"Get this dawg a bath," Black said. "He fuckin' stinks!"

Black drove through downtown and onto the freeway and exited on Westheimer Road. It was a little past midnight and the strip was full of cars. We rolled down the windows of the Navigator to let the smoke out and the atmosphere in. Houston's trademark slowed-down sounds crept from the square trunks

of long twenty-year-old sedans gleaming with candy-colored
finishes that looked wet to the touch. The music sounded as
if it were swimming through the moist air, the lyrics all *swang*
and *brang* and *grain*. For every Lexus there was a pimped-out
pickup or an old Cadillac Deville with massive steer horns
mounted onto the front grille.

I was thinking about Warehouse Jack. The math didn't
make sense to me. Finally I asked Black, "That guy's gonna
give you $250,000 for a *mixtape*?"

"He better, else I'ma have a little conversation with some
people I know over at Universal Records."

"About what?"

"There's a whole economy between the record company
and the record store, and dudes like Jack make out like ban-
dits. In order to get their CDs into the actual stores, Universal gotta go through distributors like Jack. Of course he
gonna bootleg the Universal CD, print up more copies, and
sell 'em right into the stores. But check this out: If Universal
give him a CD that don't sell, he can return it for full credit.
So come to find out he's sellin' the bootlegs *back to Universal*! As a hustler I gotta respect that. And now that I see he
gonna rob me too, he gotta pay me in advance for what it
gonna sell. At $4.25 per CD for me, $250,000 is only about
sixty thousand copies of *South Coast Creep*. He supposed to
pay me extra for anything sold past that, but we both know
I ain't gonna see no more money."

"How much does Slow Creep get from that?"

Black's cheeks bunched up into a chuckle. "Heh heh heh.
It's just like Wall Street. Buy low and sell high, know what I'm
sayin'?"

"How'd you get the tape, anyway?"

"You ain't remember I used to work up at Pump Records? I know all them niggas. I was the one kept 'em from goin' home with bullet holes in they asses. How can they refuse me?"

Black stole that tape. And Stan Ross is too scared to do anything about it.

"So how much does Tommy get?"

"Tommy gonna get his. He got a record label—he tryna sign them cats. I operate in a different arena."

We stopped at a crowded restaurant, ordered some fried shrimp and oysters, then headed back to the Hilton. The icy hotel air gave me the sniffles. I showered and knocked on Black's door. His round belly poked out of his open hotel-issue bathrobe, above his boxers. He wore cloth house slippers and a new pair of white socks.

I fell into the couch. *Dark Alliance* was on HBO, the scene where Large as Freeway Rick is gleefully stirring a huge kettle of crack with a boat oar. Black cracked the minibar and poured some Hennessy. He was snoring on his bed in minutes. I followed him into oblivion.

Insistent knocking on the door woke me up. I wiped slobber off my cheek as Black roused himself. It was still dark outside. Black removed a small silver pistol from beneath his pillow, picked up the CD off the nightstand, padded to the door, and opened it a crack. When he shut the door, a brown duffel bag was in his other hand.

The money spilled over the bed, wrinkled hundred-dollar bills wrapped in rubber bands of various sizes. Black pawed through the wads briefly, shoved them back into the duffel, then lay down with the bag under his head like a pillow. He was snoring again in seconds.

I tried to go back to sleep, but the thought of all that cash throbbed in my head. I grabbed the weed left in the ashtray, and finally it worked.

CHAPTER 37

New York was suffocating after Houston's wide, open spaces. The subway felt like riding in a can of sardines. I exited at Union Square, walked over to a restaurant, and heard Tommy Daminion's deadpan voice as soon as I walked in the door. He was sitting at a round table flanked by eight men. Chunk was there. And so was Julien.

Julien's expression didn't change when he saw me. I hoped mine didn't, either. I gave Daminion a short nod and walked around the table to take the empty seat next to Chunk.

A large guy with an earnest moon face started giving Daminion some sort of explanation. "Meyer wasn't even tryna listen to what I was sayin'. He was just like, 'The song gots to go.' That's all he kept sayin': 'The song gots to go.'"

Everyone started talking at once, except Julien, who leaned back in his chair tapping on his Sidekick. I watched Daminion. He had a half smile on his face and was rubbing the long scar that started near the bottom of his left eye. Discreet diamonds glistened at his ears and the cuffs of his finely woven button-down shirt.

I elbowed Chunk and gave him a questioning glance. He looked both ways and said, "Tommy got a song on the new album dissing Big Brawls. Now Meyer Mahl is heated."

The clamor continued for another minute. No one in the crowded restaurant paid any attention to us.

"You know what?" Daminion finally said. Everyone clammed up.

"Fuck Meyer, and fuck Big Brawls," he said, with the same half smile on his face. "When can we master the album?"

"Soon as the Slow Creep track is finished," was the reply.

"I thought that track was wrapped up Monday," Daminion said.

"It was," squeaked a yellow-skinned dude with red hair. "But the levels was all messed up, so we had to go back and redo the fill-ins, and I been waiting for Butch to get the two-inch back from the engineer over at—"

Butch interrupted. The two men argued back and forth until Daminion cut in. "Y'all cats better get it together." The sudden edge in his voice put me on alert. "You don't want me to have to settle this petty bullshit, believe that. Chunk, you finish that Spank track yet?"

Chunk took his Yankee cap off and ran his hand over the do-rag covering his braids. "Man, Meyer been putting salt in our game. He squeezing the advance money, then telling Spank we the reason he ain't got no paper. I been stayin' in Spank's ear, but Meyer is putting a hole in dude's pocket fa sho."

Now Daminion looked truly angry. Chunk stared back at him with the same look he used to give our disapproving Sunday-school teacher—*I know you're right, but I don't care.* The men at the table had the eager look of spectators at the beginning of a race.

"Y'all niggas will *not* fuck up my album," Daminion said, looking around the table. "I don't care if I have to get rid of all y'all and rap on that bitch myself. You hear me? I got too much riding on this. It represents everything I've ever gone through. I see my whole life flashing before me when I listen to it. If this album is wack, then my whole label is wack. I ain't come this far to get tripped up by my own squad. So y'all get your shit together and do what I tell you to do!"

Daminion abruptly pushed his chair back from the table and jerked his head for me to follow him. His compact frame slipped through the crowded room as if he were greased. I felt the crew's eyes on me as I walked behind Daminion to the bar.

"So what's up with your story?" he asked, eyes darting over my shoulders.

I tried to shrug nonchalantly. "It's going good. I just got back from Houston with Black."

"Word? What he got poppin' down there?"

"Umm, he was making moves with the Slow Creep mixtape."

"Oh, so y'all saw Jack, then?"

"You mean the fat white dude in the warehouse? Yeah, we saw him."

"So how much did Black get for the tape?"

I had just gotten back from Houston the night before and slept until two that afternoon. I hadn't worked out since Holliday left. My mind felt stuck in second gear. Somehow I had never thought about how to answer Daminion's inevitable question.

"Someone dropped off some cash at our hotel, but I didn't see how much was in it." It felt uncomfortable to be answering the questions instead of asking them.

Daminion's eyes stopped moving around the room and came to rest on mine. It took all my concentration not to flinch.

"What's Julien doing here?" I asked, to break the tension.

Daminion's eyes flicked toward the table. "Now that I'm out, he came to pay his respects."

"Does that mean he's off your list?"

"What list?"

The "To Kill" list. I couldn't bring myself to say it.

Daminion smiled after I hesitated. "I'm a law-abiding citizen, menh. The only thing I have time to bother with is making money with this music. 'Cause they don't want a nigga to have to come out of retirement." He smirked. "So tell me about your story. When's it coming out?"

"Right before the Baller."

"Good. That's exactly what I need." Daminion was gliding back toward his table before I could reply. I took the sight of his back as my cue to exit. As I looked back at Daminion's table once more as I approached the door, Julien looked up from his Sidekick, caught my eye, and blew me a kiss.

CHAPTER 38

The woman in my bed was breathing through what sounded like a mouthful of spit.

I don't remember her name. My days were now ending at four a.m. in some club with Chunk and Wop—Atlanta, Chicago, DC, Phoenix—all the while Chunk trying to reel Young Spank back in. I met more industry people than I ever dreamed existed and enjoyed a parade of lap dances until I decided it was time to actually have sex with someone besides Holliday.

I met her on a dance floor at Kaya, where she gave me

a whole new appreciation of why "Spank Me" was a hit. We were both drunk. Only after we exited the cab and entered the silence of my bedroom did I realize that she breathed through her teeth, which seemed to be acting as a dam for the huge river of saliva. I turned up my T Pain CD and lost myself in the contours of the body that had drawn gasps at the club. As soon the sex was over, that raspy gurgle buzzed back into my ear and her body smelled sharp and strange.

I could have fallen onto my knees and thanked Jesus when my Sidekick buzzed Chunk's name. He was downstairs.

I concocted a lie about how my home boy was having an emergency and we needed to head back over to Manhattan to solve his problem. She obviously didn't believe me. The disapproving noise she made with her mouth sounded exactly like our sweaty stomachs separating.

Chunk was at my door when I walked her to the elevator. She didn't look at him.

"You smashed that?" he said incredulously as the elevator door closed. I fell back onto the couch and the smell of my own crotch hit me in the face. I dashed into the shower, then came back out to find Chunk pacing across my living room, manically thumbing his Sidekick and yelling into a cell phone propped between his ear and shoulder.

"Chill yo, you gonna wake up my neighbors," I told him.

Chunk lowered his voice to a whisper-shout. "These niggas don't understand who they dealin' wit. . . . We just got to get that gwop. . . . Man, this is Daminion right here, you know how we do. . . . You better hope I'm dead in six months. You better hope so!"

Chunk snapped the phone shut with one hand and pocketed

it, then whipped off his do-rag, scratched the scalp between his thick braids, and dropped heavily into an armchair.

"Spank is gone," he said, still mauling his Sidekick.

"Gone where?"

"Gone to Fresh Beat. Fuckin' Meyer Mahl."

"How does that work, though? I thought you had a contract."

Chunk looked up with a disgusted expression on his face. "Truth be sold, there's a problem with the contract. I had my man I knew from the fed put it together, like, on the spot, because when it was time to sign, duke there wasn't no time to waste, kna' mean? And Meyer got enough lawyers to bust holes through a brick wall. We got a legal letter today flabbergastin' the situation all up. Tommy says he ain't tryin' to spend more money fightin' Meyer in court than he'd make off Spank anyway. Bottom line is, if Spank wanna go, he gonna go. Which is gonna fuck up my paper in a major way. I got a lotta shit up in the air right now."

I thought back to the story about the producer who got pistol-whipped for daring to defy Daminion. "I heard Daminion's contracts don't end, ever. So he's just gonna let Spank walk out on him?"

"That's the craziest thing. I ain't worry about no real contract 'cause we is who we is, kna' mean? Ain't a nigga in the industry don't know how we get down. But Tommy ain't tryna rock like that no more. He just got out, so I guess he ain't tryna go back in. He said he can't endorse me dealing with it on that level."

Chunk lurched up from the chair, boot-dragged his way to the fridge to retrieve a Heineken, and sat back down. The chair groaned under his weight, defeated. I wanted to find a bright spot for him.

"You still got the *Teflon* album, though. You gettin' gwop offa that, right?"

"Meyer squashed that, son."

"How he do that?"

"Tommy got his album deal through Soulstacks Records. Soulstacks is owned by Versatize. So when it came time to ship the album to stores, Meyer put his mack down. Twice a month there's a book that goes to retailers from the distributor. The order sheets tear out; they have the serial number of the albums on them. But the *Teflon* order form wasn't even in the book. When we hollered at Soulstacks, they said they got confused on the release date. That's bullshit. So only about thirty thousand copies got shipped, compared to anywhere from a few hundred thousand to a million for a big record. We was supposed to have thirty thousand copies in New York alone. It was impossible for people to find the record in stores."

"Wow. I thought Meyer wasn't the threatening type."

"He ain't. When you got his power, you don't need to make no threats. You just make the project go away."

"So you ain't gonna make nothing on that? I thought you told me you was an associate executive producer on the album."

Chunk made a frustrated face, got up, and started pacing. "I am. The budget was like four hundred thousand; Tommy spent maybe a hundred fifty making the record. I got a little taste of what was left over, but that money's gone now. I got to think about my next move."

"Which is what?"

He put his empty Heineken bottle down next to a pile of papers on the countertop separating the kitchen area from the dining room. Something caught his eye and he picked it up. It was the Young Spank contract I had picked up that night at Scruplex, out in LA.

Chunk looked at me and cocked his cinder-block head to one side. "Son, how you get this?"

"You left it on the table at the club that night in LA."

"What night in LA?"

"The night you showed me the D. Rex tape." Chunk gave no sign of recognition. "You know, Scruplex, Spank was there, Shortcake in the VIP . . ."

Chunk just gave me a red-eyed stare. I searched for something to bring him back to reality.

"C'mon, son, ever since I known you, you always been leaving stuff around and forgetting it."

His eyes narrowed. "But you just so happen to have this contract when we sitting here talking about Spank leaving me for Fresh Beat. How I know you ain't show this to Meyer Mahl?"

There had to be a way to snap him out of it.

"Chunk, think about all the times you left stuff places. Remember when you came to visit me at Rutgers, and you spent the night at that girl's room, and you left the bag full of crack over at her spot? Remember that?"

A reluctant smile cracked his stubbled face. He scratched between his braids and exhaled, tossed the contract into the living-room wastebasket, then bent over to retrieve it. "I prolly need to keep this, though, in case push does come to— aaaagh!"

I sprang to my feet, muscles quivering. Chunk threw the contract onto the floor and pointed at it.

A dripping condom was stuck to the front page. From that girl.

"You really did smash it!" Chunk said. "My nigga! I always knew you was a pimp. Good thing I found this nasty shit before Holliday did."

My face told Chunk to slow down.

"What, you ain't hit that?"

"No, I . . . I hit it. But Holliday broke out."

"She left you? After all this time? What happened?"

There was no way I could explain, because I didn't really know myself.

"You remember that big dude Cox at Daminion's sentencing?" I asked. "I think something happened with him. When they saw each other, they acted like long-lost friends."

Chunk sat down. "That ain't good. That's one pretty muhfucka right there. He ain't to be fucked with, especially when it come to hoes."

"Holliday ain't no ho."

"She ain't? I thought she just left you for a big diamond-ring nigga? What you call that, then?"

I thought about it for a few seconds and realized that I wasn't ready to give her up yet. "Tell me more about this Cox dude. What's his hustle?"

Chunk propped his boots up on my coffee table. "I don't really know how he gets paper. He don't sell dope that I know of. He sells some records independently, but that's obviously just the beginning of his game. And on the streets dudes respect his gangsta."

"Why?"

"Because he's just a raw, hard-core nigga. Like this one time

I was in this club with Tommy out in LA, a real grimy gutter spot, and shit was getting thick. This was when the East-West beef was poppin', so dudes was mad at you just for being from Brooklyn. We in the club and niggas is mumbling at us about this and that. Cox was there to perform. We see him backstage and he tells Tommy, 'Whatever you need, I got you. I got you, man, you hear me?' He was crazy emphatic on that point, kna' mean? Of course, soon there's a fight somewhere in the club. Door security was real tight so we knew ain't no gats up in there. But it felt like dudes was gonna use the fight as an excuse to rush us. Cox was rocking the mic at the time, and he jump offstage over to where we at and all of a sudden spits two razors out his mouth into his hands, like *Phuh! Phuh!* And he had just been on the mic—dude was rhyming with razors up in his mouth! We got up out of there no problem after that. Real talk."

By the time Chunk finished his story, his head was leaned back and his eyes were half-closed. I threw a blanket over him and gingerly tossed the condom-contract back into the trash. I headed back to my room before remembering what had just happened there. So I lay down on the couch, buried beneath my friend's snores, and tried not to think about Cox and Holliday outside that courtroom.

CHAPTER 39

You know KRS-One started his career when he was homeless. Scott La Rock was a counselor in the shelter. I could have been bigger than KRS if I had the right people behind me. I got rhymes, like:

Today's agenda
I be like Edison the inventor
Go to St. James and Fulton, tell em Dontay sentcha
Then you recognize my credentials ain't no surprise
Crack fiends like flies but I refuse to despise
In dreams I appear, embrace death never fear
This nigga right here the tragic king like Lear
All bow down to the revolution sound
Masterpieces straight from Bucktown
Brooklawn nigga
Ya hook's wrong nigga
Ya song's shook nigga . . .

Mad heads could rhyme inside the shelter system, so when I got there, I was catching wreck. We was in a cipher outside the building when something smashes into the ground a few feet away from us, like SPLAT! I heard somebody laughing from an upstairs window. I was new, so I ain't know what it was. I walk closer to take a look and then I understand why nobody else ain't looking but me. Somebody threw a brown paper bag out the window filled with human shit.

That pretty much tells you all you need to know about the shelter I ended up in. A thousand men lived there. Half crack fiends and the rest straight outta prison. I can't even describe the filth. Roaches in the showers big as my foot. No soap to be found. All you got is a bed and a locker. You gotta leave every day by nine in the morning and they won't let you back inside until five. Then they lock the door at ten.

That's why I was so stressed out when I came to your office, because it was getting late and I was about to get locked out.

If any of y'all had my back, I wouldn't have been in that position. I knew I couldn't walk around with all that money on me. That was just asking for trouble. I would have mailed it to myself—that's what I used to do—but you made me leave that apartment, so I didn't have an address. I couldn't trust you with my money. I was gonna hide the cash at Moms's house along with The Joint. But she went crazy on me, so that was out. I had to keep it over at my friend Nicky's place, and she stole it from me.

I know you don't believe me, same as you don't believe what I tell you happened at Moms's house. Same as you don't believe me that Jesus *has returned. But go ahead, don't listen. It's your fate—do what you want with it. You didn't believe Cox was my man, either. You think you Mr. Hip-Hop Fever superstar with all the connects, and here's your homeless brother doing for you what you never did for me. Play that back on your fuckin tape. You think you slick, nigga. I sacrificed everything for you. But that's aiight. E'ything will be clear in the Next World.*

CHAPTER 40

"Which one do you like?" Rosa asked. Six versions of Reddy's round, yellow face peered out at me from six mock-up magazine covers taped to the wall in Rosa's office.

I pointed to one with a REDDY TO RUMBLE cover line and Reddy gritting his teeth to reveal a set of platinum choppers, studded with cinnamon-colored diamonds that matched his hair. Rosa studied it, then leaned her head way back in her chair and regarded the fluorescent light in the ceiling. Her long black hair spilled halfway to the floor. "This is already the hardest part of my job," she said. "And now I got Reddy blowing up my phone trying to pick the cover for me."

I had my first byline for the *Fever*, the Young Dro story. The issue also had a piece about the D. Rex tape, with stills taken from the video. Rosa was treating me like family now that I kept her updated on Taylor's and Leak's activities. A half-dozen editorial staffers were on Taylor's side, judging from the conversations on Knots Landing. Taylor was promising everyone big

things when he bought back the *Fever* from Versatize. Leak's
boys said he was in the studio working on a new album.

"What's Reddy want?" I asked. My Sidekick went off:
Dontay calling, for the third time in the past half hour. I let it
go to voice mail.

"This fool wants me to show him the cover before we print
it." Rosa snorted out a laugh, still staring at the ceiling. "He's
shook because the last time Taylor and Leak had him on the
cover, they made him look like a clown with a cover line that
said, REDDY . . . OR NOT."

I remembered that cover. The article was full of complaints
from rappers that Reddy wasn't paying them fairly. "What was
up with that?" I asked.

"Leak was pissed because Reddy wouldn't let his artists rap
on Leak's album. Damn, here go Reddy again." Rosa hit a button on her buzzing Sidekick and tossed it to me.

BITCH, DON'T YOU KNOW YOU CAN END UP IN
A TRUNK SOMEWHERE? STOP PLAYING AND LET
ME SEE MY DAMN COVER.

I placed her Sidekick on the edge of her desk next to a pile
of mock-up pages. It was close to ten p.m., we were late closing the issue again, and the managing editor had us all trapped
in the office until we completed whatever amount of pages he
deemed satisfactory.

I actually enjoyed being there. I didn't have anywhere else
to go or anyone else to be with. And it seemed as though the
only chance I had to get Holliday back was to prove that my
success at the *Fever* was worth it.

"So let me tell you about my Tommy Daminion story," I said as Rosa grabbed a mock-up page from the pile. "You know this rapper Cox? Underground dude, tough guy, big muscles? He was at Tommy's sentencing. I want to talk to him, but I can't find home boy anywhere. You know how I can reach him?"

Rosa drew a huge X through a photo, tossed the page to the side, and picked up another one. "What does he have to do with the story?"

"I don't really know, and that's what's bugging me." I lied. "What's his connection? Why would he show up at the sentencing? I think it could lead to something good."

Rosa looked up at me and leaned forward, planting her breasts on the table. She rested her chin in one hand and raised her eyebrows.

"I'm not sure where that's gonna lead, and I have no idea where to find him," she sighed, "but if it's important to you, I can make it happen. Because you're a major part of the team—you know that, right?" She reached across the table and briefly squeezed my hand, then leaned back into her ceiling-watching position.

"Has anyone told you about what Leak did to me?" she asked, after a pause.

"No," I lied. Word on Knots was that Leak had smashed it.

"One day not long after I started here, he walked into my office and started asking about doing a story on him for the magazine. He had one of his albums coming out. I said I didn't think it was appropriate due to conflict-of-interest reasons, him being an employee here and all. He was like, 'An employee? I own this muhfucka!' Which says it all right there, since he didn't own it anymore. But I kept it cordial and everything, until soon he starts trying to kick it to me. Talking about how we should visit his place in Miami, how good I would look on the beach in a swimsuit, all that. I tried to play nice. Then he starts talking about buying me a 'thong wardrobe.' That's exactly what he called it: a 'thong wardrobe.' I actually had to keep myself from laughing at this point, so I turned around so I wouldn't laugh in his face, and this nigga actually sticks his hand down my jeans and snaps my underwear! Like this!"

Rosa stood up and turned around. There was a wide swath of smooth, light brown skin between her low-slung jeans and tight T-shirt. She reached down her pants, pulled up a string from her thong, and let it pop back into place.

She turned back around. We stared at each other and I almost moved toward her before the door opened and the crooked-hairline managing editor rushed in.

"Yo, Reddy is in the building!"

Rosa's head turned so fast, her hair flew out behind it. "Stop fucking with me."

"Dude is inside the office. The intern at the front desk let him in. He'll be here in about thirty seconds."

Rosa dashed around her desk and snatched the covers off the wall in one swipe. "Get the pages from the art department," she barked at Crooked Hairline, who ran out. Rosa folded the covers once, stuffed them behind some books on a shelf, then strode out and left me sitting in her office.

The door opened a few seconds later and Reddy walked in, followed by a very dark-skinned bodyguard with a football-player neck as wide as his head. Reddy plopped down onto Rosa's couch and put his feet up on the coffee table. The bodyguard stood next to the door. Reddy looked all over the room and then finally at me.

"Welcome to the *Fever*," I said, actually nervous to be alone with the superstar. "What's good?"

"Where Rosa at?"

"I don't know. I'm Marq, though. What's on your mind?"

Reddy got to his feet. His trademark reddish mini Afro was perfectly round, like a bubble, with a diamond-studded pick planted in the back. He rummaged through the pages on Rosa's desk, then looked at me again.

"Why am I even talking to you?" he said. "Y'all is *wack*. And you need to get them crackheads out your lobby. It ain't good for business."

Reddy swaggered out, trailed by his bodyguard. A few seconds later I realized what he was talking about and ran out.

CHAPTER 41

I found Dontay telling Large stories to the intern at the reception desk. Befuddlement clouded the girl's plump face.

"He was crying like a baby, yo. L was scared about his mama and it just got to him, and he broke down right there in the studio. Can you believe that? See, that's the side of Large that most of y'all don't—"

Leak burst through the door and put both of his hands on the shoulder-high reception desk.

"The fuck you let Reddy in for?" he shouted.

The girl's eyebrows furrowed into a frown, turning her cute face mean. "How I'm s'posed to stop him?" she said, wagging her head for emphasis. "He got off the elevator and walked right through."

"Why you buzz him in? Do that again, you'll be working at K-Mart!"

"You know that buzzer been broke, and I can't get up and unlock the door every time someone wanna go in there! All these trifling niggas hangin' around the office for securr-ity, why they ain't *securrin'* the front door?" She sucked her teeth and stared at her antagonist defiantly.

Leak's fists clenched. For a second I thought he was going to hit her.

"Bitch, you're fired," he said. "Get the fuck out. Now."

Her eyebrows shot up, disappearing beneath her bangs. Pure hatred flooded her face. She gathered a few things, stood up, and waddled out from behind the desk, revealing a hugely pregnant belly. Leak waited until the elevator doors closed behind her and started to boot-drag back into the office.

"That was foul, son," Dontay said.

Leak stopped in his tracks and squinted as he looked back and forth between us.

"Who this?" Leak asked me.

I think I actually took a step away from Dontay. "My brother. He's here to see me."

"Get him in check, will ya? I ain't got time for this right now." He spun around, jewelry clanking, and hurried back into the office.

I pulled Dontay into the elevator and stabbed the button for the lobby. We stood shoulder to shoulder in silence, staring at the door until it opened at the ground floor. As soon as we stepped onto the sidewalk, Dontay lit a crumpled cigarette and coughed.

"I need some money," he said, glaring at me through the smoke.

Jesus Christ. "What happened to the five grand Pops supposedly gave you?"

"Someone stole it from me," he said, looking away.

"I don't believe you."

"I don't care what you believe."

"How could someone steal your money from you?"

"When you don't have a place to live, it happens."

I don't remember exactly what I said after that. I know we yelled at each other. Who knows what would have happened next if the door to my building hadn't opened and Reddy's thick-necked bodyguard hadn't stumbled out onto the sidewalk, like a big, black bowling ball popping up into the rack from beneath the lanes.

A few seconds later Reddy walked out the door, followed by Leak and several scowling members of his crew. I tugged Dontay out of the way.

Leak spat onto the sidewalk. The circles under his eyes were darker than ever. "Stay the fuck outta here before I have to take this to the next level," he said to Reddy. His aimless crew seemed transformed. Two of them took up posts about ten yards up and down the block, scanning the crowd. Two more stood directly behind Leak, barely concealing snub-nosed pistols. Another dude walked up and down the curb, discreetly inspecting the double-parked cars, while another did the same thing across the street.

The last man spotted Reddy's Range Rover. He walked quickly up to the driver's window and pulled a nine millimeter out the front of his pants. Shielding the weapon from view with his body, he said a few words and scanned the inside of the vehicle. Then he gave a piercing whistle and signaled over his shoulder to Leak.

Reddy patted his mini 'fro and calmly regarded Leak through amber-tinted shades. His bodyguard stood behind him, one hand inside his jacket.

"Trying hard to hold on to what you got, huh, Leak?" Reddy said. "I respect your gangster. When them crackers snatch your magazine, come holla at your boy."

Reddy strolled across the street and into the backseat of his Range Rover. As the vehicle blended back into traffic, Leak's crew started laughing among themselves.

"Son, you seen the look on duke's face?"

"We shoulda thrown 'em off Knots."

"You almost shot yourself in the foot in the elevator."

They all put away their guns and went back into the building.

Dontay was literally trembling with anger.

"Please tell me you ain't writing about that worthless piece of garbage Reddy," he said.

"He is on the cover, but I'm not doing that story."

I saw hate in Dontay's eyes. "It's 'cause of rags like the *Fever* that dude can do the things he does. And now you right in there with them devils. You prolly writing about 50 Cent or some other cancer," he said with contempt.

I wanted to chop him down a notch. "Actually, my next interview is with Cox. You know him?"

The look of surprise on Dontay's face was almost like a cartoon. He was such a child.

"I don't believe you."

"So now you know what it feels like," I said, each syllable a pleasure.

Dontay's face twitched grotesquely. He bent his head and

that's when I noticed he had a new bag. It was light brown leather and narrow, as though it belonged to a woman. He rummaged around in it for a while and came out with a crumpled piece of paper and a pen. He wrote something on the paper, ripped it, and handed half to me. It was a phone number.

"When you talk to Cox, ask him about the songs we did ten years ago."

He turned around and walked up the block. I had Cox on the phone before Dontay reached the corner.

CHAPTER 42

Cox's house was halfway down a quiet residential street deep in Queens, three redbrick stories encircled by a lush lawn. Two white vehicles were parked in front of the garage, a Benz G-wagon and a BMW 750 sedan. Cox answered the door wearing a plain gray T-shirt, cotton sweats, and brand-new white socks on his huge feet. The home was spacious, airy, and immaculate. I heard a woman's voice speaking softly in the distance, but didn't see a soul.

I followed Cox downstairs to a small den in the basement. The walls were covered with signed photos and other memorabilia. He motioned me through a door that led to a large state-of-the-art recording studio. Racks of equipment stretched from the polished wooden floor to the ceiling. A full drum set and three guitars sat on a small riser. Animated fish swam across two huge, flat Macintosh computer screens.

"This is hot," I said, fingering the edge of one Mac.

"Word—Leak called me up one day and was like, 'We got a new *Fever* Internet show poppin' off; go buy yourself a nice system and hit me with the receipt and I'll reimburse you.'"

"He just hit you off for no reason? You and Leak are cool like that?"

"We've done some work together. He pays big for cameos. That's good money."

He seated himself behind an immense mixing board, leaned back in the leather armchair, and laced his fingers together across his wide chest. He had to weigh at least 260 pounds, with what looked like zero body fat. His spotless skin glowed in the soft light. And he had the same gray eyes as me.

What I really wanted to talk about was Holliday, but I decided to start with music. Cox had made numerous guest appearances on other rappers' songs and had released two albums independently. He didn't play around with intricate rhyme schemes or deep stories. His music dealt with three themes: stating his street credentials, calling out corrupt music-industry execs, and pointing out problems with society. Conspicuously absent were any references to selling drugs. According to Soundscan, his latest CD had sold a paltry 157,000 copies.

"How do you think your last record was received?" I began.

"I really don't care how it was received," Cox said calmly. "I don't rap for the industry, or the radio, or even really for the fans. I'm an artist. I rap to express myself and put out ideas to the public that nobody else is gonna say. I'm trying to wake niggas up. Nat Turner wasn't worried about how he was going to be *received*. He just saw injustice and oppression and self-delusion, so he did what needed to be done."

Famous people make a lot of questionable statements in interviews, and most of the time I let them slide. But sitting across from this man almost twice my size, I felt as though I had something to prove.

"How can you say you don't rap for the fans?"

"If they like what I do, I deeply appreciate their love and their support. But I rap for niggas rolling through dark streets putting in work. Those are my people. Everything else is secondary to that."

"Even record sales? You're happy only selling 150,000 copies?"

"After mom and pop stores, it was close to two hundred thousand. And when I cop eight dollars per copy, fuck yeah. Look around, man. What expenses you think I had making my album? None, that's what. I did the whole thing right here. I produce my own beats. The tracks I don't produce, niggas like Premier give me for free 'cause of our relationships. I made more money than a platinum rapper on Fresh Beat who got Meyer Mahl's greedy hand in his pocket recouping all kinds of imaginary charges. See, these label cats way up in they skyscrapers is scared to fuck with dudes like me, even though ain't a nigga in the game can hold a candle to me onstage. Because Meyer knows if he try to steal from me, I'll run up in his office and crack his face open."

"What happened to get you so mad at everybody?"

He chuckled and thought for a moment. "I came in the game at the top. Eric B came and got me out my neighborhood 'cause he heard I was nice on the mic. His crew was the roughest, wildest, illest bunch of Brooklyn gangsters you could find. And in all respects I held my own. I was always a big dude, and as a kid I had a neighbor who was a Navy SEAL, who tightened up my knuckle game. When I came to the Paid in Full Posse, I could rap and I could fight. This is the late eighties. Once they gave me some real weaponry, it was on. That was when I started carrying two guns all the time. I thought, 'I got two hands, so I need two guns.'"

I glanced at the wall over Cox's shoulder and read a framed passage: "Lord grant me the serenity to accept the things I cannot change, the courage to change the things I can, and the wisdom to hide the bodies of those people I had to kill because they pissed me off."

Somehow, reading that put me at ease. There was no way Holliday could love a killer.

"Eric got me a deal," Cox continued, "that put like forty Gs in my pocket. But they only gave me the deal to keep Eric happy. When the record came out, there was nothing behind it and it sank like a rock. I had already used my advance money to buy a condo and a 300 Benz. I had payments to make, and my record wasn't poppin'. When I started askin' questions, no one returned my calls. So I went up there and asked the same questions. This exec got ignorant with me, so I punched him in his face and left him unconscious on his desk."

Cox flexed his hand at the memory, revealing his blackened knuckles. I said nothing.

"I figured if the industry wasn't showin' me no love, the streets would. I got on with Cleopatra's record label, which was full of street dudes like me. I went on tour and did some shows, some guest verses. They owed me about fifteen thousand dollars, but kept giving me excuses about where my money was. Finally they told me to come over to the office, but they only had five thousand for me. When I asked where the rest of my money was, dude was like, 'That's five thousand more dollars than you had this morning.' That's exactly what he said."

The look on Cox's face made me wonder why anyone would be dumb enough to tell him something like that.

"I went home and got my Mac-10 and my two .44s. When I got back to the office, I pulled the Mac out my backpack and sprayed that muhfucka, not hitting nobody, just blasting the walls all to pieces, all the platinum plaques and everything. Everybody was on the ground screaming. And whaddya know, they went to the bank and brought back my money."

Cox was leaned forward in his chair now, elbows on knees, hands clasped in front of him, emphasizing his words with sharp movements of his shiny head. "And that was black people that did that to me. They wasn't no different than them crackers up at Fresh Beat. The rap game is finished, man. Fuck all these rappers. These niggas is frauds. I got more money than them, plus all my jewels are real. They ain't hip-hop, or else you would see DJs and B-boys and graf writers all over MTV. And they damn sure ain't gangsta. They don't bust no guns. If you selling so much drugs, why you need to rap? Why you gonna encourage kids to be on the corner killin' each other over a fifty-dollar rock? MCs control the masses, worldwide. How people talk, how they think, what they wear. But now we're doing the white man's work for him. The game got so twisted. Take Slow Creep. They got so much talent, but it's sad they talk about hustlin' to validate themselves as MCs. Why would you put yourself under that risk? I respect their music, but if you're a real artist, why would you want to sell drugs over creating your art? Why would you . . ."

Cox's voice faded to background noise as I processed this

unexpected information. I tried to think logically: Creep had plenty of drug-dealing references on their albums, but so did everyone else. So Creep's lyrics could be typical rap boasts. Or maybe they were keeping it real.

Importation my expectation
Explanation for the next vacation
You went down south stopped at the border
We Gulfstream through and place the order
Break bread with dons, gonna rub you out
Fly back get paid then flood the drought . . .

". . . sometimes I gotta wonder what's our purpose here on this planet," Cox was saying. "Do we even have a purpose? Are we really God's creatures? Because if you look at people's actions, I'm not so sure. So I decided I wasn't gonna have nothing to do with none of these cats. I'm just gonna do me. And now, all these years later, the only people that ain't stabbed me in the back is the killers and gangsters that society is so afraid of. You wanna judge me on what I did before? Fuck you—I'll just keep stacking this paper. I'm not what I was before, and I'm not what I will be in the future. So judge me at your own risk. But never, ever underestimate me. Because if you do . . ."

The room went black and I gasped. A red laser dot flickered across the room and came to rest on a far wall. The lights flicked back on. Cox was gripping the biggest pistol I had ever seen, live or in the movies. The dot was now poised on the door to the studio, head high.

"That's whassup," he stated emphatically, aiming the enormous piece of black metal but looking at me. He secured the cannon back under the mixing board with one hand and leaned back in his chair.

I tried to think of a good segue as my heartbeat returned to normal.

"So how do you know Tommy Daminion?" I asked.

"Tommy's a general, man. How can I not know him?"

"Y'all do business together?"

For the first time I detected anger on Cox's pretty face. "I don't sell dope. That's not my thing."

"So how did you meet Holliday's father, then?"

Cox's eyes got wide. He rubbed his head with both hands, then laced his fingers across his chest and spoke.

"Now I see why you really came here. But that's cool. I would go all out for Holliday too. She's a bad bitch."

I felt a flash of anger before I realized it was a compliment.

"So to answer your question, I'm all about justice, dawg. That's how I know Holliday. Justice needed to be done."

Cox wheeled his chair to the end of the console. "I'm gonna play you something from my new album," he said over his shoulder, punching a few buttons. The drum pattern reminded me of The Joint.

"So you know my brother Dontay?" I asked.

Cox wheeled around and scrutinized me, gray eyes squinting.

"That's the second time tonight you surprised me," he said. "Y'all don't look nothing alike."

"Yeah, I know. He told me to tell you what up."

Cox turned back around. "Duke was nice with the beats, I can tell you that. What's he up to these days?"

For once the thought of my brother made me sad.

"He's up to no good," I said. "As always."

CHAPTER 43

Kaya felt a lot different from the VIP section. The tinted glass enclosing the balcony muffled the music from below. I could hear the fizz of champagne tumbling into nearby glasses, the murmur of powerful voices, and the giggle of beautiful women who were not being paid to get naked. Three months ago I was downstairs in the general population, unaware that this bubble of influence even existed. I looked down into the crowd and felt as if I were levitating.

Chunk picked up a bottle of Perrier Jouët from the forest of bottles on the low table in front of our couch. He poured another glass for me, Wop, and the half-dozen other men and women around the table.

Chunk beckoned to a fat dude awkwardly posted up nearby. He had a thin chin-strap beard and THUG LIFE tattoos crawling down his foreams. Chunk introduced him all around as Young Vet, "one of my artists."

"Vet, you been in the studio?" Chunk said brusquely. "You lace that track the other night?"

He nodded.

"Good. Now lemme get that watch back."

Young Vet's eyes got bigger and his bulk shrank two sizes. "I thought you said I could hold it!"

"I said hold, not have. Now come up off that," Chunk snapped, holding out a hand and wiggling his fingers. Vet reluctantly slid the Rolex off his wrist. Chunk shoved it into his pocket and peered through the glass into the general population. "Yo, you see that one in the pink top? Right there, with the titties? Go bring her up here, plus any friends she got. But not if her friends ugly—we don't want no grackles up in here."

Vet shuffled to the door, parted the red velvet curtain, and descended the steps. Chunk started laughing. "See, that's the difference between a thug and a gangster. And here's the real funny thing. You see that nigga over there?" He pointed to the rapper Mini-Mack, surrounded by four women. "That was his watch. The homies caught duke at the BET Awards." Chunk cackled, then walked over to Mack's table, gave him a pound, and slid into a seat.

I was waiting to talk to Tommy Daminion. For the past hour he had been sitting across the room, conversing with a stream of people. Right now he was talking with two execs I recognized from Sony. He seemed in his element, leaned back with his arms spread on the back of the couch.

I felt a pang of regret that I didn't have the nerve to walk over and take a seat. But I was afraid of violating some sort of gangster etiquette. I had to be invited, especially since I wanted info about a sensitive situation. The Cox interview had convinced me there was more to the Slow Creep situation than I knew.

I looked around the room for an easier area to infiltrate. I knew about half of the faces in the room, not counting celebrities. There was a knot of *Fever* people at one table, with Rosa in the center thumbing her Sidekick. And then I heard Black's voice, his LA twang riding atop the rolling Polow beat. He was talking to a lanky, stooped-over dude with a receding hairline.

I walked over, thinking that Black would go over to Tommy's table sooner or later.

"Sheeit, one of my nuts is bigger than this muhfucka!" Black said. He was holding a piece of clear plastic wrap with a bud of weed inside. "This ain't $175 worth of weed."

The lanky dude scratched his head and said, "It is in Noo Yawk."

"Nigga, I sell hundreds of pounds of weed at a time. Don't tell me what it cost." Black pulled a knot of bills out the pocket of his slacks. "Now tell me how much you really want."

Black ended up paying $120. Lanky segued into the fact that he was a rapper. "I got skills, man, I'm tellin' you," he insisted.

"Fuck skills," Black said. "You need songs."

Lanky left soon enough. I ordered two shots of Goose. Black and I clinked glasses and he rubbed his belly beneath his untucked linen shirt.

Something clattered at our feet. I looked down and saw a small silver pistol on the floor.

"Fuck!" Black said. He quickly picked it up and shoved it into his pocket. I started to ask how he got the gun into the club, then decided to stick to my script.

"How come you ain't kicking it with Tommy?" I asked.

"Who, Tommy Daminion from Daminion Entertainment?" Black said loudly in Tommy's direction. "Not tonight. He's making big deals. I'm just a drug dealer visiting town for a few days."

"He was asking me about the Slow Creep mixtape."

Black made an exasperated face. "I told him what the deal was. Dude been acting kind of pussy if you ask me, Julien all snuggled up under his nuts."

Black was staring at Tommy's table. I followed his gaze and saw Julien slide into a seat across the table from Daminion and start whispering into a woman's ear.

"You and Julien ain't cool?"

Black drained his glass, smacked it onto the bar, and wiped his mouth with the back of his hand. It was refilled before his hand could return to his belly.

"All these niggas is fags. Everybody in the music industry is gay. Please quote me on that. Fuck him and that fat bitch Sam.

I recalled the Buddha outside of Roscoe's and the violent rooster, Emp. My hand twitched around the memory of the pistol in my palm.

"Big Sam?"

"Fat Sam," Black corrected. "I get a call from that nigga a while back and halfway through he bring up Julien trying to sign some LA groups. I'm just bein' me, you know, and I start jokin' about Julien tryna get in the game when he need to stick to robberies. Just playin', you know, me bein' me. Because the nigga do got some bad skin. He's the real pimp." Black laughed. "P-I-M-P . . . L-E. Nigga forehead look like it got herpes."

I quickly checked to make sure Julien wasn't looking before laughing at Black's joke.

"Little do I know Sam got Julien on the other line not sayin' nothing, like on a three-way call, you know? Ain't that something high school girls do?" Black downed the rest of his drink.

"How did you know Julien was listening?"

"Because later I get a call from Tommy askin', 'Remember

what you said about Julien?' I said, 'Yeah, that he's a herpes-head muhfucka?' And Tommy said, 'That shit wasn't funny. It's a problem. Jack wants to see you.'"

The way Black emphasized the word 'see,' I could tell it had nothing to do with vision. I glanced over at Julien. He was wearing a loose, aqua blue button-down shirt with thick gold vertical stripes, and had his arm around the girl now. Sure enough, he reached up to scratch his forehead beneath his linen page-boy cap.

"Maybe Sam just told Tommy what happened," I said, hoping that things weren't as serious as they sounded.

"Nah, Tommy said Julien told him, 'I heard it myself.' So I call Sam and ask him, 'What's wrong, you don't like me? Ain't our kids run track together? You tryna get me killed?' He laughed, and I was like, 'Seriously, you told Julien what I said.' He told me to stop trippin'. I was like, 'Nigga, Julien said what I said!' Then the other line beep and it's Tommy again. He was mad, talking about I run my mouth too much. . . ."

I had too much liquor in me to keep track of who said what to whom. But hadn't Black told me that he would die for Tommy? Didn't Tommy say Julien was the one who got him locked up? I thought about how on *The Sopranos* everybody was all kissy-kissy, then plotted behind one another's backs. And here I was sitting next to a dude with a target on his back. A tinge of fear scratched at the edge of my fog.

I tried to laugh. "Seriously, though, Julien ain't really tryna kill you, right? I mean, he's right over there. If he wanted you dead, wouldn't he have done something by now?"

Black looked at me, and there was no trace of a smile on his face.

"About a week ago I get a call that Julien needs four hundred pounds of weed and can I make that happen. I get it hooked up, but at the last minute it fall through. And I had no idea this nigga wanted to see me. Julien coulda got me right there, on the exchange. That's his specialty."

I wondered how a man handles being in the same room as a guy who wants him dead.

"I know Tommy loves me," Black said. "And I would back down to Tommy. Not outta fear, but on some 'I love you' shit. Tommy, Sam, Julien . . . I respect all these niggas. On some street shit, I don't discredit none of them. But Sam coulda got me killed, so I can't fuck with him, ever again. Julien—I talk shit about that nigga, but if he really wanna see me, he could see me."

I knew that facing death was a part of Black's life, but to have it so casually close . . . it made me feel a strange combination of sympathy and respect. And maybe it was the liquor, but I wanted to help him.

"Can't Tommy work this out? Y'all still cool, right?"

"Whatever is whatever, man. Dude is mad at me over the Blast tape."

"What Blast tape?"

Black signaled to the bartender. "Blast is a new nigga Tommy's managing. He a gangbanger, or so he claim. But dude was on a reality show a few years back talkin' 'bout he's a Buddhist, on some ol' Tina Turner nyah-nyah-ren-ko shit. I had a copy of the tape, and Tommy's mad that it got out on YouTube."

"Did you let it out?"

"Nah, but I ain't squash it, neither. That's what Tommy's mad over."

I looked over at Daminion's table, and he was staring directly at me. We locked eyes for a moment, his face a blank mask, and then he went back to his conversation.

Suddenly I felt so lonely it was almost a physical sensation. I took out my Sidekick and texted Holliday.

I MISS YOU. CAN WE GET TOGEHER AND TALK?

I noticed the missing *T* only after I hit the send button. I swallowed the last of my Henny and exhaled until the fire in my chest burned low. On the spur of the moment, I decided to throw my Slow Creep cards on the table. I had planned to lead up slowly to the question. But what the fuck.

"There's more to the Slow Creep deal than music, isn't there?"

Black looked out into the crowd and laughed. "That's funny."

"I was told they movin' keys." *Movin' keys.* How many times had I rapped along to those words? Only this time it felt dangerous and real, as though the cocaine were actually in the room.

"Word? Who said that?"

If I didn't give a good answer, Black could deny it. I decided on a semi-lie. "You know me and Chunk go way back."

Black looked out into the crowd again and nodded his head to the music. "This the best song Nas ever wrote," he said.

I swear, that's how we pledge allegiance to the alliance
Of underworld killers and thugs, though the science
Of a nigga's still yet to be found
So light up some green and pass it around . . .

Black turned his yellowed eyes on me. "All I got to say to you is this: Keep your eyes open at the Baller. Now I'ma go to the bathroom and roll up this weed." He slid off his stool, hitched up his pants, and waded through the crowd.

A rush of exhilaration flashed through my body, leaving me literally tingling. Black's nondenial was confirmation enough: Slow Creep was selling drugs as well as their music. My story would make the cover of the *Fever* for sure. I restrained myself from pumping a fist in the air.

My Sidekick buzzed. Holliday!

IT WOULD BE GOOD TO TALK TO YOU. CAN YOU COME BY MY OFFICE TOMORROW?

I texted her back yes. Now things were really going my way. Spirits high, I bounced back to Chunk's table. Young Vet had returned with the girls. Chunk introduced me all around, even to Wop, who didn't notice because he was whispering to a girl whose pierced nipples shouted at us beneath her tight white tank top. I waited for a hole in the conversation and then got in Chunk's ear.

"You think we could holler at Tommy?"

Chunk looked over at Daminion's table. Pharrell and Deel-ishus were sitting there, and the crowd was even thicker than before. Julien was thumbing his Sidekick.

"He looks busy," Chunk said. "Let's catch him at the office tomorrow. You need to get at some of these hoes, nigga!"

Not if I was seeing Holliday the next day. Here I was in VIP, but still fenced off from the real players. I tried to think of something that would get their attention.

"You got Julien's info?" I asked Chunk.

Chunk dug through his briefcase for five minutes before extracting some digits scratched onto a crumpled Holiday Inn receipt. I thumbed in my message:

ARE YOU REALLY TRYING TO KILL MY BROTHER DONTAY?

Julien was talking intently to Deelishus when the message arrived. He looked at his Sidekick with a frown, then leaned over and showed it to Tommy. They looked at me and I shrugged. Inside I was trembling.

Tommy said something into Julien's ear and returned to his discussion with Pharrell. Julien got up and walked to the bar. I followed him there.

His shirt was open to the fourth button, exposing the wide, flat gold chain draped around his neck. The diamonds in his ears were the size of chickpeas. His white hat sat low on his mottled forehead.

"So you and Black real good friends, eh?" Julien squeak-rasped.

"We aiight. I see you and Tommy kicking it pretty hard. So why you got my brother all shook?"

"I'ont know what you talking about, menh."

I said nothing, but it didn't work. Julien just looked at me with a half smile on his chocolate face.

"Dontay said you was trying to kill him. I know my brother's crazy, so I just need to hear your side of the story."

"Story? What story?"

"About anything that happened at Dontay's house."

"Is that his name? I'ont even know dude's name. How could I be trying to kill him?" Julien leaned forward and raised his eyebrows until they disappeared beneath his hat. "How can you be sure of anything, really?" He laughed briefly, a high-pitched cackle that sounded like a strangled chicken.

"You wasn't at his house that night?"

Julien shook his head slowly.

This was going nowhere. I needed to jolt him out of his comfort zone.

"What about that night at Junior's, when Large got shot? You was there, right?"

Julien laughed. "Who's telling you this, Black? You got it all wrong, dude. And I don't think Tommy would be too happy to read this in your story."

That brought me up short. I needed to slow down. "Tommy put his trust in me and I would never do anything to violate that. I just want to know the truth, that's all. How can I know what *not* to write if I don't know what really went down?"

A dull roar vibrated through the floor from the crowd below. A few seconds later two bulky security guards came through the red curtain and scanned the room. A guy in a suit rushed in and shooed away a bunch of girls from a table. Reddy entered, with two models towering over him and entourage in tow. They seated themselves at the vacated table, the crowd whirling in on them like water getting sucked into a drain.

When I looked back toward Julien, he had vanished into the crowd. Tommy was gone, too. I realized Julien had told me absolutely nothing.

At least I had figured out that Slow Creep had a drug

connection. I made my way back to Chunk's table and wedged myself onto the couch. Chunk was so smashed, he completely missed my glass when trying to fill it. As the liquor seeped through my pants and my brain, I closed my eyes and tried to figure out how I was going to write this story without catching a bullet.

CHAPTER 44

Holliday's law firm took up three floors of a Manhattan skyscraper. Her office was tucked into the back of the middle floor, past warrens of cubicles and conference rooms. I knew the way by heart.

It was early evening, but plenty of lawyers still walked the halls. I couldn't understand the strange looks they gave me until I saw my reflection in a tall glass wall: Yankees cap, Rocawear T-shirt, denim shorts, chukka boots—every item black. With my white headphones, I looked like one of those silhouettes from the iPod commercials.

More nervous than I had been in a long time, I snatched off my cap as I tapped on the door to Holliday's office and eased in. It was small, just a few feet wider than her L-shaped desk, which was covered with files and documents. Aside from Holliday's diplomas, the only thing on the wall was an Elizabeth Catlett print of a proud woman, skin the color of rich earth, wearing a wide straw hat. The slim window over Holliday's shoulder revealed only the skyscraper across the street.

There was one place on her desk I was scared to look. As

I sat down, my eyes darted to the spot next to her computer screen—and my picture was still there. I almost did a dance.

Holliday had her hair pinned up with two pencils. She brushed a strand away from her face and looked at me with a half smile. "Wow, a beard," she said. "It looks good. Makes you look older."

Riding the subway over, listening to Sade on my head-phones, I thought for a long time about what I could say to fix things. A lot depended on what her mood was like. The worst-case scenario was that I would have to confess everything. But she seemed receptive—no need for the nuclear option. Instead I said something I had been scared to say out loud, even to myself.

"I'm ready to quit," I said, thinking about the scene at Kaya. Once I had sobered up, the memory of Julien and Daminion disappearing together had been terrifying. I had to convince them that Black or no Black, I was not a threat.

Holliday raised her eyebrows in surprise. "I'm in over my head," I continued. "The other night I realized that you were right. I'm not built for this. So all I need to do now is finish this one story, to show Tommy that I'm not any danger to him." Better to leave Julien out of this. "When that's done, it's a wrap."

Holliday looked at me with a protective look in her eyes. She reached out and touched my face gently—and then she pulled the trigger.

"It's over," she said, eyes starting to go wet. "It doesn't have anything to do with whether you're in or out."

My heart started racing. "What do you mean it doesn't matter? I'm doing what you wanted me to do!"

"Things have changed. You've changed, and so have I."

I remained silent as I tried to get a grip on the situation. But it was about to get worse.

"There are a few things you should know. When I said Daddy went to jail for killing my mom, he wasn't really convicted of that. It was drugs. The people who killed my mom were trying to get back at Daddy. And I wasn't at the movies when it happened. I was home with my mom. And we knew they were coming."

"How'd you know?"

"My street friends told me."

"Street friends? You said you were a bookworm!"

"I was, especially compared to the rest of the crew. But the fact is, me and my mom knew. Daddy said if things ever went really crazy to call a certain telephone number. He wrote it on a piece of paper and I kept it in my wallet. That night I called it. A recording asked me to leave a message, so I did. I said people were coming to my house to get me and my mom."

Holliday didn't look at me as she spoke, shuffling the papers on her desk with her left hand and twirling a pen through the fingers of her right.

"My mom was real tough. I tried to get her to leave, but she said we had nowhere to go where they wouldn't find us, so we might as well stick it out and hope that whoever was on the other end of that number could do something for us. Whenever I asked whose number it was, she wouldn't say.

"We were in the basement when they came. Momma had left a can of hair spray in front of each door, so when they came in, I heard the can fall down and roll all the way across the floor. They searched the whole house before coming down the basement steps. I could hear men talking in Jamaican accents. When someone started down the stairs, Momma opened fire. One of them got killed and his body rolled down the steps. The other two started shooting through the floor at us. Momma shot right back up at them."

I had never felt as lost as I did at that moment. Holliday might as well have confessed that she was really a man.

"The shooting stopped and we heard their boots clunking out the house. I thought it was over until the little basement window smashed open. Someone stuck a shotgun into the little space and started letting off. I jumped into this tall wardrobe box where all our winter clothes were hung. Momma was standing by the basement steps and I saw her get it in the back. She fell facedown on the steps—I can still remember the sound her body made when it hit. I almost screamed, but I clamped my mouth down so hard, I bit my tongue. They let off a few more blasts and then knocked out all the glass in the window with a long flashlight like the police carry. They were shining the light inside when I heard one of them give kind of a wet, yelpy gargle. The flashlight dropped in the window and I heard two muffled shots from a silencer. It was quiet for a long time and then the basement lights came on. This huge dude came down the steps with a silver .45 in each hand. And that was how I met Cox."

She finally looked up at me with an expression so pained, I yearned to comfort her. She fell back in her chair as though she was exhausted.

"I've spent a long time coming to grips with everything that happened to me," Holliday said. "If I could have, I would've told you more. But it's only now that I'm figuring all this out.

That's what I had to do to protect myself. I hope you won't hate me for that."

Holliday picked up her briefcase, walked around the desk, and leaned over my chair. Her hug pushed me dangerously close to crying. I don't know how long I stayed in her office after she left. Finally I dialed up some Game on my iPod, and his angry voice gave me the courage to leave. Alone.

CHAPTER 45

At least a dozen people at the *Fever* asked if I could get them free passes to Tommy Daminion's birthday party—the same ones who had looked at me as if I were stupid for saying he was a story three months ago. I finally had respect in the office, both from Rosa's people and the Knots Landing crew. I couldn't admit to any of them that I was worried I might never talk to Daminion again. But I stayed in Chunk's ear, and he finally hit me up the day of the party, saying Daminion would talk to me at the venue.

There was a long line when I arrived at the club near Union Square. I went to the VIP entrance, said my name, and was waved right through. The bouncer gave me only a cursory pat-down and came nowhere close to discovering the half-smoked blunt in an envelope tucked inside the rolled-up cuff of my jeans. Inside was still only half full. I found one of Daminion's soldiers and asked him where to find the man himself. He spoke to someone on a walkie-talkie and directed me to a door on the side of the stage. A few narrow steps led to a twisting, low-ceilinged corridor. I followed voices until I came to a dressing room with another soldier posted in front of a door plastered with promotional stickers. His expression told me to wait. The low, raspy throb of a Buju Banton record came from upstairs. I strained for something else until finally, above the patois, I heard two other voices. One was Tommy Daminion's unmistakable Brooklyn monotone. The other voice danced just beyond my recognition.

"The tape is all over the place now," Daminion said.

"What about radio?" the voice asked, deep and slow.

"Emmis, Radio One, Clear Channel. Massive 99 been talking about it constantly. D. Rex's spins are drying up with a quickness."

Buju's chanting filled the pause.

"I told that boy," the voice said, sounding weary. "If he would have listened to me, none of this would have happened. All right, Tommy, I got to go. I'll talk to you soon. And happy birthday, my brother."

The door opened. The face that emerged was startling in its paleness, interrupted by wide, pink lips fixed in a permanent half smile. He was short, with gray eyes on the same level as mine. He looked more like a cat than any man I had ever seen.

I remembered him from Daminion's sentencing: Felix Billings.

Both our brains were spinning—Billings's trying to figure out who I was and what I was doing, and mine trying to fit his conversation into what I already knew. And then it clicked.

They were talking about the D. Rex tape. Billings used to be D. Rex's manager. They had beef and D. Rex left him. So Billings got the tape to Daminion, who gave it to Chunk, who released it to the world.

Billings stood there long enough for me to realize that I should introduce myself.

"Mr. Billings," I said, feeling an unexplainable urge for him to like me, "I'm Marq Wise from the *Fever*."

The strange smile remained but his cat eyes narrowed a tiny bit. I felt like a child whose simple lies were wordlessly exposed.

"I'm, uh, here to see Tommy. I heard your speech in court. Tommy's lucky to have someone like you in his corner. I'd love to talk to you sometime for my story."

Billings chuckled slightly, placed a black fedora adorned with a small feather on his head, and walked past me without a word. His shiny black shoes clipped quickly up the hallway, leaving me with an unsettled feeling.

I started to walk in the door to the dressing room, but the soldier stepped in front of me. "Who dat," Daminion said from inside the room. The soldier raised his eyebrows.

"It's me. Marq Wise."

Daminion was leaned back on a wide leather couch, wearing an undershirt and slacks. An assortment of cell phones and Sidekicks lay before him on the coffee table, along with a white Styrofoam container of steaming food. A bright blue shirt and sumptuous navy suit hung on a rack next to a brightly lit dressing-room mirror.

I took a seat on one of several metal folding chairs, decided against using the recorder tucked into my pocket, and instead took out my notebook. "Thanks for seeing me. How you been?"

"I'm great." He chuckled without smiling and rubbed his face. "A few months ago, I was locked up. So I'm just happy to be here. I'm happy to have artists on the radio and records in the stores. Ten years ago I was facing a life sentence. Niggas never woulda thought I'd make it to this position. But you know how the Book says: 'The last shall come first.'"

Mom flashed through my mind, holding a Bible over me. "You know the Bible?"

"I became a Muslim in prison. But coming up with the Rastas, it was a big part of that faith. We were all versed in the Bible and the Old Testament. It was insane—we'd quote from a Bible held in one hand and kill you with the other."

Daminion had a faraway look in his eyes for a moment. He returned to our room and grabbed a piece of fried plantain from his food container. "But how *you* been?" he said. "When your story coming out?"

"This the last interview I need."

"Cool. So what you need to know?"

I felt nervous, like a bank robber approaching the teller, and took a deep breath. "I got a lot on my plate right now, trying to figure out a lot of things. Let's start with Young Spank. What happened with that?"

Daminion shrugged. "Chunk let the situation get out of hand."

"Can you do anything about it?"

"*Do* anything about it? Like what?" He challenged me with hard eyes.

I backed down. "I don't really know. Talking to Chunk, I felt like he wanted to take it to the streets. I know he was counting on that Spank paper, that's for sure."

Daminion was leaned forward over the coffee table, taking small bites of chicken from a plastic fork. The aroma made my mouth water. All I had eaten that day was a hot dog and soda from a corner cart. Daminion chewed long enough to make me wonder if I needed to ask another question before he finally swallowed and leaned back in his chair.

"The Spank situation is what it is. There was a time when there woulda been some violence. And I ain't scared of that, in any way whatsoever. I been in prison half my life and it just made me stronger. I did better business in the fed and made more connections than I did on the streets. Well, maybe not as many connections in the music industry." Daminion laughed heartily. "But I'm doing business now, real business. When you have a felony on your record, the game is stacked against you. I had to learn the system in order to beat the system. Now I've learned how to *structurally* do business. Back in the day we'd buy a pound of weed and bag it out. Sometimes we'd make three hundred dollars on a pound, sometimes we'd make two fifty. Then we started to understand the grams and metrics of weights. If you know the size of the bag, you can make profit into a science. The hustle got a lot smarter. When I came home fifteen years ago, that's what kind of hustle it became. You just figured out what profit you wanted to make.

"Now I'm on a new hustle. What other industry you know where a felony don't keep you from getting in? And there's a science to this hustle too. I want to make records with people because they respect me as a music dude, not because they're scared of me or what I represent. There was a time when that was not the case, when little things turned into big things. You step on our sneakers, even if it was an accident, that was so much disrespect. It wasn't even two-hundred-dollar Jordans— we was wearing thirty-five-dollar Pro-Keds. If I thought you was arrogant, you could lose your life. It was just the mentality of that era. But that ain't the case no more. The violent part of my life is over. That's why I say it is what it is. I ain't trying to hurt nobody, not over no paper, and especially not over no Young fuckin' Spank."

"Not even after Meyer jerked you on the *Teflon* album?"

I don't know who was more surprised at that question, me or Daminion.

His words emerged in carefully considered syllables. "I got a call from Brawls when he heard the track dissing him—he said could I pull it off 'cause he didn't need that problem. I said sure, but you gotta give me one of your records to replace it. He said yes. A week goes by, then another week. I call over to see what's up, and the next thing I know Meyer Mahl is on the phone, like, 'You're trying to start another East Coast–West Coast war, why are you putting this record out, whatever whatever.' He had this real parental, teacher type of tone. And that infuriated me. Why is this dude Meyer telling me what to put on my record? Do I call over to Fresh Beat telling you what to put out? Then I get a call from the president of the entire Versatize corporation. He asks me, 'Do you really need that record on your album?' That *really* infuriated me. I realized that Big Brawls was pulling rank. He's a straight bitch. I gave him a chance to talk to me about it, man to man, but he'd rather have the big bosses tell me to take it off."

Daminion realized he was scowling. I watched him relax, the wrinkles smoothing out of his forehead. He gave a genuine smile.

"So I said fuck them and put the record out. I made money off the budget anyway."

It took me a while to scribble all that down. As I wrote, I

tried to think of a way to ease into my next question. But it still felt as though it came out wrong.

"I been seeing you with Julien a lot, and I can't figure that out. I thought he was on your 'To Kill' list?"

"Sometimes you gotta live and let live, menh," Daminion said, spreading his hands generously. "You know why I love dude? He always overshadows me. There's a purpose for a Julien. He's that dude with the alligator jacket or the forty-inch rims. I go to his house and he got a red refrigerator." He laughed and shook his head. "A red refrigerator! He's so Brooklyn, so cocky and confident. Niggas know he'll bust his gun. Who else is gonna overshadow me? If niggas affiliate him with me, they might leave me alone. That's the only use for a Julien, and I think it's a good one."

"What about Black? Y'all don't seem as tight as you used to be."

"Black is still my dude. He just got a big mouth and don't know when to close it."

I stayed silent, wanting him to say more and scared to push him further. But Daminion waited me out, slowly chewing his food. My mind traveled to the half-smoked blunt hidden in my cuff. Finally I decided to throw caution to the wind.

"So I ran into Felix Billings on my way in here. Did he have anything to do with that D. Rex tape getting out?"

My words hung in the air, mingling with the reggae beat rumbling from upstairs. Daminion looked at me with an utterly blank expression, then went back to his plate of food for what seemed like forever. This had to be one of the worst interviews I had ever done.

Daminion tossed the Styrofoam container into a trash can next to the couch and looked back at me.

"So when is your story coming out?" he asked.

"This is the last interview I need."

"So when is it coming out, menh?"

"The issue hits newsstands in a few weeks."

Daminion got up and walked over to the lighted mirror. He opened a small leather case, removed a brush, and began to pull it over his close-cropped hair. "You remember what I said when we first met, right?"

"Uh-huh," I lied.

"So then you understand that I need to look at the story when you're done."

I hoped he wasn't saying what I thought he was saying. "The issue comes out at the end of August."

"Nah, you ain't understanding me. I need to see it before it's printed."

The blood in my veins came to a stop. Showing someone a story before it was published was forbidden. "Um, I guess I could ask if we could do that."

"What you got to ask about? Just hit Chunk off with it. Aiight?"

He looked at me in the mirror, the halo of lights encircling his gleaming brown face. He was the cat and I was the mouse.

There was a knock at the door. "The photographer's here," a voice said.

Daminion took his shirt off the hanger. "Aiight," he said, dismissing me from his presence. "Enjoy yourself at the party."

CHAPTER 46

I stumbled upstairs in a daze, looking for a place to light my blunt. But there was no one else smoking, so I went to the bar and ordered a Henney. The liquor didn't erase my sinking feeling. I got the distinct feeling that someone was watching me and looked around, but the club was a forest of bodies now, filled to capacity. It was a smallish space, with a roped-off VIP section raised to one side, a small stage, and the dance floor in the middle. I tried to lose myself in the rolling thump of R. Kelly's "I'm A Flirt," but the music fell to pieces beneath extraneous conversation spinning through the air like sand in a windstorm. As I ordered another drink, the music lowered and the DJ's voice came through the speakers.

"Big shout-out to the guest of honor, Tommy Daminion, in the building. Happy birthday, my brother. Keep making them hits. And now everybody stand up for tonight's special surprise guest, in the building, Ton-Ton!"

The rapper swaggered onto the stage to the "Hips Don't Lie" beat, mic in hand, and launched into a verse.

> Happy birthday to Damin-ion
> Of all the kingpin he's number one
> Happy birthday to the king of kings
> Brooklyn to Kingston him runnin' t'ings . . .

The crowd surged forward and space cleared at the bar. I looked around again and there was Dontay.

He was staring at me from a few feet down the bar. Despite the heat he was wearing a heavy denim jacket and corduroys. We looked at each other, neither wanting to make a move toward the other. I was actually relieved to see a familiar face, so I finally walked over.

"What are you doing here?" I asked.

"I followed you."

"Why?"

"There's something you need to see."

"Aiight, show me."

"It's not here. You have to come with me."

"C'mon yo, forget the games. Just tell me what it is."

"I've already told you that. Now you have to see it for yourself."

No way I was following my brother anywhere. I leaned back against the bar and turned my attention toward Ton-Ton onstage.

. . . make way for the champion sound
them get inna de way and them get laid down . . .

Get in the way and get laid down. But hadn't Daminion told me that he was done hurting people? Even if he really wanted to change, would his world allow him to?

"C'mon, Marq. Let's go," Dontay said.

Suddenly that didn't seem like such a bad idea. I knocked back the last of my drink and followed Dontay out of the club.

When we hit the warm night, Dontay stopped, pointed up at the clear, starry sky, and said, "Those things of beauty heaven bears." He started walking down Broadway and I followed down the crowded sidewalk.

"You know the Bible is all metaphor and prophecy," Dontay began. I silently groaned to myself. "But everybody takes it literally. That's why so many people have overlooked the Promised One, better known as the return of Jesus Christ."

"You're crazy," I said. "When Jesus returns, it will be obvious to everyone." I dug way back in my memory to Sunday-school lessons. "The sun will be darkened—the stars will fall from the sky and everything. The Bible is real clear on that."

"That's all allegorical," Dontay retorted. We turned off Broadway onto Eleventh Street, his long legs striding so quickly, I had to hurry to keep up. "Genesis says God made the sun on the fourth day. But how could there be days one through three if there was no sun?"

"So the Bible is wrong, then," I challenged.

"Absolutely not. God created the world and the Bible is God's word made manifest. But after two millennia people are misunderstanding the Bible. So God sent Bahá'u'lláh to make things clear."

"Do I gotta drink carrot juice every day to understand the Bible?" I cracked. "And how come I never heard of this religion before? Why you the only nigga in Noo Yawk running around talking 'bout Jesus has returned?"

Dontay stopped walking and turned to look at me. And for the first time I could remember, he smiled.

His teeth were yellowed and his face unshaved. He was wearing that ridiculous women's leather bag strapped across the chest of an ancient WU-TANG FOREVER promo T-shirt. But as I studied my brother's ruined face, it dawned on me that he actually seemed happy.

He was standing next to a plaque reading BAHÁ'Í CENTER. I followed him through a metal gate and down a long corridor. There was music playing inside. Several people greeted him warmly, and two actually embraced him with strong hugs. We went through a doorway, walked up a few steps, and entered a small auditorium filled with people of all ages and races, singing along with a dreadlocked young brother onstage.

They were singing about Bahá'u'lláh—that's about all I remember. Because once I finished enjoying the fact that Dontay wasn't asking me for anything, my mind traveled back to the fact that if I didn't show Tommy Daminion my story before it was published, who knew what could happen. Then my thoughts traveled down my leg to my rolled-up cuff and the blunt hidden inside. I could almost taste the smoke on my tongue.

CHAPTER 47

I heard murmurs of respect as we gathered in the *Fever* conference room for dinner. The issue was even later than usual and Crooked Hairline wouldn't let us go home.

"Yo son, you doing big things with that Daminion story," someone said.

"That intro was hot to death."

"I ain't know you was that kinda beast with the pen, son!"

The praise washed over me in a warm wave. The story didn't come easily. I wrestled with the lead for a good week until I fell asleep on my couch with the Teflon album on repeat. I dreamed that Chunk and I were walking up a wooded hill. We came over a ridge and saw a valley full of rappers scraping and scratching at one another, their rhymes piercing my eardrums like arrows barbed with desperation. Dontay was in the middle of the throng on the turntables, headphones clamped over his ears, oblivious to the tumult. When he zigga-ziggaed into The Joint, I woke up with the lead in my head:

He wears the Black Steel like a badge. These bars made him. But Tommy Daminion is known to flip things, and now them bars are working for him. A few short months after I met him in federal custody, Daminion is the king of kings this night. . . .

I had stayed up all night and turned in the story this morning and sent a copy to the research department for fact-checking. Everything was a huge rush. By this afternoon, it seemed as though everyone in the office had read it. I was still trying to decide whether to send it to Daminion.

Rosa strode into the conference room atop a pair of massive Nikes with the *Fever* logo embossed onto the heel. She tossed a few advance copies of the new issue onto the table. Reddy peered up at us from behind diamond-studded glasses, like some sort of black Liberace.

"Aiight, we did well with the Reddy cover," she snapped, seizing a slice of pizza. "Now who's the next cover gonna be?"

There was silence around the table.

"Y'all need to get your minds off Knots Landing and into the game," Rosa said, her voice rising. "There ain't a single idea in here?"

"How about T.I.?"

"*XXL* got him already."

"What about Tupac?"

"Again?" three people said at once.

"Young Spank."

"One-hit wonder," was the chorus.

"50 Cent."

"Overexposed."

"How about a woman for once? Beyonce's new record is coming out."

"Her daddy promised *Vibe* an exclusive. But doesn't Missy Elliott have a new album?"

"Missy on the cover won't sell," Crooked Hairline said, glancing at Rosa for approval. She was thumbing her Sidekick.

"Too ugly," Rosa said without looking up. The women in the room exchanged eye-rolling glances.

"I think Missy is sexy," a guy said. "I'd smash that."

"See, why do men have to be so violent. 'I'd smash that.' No wonder we don't wanna give y'all no lovin'."

"Yeah, I should be more sensitive. I shoulda said, 'I'ma *hit* it.'"

Everybody laughed and the joke escalated around the room as Rosa continued to thumb her Sidekick.

"I'd kill that, yo."

"I'ma stab it."

"I was digging her out."

Jamaican accent: "Mosh it up!"

"I smacked that."

"I blew her back out."

"I blazed it."

"I blazed them skins, son."

"That's enough!" one woman finally yelled. "We are not going back to 'skins'! I thought we got rid of that fifteen years ago. I will *not* allow us to reduce women to the sum total of the skin around the vagina."

There was silence.

"Didn't Don Imus get in trouble for saying 'nappy-headed skins'?"

The room exploded with laughter. I waited for the noise to subside.

"What about Tommy Daminion on the cover?" I asked, excitement tingling the back of my neck.

Rosa looked up with a hungry smile.

"Now we're getting somewhere," she said. "Marq, come see me after the meeting. Aiight, now let's talk about the new Cash for that Ass contest. . . ."

Rosa was leaned back on her couch when I walked into her office, the page proofs for my story spread out around her. She shuffled the papers into a pile and patted a space next to her. I closed the door behind me and sat down.

"This is a great story," she said, leaning toward me. "I knew it should be the cover all along. I just wanted to see if you would say so."

"Aiight," I said. I wished I had showered after pulling the all-nighter.

"I'm glad to see that you believe in it. But to make the cover, it needed a little extra pop, just a little sump'n to give it that extra bang. Here, tell me what you think." She handed me the stack of pages.

It took only a glance to realize that I was dead.

The layout had a big picture of Tommy on one side of the page, looking to his right. Black was on the other side of the page, looking to his left. They were separated by a huge, blood-red headline: BLACK WILL SHOOT.

The subhead read, "Tommy Daminion has emerged from behind bars to reclaim his spot in the rap game. Now he's about to bag Slow Creep . . . unless his old partner Black bags him first."

Rosa put her hand onto my shoulder. "Don't worry. This is just a quickie layout and edit. Before you jump to conclusions, look at this." She handed me a mock-up of the cover. Tommy was seated in the same club dressing room I last saw him in, gazing into the camera with eyes that hid unknowable secrets. The photo must have been taken shortly after I had left. The scar on his face beckoned like a crooked finger. And there it was again: BLACK WILL SHOOT.

Beneath the cover line, smaller letters shouted out: BY MARQ WISE.

I tossed the page aside and read through my story. The Black Steel lead was intact, but the rest of the story had been edited to play up the conflict between Black and Tommy. And they had twisted the context of the "Black will shoot" quote to make it apply to Tommy instead of the vague population at large.

"Who edited this?" I asked Rosa.

She gently rubbed my neck. "I did, Marq. Do you like it?"

"There's no way it can run this way. You want me to get shot or something?"

"C'mon, baby. Nobody's going to shoot you. I know you want to get that cover, right?"

"I gave my word to these dudes that this kind of thing wouldn't happen."

"We can work it out with them—I know we can. You proved yourself with this one. I need someone like you on my team, Marq. I need you."

Our faces were so close, I could feel her warm breath. Her hand came to a gentle stop at the nape of my neck.

"We would be so dope together," she whispered.

As the blood rushed through my body, I let myself teeter on the edge of the possibilities. It felt warm, helpless, and deliciously dangerous, like when I let Wop buy me some head from a stripper two weeks ago. But when I opened my eyes, it felt so wrong.

I stood up and grabbed the pages. "I can't let this happen," I told Rosa. She dropped her forehead into one hand, her black curls spilling forward, then flung her hair back and looked at me with hurt eyes that quickly reverted to ice.

"Think about it," she said. She started to walk over to her desk, then stopped in front of the window, the light from the streets glowing behind her. "Isn't this what you've wanted ever since you walked through that door? So don't bitch up now that it's staring you in the face."

CHAPTER 48

I hate music videos. They take the focus away from the music, where it should be. I only saw one of Large's videos, just one. Him and Reddy was on a boat tossing money into the water, and then a bunch of mermaids swam up and had the money plastered all over their fish bodies. Can you believe how stupid that is, with people starving in the world? To actually throw money away?

I coulda been rich if I wanted to, but I gave that up for you and for the sake of keeping my music pure. "He is my true follower who, if he came to a valley of pure gold, will pass straight through it aloof as a cloud, and will neither turn back nor pause." That's what Bahá'u'lláh says. "And if he met the fairest and most comely of women, he would not feel his heart seduced by the least shadow of desire for her beauty." Can you claim that for yourself, yo? How many dudes you know like that besides me?

I always knew the only way I could regain your respect was to get money. Which has never been a problem for me—I'm a moneymaking machine. That's why I decided to finally sell The Joint after all these years. When that song comes out, it'll make me the person I'm supposed to be. Artistically speaking I'm greater than Large. And when you put him on a song with me, it's bananas. If I was to walk into a studio and sell that track, I could charge about a hundred, a hundred fifty thousand for the music alone. Then add Large's voice on top of that, plus the historical value since it was his first record, and it's worth at least five hundred thousand dollars.

Once I decided to sell it, I knew I had to go to the Baller to make that happen. But even though I'm

sitting on close to a million dollars' worth of music,
I didn't have a dime to my name.

I'm gonna try and make this next part as brief
as possible, although I know it won't be brief enough
for you. My entire insides is built on the feeling that
no one cares about whether I succeed or not. Right
up close to that, hugging that, is the feeling that
you are the only person I've experienced any real
love for. But if there's a choice between putting me
first or something frivolous that you want, I might
as well forget about it. But you wouldn't be who you
are without me, cause it sure ain't come from your
mother. I had to fight her over that. I don't get
no pleasure taking a dollar from you. It destroyed
me. The man I was before is gone. But I did it anyway, and I did it for you, to teach you how to have
responsibility. And I get a lot of satisfaction from
the fact that because of me, not nobody else, you'll
be able to make your way in this world, even though
you never used the juicer and I have questions about
your spiritual growth.

The last thing I want to say is this: There are
ways that I hurt you. Not fundamentally, but still
it hurts. So if you take my sincerity and couple it
with my religious beliefs and roll the whole thing
into my ability to produce music, it would have been
very cost effective for you to bankroll me. If you
looked at me like a company that makes beats, my
rate of return would have been more than the biggest
bank in America.

That's what I was trying to tell you when I came to your office that day. But of course you didn't listen.

I'ma be perfectly honest with you. I'm not always honest. I try not to lie, but I keep things to myself because I grew up alone in a house full of foster kids who got more love than me, even the worst of em all. But real talk, yo: I'm terrified of the time when I'm not working. When I'm looking at seven days before you give me more money, and I don't have meaningful work to do, and I don't have food, I can't help it. I fight against it and still bad thoughts come. And then when anything more than a dollar bill comes along, I just can't handle it. And that's when I get high.

This world is just temporary dust. The Next World is eternal. That's where God is, and that's what we have to prepare for. We're like babies in the womb waiting to be born. Most people are worried about self. Everybody wants to make themselves feel good with material things—houses, money, vacations, jewelry, drugs, women, whatever. Look at yourself. But that's no better than animals acting on animal instinct. What separates us from animals is knowledge of the spiritual world. And to get to the Next World, to get closer to God, we have to forget about all the material things. "Loose thy soul from the prison of self. Seize thy chance, for it will come to thee no more."

That's what I'm trying to tell you, Marq. Forget about this life. I know I have. Everything you think is important really means nothing. We got to get ready for what's next.

CHAPTER 49

I left Daminion a half-dozen messages after leaving Rosa's office, to no avail. Then I texted Chunk. The only chance I had was to get Daminion the original version of my story.

It felt like forever before Chunk pulled up in his Benz. I ran out of the lobby, hopped into the passenger seat, and dropped my real story onto his lap.

Chunk glanced at the pages as he pulled into traffic. "Tommy already seen your story. What was you thinking? You got a death swish or something? You fuckin' me up with this, son. I vouched for you."

"He has the wrong version! They edited it all crazy. He needs to—hold up! How he got the story already?"

"Somebody at the *Fever* e-mailed him a copy. I dunno who it was. Tommy called me right after, and he ain't happy."

Chunk swerved around a cab and accelerated through a yellow light. We were headed downtown, the evening sky turning purple as the Benz surfed the river of yellow cabs. The Game's raspy voice scraped from the speaker. I leaned the seat back and tried to let the beats pound the tension from my body. I can handle this, I told myself. It's gonna be aiight.

"I just need to talk to Tommy and straighten this out. Where's he at?"

"Miami, son. Gettin' ready for the Baller."

"Fuck. I been trying to get dude on the phone, but the message says his mailbox is full."

Chunk pulled out his cell and hit a few buttons. "What up, Tommy. . . . I got him with me right now. . . . Here he go."

The phone was in my hand. I sat up straight and took a deep breath.

"Tommy, it's Marq. Listen, you got to trust me on this. They screwed up my story, edited it to make it something that it wasn't."

His voice crackled in my ear. "Who did that?"

The thought of Rosa's soft touch made me pause. "I don't know exactly who, but the story you read is not what I wrote."

"What about the headline?"

"I definitely didn't write the headline. When you see the original version of what I wrote, you'll see that I held it down like we said."

"How come I had to get the story from somebody else, though? *You* were supposed to give it to me."

"I was about to. I just turned it in at the magazine this morning."

Tommy was silent for so long, I looked at the phone to make sure the call wasn't dropped.

"Listen," he finally said. "Give whatever it is you got to Chunk. But it really don't matter now, because how the story ended up can't happen. You unnerstand me? It can't happen. Tell them *Fever* muhfuckas they don't want me to live up to everything they heard about me."

The call went dead. Chunk tugged the wheel to the left and we shot onto the Brooklyn Bridge. I pulled out my Sidekick and messaged Taylor.

YOU HEARD ABOUT MY STORY?

The Benz hurtled up the bridge so fast, I thought we would launch into space at the apex. "Where you rushing to?" I asked Chunk.

"I'm pickin' Spank up."

"Spank? I thought y'all was through."

"We got unfinished business."

Taylor hit me back.

I HEARD. DON'T WORRY, WE CAN HANDLE THE SITUATION. I'LL HOLLER AT TOMMY. SEE YOU TOMORROW AT THE HOOP GAME.

"Taylor says he's gonna holler at Tommy," I told Chunk.

"None of that's gonna help unless y'all get that story straight. Real talk."

Chunk jerked to a stop in front of the Marriott hotel, pulled out his Sidekick, and started thumbing. I turned up Nas— *heard you was a thug with a good disguise*—and let my tired eyes close until I felt Chunk poke me in the ribs. He pointed to the front of the hotel. The doors slid open and Young Spank shuffled out, followed by a smallish guy in a SPANK ME T-shirt. Chunk got out the car, gave pounds, and leaned his seat forward. Spank and his boy slid into the backseat, the S medallion at the end of Spank's long chain clanking against the side of the car as he entered.

"Let's drive around the block so we can blaze up while we handle this business, aiight?" Chunk said. He produced a blunt from the center console and held it back over his shoulder. I watched Spank's faint reflection in the window as he lit the blunt, took three deep pulls, and passed it to his boy, who took three pulls and passed it to me. I thought the rule was take two—puff, puff, pass. But I took three since that's the way things were going.

We took a right onto Tillary. I cracked my window, exhaled smoke into the warm night air, and looked over at the basketball court. I needed to get my workouts back on. The lights were on, and a young boy was dribbling alone down the court, his huge T-shirt billowing out behind him. He missed the layup.

We stopped at the light at Flatbush Avenue as traffic crept in front of us onto the Manhattan Bridge. Chunk reached into the console, pulled out a knot of bills folded in half and secured with a rubber band, and tossed it into the backseat.

"That's twenty right there for the show I told you about," he said, glancing in his rearview. "They got another twenty for you before you go on. Forty grand for thirty minutes—you can't beat that. I told you I got this, man, I got this."

Spank grunted with the blunt in his mouth and started counting the money. The light turned green. We drove across Flatbush and beneath the Brooklyn–Queens Expressway. The Lafayette Gardens projects loomed like a brown fortress to our right. In Spank's window reflection, the streetlights scrolled across his face and the blunt throbbed like an orange taillight.

"Fuck Fresh Beat, kna' mean?" Chunk said as we stopped at a light. His window was rolled down, arm hanging out. "I know they talk a good game, but they can't hold you down like—what the fuck?"

The Benz jolted forward, snapping my head painfully backward. Someone had rear-ended us. Chunk pulled over and sprang out of the driver's seat. Spank, his friend, and I all piled out after him. A blue Tahoe was behind us, one headlight smashed.

"Aww, man!" Chunk yelled, looking at his dented rear end. "The fuck y'all doin' back there? Y'all better have some insurance!"

A brother wearing a button-down shirt tucked into khaki pants climbed down from the Tahoe and inspected the damage with Chunk. Khaki Pants argued with Chunk for a minute, then they retrieved their respective insurance cards and laid them on the roof of the Benz to exchange information. Spank, his boy, and I stood on the sidewalk finishing the blunt.

All of a sudden I felt something poking my back.

"Say one word and you dead," a voice hissed from behind me.

Out of the corner of my eye I saw two other guys close behind Spank and his boy. I looked over at Chunk to save us.

Khaki Pants was standing behind Chunk, his face twisted into a violent snarl as he whispered something into his ear. The assailants shoved the four of us into the street and made us kneel down between the Benz and the parked cars on the side, hidden from view.

My intestines squirmed as though I had just mainlined Ex-Lax.

"Nigga, you know who you fuckin' with?" Chunk growled. "This is Daminion, bitch. You got a death swish or sump'n?"

I felt cold steel jammed against the base of my skull, the same place Rosa's hand had rested a few hours ago. A rough paw rummaged through my pockets, extracted my wallet, and yanked the Sidekick off my hip. I stole a glance over at Chunk.

He was staring at the ground, still as a stone, shoulder muscles popping out from his tank top. I wondered if he was going to make a move, and I tried to plan what I would do if he did. But the weight of the pistol kept jerking my thoughts to bad places, up the gun barrel until I was facing the bullet waiting to explode into my brain. Mom's stern face materialized before me and I saw Dontay laughing with a mouth full of yellow teeth. I thought about the last time Holliday and I made love, and then her face was crowded out by a thousand grotesque strippers. Mom came back, dragging the Lord's Prayer with her. I asked God's forgiveness for ignoring him until this moment, and then I began to beg for mercy. *Our Father, who art in heaven—*

"I'll take that," said Khaki Pants, clutching the wad of bills Chunk had just given Spank. "Oooh-wee! Look like we got some ballers here. Now come up off all that jewelry." Chains and watches clink-clanked as they were handed over. Khaki Pants looked at Spank's giant S medallion and snatched off the rapper's sunglasses.

"You that nigga Young Spank, aintcha," he said. "The fuck you doing around here, nigga? They ain't told you Brooklyn keep on takin' it?"

Cars were driving past without stopping. The thought crossed my mind that we were about a dozen blocks from my house. I had driven down this very street plenty of times when the BQE was jammed.

"Gimme all that gwop, rap star. I know you got more than that. Yeah, man. That's what I'm talkin' 'bout. Gimme all that. Now lay the fuck down."

Spank and his boy fell to the street. Two assailants jumped

into the Benz, the other two climbed into the Tahoe, and they all screeched off. Chunk sat in the street, leaned up against a parked car with a dazed look on his face, shaking his head.

"I need to get high, man," Spank said. "I need to get high right now."

I felt the same way. I glanced at the street to see if the blunt had fallen by the wayside. No luck.

Spank's home boy ran into the street and looked down the block at the disappearing Benz, then bounded back in front of Chunk. "What we gonna do, man?" he bleated. "We gotta get them niggas!"

Chunk heaved himself to his feet and looked both ways down the street. "I can't believe I got got," he said in amazement. "That shit never happened to me before."

A young woman walked by wheeling a snoring baby. She hardly gave us a glance.

"Tell you what," Chunk told Spank, who was slumped on the curb. "Y'all two head back to the hotel. It's only a few blocks. I know niggas in these projects. Me and Marq's gonna head up in there and find out who did this."

Ain't no way I'm going up in there, Chunk or no Chunk. Before I could open my mouth to tell him that I was about to walk home, he glared at me to stay quiet.

"Aiight? Y'all wait for me back at the hotel. I'ma see y'all soon with some good news." Chunk stepped into the street and flagged down a gypsy cab. "This here's Young Spank the rapper," he told the driver. "He going to the Marriott right up the street. He ain't got no cash on him now, but if you wait outside the hotel, he'll come down with fitty bucks."

When the cab was out of sight, Chunk looked up and down the street and then turned to me with concern on his face.

"You aiight, man? You ain't shit on yourself or nothing, didja?"

My ass had spasmed for sure, but it was clean.

"I'm good. But no way I'm going up in them projects."

"Neither am I, nigga." Chunk pulled out his Sidekick and thumbed in a message. Chunk's Benz drove down the other side of the block.

How did he still have his Sidekick? How did the car get back so fast?

I saw Wop at the wheel. Chunk jogged across the street and looked back at me.

"You better come on," he said with a laugh. "These project niggas get hungry after dark. And them cats won't fall for no okey-doke."

Back at my apartment, Spank's chain sat on my coffee table as Chunk and I leaned back on the couch, ogling Trina on BET.

"It's like this," Chunk said, sipping from the icy Belvedere I had retrieved from the kitchen. "I don't start out planning no jooks. But if I do a deal with you, at the first possibility of something going wrong, I start thinkin' 'bout robbing you. If it's convenient, then you subject to get tooken. But I'ma okey-doke you and act like I'm the victim, too."

"How often do these deals go wrong?"

"About half the time. Maybe more."

As the icy liquor trickled down my throat, Trina seemed more real to me than tonight's robbery. Then I looked at Spank's chain and remembered the gun on my skull.

"What if tonight didn't go as planned?" I asked. "What if one of them cats woulda acted up?"

"They woulda got dealt wit."

"Just like that? It's that easy for you to kill somebody?"

Chunk tipped back his glass and looked at the TV for a long time before I realized that Young Spank's video was on. He was swaggering through a club, surrounded by women and his SPANK-shirted homies. When he grabbed his S chain and pushed it into the camera, Chunk and I busted out laughing, slapping hands and elbowing each other with glee. Chunk grabbed Spank's chain and put it around his neck. Then his face froze into a frightening mask. He leaned back into the sofa and stared at the ceiling.

"It's never easy," he said. "It's not like the movies. People don't die quick—they scream and beg. There's a lot of blood inside a person. And think about if you actually know him. Now there you are getting ridda they body."

"Is this life what you want, Chunk? Is this success?"

"Sheeit." The thought seemed to drag him out of a dark place. "Success is being free and not dead. And I'm stackin' paper on top of that? I'm doing what I wanna do, being creative, getting in the studio, bringing music into the world. Damn right this is success. But what about you, though? I bet you never thought you'd be sitting with me counting a pile of illegitimate bills. I guess things was going good for you until they fucked up your story. Don't worry, though."

Chunk reached into the front of his pants and removed his nine millimeter, placed it on the table, and fell into a sleeping position on the couch.

"Them *Fever* cats gon' come around, you'll see. 'Cause they know they can get dealt with just like anybody else."

CHAPTER 50

Diddy was demanding the basketball. I waited for him to catch the pass and then forced him left. He missed a layup, Crooked Hairline grabbed the rebound and tossed the rock to me, and we were off to the races.

All my problems evaporated as I flowed down the court, ball in my hands, operating on instinct and reflex and muscle. Even better, half the music industry was lined up around our court to watch the *Fever* play Diddy's Bad Boy Records. Except for the street-ball star Main Event, who was running with Bad Boy, I was the best player on the court. *You now rockin' with the best, B-ball on a string, number nine on my chest. . . .*

Main Event dunked, drawing awed oohs from the crowd. I dribbled hard down the left side with Diddy on me, then stopped on a dime. Diddy's momentum made him sail past and the crowd erupted, a hundred voices rising as one. I bounced the ball over to my right hand, drove toward Main Event, and jumped. He leaped to block my shot and I passed in midair to Taylor under the hoop for an easy bucket.

Go, boy! Was that Rosa's voice? She was in the crowd, her first time at one of our games. My backpedal got a little extra bounce.

The next time down the court Diddy wasn't guarding me anymore. I guess he didn't want to get embarrassed again. My new defender was tall and slow, and all he could do was foul me. But we had no answer for Main Event, and at halftime the score was tied.

As we rested on our bench, Diddy walked over, plopped down beside me, and draped his arm over my shoulder. "Nice half, playboy."

A tiny part of my brain was incredulous at being next to the infamous Sean Combs, but the rest knew that I deserved it.

"Thanks, Puff. You gonna guard me anymore today, or am I gonna foul your boy out? 'Cause you know I ain't switchin' off you."

He laughed. "I'm getting too old to chase y'all youngsters around. But check it, I heard Tommy Daminion was lookin' for you. You sure you aiight? I wouldn't want you lookin' over your shoulder or anything like that." He peered over his shoulder at the throng beginning to close in on him. "You never know who could be in the crowd at one of these games."

Diddy got up, smacked me on the shoulder, and went back to his team. "Nice try, Puff!" Taylor shouted at his back. "My squad don't get shook."

Word, I don't get shook. No nuts, no glory.

More people came in the second half. Players from other games flocked to our court. Rosa was standing on a chair so she could see over the people packed three deep on the sidelines. I got a little tired and picked up some fouls trying to reach in and steal the ball from their point guard. He had a weak handle. Diddy was taking more shots than he should have, and I could see his squad getting frustrated. But Main Event was a solo highlight film, at one point throwing down a two-hand jam so hard that the crowd spilled onto the court and stopped the game for five minutes.

I was grateful for the rest, so I sat down on the court and breathed in the bedlam. Young men hopped and whooped across the gym. One grabbed the ball and tossed it over the crowd's head into the adjacent court. A dancer's limbs jerked like a puppet's.

The game resumed, about two minutes left. They were double-teaming me, so I dished more than I shot. Diddy hit a bucket and Main Event drained a long three. I made two free throws, the routine unconscious: bounce, bounce, bounce. Breathe, bend, flick, swish. Bounce, bounce, bounce. Breathe, bend, flick, swish. Game tied. Then I was on the line for two more free throws.

Bounce, bounce, bounce. Breathe, bend—

"You know Tommy got a price on your head," Diddy said, just low enough for the ref not to hear.

Flick. The ball thudded on one side of the rim, then the other side, then fell through. The crowd made a sound like a barn door on rusty hinges.

Diddy's earrings flashed. Who wears earrings in a ball game?

Bounce . . .

"I read your story. It was wack."

Bounce, bounce . . .

"Taylor, you ain't school this kid? You tryna get him kilt?"

Breathe, bend . . .

"See, if you put me on the cover, you wouldn't have these problems."

Flick.

"'Cause I don't—"

Clank.

I missed. Main Event grabbed the rebound and handed the

ball to his point guard with the weak handle. I glanced at the clock: thirty seconds.

It's okay. We're still up one. Play defense. It's okay.

As Weak Handle approached midcourt under pressure, I could tell he was about to pick up his dribble. Puff ran toward him calling for the ball. I stayed a half step behind Puff until the ball was in the air, then darted forward. It was a lazy lob. Time to snatch the ball and this game.

Puff and I both leaped. The whistle blew. I picked myself up and headed to the foul line to ice the win. Then I saw Puff headed to the other foul line, and all the other players were walking with him.

"Foul on number nine," the ref said.

I ran up to the ref, a gray-haired Puerto Rican who had been doing my games for years. He wasn't hearing me. The crowd's noise grew louder. A tiny voice whispered that this was my fifth foul—I was out of the game.

This is so wrong. They just gave the call to Diddy because he's Diddy. It's Rosa's fault—I can't sleep because of this story drama. I shoulda hit the last free throw. If Dontay wasn't giving me so much grief, I'd be in better shape.

I retreated to the opposite sideline and watched Diddy make his first free throw. The sweat felt like syrup rolling down my body. I couldn't watch the second free throw. My chest felt as if it were going to burst. I turned around and saw an empty chair. The crowd was flowing toward Diddy.

I grabbed the chair and threw it as hard as I could at the wall.

Diddy's second free throw clattered off the rim. I heard the faraway sound of a whistle blowing and a technical foul being some of your favorite haunts." Wilkins pulled up in front of the A.C. and put the car in park. The doorman walked up to the driver's-side window. Wilkins pulled his badge and the doorman scuttled inside the club like a roach into a crevice.

As scared as I was of being seen with Wilkins, every second with him was a second I didn't have to think about the ball game.

"So I go to strip clubs. That ain't no crime."

"What about that weed stashed in that gym bag of yours?" Wilkins said, watching a group of drunk Wall Streeters enter the A.C. "What's that weed delivery service all y'all *Fever* boys like to use, that 917 number? Maybe you'd rather talk about that, huh?"

I said nothing. It was all I had left at that point.

Wilkins reached into his pocket and handed me a picture of a man wearing a Pittsburgh Penguins jersey and standing on a street corner. One of the jersey's arms hung empty at his side.

"Maurice Milligan was a local DC promoter when Taylor was at Howard. After Taylor started the magazine, money was real tight and he got a ten-thousand-dollar loan from Maurice. After a while Maurice decided that he was entitled to a piece of the magazine."

Wilkins pulled out a pack of Newports and offered me one. I scrunched up my nose, wishing I had a blunt instead, and he lit it for himself.

"Leak caught Maurice coming out of a strip club just like this one. He held him trapped in a basement for three days. Maurice considers himself lucky that all Leak did was smash his arm to bits with a sledgehammer."

called on me. Two more shots for Bad Boy, plus poss
the ball after that.

I slunk out the gym as Main Event drilled the fre
to seal the win.

The hot night fell on me as I pushed through tl
doors. I wanted to dig a hole and climb inside.

"You look kind of lost," a voice said. I turned ar
an older black man, square-shaped, wearing a suit and
Afro.

"You don't remember me?" he said. As soon as he ext
his card, I remembered the FBI agent's name: Wilkins.

The inside of Wilkins's car smelled like chicken and cigar
this time. I leaned my head against the window as he d
across town.

"We know that some rappers are trying to import a
load of heroin. What we don't know is exactly who."

"Neither do I."

"Are you sure? Maybe it's Leak. There's no talk in t
office about it? No people from out of town you've never se
before?"

The air-conditioning was making my nose run. I pulled o
my sweat-soaked jersey, blew snot into it, and stuffed it int
my bag. I took a new white T-shirt out of the plastic and pu
that on.

"I can't talk to you, man. You know what they do tc
snitches? Matter fact, you're driving too close to the office. I
can't be seen with you, man. I got nothing to say to you. You
need to let me the fuck out."

"I'm not going near your office. I thought we'd spin by

I rolled down my window and the cigarette smoke seeped out, replaced by the scrambled sounds of the night.

"Why did Taylor really hire you, Marq?" Wilkins said. "It wasn't for your writing, I'll tell you that. It wasn't for your hoop skills—I thought the ref made the right call tonight, by the way. You went over Diddy's back. But Taylor's using you, and Taylor is in Leak's pocket, which means that Leak owns you. Is that what you want?"

Is that what I want? I want to grab hold of my life, that's what I want. I want to go to sleep for a week. I want to go home to Holliday and watch movies and make my free throws.

The photo nudged a few things around in my brain. I handed it back to Wilkins, pulled out my Sidekick, and sent Chunk a message.

CAN YOU BELIEVE THE FBI IS HAWKING ME?
I'M AT THE A.C. COME THROUGH SO WE CAN
GET AT SOME OF THESE HOES.

"Check this out," I said, turning to look at Wilkins. "I'll keep my eyes open. I got a lot on my mind right now, and maybe if you can help me, I can help you. Now if you'll excuse me, I got to go smoke some weed before I lose my muhfuckin' mind."

CHAPTER 51

"Taylor got a Ferrari?" Chunk exclaimed as we stumbled out the A.C. It was a vicious yellow beast, with a threatening rumble even at rest. The passenger door was raised up like a bird's wing. I gave Chunk and Wop good-bye pounds and fell into the smooth leather seat.

"Don't worry about tonight's game," Taylor said. "It wouldn't even have been close without you."

I was so bent, the nighttime neon left smudgy trails across my vision. I forced myself to think about what was happening to me.

"What were you hoping to get out of all this?" I asked.

"All of what?"

"Stop playin' with me, man!" I yelled. Taylor blinked his long eyelashes, hard. "You know what the fuck I mean. What did you want out of this Daminion story? You need to come clean before I start listening to what the FBI is saying."

I tossed Wilkins's card into his lap. He took a hand off the wheel to examine it, then tucked it into the breast pocket of his shirt. When he spoke, he sounded genuinely remorseful.

"I messed up, Marq. I was supposed to snatch that story before Rosa could get it. I didn't even expect her to still be here at this point. So I let you down, and I'm sorry for that. I really am. But we can fix this. What Rosa did is grounds for dismissal, so now's the time to get her outta there. And I spoke to Tommy yesterday and told him it's not your fault. You did your thing with this story, and we're gonna publish it just the way you wrote it."

We were stopped at a light on Forty-fifth and Broadway. Even at this hour the street was filled with pedestrians. I wished I were one of them, innocent and unaware.

"Taylor."

"What's up?"

"You didn't answer my question. Why did you want me to write about Tommy?"

We rumbled into a parking garage. The attendant's eyes gaped when he saw the vehicle. "We're gonna be a while," Taylor told him, handing him three twenty-dollar bills with the keys.

"When I sold the *Fever*, I thought that was the pinnacle for me," Taylor said as we joined the sidewalk traffic. "I was looking forward to kicking back and having someone else deal with all the pressure. But then I found out that I was addicted to the game. I couldn't sit there and watch when I knew I could do it better. So we started putting together a crew to buy back the magazine. And the first person on board was Meyer Mahl. We're starting a record label slash magazine company. It makes perfect sense—we can cross-promote all our own artists."

We walked into a small vestibule and Taylor pressed a button.

"So you guys wanted to sign Slow Creep," I said, "and you thought a negative story on Tommy would knock him out of the running."

The door buzzed and we walked through. The elevator dinged its arrival.

"I didn't want it to be *that* negative. Just the truth, which would be enough to slow him down until we signed Creep." We got off at the twentieth floor and walked down the hall and through a door marked HILLTOP PROMOTIONS.

Tell them Fever *muhfuckas they don't want me to live up to everything they heard about me. . . .*

"You weren't worried about what Tommy would do if he found out?" I asked.

Taylor shot the cuffs of his suit jacket, smiled, and put his hand on a door marked STUDIO. "It was a miracle that Tommy beat that case. And even if he did, so what? The *Fever* ain't to be fucked with."

The door opened to a dim, pulsing mist of sound and smoke. The room was oval, larger than I expected. The entire thug half of the *Fever* staff was spread out on couches that ran along the side walls, with a dozen women mixed in, several with their shirts off. At the center of the room was the biggest mixing board I had ever seen, with a rainbow of LED lights dancing to the thudding beat. In front of the mixing board was a wide window looking into a sound booth.

Leak was at the microphone, sweat pouring down his bald head and soaking through his wifebeater, eyes closed.

> Dealing wit me you best stay suspicious
> Slugs hit yo' chest and you be like what is this
> Vultures of the industry, we mean business
> Chicks ride the triz-nain ma watch me twist this
> Bitch-ass niggas talk foul behind my back
> Acting like the four-fifth won't clap
> I got all I want from guns to cars
> In the pages of my magazine, son makes stars
> Snitch bitches I'll make you pay
> Bullets fly you spring a Leak then pass away
> I'm a thug from my head to my Timberlands
> The way I shine make you wish that you is my man . . .

Taylor took a seat in front of the mixing board and accepted a blunt from the engineer. He took two pulls and passed it to me. The bright light behind Leak made the sound-booth window look like a TV screen.

Leak finished his verse and opened his eyes. He pulled a small towel from his back pocket, mopped his face, and disappeared through a door in the back of the vocal booth.

"Lay-Lo, you up!" the engineer said. A dude got off the couch, clutching a legal pad. Taylor led me out of the room, down the hallway, and through another door into a small kitchen. Leak's slim frame was standing before a square table, a silver pistol handle adorning the front of his waistband like a rodeo belt buckle. Flanking the pistol, two Sidekicks and a BlackBerry were clipped to his belt. Leak poured three shots from a bottle of Goose and we all sat down.

"Salud," Leak said. We clinked glasses. Leak closed his eyes while he knocked back his liquor, then opened a cigar box filled to the top with prerolled blunts. He sparked one up and we passed it around once before he spoke.

"Welcome to the fam, son. You been holding us down, and now it's time for you to reap the benefits. Ask any of my niggas about what this here means." He wrapped a fist around his chain and shook his FEVER medallion.

I didn't know where he was going with this, so I nodded and said nothing.

"The feds had a hard-on for me ever since I was in them Pittsburgh streets, running shit up on the Hill. They had niggas snitchin' on me for years, but I'm still here, ahead of the game, rich as hell. And this Wilkins nigga the weakest of 'em all. I bet he told you them same lies he been telling the last ten years, showed you that tired-ass picture."

"So was his story true?" I asked. "About the sledgehammer?"

Leak put flame to another blunt. "Damn right it's true. Dude was fuckin' with my family. Taylor paid Maurice back, but then Maurice got greedy. Let me tell you something. All these niggas talk about I did this to Taylor, I did that, but this man right here is my brother. I'm holding Taylor down to the end of time—I put that on my *life*. Ain't nobody showed me more love than this man right here, and I will always love him, to the death."

Leak wore the same intense expression he had in the vocal booth. The harsh fluorescent light made his teardrop tattoos stand out like lint under black light. Taylor sat back nursing his drink, his pretty features arranged into a serious face. My mind trudged back over all the information I had gathered, looking for a leverage point, something that would help me.

"So what about the time you had the gun on Taylor?" I said.

Leak was now keeping the blunt to himself. "Like I said, we family. Family fight, they beef, but at the end of the day we always stand together. I got a real dark side, man. I try my best to control it, but that ain't always possible. That's why I stay smoking, so I won't wild out."

I poured myself another drink. I had been plenty drunk many times before, especially in college, even to the point of passing out. But I had never been as intoxicated as I was right then. The only way I could stay conscious was to keep imbibing.

"But sometimes I think cats *want* me to wild out, the way they come at me. When that happens, I'm a problem. I'm a real muthafuckin' problem." Leak's voice rose and I could see the veins in his neck jumping. "Niggas know they fuck with me or my squad, I'ma see you, and at that point it's a wrap. I don't care if you a kingpin or a peon, I'ma see you, personally.

Niggas know that. There ain't a dude behind the microphone realer than me when it come to these streets. I been grinding more than twenty years, man, from the vinyl era. We built this thing right here show by show, block by block. Nobody ever gave me nothing when it came to music—the opposite, really, because I had the magazine and all the conflicts and hate that came with that. So these fancy-ass rappity-rap cats can say what they want. Until they earn stripes like me, they can suck my dick. I'm the realest nigga on the mic since Tupac, ya heard?"

Leak picked up his towel from the table and mopped the scowl off his face.

"That's how we do it at the *Fever*, son. Haters say what they want, but we still here, stackin' paper. You can't ignore us. Now you part of the team, kid, so act like you know. Represent that shit to the fullest, ya heard?"

There was a long, flat velvet box on the table. Leak opened it and gently removed a long platinum chain with the gleaming *Fever* logo dangling from the end, three fists clenching one another tightly. He stood up and I instinctively bowed my head. The chain fell onto my shoulders. We drank and sparked.

"Go 'head, nigga. You know you wanna look," Leak said, motioning toward a mirror over the sink.

The pendant banged against my stomach as I walked. In the mirror the diamonds pulsed and flashed, brilliant against my white tee. Taylor clapped a hand onto my shoulder and nodded his head. "That's good money. You doing it big right now." Leak was on his cell phone behind him. *Tell 'em they ain't allowed in Pittsburgh, period. . . .* The diamonds rose and fell with my breath until my eyes traveled up the chain to my face.

A red-eyed stranger looked back, dry sweat-salt caked above stubbled cheeks, a fresh scratch from tonight's ball game etched below one ear. The thudding beat from the studio dragged a sick taste up from my stomach. Behind my head the kitchen was tilted like the deck of a ship at sea. My life rushed into the present. If I could have, I would have collapsed onto that cold floor and passed out.

"So what's the plan?" I said in the mirror to Taylor. "I'm lookin' at the FBI, Tommy Daminion, Rosa. . . . It ain't pretty. How we gonna do this?"

Taylor smiled, reached into his breast pocket, and pulled out a plane ticket. "The Baller, baby. It's like I told you. That's where it all goes down."

CHAPTER 52

Black folks have an old saying that will touch your soul: He and He alone knows how much I can bear. So only God knows how I survived a three-day bus ride to Florida with no food, no money, not even no batteries to listen to my music, just a pen and a pad and a life full of hate. It was hell on earth, a stinking, rolling hell, and I cursed you every mile.

But here I am. Large told me a lot of different ways that he went through hell and it gave him greater power in his own work. So my music will be even more powerful from all this. I'm ready to make another joint now. I'm ready to make twenty joints. This is when I'll decide what kind of celebrity I want to be.

Your father was a celebrity. He was somebody, had to be. And you never even knew. You the fact finder, the investigator, always trying to catch me in a contradiction when that's where my art comes from. I can look at something two different ways and see the beauty in both sides. Maybe that's because nobody ever taught me no discipline or boundaries. Anything I ever wanted I had to go get for myself. If I was hungry, I found me some food. So when I saw the feather in his hat, I just had to touch it. It had every color in the rainbow when my world was all gray. I was just a little boy—this was before you was born—but on some level I connected it to a real man made of flesh and blood who maybe could do something for me.

I looked at the feather through the crack in my door for about an hour that night before I crept out my room. The hat was on the couch. At any minute I thought the light would come on in Moms's room and she would come out and tear me to pieces. When I finally got the hat in my hands, I was disappointed. The feather was stiff and scratchy and slid down in the hat band when I touched it. I put the hat on my head and it smelled like cologne. I tried to remember what my daddy looked like, but I couldn't see anything. The hat was down over my eyes on my little head and I got so caught up, I didn't see the bedroom door open.

I felt a tap on the hat and froze. It raised up off my head on its own power. I kept my eyes shut tight. I felt a rap on my forehead and cracked my eyes open to see the strangest-looking dude I ever laid eyes on before or since. Pops is dark and handsome, I knew that much. This dude was . . . well, he looked like a cat. He had gray eyes like yours, big pink lips, and a white man's skin. He was fully dressed, down to his tie. He looked at me with his cat eyes and said, "Gimme my hat, lil' man, before I have to tell yo' mama on you."

He took his hat and left without another word. I dashed to my window so I could see him leave out the front door. There was a long black car waiting in front of our stoop. He got into the backseat and I never saw him again. But whoever he was, that man was your father.

Not my father, Marq. Yours.

I know what you're gonna say. Think about it, though: Did Moms ever come straight out and say who your daddy is? She let you think we have the same father because that was the easiest thing. I'm tryna save you here—you can't see that by now? If you woulda just listened to me, none of this woulda happened. Because my problem is not the drugs. My problem is you.

CHAPTER 53

Dozens of Tommy Daminions glared at me from the glass wall of a newsstand inside the Miami airport. I removed my sunglasses and absorbed the impact of the words on the magazine cover beneath Tommy's cipher of a face: BY MARQ WISE.

I pulled out my Sidekick in the taxi to the hotel and texted Rosa:

I CAN'T BELIEVE YOU DID THIS TO ME.

She had been avoiding me ever since the meeting in her office. I thought Taylor might prevail and get her to use my original, but Rosa's version was the one that was printed. Now I had no choice but to roll with it. And I felt like, Whatever is whatever. Just bring it.

The escalator gently lowered me into the hotel lobby, a glittering pastel fishbowl. All of the New York industry was there, plus an eager swarm of strangers. Every hat brim, shirt button, and untied shoelace had been set with precision. Familiar faces turned my way, pinky-ringed hands extended, greetings exchanged. But something felt different. People's energy changed around me—they had seen my story. Plus I had the ill chain on. *You got that swagger, son. . . . Black Will Shoot—sound like a hit record. . . .* I posted up near the bar with the Knots Landing crew, marinating my anxiety in alcohol, VIP laminate hanging around my neck next to the heavy FEVER pendant. The low roar of conversation wrapped around us like fog. People peeked at our badges and offered CDs, flyers, business cards, T-shirts. The check-in line was outrageous. Briana took me directly to the manager, who retrieved a room key as I listened to two guys try to convince a desk clerk that their reservation had been lost in the computer system.

The Baller convention program listed dozens of panels with names such as "How to Increase Your Spins," or "Downloading 101," or "Dirty South Marketing," and "The MySpace Revolution." I marked the ones featuring my favorite rappers and made plans to meet the *Fever* thugs before the unsigned-artists showcase.

The elevator doors were spaced three on each side of the vestibule, like domino dots. The area was so packed, I thought there must be some kind of disturbance. But it was just solid people, sweating despite the air-conditioning, waiting for a door to open. And waiting. Curses and body funk seeped through the air. I couldn't believe how long the elevators were taking—apparently too many people were waiting to descend. Maybe I could take the steps. I pulled out my room key and saw I was on the forty-third floor.

I texted Rosa again:

I USED TO THINK THE FEVER WAS FUCKIN SPECIAL.

Fifteen minutes later, my shirt soaked with sweat, I slid the key into my door, opened my room, and saw a strange set of luggage on the far bed. I checked the bathroom—empty. But the closet had a yellow suit and four silk shirts hanging in it, and there were empty Popeyes chicken containers on the table next to the TV.

I went back to the manager, a white dude with a black haircut, and told him that my room was still occupied. He apologized, checked his computer, and ordered me up a new key. The trip back upstairs took exactly twenty-seven minutes, but it went faster because a freestyle cipher jumped off by the elevators, a half-dozen dusty fellas in matching green T-shirts bouncing mediocre Southern boasts off one another until a California kid broke their rhythm with an improvisational challenge.

Count the best MCs, I'm top fifty in the nation
You been tryna get signed longer than this elevator's takin'
Now you at the Baller hopin' to catch notice
Claimin' Dirty South but sound like South Dakotas . . .

My new room also had someone else's luggage inside. Now I was mad. The manager upgraded me to a suite.

"I'm really sorry," he said, frazzled. "People are checking in for one night, but then they don't leave."

The *Fever* crew had three blunts circulating. Fully buzzed, we all mashed through the lobby, descended escalator after escalator to the bottom of the hotel, then headed for the unsigned-artists showcase. A distant thumping led us to the ballroom. We flashed our laminates, skirted the line, and entered the echoey space. The stage was empty but the room was full of familiar voices.

"We came all this way to see the same cats," someone observed.

"Nah," was the response. "We came here so all these wannabe niggas can see *us*."

A six-man crew clutching red plastic cups took the stage to general indifference. The ringleader had braids that slid sideways down his head, framing gangbanger sunglasses. The DJ zigga-ziggaed into a beat that eluded recognition. Sideways Braids chanted, "Boom! Boom! Put yo' hands up! Boom! Boom! Put yo' hands up! If you wanna hear Pimptastic, put yo' hands up!" A few girls in the front complied, apparently imported just for that purpose. For everyone else it was business as usual. An anonymous figure emerged from stage right and launched into an unintelligible flood of rapid-fire syllables. His associates paced behind him, reduced to gestures since Sideways Braids gripped the only extra mic.

Sideways Braids said, "Everybody in here feeling my man Pimptastic, I want you to throw the *P* in the muthafuckin' air. . . ."

No *P*s were thrown. After a few more futile minutes they were through.

That's when I heard the cough.

The rest of the world receded to a distant throb. Dontay coughed again, hacking up what sounded like a golf ball of phlegm, and I realized the sticky echo was coming from the tower of speakers on each side of the empty stage. I shook my head and the room swam. When it came back into focus, Dontay was behind the turntables, which sat atop a low platform to the left of the stage.

The top of Dontay's headphones dug a trench in his half-fro. He lowered chalky lips to the slim mic rising from the mixer and said, "Can we please have a moment of silence for the greatest MC in the history of hip-hop—the late, great William Christopher."

On the last word Dontay turned on the echo chamber. Conversation ebbed as the name reverberated through the ballroom.

"Large," he said, "rest in peace . . . peace . . . . peace . . . peace . . .

Someone flicked a lighter alive and raised it high in the gloom.

Dontay's hands moved above the turntables and Large's voice rang out, a cappella.

A black man stands in the belly of the beast—

Dontay spun back the record, let it go, then snatched it up and scratched it.

A black man stands—
A black man
Bikki-bikki-black man
Bikki-black man
Bikki-bikki-black man—

Someone started to clap. When it spread, Dontay freed the record and Large's voice swam atop the beat of the crowd.

A black man stands in the belly of the beast
Trapped behind bars built with foul speech
A three-piece dinner goes to the winner of the question
When'll y'all niggas learn a lesson
Stand around frontin' clutchin' on a Smif & Wesson
Straight hostile is the shape of your expression . . .

I immediately heard Dontay's voice beneath Large's aggressive baritone. At first he mimicked Large's every intonation, then added a mournful, harmonic tone. Then his hands moved above the mixer, fading out Large's voice until all that remained was Dontay's angry, accusatory rasp, riding the thunderous claps of the audience.

The words weren't from any Large record. They were Dontay's own.

> The equation, of the situation
> More devilish than a slave plantation
> A few good men had to be persecuted
> So the greedy man could have his plan executed
> In the process the truth got diluted
> My man L's legacy got convoluted
> Traitors perpetratin'
> Murderers skatin'
> Money change hands but the needy kept waitin'
> This is actual facts, son, no need debatin'
> The truth will make you sicker than a Muslim eatin' bacon—

A roar rose from the crowd. Dontay's slim figure bobbed deeply to the clapping hands, face down, staring at the turntables, headphones clamped over his ears. He had the attention of every single person in the room.

> Black music used to plead with a power that's higher
> Could the Lord please make my black burden lighter
> Now we spend lifetimes trapped in the gutter
> Sell crack to mothers, be the Number One Stunner

Hey little brother, did you ever ax your mother
'Bout your father
Nah son, you didn't bother
Whole generations had to raise ourselves
Might as well have grabbed the gat and just sprayed ourselves
I'm an old-skool nigga wit old stories to tell
And if you love my man Large, I wanna hear you yell

And right on beat, Dontay dropped The Joint.

The bass crushed the room with palpable force. There was a millisecond of stunned silence, and then the ballroom was a volcano of noise. Large's voice pummeled bodies into motion.

Africa to the Louvre
Large stay smoove
Large pay dues on boulevards they cruise
Souls I bruise, wise men turn fools
Ay yo, Dontay, make the beat jam on the groove . . .

Dontay slipped in the instrumental, spun back the vocal version, and then cut up his name to the beat.

Ay yo, Dontay
Dikki-Dikki-Dontay
Ay yo, Don-tik-tikki-tikki-tay
Ay yo, Dontay
Dikki-Dikki-Dontay
Dik-Don-Dik-Don-Dik-Dontay

My brother dropped the beat out and turned on the echo. He lifted his head and stared defiantly into the crowd as his name rang infinitely.

Dontay . . .
Dontay . . .
Dontay . . .
Dontay . . .
Dontay . . .

CHAPTER 54

"My first single has to be about Abraham," Dontay said.

The man laughed. He was tall and bald headed, with golden brown skin beneath a well-tailored pink seersucker suit with a crisp white shirt and white pocket square. The three of us were sitting in an empty Baller conference room.

There was a recording contract on the table.

"Abraham?" The man chuckled. "Who's that? Somebody you and Large used to run with?"

Dontay leaned back stiffly in his chair. His face was gaunt and unshaved, eyes wild. I cringed expectantly, then pulled out my Sidekick to distance myself from the situation and texted Rosa:

THE LEAST YOU COULD DO AFTER STABBING
ME IN THE BACK IS CALL ME BACK.

"The prophet Abraham," Dontay said. "The first of God's Manifestations. There's gonna be nine songs on my album: first Abraham, then Krishna, Moses, Buddha, Zoroaster, Jesus, Muhammad, the Báb, and Bahá'u'lláh."

The man leaned back his head and laughed deeply, exposing a mouth full of long white teeth. He leaned forward and wiped his eyes.

"Tell you what—if you can rock that like you killed it today, you can rap about Scientology all I care. I ain't never seen nobody turn out an industry crowd like that. I was thinking we could get Lil Jon to do the remix of that Large song you got."

Dontay's eyes narrowed. "I ain't releasing The Joint."

"You been talking about putting that out the past ten years!" I blurted.

Dontay got up and started pacing, rubbing the chest of his stained T-shirt as he walked. "Everything is beneficial if it's joined with the love of God. But without that love everything is harmful. Music can bring the spirit of life to someone who loves God. But to someone caught up in the material world, that same music can stain his heart with lust and hate. My music has to be spiritual food. Sounds are just vibrations that pass through the air and come into contact with the nerves inside your ear—that's what Abdu'l Bahá says. These vibrations are just chance phenomenons, but even so, they can move the heart and make your spirit tremble with joy."

The man raised his thick black eyebrows, wrinkling his smooth forehead. He waited for Dontay to sit back down before he spoke. He tried to look Dontay in the eye, but my brother had pulled a small, slim book out of his bag and was rapidly flipping through the pages.

"Look, man, you need Large on your record," the man said. "That's the difference between platinum and peanut butter, you feel me? So we gonna do this or what? You wanna get this money, or you wanna sit around talking all mystical? Because without Large we got nothin'."

Dontay stopped flipping pages. As he began to read, I got a familiar sinking feeling.

"With all his heart he should avoid fellowship with evildoers and pray for the remission of their sins," Dontay said in a trembling voice. "He should forgive the sinful and never despise his low estate, for none knoweth what his own end shall be. How often hath a sinner attained, at the hour of death, to the essence of faith and, quaffing the immortal draught, hath taken his flight unto the Concourse on high! And how often hath a devout believer, at the hour of his soul's ascension, been so changed as to fall into the nethermost fire!"

Dontay looked up from the book. Tears had painted wet trails down his ashy cheeks.

"Bahá'u'lláh," he said.

"Baha what?" the man asked.

"The Glory of God. Those are the words of the Glory of God."

The man stood up, gathered the contract from the table, and slowly put it back into his shiny black leather briefcase.

"And here I was thinking you wanted to be rich." He shook his head.

Dontay's face twitched, but he stayed silent. The man walked out. As soon as the door closed behind him, Dontay's frame sagged as if exhausted. He reached into his bag, removed a rickety pistol, and pushed it across the table to me.

"You better take this," he said. "I don't want to fall into that fire."

CHAPTER 55

I found Chunk in a suite on the thirty-third floor. He was alone in the spacious front room, leaned back on a couch, celly to his ear, piles of papers and clothes and CDs strewn about. The heavy drapes were wide open, ocean stretching to the clear blue horizon. On the coffee table was a huge Ziploc bag of weed the size of a loaf of bread. Stacked next to the table were six new Macintosh laptops, still in the boxes. Loud music throbbed from behind the bedroom door.

I waited until Chunk snapped his phone shut. "He's here," I said.

"Who?"

"My brother Dontay."

"Stop playin'."

"Nigga just rocked the unsigned showcase, had rhymes and everything."

"Dontay was on the *mic*?"

"That ain't the half. He tore it down! Some cat offered him a record deal on the spot. And he gave me this."

I untucked the gun from the small of my back. Chunk leaned forward with his mouth ajar.

"I'ont know what's more bugged out," Chunk said, taking it from my hand, "the record deal or this prehistoric pistol." He flipped open the cylinder. "This thing is loaded!" he exclaimed. I hadn't thought to check. "You better lemme hold this for you. He brought this down on the plane?"

"He took the Greyhound."

"I told you stop playin'!"

"Dude is out his mind. He had a record deal on the table in front of him and was talking straight gibberish so the dude just left. After that he was about to pass out, so I had to take him back to my room. Like I don't have enough to worry about already."

Chunk leaned back on the couch and contemplated the ceiling. I sank into an armchair, trying not to look at the sack of weed, still in shock that Dontay was in Miami. He didn't even have a suitcase, just his shoulder bag with a few CDs and a half pack of Newports. I had plenty of room in my suite, but there was no way I could give him a key. I needed to get rid of him, fast.

"Aiight, first things worst," Chunk finally said. "You ain't in no danger. Tommy's heated about the story, but he believes you that you didn't write it that way."

The memory of my betrayal made me pull out my Sidekick and message Rosa:

BITCH, WHEN YOU GONNA ANSWER ME?

The bedroom music got louder for a second as the door opened and closed. A sweaty older dude emerged with his shirt unbuttoned, exposing greasy chest hair and a potbelly. He gave a mock shiver, lips flapping from side to side.

"Damn, that was crazy, kinfolk! What you feeding them girls?"

Chunk laughed and gave him a pound. "You know how

we do. Don't forget this here." He took a laptop off the stack and put it into a large plastic shopping bag. "I'ma call you next week about that record."

The front door closed. "What was *that* about?" I asked.

"Spins, nigga. I'm in the independent promotion game now. We get your records played. Dude runs the biggest station in Houston."

The bedroom door opened and another man came out. He exited the suite without a word.

I sized up the situation. "So if you gotta buy weed and computers, plus dole out cash bribes, where's your money in this hustle?"

Chunk laughed, his beefy shoulders bouncing up and down. "The labels, nigga! They can't be associated with all this. So they pay the promoters to get their records played. And that's where—"

There was a pounding at the door. "Poh-leece! Open up!"

I put as much space between me and the weed as I could.

Bang bang bang bang bang. "Poh-leece! Open the damn door!"

I darted into the bedroom, looking for a way out. The drapes were drawn, with just a hint of sunlight leaking in around the edges. Smoke and a strong wet-grass aroma hung heavily in the air. When my eyes adjusted to the darkness, I saw a half-dozen men gathered in a semicircle, sitting on chairs and the edge of the bed. In the middle of the circle was a single chair, somehow bearing the weight of an immensely obese man naked from the waist down. The folds of his doughy, pockmarked buttocks reminded me of a circus elephant sitting on a stool. A woman's face was buried in his lap. The man shuddered and she raised her head.

It was Shortcake.

"What up, Marq," Wop said from the corner. "Wanna quick dick suck?"

My stomach lurched. Shortcake hustled into the bathroom, exposing her perfect thonged ass, and I felt aroused despite my revulsion. I heard laughter from the front room and opened the door. Squinting against the light, I recognized Black sitting on the sofa, rolling a blunt, and grinning.

"How you gonna give me a pound of shake from all that weed you sellin'," Chunk was saying, "then come smoke up all my profit?"

"Because you cain't leave nary scrap of weed around me, just on principle," Black said jovially. "You got to keep the grass far from the goat."

Black noticed me and chortled. "What up, my nigga. So now it's your turn in Tommy's doghouse, huh? I thought your story was hot, myself. Y'all coulda got a better picture of me, though. Y'all tryna make a nigga look fat."

"You *are* fat," Chunk said.

"Nah, I'm just prosperous. Ay yo," Black said, looking at my face, "what's wrong with you? Tommy ain't gonna kill ya. He's practically a law-abiding citizen these days."

"Nah, it's his brother," Chunk said. "You know, that *dude*. The one your boy got a problem wit." Black and Chunk exchanged a meaningful glance. Black stroked the graying hairs on his chin.

"That's really your brother? Y'all don't look nothing alike," Black said. "What happened with him and Julien?"

"I'ont really know," I said. "You can never tell what's real with Dontay."

"You know Julien is tryna see dude."

"See him like *see* him?"

"Word. What you think about that?" Black and Chunk studied me with identical blank expressions.

I already had enough problems. I didn't need to add a guy like Julien to the list.

"I ain't my brother's keeper," I said. "He's a grown-ass man. He gotta take care of himself."

"That's what *I'm* sayin'," Chunk said, looking at Black.

The music got louder in the other room. Black and I sat on the couch passing the blunt back and forth. "So how did your story get all twisted?" Black finally asked.

"The editor did it." I felt Rosa's whisper on my ear—*We would be so dope together*—and then my Sidekick was in my hand.

YOU AND THE FEVER CAN KISS MY BLACK ASS.

I let the anger ebb from my chest and forced myself to think. There was still one last thing I needed to know.

"So who's gonna sign Slow Creep?"

Black and Chunk made eye contact. Black silently began rolling another blunt—rotate the cigar leaf with the weed inside, lick a section shut, rotate and lick, rotate and lick. Chunk picked up his cell.

Something was going on, and this time I wasn't going to get played for a sucker. I thought back to the last time I had seen Black—at Kaya, when he had all but confirmed that Slow Creep had a drug connection. And there was Agent Wilkins sniffing around.

"Creep is selling more than music down here, ain't they," I said.

Black scrutinized his completed blunt like a scientist peering at a test tube. I turned to Chunk, who had his phone pressed to his ear.

"So where they at?" I asked.

Chunk waved me off and put a finger into his free ear. I knocked the phone out of his hand and stared at him. "What's wrong with you, man?" He bristled. "If my cell is broke, you buying me a new one."

Black was leaned back on the couch blowing smoke rings toward the ceiling. Black the hustler . . . *I sell hundreds of pounds at a time.* . . . *Our lives depend on this.* . . . *The science of a nigga's still yet to be found.* . . . *Especially yours* . . .

That's when I knew. I knew what was going down, and I knew what I wanted—to be like them. I wanted to live without rules, to show Holliday that I was more like her daddy than she knew, to stand unconquerable before a world designed to defeat me.

I took two pulls off the blunt but didn't pass it back to Black. That got his attention.

"I need to roll with you when you get at the Creep."

He gave a short chuckle. "Yeah, right."

"Nah, for real though. I need to roll."

"You crazy."

"I never been more serious in my life." I searched for something in this situation that would benefit him. "Think about how useful a guy like me could be."

Silence.

"You can trust me. Remember when I picked up your gun in LA? Remember Emp? You can trust me."

"Maybe I can. But you told Tommy the same thing, and look how that turned out."

My Sidekick buzzed. Rosa!

```
YOU TALK ABOUT BACKSTABBING AND YOU'RE
ROCKING ONE OF LEAK'S CHAINS. WHEN YOU
GET BACK TO NEW YORK, DON'T BOTHER COMING
TO THE OFFICE. YOU'RE FIRED.
```

I shot up off the couch to hurl the Sidekick through the window into the ocean, then somehow stopped myself. I clenched my eyes tight and forced my mind to slow down, to search for some escape from what my life had become.

Black was watching me from the sofa. I showed him Rosa's message.

"Check it," I said, taking a deep breath. "As you can see, I'm looking for a new situation. I'm a loyal dude with unique skills. And I know what's going down with Slow Creep regardless. I don't work at the *Fever* no more, so ain't like I'ma write about anything. And even if you don't take me to see them, you know I can get enough information to probably show up uninvited." Black's eyes narrowed. "And that wouldn't be a good idea at all," I continued. "So just tell me—how can I be down?"

Black and Chunk exchanged a long, cryptic look. Chunk finally shrugged and said, "Can't hurt in this situation. Might even help."

"Aiight, fuck it," Black said, hefting himself to his feet. "But I'ma let you know. Our lives depend on this—especially yours!"

CHAPTER 56

Black and I were standing in the valet-parking area of the hotel when I heard a clatter by his legs. I looked down and saw a sleek little black pistol next to his Reebok. Compared with the gun Dontay had handed me, it looked like something from the future. My hand itched for it.

Black grabbed at his waist, then shook his leg like a dog and accidentally kicked the gun. It skidded across the pavement, coming to rest in front of several red suitcases belonging to a blond-haired family of four.

Black shot me a mischievous glance and sauntered over to them. "Welcome to Miami, everybody," he said. "Y'all coming or going?"

"Going," the parents said in unison. The whole family was holding hands. The boy looked about nine and the girl a few years younger. He was staring at the pistol at Black's feet.

Black followed his gaze and cracked a big smile. He picked up the gun, twirled it around his finger like a cowboy, then lifted up the front of his shirt and stuffed it into the waistband of his sweatpants. The boy's mouth dropped open.

"Are you 50 Cent?" he asked.

Black tilted back his head and laughed as the valet handed him the keys to a silver Lexus convertible. He popped the trunk, which was tightly packed with boxes of CDs, and removed a handful of loose discs. He slipped them into a blue nylon gym bag and tossed the bag into the tiny backseat of the convertible. I got into the passenger seat and leaned back into soft leather.

Before Black pulled off, he rolled to a stop near the family. The boy's wide blue eyes were level with the top of my door.

"50 Cent don't got as much money as me." Black chortled, then took off.

Top down, hot air beating on my numb face, we drove into the setting sun along an elevated highway that led over the water from Miami Beach back to Miami. I had on a new pair of Air Jordan Vs, and they were a bit too large at the ankle. I tucked my digital recorder in there, just in case. The radio was off and Black was silent. I thought about how I could pry Dontay out of my room. He had to leave sometime. Maybe I could switch to another room and just disappear. But that would mean losing the suite.

The navigational system told us to exit the highway. We turned onto an avenue lined with decrepit commercial buildings that gave way to blocks pocked with empty lots. Black faces stared at us as we slid past, their gazes bouncing off our mirrored sunglasses. We passed a park with shirtless youngsters flitting across a dusty baseball field. The neighborhood turned residential and more upscale. Soon we drove into a parking lot fronting a row of new town houses.

I saw Slow Creep's truck, painted flat black with those huge slitted eyes. It was the same truck I had seen back in New York, outside the first club Taylor had taken me to.

Black killed the engine. The truck's passenger door creaked open. A slender guy in wrinkled linen jumped down, walked over to us, and gave Black a pound.

"This is Slow Creep's manager, Foochie," Black told me.

"Foochie, this my man Marq. Let's go inside. Where your boys at?"

On cue Trophy and Bizack emerged from a side door of the truck. Their pale faces were young and serious, with wispy mustaches and thin tufts of chin hair. Oversize T-shirts swallowed their thin torsos and denim shorts hung down to their calves. The major difference between them was that Trophy wore white crew socks beneath adidas flip-flops, while Bizack sported red and black first-edition Air Jordans.

I was dumbfounded by the Jordans. I had never seen a pair of first editions except on the Internet. My feet felt hot, and the hidden recorder chafed my ankle.

We all followed Black up the steps of a town house. He pulled a single key from his pocket and opened the front door. We walked past a spotless kitchen and dining room, down a long, high-ceilinged hallway, then turned a corner and descended four steps into a sunken living room. It was sparse and modern, two stories high, dominated by a huge flat-screen TV and an even bigger empty fish tank. Bizack turned on BET and leaned back on the couch as the "So Crispy" video played. Trophy stood two feet from the empty tank, staring intently inside. I sat nervously on the edge of an armchair.

Black plopped down onto a love seat. "So we gonna make some history or what?" he said. "Like I been sayin', nobody else got my connects across the board, you feel me?"

"Word, 'cause I'm looking for other ways of making paper besides music," Bizack said, staring at the plump blue gym bag at Black's feet. I was surprised to see that Bizack's eyes were bluer than the boy's at the hotel. Black followed Bizack's gaze and grinned.

"Yo, this is *ill*," Trophy said, staring into the cavernous tank. Jittery, I popped up and went over to look. The bottom of the tank was a carefully constructed rocky landscape, punctuated by ceramic human figurines, all naked, sculpted into various frightened poses. Live snakes of various sizes and colors were intertwined among the figurines. I shuddered and returned to my seat.

Black reached inside the gym bag, drew out a handful of CDs, and handed them to Foochie. "Here's how your *South Coast Creep* mixtape came out. Your lawyer has the countersigned contracts. And *here*"—Black shoved his hand inside the bag again—"is an eighty grand advance on the tape." He withdrew eight bundles of bank-fresh money and tossed them onto Bizack's lap. Trophy left the tank and sat down next to his partner. "You gonna see plenty more paper on the back end once that joint start sellin'."

My mind flashed back to the Houston hotel room. Black had gotten two hundred fifty thousand dollars for the tape— and said there was no more coming.

I looked at the gym bag. It was still full.

"So," Black said, "why don't we get down to the real business of the evening? I need to know where all this is coming from."

Trophy rubbed his hands together with a hungry expression. Both rappers started to speak at once, stopped, then started again. They looked at Foochie and he nodded. Bizack shoved Trophy with one hand and spoke alone this time.

"Aiight, so Foochie is from Detroit and know these Ay-rab niggas who own a store, right? Turns out they got connects back in Afghanistan—"

"Some real Taliban shit, ya heard?" Trophy interrupted.

"And you know what they grow in Afghanistan—"

"Poppies, son—that's what the H comes from."

"So the Ay-rab hooked it up. It's all in the truck outside."

"Where'd you take delivery?" Black asked.

"Here in Miami," they said in unison.

"You brought the connect's info? Like we said, I can get a better price next time 'cause I got Mexican friends."

Foochie pulled a folded piece of paper out of his pocket and handed it to Black.

"Now what you got for us?" Trophy said, rubbing his hands together again.

"I got what I said I'd get," Black said. He grinned, zipped open the bag, and held it upside down. Bundle after bundle of cash spilled to the floor.

Bizack dropped to his knees in the middle of the pile, like a parched man who stumbled on an oasis. Trophy had a dreamy look on his face as he started neatly stacking bundles on a low coffee table.

I felt a hot flash of envy toward these two rappers who were sitting on what seemed to be at least a million dollars.

Black looked at his watch. "This is a big day, my niggas. We gonna make history and a lotta money together. This is the start of a beautiful—what the fuck?"

Two men in ski masks were standing at the top of the living-room steps.

CHAPTER 57

"You know what this is," the first ski mask said, pointing a shotgun at us. "Lay down and don't nobody play hero."

My muscles were frozen with fear. How could Black get caught like this? "Is you crazy?" Black said, stepping forward. "You don't know who I am?"

Ski Mask Number One hopped down into the living room and shoved his shotgun into Black's chest. Black shrank back until he was up against the far wall. Ski Mask Two stood at the top of the steps, silently pointing his own shotgun at Trophy, Bizack, Foochie, and me.

Black's hands were inching toward the place where he had shoved his gun. I pleaded with my eyes for him to stop. "I'ma ax you one more time," Black said. "Do you know who you fuckin' with? This is Six-Oh Crip right here, muthafuckin' South Central Los Angeles killer. Black will shoot, nigga—you can ax anybody. I got a hundred muthafuckas in my hood ready to kill up shit for me. And even if y'all murder me, my niggas gonna get payback."

Ski Mask One shoved his firearm into Black's pillow of a belly, freezing Black's hands. "I said don't play hero. I'ont care who you is," he growled. "If everybody don't lay facedown on the floor, I'ma start pullin' this trigger."

Black lay facedown—but Ski Mask One didn't take Black's gun.

He didn't take the gun.

It was another setup. Just like Chunk robbing Young Spank in Brooklyn. I waited for relief from the tension filling my body, but instead I regretted ever asking to ride with Black. What if Slow Creep made a move and someone got shot? What had I been thinking asking to ride with Black? I felt an almost physical yearning to be back home in Brooklyn, sitting on the couch with Holliday, watching TV, reading the newspaper, living a normal life.

Ski Mask One forced us to lie facedown on the carpet with our hands behind our heads. He patted everyone down and removed guns from Slow Creep and their manager. Then he scooped the cash into Black's gym bag and tossed it to Ski Mask Two standing at the top of the steps.

The fibers of the beige carpet scratched my cheek. I was lying between Black and Bizack. The acrid stink of Bizack's armpits hit my nostrils.

"Yo, son, you got to do something!" Bizack whispered, heightening my fear. I thought he was talking to me until Black whispered fiercely back, "They got the drop on us, cuz! Right now it is what it is. Cool out and we'll clean this up later."

"That's my money they got!" Trophy whispered from the other side of Black.

"Somebody musta followed your stupid truck," Black said. "Or the connect is settin' y'all up. I can't believe y'all rookie muthafuckas is gettin' me ganked like this."

All of a sudden Bizack flipped over and lunged for something. My heart almost jumped out of my chest. There was a sickening crunch and Bizack's face bounced off the floor, inches away from me, leaving a bright red stain on the carpet. When he opened his mouth, teeth fragments spilled onto the floor.

"I thought I told you to lay your cracker ass down," Ski Mask Two said. The voice was a familiar squeak-rasp. "This a black man's world right here. Stop tryna act like y'all bruddahs!"

I remembered the voice. It was Julien.

Heart pounding in my ears, I caught a glimpse of Bizack. His eyes were closed, long brown eyelashes lying wet against his pale skin. Snot dripped from his narrow, sharply pointed nose.

Footsteps faded down the hallway. Black scrambled to his feet. Trophy knelt over Bizack and tried to shake him out of unconsciousness. On his knees, Foochie screamed with anger and shook two middle fingers at the sky. Black ran to the front door, then walked slowly back into the living room, a picture of dejection.

"I never thought I'd see the day *I* got got," he said. "I guess there's a first time for everythang. But this ain't gonna be the first time I kill somebody who took something that's mine. Foochie, y'all can stay here and get cleaned up. Me and Marq gonna go handle this business."

CHAPTER 58

Slow Creep's truck was gone from in front of the house. We hopped into the Lexus and sped through the humid streets. I waited until we were back on the freeway to ask Black what happened. He just smiled and turned up Rick Ross on the CD player.

A picture of Bizack's smashed mouth kept playing through my head, making me cringe all over again. . . . *Slap ya in the head I'ma open one* . . . Rick Ross rapped. I wondered how Bizack would be able to rap with all those broken teeth. Violence sounded so abstract on records, but up close it was horrifying.

Black dropped me off in front of the hotel and went to park the car himself. As the hotel doors slid open, the sound of a thousand hungry voices smacked me in the chest. The lobby was even more crowded than before, filled with people whose lack of laminates branded them as outsiders. The escalator lowered me into their midst. I waded to the bar, pushed to the front, and ordered a Heineken and a double shot of Hennessy.

A heavy hand clamped down on my shoulder. "THE FUCK YOU DOIN' HERE, SON?"

Without thinking I knocked the hand off me, whirled around, and cocked back my bottle, ready to smash it into somebody's head.

Looking back at me was Chunk, eyes wide. I felt beer dripping down my arm.

"Yo, son, you should see your face!" he said. "You need to go spark a blunt or something, 'cause you scaring me right about now." Chunk slid up to the bar on one side of me, wearing slacks, a crisp white flat-collared shirt, and big diamonds in both ears. Wop took the other side, dressed in lime green from hat to gators. I put my glass back on the bar and the bartender refilled it.

"Shit is really real right now, son." I started to tell Chunk about the Slow Creep jooks, but he put a finger to his lips.

"So you ready to go to the Willie Awards?" he asked. "They started a half hour ago."

"Hell naw. I'm going home." Now my desire to live Chunk's life seemed absurd, another wrong turn in this doomed summer.

"Home? Why you say that?"

"I'm done, yo," I said, trying to keep the quaver out of my voice.

"It's only tight for us to flow through the Willies real quick," Chunk insisted. "It's the big bash, son, where the big dawgs run. Three months ago you wouldnta been allowed in the building. You come a long way. I'm prouda you, my nigga. Let's go celebrate and then you can be out."

I had every intention of going back to my room until I remembered that Dontay was there. So I knocked back my drink and followed Chunk as we struggled through the throng, stopping every few feet to greet someone. The ballroom was dark when we entered, a sweating comedian spotlighted onstage.

". . . y'all know he the only cat in the industry who recoups off bootleggers," the comedian said. There was a swell of mirth in the room. "For real though. I seen a line of Africans outside his office with crumpled bills stuffed into some fake Louis Vuitton bags, talking 'bout, 'You can haf de bag, too! I sell Kanye Wess dis same bag—it is real!'"

I scanned the room as laughter danced in the air. Dozens of round tables were packed into the huge space, each ringed by about twenty chairs. Resting atop bloodred tablecloths was enough champagne to drown France. The guests wore their finest—suits and linens, cuff links and gators, derbies and bowlers and fedoras. Diamonds glittered like city lights seen from an airplane.

"And the payola, man—forget about it," the funnyman continued, grinning into the lights. "You wouldn't believe the stuff he's giving the radio cats. Money, drugs, cars, jet planes. You remember Big Brawls's last record? They was givin' away virgins for that one, dawg. For real though. Virgins. I know because there was a bunch of Al Qaeda suicide bombers outside the station that day, talking 'bout, 'I don't want to die! I just want to hear the new Big Brawls record!'"

The comic waited for the laughter to die down, then said, "They tried that virgin trick with the new Trina joint." He chuckled to himself. "But once the virgins heard the record, they wouldn't give it up unless somebody bought 'em a Benz."

This time the comedian shouted over the avalanche of hilarity. "And then Meyer leased them hoes some Hondas and recouped Benz money from Trina's record sales!" The room detonated. "Ladies and gentlemen, the guest of honor, the Big Willie of the Year in the building—everybody give it up for Meyer Maaaahl!"

The spotlight zoomed to a table in the front of the room. Meyer was sitting there with a half smile on his face.

Sitting next to Meyer was Tommy Daminion. Sitting next to Daminion was Black. And sitting next to Black, wearing a bright red alligator-skin jacket, was Julien.

Applause cascaded through the room as Meyer walked to the podium, shaking hands along the way. Back at the table Black leaned over and said something into Julien's ear. Julien cracked up. Daminion poured champagne for Black and Julien. They all toasted and drank.

I looked around the huge room and contemplated that I was the only one who knew the real Slow Creep story. I waited for the familiar sense of satisfaction that usually accompanied my solving a story. But instead there was an empty feeling at the knowledge that I could never publish what I knew.

My Sidekick vibrated. It was a message from Daminion.

WHY DON'T YOU STOP BY MY TABLE FOR A MOMENT.

I started walking alone toward the head table as Meyer leaned down and lifted the microphone on the podium to his height.

"All right, all right, settle down everybody, let's not get carried away," he said in that peculiar enunciated accent, squinting as his eyes got used to the lights. He removed a missile of a cigar from the inside breast pocket of his sleek navy suit. "I know a lot of you never expected to see me here. And now here I am. So Tommy . . . can you please let my wife and children go now?"

That brought down the house. I was halfway across the room as the spotlight flashed on the head table. Daminion was leaned back in his seat, smiling broadly with his thumbs tucked behind the lapels of his pin-striped suit. Black was doubled over with laughter, and Julien was slapping Black on the back with one hand and covering his mouth with the other.

"Okay, okay, all jokes aside," Meyer said. The corners of his mouth returned to their default frowning position as he leaned forward with one hand on each side of the podium. "It's great to be here among so many people we've done business with over the years. These are hard times in our business, hard times indeed. Downloaders are stealing our property as I speak this sentence. Record stores are closing their doors. The competition for our customers' time and money has never been tougher.

"But there is something special about what we do. We provide a product that you can't get from a video game or a DVD or a fucking computer screen. The world *needs* music. And the world needs us to find the genius buried in the millions of untalented schmucks out there, and to polish and refine that genius, and to put that sound on people's car radios and concert stages and iPods and ringtones and wherever else this crazy world takes us. There is value in our business. There is meaning. There is *soul*. Never forget that. . . ."

I slid into the empty seat next to Daminion. His calm eyes flicked over me and I became painfully aware of my sneakers, sweaty Sean John polo, and creased linen shorts. But whatever. I'd be out soon anyway.

"Which brings me to the fact that there are still some superstar acts in this business," Meyer was saying. "There are still some artists who can send people running to buy their record when it comes out. And I'm very pleased to say that we have plenty of this type of artist at Fresh Beat Records."

Meyer looked out over the crowd. He had everyone hooked.

"We have just signed Slow Creep to Fresh Beat Records." The room inhaled. "Their album will be dropping this fourth quarter. I look forward to working with all of you on this historic release. . . ."

I felt a poke in my ribs. Daminion was looking at me with his unreadable eyes.

"Here's a story for ya," he said. "Black signed Slow Creep to a production deal with Daminion Entertainment. And I signed them to Fresh Beat. Taylor thought he could knock me out with your story, but it's obvious now that was a miscalculation." He allowed himself a small smile.

I looked at Black and Julien. "You don't have to worry about me telling," I blurted.

"Tell what?" Black chortled. "That someone got robbed for some mixtape money? I ain't see no contraband. Did you?" he said, elbowing Julien.

"How could I see something when I wasn't there?" Julien said, staring at me intently.

"Now, my brother," Daminion said quietly, "you need to get out of here and clean yourself up."

Daminion pointed at my shirt. I looked down and saw the stain. It was Slow Creep's blood.

CHAPTER 59

I'll never forget the night we made The Joint. It was in one of them classic Brooklyn basements, the floor more dirt than concrete and rough walls that looked like a cave. Niggas was down there weeded up, smoke so thick you could barely see through it. I hooked up my drum machine and started banging out the beat. The idea had jumped into my head coming over the Manhattan Bridge. I was in the last car of the train, all alone. I saw the skyline—this was when the World Trade was still up. And them two towers just got to me, man. Cause if you actually stop to think about them, it's incredible! How could a man build something like that? A hundred, hundred fifty, years ago, wasn't no building in New York more than a couple stories tall. It ain't no accident that skyscrapers was invented after the Promised One came. We living in a New World Order. And when I looked at all them buildings, I got a strange sensation, like power and ambition. It was like I had a purpose. That's where the song came from. But it never came out of me until I was in the basement with Large.

He was just kicking rhymes as I played with the drum machine. Niggas was passing blunts around. There's a reason so many rap dudes smoke weed—because it expands the way you think and what you believe is possible. Ain't nothing really wrong with weed—it ain't bad for you. It lets you make connections that you can't normally put together. And when you add that to my music, Large was inspired. It was the best song he ever wrote.

> Tall nigga, name of Dontay
> I rap tight like turbans in Bombay
> Best restaurants, the best entrées
> Blow like volcanoes in the land of Pompeii
> I say, borough to borough
> Nuts like a squirrel
> Fight the power like COINTELPRO heroes
> Intellectual
> But I'll stab you with a fork
> Magnitude greater than all New York
> Never eat pork or swine, know what I'm saying?
> The brothers is seekin' justice, wit no delayin'
> Like water from a hose is how this knowledge be sprayin'
> I want my music what the whole world be playin'
> Africa to the Louvre
> Large stay smoove
> Large pay dues on boulevards they cruise

Souls I bruise, wise men turn fools
Ay yo, Dontay, make the beat jam on the groove . . .

Dude laid it down in one take! One take! You know how hard that is? After we listened to it, everybody realized that we just made history. So we start celebratin, Private stock and weed and all that. And right there is when I first smoked cocaine.

I never woulda touched it if Large hadn't pulled it out. He had a single vial, with a blue top. I kept that vial with me every day since then. It means the world to me. Large took it out and sprinkled some crumbs into the blunt. I knew I could handle it, and I did. Wasn't no big deal—I didn't feel like I could go jump off a roof or anything. Cocaine still ain't no big deal to me. It's just a symptom of all the stress I've been forced to deal with all my sorry life. Soon I'm gonna have to face the consequences of every-thing I did. And I'll have to face them alone.

CHAPTER 60

Dontay was kneeling in front of the coffee table when I opened the door, pounding out a beat with his fists. A burning ciga-rette dangled from his lips. Room-service trays and a bottle of cognac were spread around the floor.

He had a smile on his face. "I got a new song," he said, keeping the beat going on the table. "Another classic. Check out the hook."

Who's that knocking at my back door
It's a face I seen before
Who's that knocking at my back door
Looks like a sinner to me

He was singing more than rapping, sounding like a bluesman, eyes closed, swaying to the sound of his own voice. Oblivious to the world. I started throwing my clothes into a duffel bag and contemplating my options once I got back to New York. Somehow Dontay seemed to be worthy of blame for my predicament. I started to cut him off but he raised his voice and kept on.

Who's that standing in the cocaine house
Death coming from out their mouth
Who's that standing in the cocaine house
Looks like a sinner to—

Dontay abruptly coughed, long and wet, then swallowed. "Lemme get that piece back," he said.

"Piece of what?"

He laughed and shook his head condescendingly. "My gun. I need my gun back."

I had forgotten all about that relic. "I ain't got it on me."

"What? Who got it, then?"

I didn't want to say Chunk. "My man is holding it for me."

"What the hell is wrong with you, son?"

"I ain't your son! If you ain't want me to get rid of it, you shouldnta gave it to me!"

Dontay stubbed out his cigarette on one of the room-service plates.

"So you'd rather I shot that dude, huh?" Dontay said.

"I'd rather you signed the record deal. How many years you been after that?" I ripped my bloody shirt over my head, flung it into the trash can, and retrieved a clean one. "Then when it lands in your lap, you throw it away. Just like you been throwing away your life all these years, smoking that crack."

My brother's eyes narrowed. He took a swig from the cognac bottle and started banging on the table again.

Who's that knocking at my God's door
It's a face I seen before
Who's that knocking at my God's door
Looks like a sinner to me . . .

Ironically, there was a knock on the door of the suite. I peered through the peephole and saw a short man with a wide, squat cart. "Room service," he called out.

Dontay was spending my money like water, as usual. A sharp hunger pang reminded me that the last time I had eaten was that morning on the plane. Had I really been in Miami for only one day? It felt like weeks.

I turned the knob and the door knocked me off my feet.

I tumbled backward as three men with bandannas tied over their faces barreled through the door. From the floor I saw a herd of Timberlands. I was trying to scramble to my feet when a hard kick to my ribs knocked me over again.

Except for a shoving match or two, I had never been in a real fight before. Not that you could call this a fight, since I never made it back up off the floor. As the Timbs rained down on me, I covered my head with my arms until a hard toe found the top of my right cheekbone, just below the corner of my eye.

The world turned white, but I didn't black out. The few seconds I spent drifting in a haze felt warm and comfortable. The reverie was punctured by a sharp, fast sound, like a six-foot zipper being closed in an instant. Dontay shouted in pain. The beige patterned carpet came into focus and I rolled over. One eye didn't work. Out of the other I saw Dontay slumped over, holding his leg. A man was standing over him with a long pistol. Smoke was coming out of the silencer.

"Oh, shit!" one of the men said. "Hold up!"

The speaker squatted down next to me and took hold of my face. I saw his green eyes wince as he turned me from side to side.

He pulled down his bandanna. It was Wop.

"The fuck you doing here, son?" he said. "You supposed to be at the Willies!"

"You want me to do this nigga or what?" growled the man next to Dontay from behind his black bandanna. He looked down at Dontay, pointed his gun, and said, "Boom."

"Nah, B, hold up," Wop said. "We got a problem. This my man right here."

Wop started pacing back and forth as Black Bandanna kept his pistol pointed at Dontay. The third man stood near the door, holding a silver pistol in both hands like a cop stalking a suspect in a movie.

Wop pulled out his Sidekick and started thumbing. I heard a low tune coming from someplace. Was a radio on somewhere? I strained to hear the source until I realized it was Dontay, humming a foreboding melody. Then his lips started moving in a whisper nobody but me could hear.

Looks like a sinner to me
Looks like a sinner to me

My Sidekick vibrated on my hip. I instinctively reached for it and the man standing by the door pointed his gun at me.
"It's aiight," Wop said. "Answer it."
Chunk.

YOU WEREN'T SUPPOSED TO BE IN YOUR ROOM. I WAS GONNA DO YOU A FAVOR BUT NOW THINGS ARE FUCKED UP. I THINK I CAN FIX IT THOUGH. MY BAD.

I started to text him back when Wop knocked the Sidekick out of my hand. It tumbled into the corner next to my duffel. "Sorry, home boy," Wop said. I heard footsteps behind me. The *Fever* chain was ripped from my neck and a blast of pain exploded at the base of my skull. It was such a relief to finally pass out.

CHAPTER 61

I shoulda made you listen to me from the jump—that's what I woulda done different. You heard me? You got that short-nigga attitude, always been hardheaded. And there you go talkin greasy. I

can't even feel that no more. I'm too tired to hurt.
It's time to think about the next life. And you
need to think about what's left of yours. Cause
there ain't but one street nigga in this family, and
that's me.

You love hip-hop, I can tell. That's why I always
steered you away from it. You ain't built for it, never
was. Most people think if you ain't down with hip-hop,
you're soft. Man, if you ain't down with hip-hop, you're
smart. What's hip-hop gonna do for you? Make you
some money? Get you on TV? Those things will take you
further away from God, guaranteed. You can't glorify
God in the rap game. Can't be done, not without being
a hypocrite. Well, I can do it, but I got skills no one
else has. And I have the Blessed Beauty.

I ain't scared of death, yo. The Blessed Beauty
has a special place for me in the Abha Kingdom.
Everybody will be there. My man Large is waiting for
me right now. He understands what happened—with
me, with him, with all of us. You wanna know what's
happening with black people? Just listen to our music.
What does it say about us? If you put the top ten
bestselling CDs into a time capsule, and a thousand
years from now told somebody that this was the most
popular music in the world during the new millennium,
what would they think about the people who created
that music? I'm scared to even contemplate it.

Cats like me are the only ones who can change
things. I was part of the foundation of the rap
game—I was there in the places where it all began.

You gotta remember, I done rocked wit the best. The Cold Crush Brothers. Grandmaster Caz, KRS, Rakim. MCs, one and all. A rapper is someone who wraps gifts. Big Daddy Kane—niggas still can't touch Kane to this day. I watched Kool Herc spin record—can you imagine what that's like, being next to the man who invented hip-hop? This was when rap was free and pure, a beautiful thing. Back then it was a way for us not to kill each other. Afrika Bambaataa had all them wild dudes putting down they guns to come to the party. Nobody ever imagined all this money would come. And that's what ruined it, the money and the cocaine. They came simultaneously, and it was the kiss of death for the whole thing. The cocaine gave us so much cash, we didn't need the white man to make our music. I don't think you really understand what I'm telling you. You think Louis Armstrong could just put out a record whenever he wanted? Chuck Berry, Howlin' Wolf, Charlie Parker? Crack money let my generation take control. And then look at what we done with the music. Ain't no white man to blame for all this. We did it to ourselves.

My situation is what it is, man. I made choices and I got to live with them. But I know why all this happened, and now I'm ready to reap the rewards. "From time immemorial even unto eternity the Almighty hath tried, and will continue to try, His servants, so that light may be distinguished from darkness, truth from falsehood, right from wrong, guidance from error, happiness from misery, *and roses from thorns." That's what Bahá'u'lláh says. I smoked crack for a reason. I really didn't have any choice. It was meant to be from the moment my mother first laid eyes on me. But I was being prepared for something greater. "Do men think that when they say 'We believe,' they shall be let alone and not put to proof?" What do you believe, Marq? For real though. What do you believe?*

CHAPTER 62

I awakened in a tiny room—four paces square, low ceiling, concrete walls and floor. The buzz in my eardrum told me it was busted. Usually I heard so much in silence.

"Wake up," rasped my brother, Dontay, slumped against the far wall. "We in the basement. They taped us up but I got loose and untied you. Them cats ain't too smart."

"Smart?" My voice hammered the inside of my skull. The pain made me feel alive. "They was smart enough to get us."

"They ain't get *us*. They got *you*," Dontay spat.

"Nigga, they came to kill *you*!"

I lurched to my feet and staggered toward Dontay with violence in my heart. I don't know what I would have done if I hadn't seen his leg stuck out at an odd angle. There was a hole in the inner thigh of his jeans, surrounded by a huge, wet stain.

"It's still bleeding," Dontay said. "It won't take long."

"Won't take long for what?" I said, unthinking.

Dontay said nothing.

Relief and guilt fought within me as I contemplated Dontay's

death. I could have done so much more. Then crack dragged millions of white rocks and green dollars and yellow teeth and blue-
topped vials and blackened lips through my mind. He could have
been so much more. I smelled the stench of smoke and anger and
betrayal, searched for distant moments of love, heard The Joint
and felt the beat of pride and wonder and fear of this life-giving,
soul-draining music that made my brother who he was.

And no one would even care he was gone.

That's when I decided to write this book. There was some
self-interest involved, because I no longer had a job. But I didn't
want Dontay to leave without a trace. At least, that's what I
told myself as I hid the recorder behind his back.

I hit record, leaned against the opposite wall, and half listened to him ramble while the buzzing grew in my ear. Every so
often I tuned in, and then faded back into my own thoughts.
My face flashed hot and cold, my ribs ached, and my tongue
begged for water. I finally passed out for an undetermined
amount of time and awakened to a melody.

Who's that knocking at my *God's door*
It's a face I seen before
Who's that knocking at my *God's door*
Looks like a sinner to me
Who's that kneeling in the holy place
Tears running down his face
Who's that kneeling in the holy place
Looks like a sinner to me
Looks like a sinner to me
Looks a little like me
Looks exactly like me . . .

I returned to a sleep filled with car chases. Dontay was smacking someone with a bat and the noise made my head hurt. I roused myself and realized someone was pounding on the door.

"Who's in there?" a deep voice asked.

I croaked out something unintelligible.

"That you, Marq?"

"Yeah."

"Move away from the door."

I crawled to the far corner. Two shots blew the hinges to pieces. The door crashed to the floor inside the tiny room. An immense figure ducked his head beneath the door frame and stepped inside, holding an enormous pistol in each hand.

Cox squinted at me through the whirling dust and smoke.

"Let's get busy, yo," he barked.

I struggled to my feet, confused and weak. "What are you doing here?" I rasped.

Cox was squatting next to Dontay, one hand on his neck.

"He's gone," Cox said, raising himself off the floor. "Let's be out."

I was halfway out the door when I remembered the recorder. I had to look Dontay in the face to get it. His eyes were closed, dark skin ashen, mouth slightly ajar. I wish I could say I cried. God, I wish I could say I felt something. I searched my heart, because I knew what was missing. More than anything, that's what I regret, and that's what I'll remember. That terrible nothingness will stay with me the rest of my life.

I reached over Dontay's body, grabbed my recorder, and exited the room. Cox was standing in a long gray hallway lined with doors, carts, mops, and buckets. He was wearing a black vest with several flat pockets, a black T-shirt, and black jeans tucked into calf-high boots laced tight. The dim fluorescent light gleamed off the taut manila yellow skin of his bulging arms.

There was a body on the floor wearing a blue jacket, sideways braids framing gangbanger sunglasses. Blood was running down his head.

Cox looked into my horrified eyes. "I just knocked him out, that's all," he said. "I ain't no monster."

"What are you doing here?" I repeated.

"Holliday called me." He shoved one pistol into a leather backpack, slung it over his shoulder, and held the other gun low as he moved silently down the hallway. I followed unconsciously.

"Why you?" I asked.

"You can ask her that. She's waiting outside. Now shut the fuck up. There might be more of these niggas around here somewhere."

We crept down the hall to a doorway that opened into a tall concrete stairwell. I heard stealthy footsteps coming down the stairs. Cox pulled me back out the doorway and pushed me behind him as he waited to one side of the door. The pain in my head returned with a dizzy rush and I had to stop myself from retching.

As the footsteps came through the door, Cox reached out with a huge arm and snatched Holliday through the opening.

They stared at each other with shocked eyes.

"I told you to wait in the car!" Cox hissed. Holliday just glared at him defiantly until the big man's gaze relented. Then she turned her attention to me. It felt like sunshine.

"Oh my God," she breathed, touching the busted side of my face. Her hair was pulled back into a ponytail. She wore a powder blue tracksuit and no makeup. "I can't believe this. Where's Dontay?"

I didn't say anything. Holliday closed her eyes with a sadness that I yearned to share.

"We got to be out," Cox murmured. Holliday and I spoke in whispers as we followed him up the concrete stairs.

"Taylor called me," she said.

"How could Taylor have called you? Did he have something to do with me getting got?"

"No, I gave him my card the first night we met him, remember?"

"But how would he have known what happened to me?"

"Remember when Taylor gave you that ghetto laptop? The Sidekick? Well, him and Leak had all of them monitored. Every message in and out went right to those guys. Taylor saw something that got him worried. When you didn't return his message, he called and said you were in trouble."

But how had she gotten here so fast—and with Cox, no less? I was afraid to ask for the details.

"I spoke to your boy Chunk," Cox said as he ascended the steps. "He said it was all a big mix-up. Julien had money on your brother's head. He figured since you always said you wanted Dontay dead, he'd do everybody a favor and take care of it."

Cox turned and laced me with a disapproving stare that burned right through me.

"But Chunk didn't shoot Dontay. He wasn't there."

"Nah, he subcontracted the dirty work to some other

niggas. Amateurs and weed-heads, mostly. A real bad combination. They shoulda just took your brother and let you go.
They dumb asses just panicked."

I heard scuttling beneath us. A single shot ricocheted up the
stairwell, then another. Cox grabbed my arm as though it were
a chopstick, yanked me into motion up the steps, and then ran
to the next landing. Holliday was in front of him. "These niggas is stupid!" Cox muttered. "The dude they want is dead!"
At the top of the steps was a set of two swinging metal doors.
Holliday ran through them. Cox and I followed abreast.

The three of us stopped. What seemed like a hundred
Hispanic faces were staring at us, frozen at their positions in
the hotel kitchen. Music thumped in the distance.

Cox sprang into motion. "Ándale, ándale!" he shouted,
scattering the people like bowling pins. The music got louder
as we skirted a long stainless-steel table. Cox stopped in front
of another set of swinging doors, beckoning Holliday and me
through.

We were back at the Willie Awards. Lil Jon was screaming behind the turntables and the entire ballroom was packed
tighter than a subway at rush hour. Couples were pressed up
against the walls, women with their legs up or asses out, partners melting into each other as the bass pounded with a wild
energy. It was a solid mass of hundreds of bodies. Not one of
them realized we were there.

Chaos grew louder behind us. Our pursuers were smashing
their way through the kitchen.

I reached out to grab Holliday's hand. Just as our fingertips
touched, Cox strode between us, holding a giant gun in each
hand. He walked two paces into the room, jumped up onto

a table, and raised his two cannons skyward in a champion's pose.

KABOOM! KABOOM! KABOOM-BOOM-BOOM!

The rap industry ran for their lives. We stepped aside as the hordes flooded through the kitchen doors and every other available exit. As the room emptied, Cox shoved his guns back into his bag and walked calmly through the melee, Holliday and I trailing in his wake.

EPILOGUE

I see Dontay all the time when I walk the streets at night. The midnight street-corner transactors, the little boy solo subway riders. The homeless brothers and the would-be rappers. I hear his rhythm from cars, iPods, bars. Sometimes it helps.

My cover story was one of the worst-selling issues in *Fever* history, so I've heard. They said the photos were too scary. Teenage girls want something to tape to their bedroom walls. But I got eight months' severance, which is holding me over until I get this book done. My agent said nonfiction would get me a much bigger check than a novel, but there was no way I could snitch like that. So I changed the names and details to protect the guilty, the innocent, and the rest of us, as Willie Stripp used to write back in the day.

Taylor and Leak were about to get fired for misuse of corporate funds, but they resigned first to go work for Meyer Mahl. *Fresh Beat* magazine is launching this summer.

Black's phone number went dead right after the Baller, and I haven't spoken to him since. I've seen Chunk only once. He told me to come by the office so Tommy could give the book his blessing. Daminion never showed, though, and it was real awkward between Chunk and me. He talked about all the deals he had going and the money he was making, then finally asked if he could read the book before it came out. I still haven't given him an answer.

And Holliday still hasn't responded to my offer for her to move back into our apartment. We've been talking, though, even about her family. Now I understand her attraction to Cox—he reminds Holliday of her father.

The mystery of my own father continues. I've listened to Dontay's tape a hundred times, trying to figure out the guy with the feather in his hat. The physical description sounds like Felix Billings, but that's just too impossible for me to believe. Especially since all my attempts to find Billings have failed. He's like a ghost—no official records, never seen in public, never in his office. I will find him one day, though. That's what I do.

It took me a long time to get rid of Dontay's belongings from my apartment. I sold the CDs online and threw out all his Large mementos except for the blue-topped crack vial. It sits on my nightstand, next to the book with BAHÁ'Í PRAYERS on the cover. I've cracked the book open a few times. It was disappointing at first when the answers to all my problems didn't jump right out at me—I guess I was looking for some kind of specific directions. But there are some jewels buried in that book, and I see Dontay when I read it. I see him for who he really was.

ACKNOWLEDGMENTS

I always scoffed at the sincerity of artists who thanked God on rap albums filled with street stories. But look who's thanking now: Praise be to God, the Lord of all worlds.

The original editor of and believer in this book was my sister, Elizabeth Curlean Washington. I'll never doubt you again, Liz.

Very few people were willing to take a chance on this project. I'm extraordinarily grateful for two who did: my agent, Paul Bresnick, and Tricia Boczkowski at Simon Spotlight Entertainment. Special thanks to my editor, Ursula Cary, and especially to my copy editor, Susan T. Buckheit, who saved me from untold embarrassments way beyond mere punctuation.

There are three individuals without whose insight and generosity this book would not have been possible. They know who they are. But my man Tone Boots played the biggest role of all, from the beginning to the very end. Boots, I'm just as glad as you are that we met.

I would be a different person today if I hadn't encountered several writers as a young man. The first was Darrell Dawsey, whose black-as-night features and Buck Whylin' columns for *The Detroit News* revealed a new world of journalism to me. Other primary inspiration for this book came from the writings of Bönz Malone, Harry Allen, Joan Morgan, Rob Marriott, Kevin Powell, Ronin Ro, Greg Tate, Reggie

Dennis, James Bernard, the late Ralph Wiley, Dante Alighieri, dream hampton, Davey D, and Sacha Jenkins, as well as Elliott Wilson's *XXL* magazine.

I am indebted to Frederic Dannen's *Hit Men* and Nelson George's *The Death of Rhythm & Blues*, which definitively chronicled previous eras of the music business. Dontay's statement "You wanna know what's happening with black people? Just listen to our music. . . ." on page 3 is an homage to a concept I learned from George's book; and Meyer Mahl's "let my wife and children go" joke on page 357 was inspired by an anecdote in *Hit Men*.

Dontay's lyrics on pages 362–369 were adapted from "My God's Door," written by Mike Rogers of the Salt River Trio, www.harmonicaworkshops.com. The lyrics on pages 138–140 were written by Freddie Foxxx. Common authored the song on pages 165–166, and Nas wrote Black's favorite song, on pages 92 and 93–94.

Nuff respect to John Schecter, Dave Mays, and Ray Scott, for creating *The Source* magazine, which changed my world. Thanks to Chris Wilder, for assigning me my first article there, and to Kierna Mayo, for deft editing that saved me from playing myself with my first feature. *Source* alumni Scheck, James, Rob, Matt Life, Julia Chance, Shawnee Smith, and Dmitry Leger helped me immeasurably; Wilder and Reggie Dennis were beyond generous with their time and assistance.

I owe a huge debt to Rob Kenner, for giving me my first assignment at *Vibe* magazine; to Carter Harris, for dropping my name at the right time to get me hired there; and to both of them, for teaching me how to be a magazine editor. If anyone wants to know what really happened to Tupac, read what